The Divide

THE DREAMLAND SERIES BOOK II

E.J Mellow

Published by Four Eyed Owl, Village Station PO Box #204, New York, NY 10014
Editing by Julia McCarthy
Editing & Copy Editing by Dori Harrell
Cover Design by E.J Mellow
Cover Photography by Dmitry Laudin

ISBN 9780996211437
ISBN 978-0-9962114-2-0 (ebook)

Printed in the United States of America
ISBN: 0996211438

For those who don't think they can,
but will.

Prologue

HE LEANED AGAINST the wall, studying the bare table before him. The surface was white, smooth, and looked entirely uncomfortable. How would it feel to wake up on such a thing? He couldn't imagine it being pleasant, but then she'd dealt with worse than lying on a cold surface. Frowning, he wondered if she was scared to come here or if she was entirely fearless as she closed her dark eyes—eyes that he'd seen burn with determination—only to open them to an unknown beginning.

Staying perfectly still, he was unable to look at anything but the emptiness. How long had he been waiting? How long had he been trained to the same fixture? The answer didn't matter. He would never miss this. He promised her he'd be here, promised he'd never let anything happen to her. A promise he failed to keep with someone else.

"Dev, you can wait outside," said a soft feminine voice. "You don't need to stand around counting the seconds. I'm sure you have responsibilities you are neglecting."

"If I leave, I would be neglecting my greatest responsibility," Dev said evenly.

Elena sat on the other side of the room, a small smile touching her features. She wore the traditional white robe of the Vigil elders, and her posture was straight but relaxed. Her composure was something that always, ironically, unnerved him.

"Does she return these feelings?"

At her disruptive question, Dev snatched his eyes away from his target and latched on to another. She regarded him collectedly, like she did all things, with an expression that suggested she had seen into his future, flickered through his past, and held his current desires, wondering how much he might know of them.

He stayed silent, both unwilling and unsure how to answer.

"I must speak freely," she went on. "I am both happy and saddened by your situation."

His brows pinched in. "What do you mean?"

She tilted her head curiously, looking straight into his soul, and he did his best to seem calm, to not show how her ominous eyes affected him. Terra only knew how her guards dealt with being around her so much.

"I see your path as one that forks. As to which road you follow, that is still to be determined."

Dev breathed out a laugh. "Aren't most things in life still to be determined?"

"Perhaps for some."

"Well then, is it safe to assume the cliché that one of these roads is happy and the other sad?" he asked, quickly growing tired of this vague game of prophecies.

"That all depends."

"On what?"

She regarded him evenly. "On her." She paused for a moment. "And on you."

"Me?"

She nodded.

"How?"

Elena smoothed a nonexistent wrinkle from her dress. "I think the more important question is whether your heart is willing to sacrifice again to find out?"

Dev's stomach tightened, and he dropped his eyes back to the empty table. Memories he'd buried deep within the ocean of time suddenly gasped for the surface, but he smothered them quickly. A shiver of past regret clicked down his spine. But that's all it was, the past, and it could no longer bar him from having a future. *Is your heart willing to sacrifice again?*

He swallowed. "Was it ever willing?"

Elena stayed silent, allowing his question to echo through the room, and after a moment, Dev went back to staring at nothing and waiting for everything.

What I want to do is travel deep and deeper into the dreamlands,
to find that place that I know is waiting for me here.
My home.

—*Charles De Lint*

Chapter 1

THE WORLD IS dark, as it always is, and the sky seems to spin on an axis as millions of shooting stars dance across its abyss. With hands gripped tight, I attempt to race them forward. My eyes tear as cool night air slaps across my face and filters through my hair, sending it flapping out behind me—a flag in the wind. My feet sway left and then right as they dangle above a city of sleepless souls, my body barreling ahead at the whim of a predetermined path set by a zipline. With my heart pounding in my ears and my stomach tightening where my throat should be, I prepare for the rapidly approaching landing. It looms in the distance, getting larger as I shrink, the buildings around me reclaiming their majestic height and returning me to my human one. The glowing bulls-eye in the center of the square platform pulses blue, a beacon telling me to come home, and all too quickly I'm touching down, ending my flight. Retracting my Arcus from the line, my legs wobble for a second, reacquainting themselves with something solid beneath them before they are moving forward again, continuing to follow the man who's been leading the way. He hardly spares me a glance as he nods to the zipline's attendant and descends the stairs to the street. Tucking my

Arcus back into baton shape, I drop it into the quiver strapped to my back and hurry to catch up.

Hitting the street, we follow the soft blue glow emanating from evenly patterned lampposts, my footsteps quiet against the pavement. This, of course, is from no grace of mine—the boots I wear are constructed to muffle sounds.

Gazing from building to building, I take in the strange mixture of old and new in which this section of the city is styled. As if the architects suddenly stopped in their construction, skipped a century of design, and began building again in mostly modern material. Brick facades rest next to smooth white walls, Victorian light fixtures are positioned evenly down concrete sidewalks, and wrought iron fences are placed in front of all-glass buildings. What should probably appear like a hodgepodge of forms surprisingly blends together rather well.

I step to the side as a man on a bicycle passes by, and in the process I almost collide with another on a skateboard, the streets holding their usual constant hum. Straightening my black T-shirt and pants, I resist looking up to what I know will be more civilians careening above on lines, where I just was.

I still can't believe I'm here.

After falling asleep in an alien white room, in the back of a closet, in a spiritual bookstore in New York City (yes, this is all true), I awoke only moments ago in another brightly sterile room.

It's the first time I'm here knowing Terra is indeed real. That everything around me exists in another dimension, not a figment of my imagination or the creation of a dream.

Fiddling with the pockets on my pants, I glance up to another form that greeted me upon my arrival, a man who still walks a few steps ahead. His confident, graceful strides glide silently over our path, and the quiver on his back hardly moves against his broad shoulders as it blends in with the rest of his black attire. As much as I'm enjoying the view from behind, it's the color I know rests in his gaze that I find myself craving. My guide is one of Terra's inhabitants, a Nocturna, and one of the first people I met here. He's part of a race I've learned are the watchers of the Dreamers, the caretakers of our sleeping minds, and so far a person who takes up a large portion of my thoughts, both good and bad.

We haven't spoken since before traveling the ziplines, and I would ask how much longer until our destination, but I'm enjoying the silence. Using this time to reacquaint myself with the city. Something tells me he knew I would need this.

Eventually we turn down a small street and make our way through the entrance of a more modern apartment building, where we quickly ascend a few flights in an elevator. My skin buzzes with each second I stand alone beside him, and I keep myself from being dramatic by thanking God as the doors finally open, granting me a sense of escape.

After a few more steps down a dark hallway, he leads us to an apartment at the end. Pausing, he grasps the door handle and turns to face me, finally giving me what I was hungering for all those minutes ago. With my heart ricocheting in my chest, I look into his unnatural blue eyes and dangerously handsome face, seeing the smile tug at the corner of his mouth. "Welcome home, Molly," Dev says as he pushes open the door.

Everything is the same as the last time I was here. The interior is sparse of any real décor, but simple in off-white and gray coloring, and the familiar large beige couches sit in the lower portion of the living room. The warm light of the fireplace mixes with the cold blue-white of the fixtures around the apartment, fixtures that burn with the energy of the Dreamers, the *Navitas*.

Dev walks toward me while removing the strap across his chest and indicates that I should do the same. "Where are Tim and Aveline?" I ask, handing him my quiver before searching for the roommates who share this space with him.

"Tim is at City Hall, and Aveline is somewhere of equal unimportance, I'm sure," Dev says casually as he places our equipment away.

I'm not exactly positive what Tim is to these two, except a sort of father figure. Aveline is Dev's Nocturna partner. Not in a romantic sense, but his companion in their duties here in Terra. All inhabitants of Terra train for combat, Vigil included, but not every Nocturna decides to become a warrior and guard the land's borders as Dev, Aveline, and Tim do. Others filter into the various duties required in the city, including helping to monitor human dreams to spot potential developments for new technology and advancements in society.

"Let me show you your room." Dev is suddenly by my side and places his hand on my back to guide me forward.

I swallow, forcing away the shivers that threaten to course down my body from the contact. I was hoping something would have changed when I met with Dev again. That a brotherly affection would have taken hold between us once my boyfriend, Jared, and my relationship was more cemented.

I barely hold in a snort from my naivety.

Dev's body next to mine is like being near a giant magnet, specifically one that's annoyingly good looking and radiates confidence, self-composure, and desires that are usually found in dark, danger-ous places.

I've never met anyone like him, and all that he is intrigues a part of me I never thought existed. So as happy as I am with Jared, I can't ignore what Dev does to me, though that's exactly what I'm going to try *really* freakin' hard to do.

After passing closed door after closed door—with me won-dering if Dev's quarters are nearby—we stop at the end of the hall. I peek into a room much like one I'd expect to find in this apartment—simple and clean. It has the same wooden floors as the rest of the place, a white modern dresser on one end with a circular mirror above, two decent-sized windows on the adjacent walls, which are lined with sheer white drapes, and a plain queen bed resting in the center. There are a few unembellished lamp fix-tures around the room, as well as a ceiling light that swirls with the Navitas and casts the area in a low blue glow. It gives off a cold warmth that's surprisingly comforting.

"This is one of our extra bedrooms," Dev explains as I walk in. "Mine is just across the hall." The suggestiveness in his voice isn't lost on me, and I refuse to turn and catch the smile that I know matches his tone.

The thought of Dev so near to where I'll be sleeping has my stomach in a fluster, but I play it off like it's the most unimportant news in the world. "Why do you guys have beds when you don't need to sleep?" I run my hand over the pristine white comforter.

Dev gives me a look like I can't seriously be asking that ques-tion. When I stay silent, waiting on his response, his mouth twitches from suppressing a grin. "Beds can be used for things other than sleep."

Oh.

Oh!

I can't help it. I go crimson.

"Don't tell me *you* just use them to sleep?" He raises a brow. "That would be…disappointing to find out. Actually"—he scans my body with no shame—"that would be rather interesting."

I shoot him a glare. "You are disgusting."

"I can be a lot of things, Molly." He leans against the doorframe, the corner of his mouth inching up. "Especially in this room."

Oh Lord.

"Very mature." I eye roll. "Now please, if you're quite done…" I step up and give him a light shove toward the exit "I'd like to have some privacy while I settle in. Let me know when it's time to train."

His smile widens at my annoyance. "I'll be back to bring you down. If you end up taking a nap, try not to dream about me *too* much," he says with a wink before I shut the door in his face, which does nothing to block the sound of his chuckle as he walks away.

If this is how it's going to be the whole time I'm here, I might not make it.

Slouching on the bed, I think about everything that's happened to me up until this point, and how here I sit in a dimension that is connected to my own like the very nerves that run through my body.

I can still see the white room at the spiritual bookstore Rae led me to, the one way to enter Terra where my actual body stays sleeping for days so I can train here uninterrupted. It will be weird returning to my day job. Even when I'm unsure of the things I'll be doing here, I know they will feel much more important than what I do at the marketing firm back on Earth. Well, I don't think anyone can really argue that, given that I'm basically meant to save all mankind from a possible world war. Yeah, a smidgen more important, I'd say. I still have no clue how one Dreamer is meant to make a difference in helping ease the growing number of Metus, which feed off of the corruption of human minds.

Lying back with a sigh, I study the swirling light above my head, my thoughts drifting with the rhythm of the liquid that fills it. Thinking about what lies ahead, I can't help flying back to the past, to the moment of recently closing my eyes in my world and feeling my body shift away, searching for another place.

⋆⇨≡◉ ◉≡⇦⋆

There was much of nothing as I waited in the abyss. I could sense my restlessness to open my eyes and begin, to accept my role as the Dreamer and embark on learning my abilities and powers. But my body resisted, taking forever to catch up with my thoughts and keeping me in blackness.

Eventually the void began to take shape, and I sensed my surroundings—a cool surface against my back, a bright light under my lids, a hand against my own, and the whisper of voices.

Blinking my eyes open, my heart stuttered at the figure before me, and a grin formed on my lips. Constant day-old scruff, buzzed raven hair, and piercing eyes all rested in an otherworldly handsome face hovering above mine.

"Hi," I said after a moment of us staring at the other.

"Hello." He smiled.

"Fancy seeing you here."

Dev raised an eyebrow. "Were you expecting someone else?"

"Actually, I was expecting many someones—oh, you are here." Sitting up, I found Elena, a Vigil and one of Terra's elders, standing at the end of the table I was on. Wrapped all in white, her perfect shoulder-length blonde hair was swept back to reveal her very *not* elderly glowing complexion. Before I knew that Elena was one of the more powerful Vigil—another Terra race that interacts with Dreamers in their awake states as a sort of guardian angel to their destinies—I could tell she was important. She seemed to radiate the power of the sun, making her a force that you desperately wanted to look at but strained your eyes if you did.

"Welcome, once again, to Terra Somniorum, Molly," she said in her authoritative, calm voice.

"Thanks." I turned distractedly to take in the stark white room. It reminded me of the holding cell I found myself being escorted to the time I tried to make my way into a Council meeting unannounced. The similar surroundings allowed me believe we were in, or close to, City Hall—the center of Terra.

"How do you feel?" she asked.

"Fine." I glanced between her and Dev. "Why? Should I be feeling differently?"

"No, fine is perfect. I take it Rae did a proper job of guiding you here?"

"Yes."

Elena nodded contentedly and glanced toward the door a beat before Rae strode in. He let out a small sigh of relief at seeing me and smiled his radiant, sunny smile, teeth white against his dark skin.

"That was fast," he said, brushing his fingers through his tight blond curls.

"Was it?"

"Yeah, you pretty much just closed your eyes in New York when I portaled here."

"She was ready," Elena said, staring at me with her ominous eyes.

"Can you stand?" Dev offered his hand, helping me hop off the table. "This is an interesting sleep ensemble you have on today." He smirked as he appraised my baggy sweatpants and tee.

"I thought it was rather amusing myself," Rae agreed.

I regarded them both peevishly, and without another word quickly brought up the image of the black T-shirt, pants, and boots that are the uniform of the Nocturna.

Surprised, they both stepped back as my clothing rapidly changed shape and settled into what I desired. Elena watched with a spark of intrigue.

"Is that better?" I eyed them sweetly.

Dev was the one who recovered faster. "If only you could change into what *I'm* imagining."

I made a face of disgust as Rae chuckled next to him.

"All right, gentleman," Elena began, "I would like to escort her out and explain a few things before she leaves with you, Dev, and is taken to her quarters."

"I'm not starting my training now?"

"You will, but first I'd like you to rest a little. Much of what we'll be doing today will take a lot out of you, and it would be preferred if you were settled before we began."

"But aren't I technically resting now?"

Elena smiled. "It would also be best if you stopped thinking about your body in New York and thought of your body here as its own."

I nodded, though still not understanding how that would be possible.

The four of us traveled down the white sterile hallways of what Elena explained was the Dreamer Containment Center—a building not far from City Hall that resided mostly underground. Two Vigil guards walked in front and two behind. It was hard not to feel like we were being led through a prison.

Elena stopped in front of a new hallway connecting to the one we were walking through. "Down there is where your physical training will be held. It's fitted with all the material and rooms that are required," Elena explained as she began to move again. "I believe Rae will do your physical lessons today."

I looked to Rae, who shot me a wink.

After making our way down a plethora of nondescript corridors, and losing my sense of direction more than once, we stopped in front of an all-white door with a glowing blue lightning bolt resting in its center. It was a symbol I noticed also decorated the armbands of our fellow Vigil guards and something I'd seen a few Nocturna wear as well. I wondered more than once if it was the emblem of Terra Somniorum.

After a nod from Elena, one Vigil quickly pressed a code into a keypad, and with a huff of air the door retracted into the wall, and she stepped through. As soon as I entered the room, an on-slaught of pressure formed in my head, and I shivered. Glancing down, all the hairs on my arms now stood on end, and a strange wave of euphoric energy rushed through me. Something in the air made me want to take in large breaths, like I couldn't get enough of it.

"You okay?" Dev was suddenly by my side.

Glancing at him in a daze, I found myself thinking how small he looked, how fragile—a thought that went against everything I knew Dev to be. But yet I couldn't stop thinking it. Like a shift in eyesight, I could suddenly see through his skin, a strange-colored blood running through his veins, red mixed with glowing white strands of energy. I saw where it entered his heart and felt it beat in my head. I watched his glowing lungs expanding and contracting with each breath. How beautiful it all was, but how simply it could be snuffed out. How easily *I* could snuff it out if I merely wished the energy to stop flowing, for his heart to stop beating.

"Molly?" Dev's concerned voice shook me out of my trance, making the energy I saw so easily flowing through him disappear— my eyesight returned to normal.

What was that?

A hand was pressed lightly against my shoulder, and I spun around, feeling a tug in my core. Elena stood before me, eyes penetrating my own and shifting through thoughts I was unsure belonged to her or me. Whatever she was searching for, she seemed to have found, for her lips pursed and then relaxed. "Interesting."

"What is?" I asked with worry.

"Soon, Molly Spero. We'll get into it all soon," she said quietly and motioned me forward.

Before following Elena, I stole a glance back at Dev, who was regarding me with uncertainty until Rae drew his attention away. Swallowing away that strange moment, I returned my focus to the room, taking in the massive domed space and alabaster square paneling lining its entirety. Searching for the light source, I found none—the room seemed to be lit simply because it wished to be.

As Elena and I walked forward, a shape began to rise and unfold from the center of the room, snapping and shifting to finally settle into a chair you'd find at a dentist's office, except this chair was all sleek and simple in design. It appeared to be wrapped in the soft white material of the sleeping pod I laid in at the bookstore. Despite the presence of that comfortable addition, the object terrified me. What was it for? Was I to lie in that thing? And if so, what was to be done with me in it?

I searched for Dev again, to see him studying our surroundings with narrowed eyes, his expression openly revealing he didn't like this room, which did nothing to help my unease. Rae was off to the side, talking to another Vigil guard.

"Molly," Elena called as she rested her delicate hand on the chair, "this is where you will train with me on using your Navitas as well as accessing the memories of your predecessors."

"I'll have to sit in that thing?"

"Don't worry. It's not as bad as it might appear. You will need to be in this when I give you memories, but we won't need it when we practice with your powers."

I gingerly poked the seat's material. It molded to my fingers effortlessly, just like the white coffin. "How will I receive the memories?" I couldn't help but imagine ancient torture devices and pliers.

"I shall give them to you."

I laughed at her simple reply. "Yes, but *how* will you give them to me? In sandwich form?"

Elena merely smiled politely. "No, I shall send them into your mind."

I balked. "How will you do that?"

"You will see later today—nothing to get worked up over. It's very painless, and you will take to it naturally, as I have already seen."

I frowned. *How has she seen this?*

"All the Dreamers before you have easily taken the memories of their predecessors." Elena answered my unasked question. "This room is where many past Dreamers have come and learned of their history and the power that resides within them. It is specifically made to contain the almost-limitless energy you hold." She stepped forward. "You've felt what I speak of," she said without question, and I slowly nodded. *Is that what I felt when I entered the room?* "And this is all safe?" Dev asked from behind me.

"Yes, very safe."

"Hunh" was his dubious response as he ran his hand over the material of the chair.

"Come, I have a bit more to show you." Elena ushered us toward the exit.

Before I followed the rest of the group out, I glanced back at the lonely chair in the middle of the room. As if knowing we were leaving, it began to fold itself up and disappear into the ground, leaving the space empty and bare, like it never existed.

I shivered, exiting the room, just as I shivered when entering.

⇥≡◉ ◉≡⇤

A knock sounds at my door, and my eyes shoot open, the memories of my earlier moments in Terra fading away. I must have fallen asleep after all. How strange.

"You ready, Molly?" Dev's voice is muffled.

I roll off the bed and straighten my shirt, surprised I don't feel my usually grogginess when waking from a nap. "Yeah, one sec."

Quickly tying my hair in a ponytail, I steal a look in the mirror above the dresser. I hardly recognize myself in my black garb and flushed cheeks. The nerves that flutter inside me are obvious. What am I about to experience? How will it change me? So many questions spin around as I breathe in deep and walk toward the door.

Dev stands in the inky shadows of the hall. Blue eyes like liquid topaz gaze down at me, the indication of his Nocturna night vision apparent with their reflection.

He holds out a quiver and Arcus. "Ready?" His question clearly inquires beyond the obvious.

"Ready." I nod and take the outstretched objects before following him through the dark hall and toward the light.

Chapter 2

TRAVELING DEEPER INTO the city, Dev and I walk down a cobblestone road, stopping outside a building that is offset from the main plaza of City Hall. The area is filled with life, and if it wasn't for living in Manhattan, I might have found the constant hustle and bustle strange and overwhelming. Instead, I find it a comfort.

The building is modest in appearance, and a small lobby with an elevator is visible through the glass doors. If I hadn't already been here, I would have thought it was nothing more than an administrative outpost from City Hall. Instead, I know the real purpose of this facade resides underground, stretching an unknown length and depth.

I'm about to enter, when someone steps out of the tree-lined path close by. Straight blonde hair stops midwaist, and her willowy form glides with purpose. "You're thirty minutes late," she quips as she stops next to us.

"Hey, Aveline," I say, and she gives me a curt nod before settling her attention back on Dev. At least she didn't completely ignore me. *Baby steps...*

"And the world is still standing," Dev says dryly, opening the door. "I'm dropping Molly off, and then we can start our rounds."

"Well, hurry up. You're not the only one with things they'd rather be doing."

He raises a brow. "And what *things* would those be?"

"Just hurry," she snips again before turning to lean against a lamppost.

Dev waves her off as we walk into the stark lobby, and he calls the elevator. As we wait, an awkward silence settles in—awkward for me, anyway.

"So…is Aveline always so…succinct?" I ask to fill the quiet.

His lips twitch. "No, not always. Just around you, it seems." He studies me. "Why do you think that is?"

"Well, it's obvious she doesn't like me."

"Hmm."

"What?"

"I just wonder why she wouldn't."

"Wouldn't what?"

"Like you."

I laugh without humor. "I don't know. Maybe because I make you thirty minutes late?"

The side of his mouth tips up. "Maybe."

The opening ding of the elevator doors cuts our conversation short, and a Vigil guard dressed in white steps out. He's a bear of a man with short brown hair and dark skin. Creamy caramel eyes look down at me from a crooked nose that has obviously been broken one too many times. "Your name?" he asks with rigidity, his deep voice booming through the small space.

"Oh—uh, Molly Spero."

He nods to my companion. "Dev," he says while stepping out of the car and allowing the doors to shut behind.

"Alec," Dev returns.

I glance between the two. Does Dev know everyone here?

"I'll need you to call the elevator for us," Alec explains.

"Um, okay." I reach to push the call button, wondering why he let it close in the first place, but he stops me.

"Not like that." He shakes his head.

Seeing my further bemusement, Dev leans in and whispers, "You need to show proof of your power."

"Oh, well...why didn't he just say so?" I mumble, feeling a bit foolish.

Concentrating on the elevator, the familiar sensation of warm-to-cool energy swiftly travels through me, and the doors ding open. I smile, feeling like a Jedi.

"Thank you, Molly. We are cleared to proceed," Alec announces into a band around his wrist, which I assume is a radio.

We enter the car, and I turn to Dev, who hasn't followed.

"You're not coming with us?" I ask, growing a little panicky that I'll be left alone to experience what waits below without the reassuring presence of Dev. When Dev's presence became reassuring is beyond me.

"Don't miss me too much." He grins right before the doors close over his face.

Alec and I walk the halls that must sit a few stories below ground, given that my ears popped on the way down. He's been filling me in on how this compound is guarded and how I will only be able to use my powers to open doors that don't have the glowing blue lightning bolts on them. When I ask why this is, he simply says for security reasons. His lack of an answer has me noticing how many doors we've passed that have the mentioned symbol—so far, four. What would be in there that needs guarding? More specifically, what would be in there that needs guarding from me?

We see few people as I'm led forward, but each has been Vigil and each has nodded in a slight bow upon my approach.

"Why are they doing that?" I ask after walking past two more Vigil who stopped their conversation to greet me as such. I also notice Alec's proud, tall stance beside me.

"You are the Dreamer," he says.

"Yeah...and you're a Vigil, and these halls are white. So?"

Alec seems to work hard in suppressing a smile. "You are not the same as I."

I don't know how to respond to that. I understand we come from different worlds, but the people here seem awfully similar to humans—well, despite the long lives, no sleeping, night vision, and I'm sure a handful of other talents that I have no idea about. Yeah, okay, I'm not the same as Alec. Is that why Aveline dislikes me? And why would that cause them to bow to *me*—shouldn't I be bowing to them?

"Here we are." Alec stops in front of another door with the glowing symbol and punches a code into a keypad set into the wall. The entryway opens with a huff, and I take in the same giant room I was showed earlier. Elena stands small in the center, the same white chair in front of her, and I wonder for a second how long she's been waiting for me. But something tells me she's not one to show up a moment before she's needed.

"Pleasant training," Alec says while bending slightly at the waist, and I shuffle uncomfortably, still uncertain how to return such a gesture, before watching him rigidly depart.

As I enter the large room, the door behind me closes oppressively with a *whoosh*, and I swallow down the nerves that have suddenly risen. The odd euphoria I felt earlier when walking in bristles along my skin—a sensation similar to when a wall of Navitas surrounded me before it channeled into my back, tore apart a Metus, and blew Dev and I backward with an explosion. Yeah, nothing to worry about, I'm sure.

"Did you get some rest?" Elena asks as she steps closer.

"Yeah, I actually ended up taking a nap," I say while looking around and wiping my clammy palms on my pants.

"I can tell you are nervous," Elena says, taking my hands and instantly setting off the strange tugging in my stomach, "but there's nothing, nor anyone here, that will do you harm. Think of this facility as your sanctuary. You are revered here. Your importance known and respected."

They respect me? But they don't even know me. I frown, uncomfortable with that kind of unsolicited reverence.

"Let me help you," she says, and without warning, a strange energy flows from her hands into mine, soothingly traveling through me. I grow sleepy for a couple of heartbeats, and then I'm wide awake. Any prior nervousness within me is gone, and when I try to poke around to find it, it stays hazy, hidden from my reach.

How strange.

"What did you just do?"

"I calmed you." She removes her hands from mine, and the pulling sensation in my gut flickers out.

"But how?"

"I have powers similar to yours," she says as she moves around the chair. "They are not as powerful or limitless, but as the

Dreamer's *Dux Ducis*—" She sees my confusion. "As the Dreamer's *Guide*, I'm created to work with you and your power, to teach you its proper use and how to control it. When we touch, I can tap into it and gauge its strength." She regards me a moment, calculatingly, before she goes on. "Yours is the strongest I've ever felt."

My eyes widen. "Really? Why?" I ask curiously rather than nervously, given that that sensation has recently been removed from me.

"I have some theories."

"What kind of—"

"Come," Elena says with a quick smile, closing that particular conversational topic and patting the seat between us. "Like I explained before, this is a Memory Chair. We'll be simulating certain past Dreamers' memories to merge with your own. This is so you can learn faster and pick up skill sets you otherwise lack. It's how we catch each Dreamer up to speed on fighting techniques, uses of their power, and situations that have come before them. Think of it as an advanced study session." Her mouth twitches with a grin, and I'm impressed with her attempt at a joke.

"So I'll be able to see the Dreamers that have come before me?" I ask, astonished that such technology exists.

She nods. "Yes, you will inherit their memories, their talents. It will feel like your lives are merging into one. That's why we have to pace these sessions. It's a lot to take on—another's thoughts and feelings. If done improperly, it can have severe consequences for the active Dreamer, mainly in their waking life."

I work my bottom lip, wishing I could find my uneasiness again instead of this detached interest. I'm starting to think Elena had ulterior motives in doing that little calming trick of hers. "What kind of consequences?" I cautiously touch the white material of the chair.

"If oversaturated, you could become confused of whose body you are in possession of, inducing schizophrenic or bipolar tendencies."

My gaze whips to hers. "Uh, what now?"

Elena smiles. "Don't worry. This is not my first time doing this."

"Still." I glance warily back at the seat. "That's not exactly news that has me jumping into this thing."

"You'll be fine, Molly. I promise we'll be pacing these sessions properly." She gestures for me to sit. "Now, please."

I eye her a moment more, weighing my options, but ultimately end up crawling onto the recliner—probably after more of her voodoo calming magic. Elena presses a panel in the floor, and a square podium rises next to her. The top surface glows, revealing a keyboard with strange symbols—all straight lines and edges.

"What language is that?" I ask as certain panels lining the walls illuminate with similar lettering as she types.

"It's a form of Latin," she explains. "I will need you to relax on the headrest, Molly."

I do, not liking that I'm limited to the view of the domed ceiling. I turn slightly and watch four small boxes with glowing script pop out of the wall like drawers and float toward us. Besides the fronts, the rest of the containers' sides are see-through glass revealing the swirling blue-white liquid that fills them. As they draw nearer, the hair on my arms jumps, and I know this is Navitas, but something about these particular boxes has the power in me thrumming.

"This is one of the rooms where we store the memories of the past Dreamers. It's a sort of library," Elena says as she gently plucks the floating objects from the air and places them on their own pedestals that have risen around her.

"So these walls are filled with Dreamers that have come before me?" I rake my gaze over the hundreds of panels lining the space, unable to keep the awe from my face.

"Their memories and minds' power," she specifies. "Parts of their energy. I'm sure you felt the presence of so much Navitas when you entered."

I nod. *So that's what those shivering sensations were all about.* Man, talk about ghost chills.

"One day your memories will be held here too. Adding to our history and the chosen Dreamers'."

I swallow, wondering how they'll retain those memories and how much of my personal thoughts would be revealed in them.

"Oh, I've been meaning to ask, about the last time I was here with Dev in the—"

"Yes." Elena nods. "Dev spoke with me earlier about what happened with the energy wall and the Metus. All of it will be explained soon."

I worry the ringless spot on my index finger at the mention of the creatures that create and live off of nightmares in Dreamers. How long will I go before running into one of those lava-goop things again? With the memory of their decaying stench forever clinging to my nostrils, I hope not very soon. But something tells me acquiring Dreamers' memories will be dashing away this hope in mere minutes.

"Look forward please," Elena instructs as she continues to type. *Change that to seconds.*

Taking a deep breath, I turn back to the ceiling, trying to come to terms with everything I just learned, as a projected grid screen wraps around my face and locks my head into place, an invisible barrier holding me down.

Okay, so I've found that misplaced unease.

"The grid is a transmitter," Elena explains. "It's nothing to fear, merely keeps your head steady against unwanted movement when you're receiving memories." A cold material touches the tip of my finger. "I will be monitoring your heart rate as well."

Something tells me that if this were as safe as she says, none of these precautions would be necessary.

"Will it hurt?" I ask, my voice sounding small.

She places her warm hand in mine. "There will be no actual physical pain."

Not very reassuring.

"We'll start slowly with one Dreamer, let you get used to the transmittal sensations before I send you a few more. Does that sound agreeable?"

"Um, s…sure," I breathe out, a tightness clenching my chest.

The gleaming screen pulses above me, and a blue-white liquid inches across to cover its surface. It's thick like oil but as beautiful as refracted light from a crystal. In a trance, I watch it move, when two areas of liquid directly above my eyes begin to drip down. Panicked, I push my head farther back, trying to close my eyes, but I'm unable to.

"And now let us begin." Elena's voice comes out muffled at the moment the strange liquid touches my eyeballs, latching on and forcing them open.

It's cold. *So cold*!

And then it's nothing as everything around me explodes in white.

Chapter 3

I'M WAITING IN a matted room for Sensei Sonjirou and stretching as he instructed I do before our sessions. My drape of black hair falls into my face as I bend forward, and I impatiently push it away. Despite my constant complaining to Mama, I'm never allowed to cut it. Holding on to my small toes, I know I'm a young Japanese girl named Riki in my fourteenth year.

I am also Molly looking out of the eyes of Riki. I have no control over my body or emotions. I feel what she feels, I move as she deems to move, yet I'm somehow separate. I know I am not this girl, but at the same time we are one.

I know Papa is a street vendor in Edo, and I have a younger brother who is sick at home. I know the year is 1589 by human standards, for Sensei Sonjirou told me so when I met him in that strange place when I fell asleep, after the terrible flashing that left me alone and burning. I'm awake now and waiting for Sensei Sonjirou in my town at a neighborhood temple school. The monks have given us this room to practice. They seem to know more about what I am than I do. Mama says I have been chosen and have made the family proud, honored our name.

The room I'm standing in shifts into an all-white space with a padded floor. I'm panting and brushing the sweat from my brow as Sensei Sonjirou twirls toward me with his sharpened Ninjatō. I block it with my own, the metal *clank* vibrating down my arm. He retreats before striking straight, the square-tip blade aimed at my chest. I bend back as it kisses the material of my black clothes, and I roll away, exhilarated with my sure strides.

"Good, Riki," Sensei Sonjirou calls to me, his bald head glistening with perspiration and reflecting the strange liquid lights above us. I swim with elation from his praise.

The white room drops away, and I'm kneeling by my brother's bed. His cold, pale body lies lifeless as Mama holds his hands and cries. The thickest despair settles inside, and my throat burns. I run from the house.

I'm sitting in a stark white hall, after waking in the strange place again. I don't care who passes and sees—I wrap my arms around my knees and cry.

Riki cries.

Molly cries. The loss of her brother—our brother—is too great. A hand settles around our shoulders, and though we don't look up, we know who it is. He gathers us into his arms and we sob harder. He says nothing as he rocks our body, but his presence is everything.

My surroundings change again. Time has passed. I'm older, and there is darkness in both my worlds. My mind burns cold with the sensation of power and anguish. Before me is a giant twirling tornado. I scream like an animal full of rage, seeing red and vengeance as I move the swirling mass to sweep over the orange monsters that spread out before me. I can still see him from the corner of my eye, lying still. His bald head caked with dirt, skin melted to the bone, gaze seeing nothing. I roar, hot tears falling from my cheeks. With one hand controlling the tornado, I move the other to call up the white power and send it barreling into the chest of a monster. It howls and explodes, dripping its burning flesh on my skin. The pain is nothing. The pain is everything. I use it. I channel it. I put an end to it all.

The world goes white. I'm Molly, shaking and standing in emptiness. The anger and utter despair still racks my body. Sensei Sonjirou—how could he be gone? How could they get to him? I drop to my knees, broken. The control of my body is foreign. My hands don't seem like my own, but they are. No longer are they small and callused, but long and thin.

"Molly, we must continue," a voice speaks through the void.

Continue?

"That was your first Dreamer. I am sending you another."

Before I can protest, the blank world is painted with new colors, and we go on.

The memories keep coming in an onslaught of emotion and tactical information. My head buzzes with ice-cold pain, and my joints spasm in random reactions to situations I find myself reliving through another's eyes. I am a young black man from a small town in Ethiopia, surrounded by a charred landscape, doing back flips away from a group of growling Metus. I'm a little redheaded girl from Croatia practicing her power in an all-white room—the freezing sensation envelops both our minds as she brings forth lightning from thin air.

As soon as one Dreamer's memories stop, another's begin, and even though the visuals vanish as soon as I register them, each and every emotion and ability seeps through my cortex, easily becoming my own. Who I am and who they were interweaving with my DNA.

As the experiences of my predecessors zip through my mind, I begin to see a pattern, something they all share. They are all young. The thoughts and images of them don't extend into any life with gray hair and wrinkles. Some are barely past adolescence. I shiver and push away the idea that none seem to have lived beyond their youth.

Finally, after what feels like forever, and at the exact moment I sense my body rejecting any more stimulation and becoming sick, the images stop. My brain, which was tensing in a panic of frostbite and white light, grows warm. I gasp at the sudden shift, and blink to the empty space in front of me, my eyes released from their prison. Breathing heavily, I take in my surroundings.

I know I never physically left this room, but it's as if I've been everywhere but here. My body feels foreign, my memories fuller. I have lived more lives than I can count, and I'm sifting through which one belongs to my current body. My stomach twists with motion sickness, and my mouth holds a metallic taste. I have a strong urge to close my eyes and experience only blackness. I have an even stronger urge to vomit.

"That will be all for today." Elena rests her warm fingers to my wrist, activating the strange tugging within me.

"We will feed you a similar amount of Dreamers once your mind and body have rested. Tomorrow we will work on your power." She smiles gently. "How do you feel?"

"Different." My voice sounds unfamiliar after speaking through so many others.

"Drink this." Elena extends a clear liquid in a glass tube.

I eye it dubiously.

"It will help," she explains.

Trusting her words, like I always seem to, I shoot it back. It's sweet but refreshing.

After a moment my body quickly settles into itself, feeling grounded. Even so, I am not the same as I was before I sat in this chair. I have fought countless battles, created things with my mind I have never dreamt possible, and experienced the shock of becoming what I am over and over through many different lives. A strange peace and confidence settle over me, but with them a heavy foreboding of what's to come. I am no longer *just* Molly Spero, yet I have never felt more like myself.

"I must warn you," Elena says, taking the empty tube from my hand, "when you wake in your world after these next few days, you will be very different."

I swallow. *Will I like this different me? Will my friends and family?*

"I know there is a popular saying 'ignorance is bliss.'" She eyes me sympathetically, as if she knows my thoughts. "But I also know there is a better one that says 'knowledge is power.'"

I'm currently unsure which one I agree with.

As the Memory Chair folds into the ground Elena, explains that the next stage is meditation. I must calm my mind and body, center myself, and learn to compartmentalize the memories of those who have come before me. The liquid I drank expedited the process, but I must still go through this exercise.

It's an understatement to say that I'm not very good at this. I'm not an avid practitioner of yoga, and the few times I go, I always fall asleep during the meditation portion at the end, usually nudged awake, by a disgruntled participant, for snoring.

Namaste to you too, lady.

Elena instructs me to concentrate on my breathing, which I do, but not without seeing flashes of another Dreamer doing this exact thing. I find myself traveling into Riki more than once, Sensei Sonjirou replacing Elena. I worry this is a sign of the schizophrenia she was talking about earlier, but again, I'm susceptible to bouts of hypochondria.

Eventually I find my center, and pieces of my own life come to the forefront. My parents, my best friend Becca, my boyfriend, the house I grew up in, they all push forward, allowing the memories of the past Dreamers settling like multicolored sediment below.

Elena's soothing voice stirs my eyes open. "You have done wonderfully, Molly." We both sit cross-legged in the center of the room. Her body emits a beautiful shine, even more than it did prior to our meditation.

"Do you feel up to your physical training now?" she asks as she gracefully stands.

"I think so."

She smiles. "Good."

As if on cue, the airtight door on the far wall *poofs* open, and Alec stands in its frame.

"I'll see you for our second session, and please be sure to eat and get some rest after training," Elena says.

"Yes, I will. And thanks for um…this." I awkwardly gesture around the room.

She nods. "Of course."

Walking up to Alec, I stop when Elena calls my name, and I turn to meet her bright-azure eyes. "Remember," she says, a secret grin in place. "Go easy on Rae."

⋯⫸ ⫷⋯

The training room Alec brings me to is large, white (surprise, surprise), and void of anything but a wall-to-wall thinly matted light-gray floor, reminding me of a gym without the equipment. The space is vaguely familiar, but I'm almost positive it's because of a memory I've just gained and not from personally ever being here before. A lot on the walk over had the same sense of déjà vu. It was rather unsettling.

Rae stands off to the side, stretching. He's barefoot, wearing loosely fitted black pants and Terra's standard black T-shirt. The lighting in this space is dimmer than in the Memory room, and my eyes travel to the ceiling, which is lined with panels of swirling liquid. For the first time I realize why I always feel like I'm looking at something secretive while watching this energy. It's the very energy of the imagination, raw and pure and vulnerable to my abilities here. The memories I gathered from Elena allow me to understand how I can call upon the Navitas in this room and use it to my will. How it whispers to me currently, almost pleading to be freed and created into so many wonderful things. But within that light I also sense a darkness, a tempting snake that curls around ideas and desires that are black and twisted, that murmur of a strength surpassing all creation but used at a great cost. Even with that hint of a demon, and maybe because of it, I yearn to join with the light, to take care of it, and keep it hidden. The feeling is similar to when Dev and I were standing in the protective ring against the Metus, but not as all consuming. I wonder if the change in the level of my desire is from the experiences I was just given.

A throat being cleared dashes away my entrancement with the Navitas, and Rae stands before me, hands on hips, wearing a questioning expression. "Doing okay there?"

I blink, removing any last remnants of those strange feelings. "Yup, doing great." I walk forward. "Just trying to get used to about a handful of other people's memories in my brain."

Rae grins. "And this is just day one."

Chapter 4

Stretching on the mat, I find myself more flexible than normal. An ability I'm pretty certain was also retained from the past Dreamers, as if my body also took on their collected muscle memory. Whatever the cause, it's pretty sweet, and as I bend forward, easily grabbing my heels, I glance to Rae, wondering if he'd laugh or yell at me for pausing his warm-up to see how truly bendable I really am.

"You'll need to do these stretches before and after each session," Rae explains, his tone serious and professional. "The training you'll endure will be intense, and if you don't properly—Molly, what are you *doing*?"

"Check it out! I've never been able to do a split before!" I throw out my hands dramatically, like I've seen Olympic gymnasts do on TV, and hold my pose.

Rae blinks at me, deadpan.

"Not the right time?" I ask, continuing to hold out my arms.

He shakes his head while pressing his lips together, as if to keep from smiling. "You're not going to make this easy for me, are you?"

"But..." I look down. "Split."

Rae's composure finally cracks, and he laughs. "Okay, get up." He walks over, still chuckling. "Come on, get up. If you stay like that any longer, I won't be able to wipe the image of your goofy, proud smile from my mind for days." He helps me stand. "And I already have issues with concentrating as it is."

"We call that ADHD on Earth, and sorry," I say sheepishly. "Just found that to be pretty cool."

He pats me on the back. "Trust me—that's only the beginning of cool."

"I don't know. Splits are high up there on the cool scale."

"All right." Rae rolls his eyes. "Enough with the horse dancing."

I blink at him. "Uh, horse dancing?"

"Yeah, you know, fooling around—horse dancing."

"Rae." I hold back a snort. "I think you mean horsing *around*."

"Never heard of it. Now get over here." He positions me in the center of the mat as I swallow back a grin. *Horse dancing.* "Okay, we're going to see what you've obtained in your lessons with Elena. I'm going to come at you with no instruction at first." He takes a couple of steps back and stands with his legs apart, looking like a predator about to pounce on its prey. Fun time is clearly over.

Taking in his new posture, I surprisingly find myself balancing on my heels, ready to move with his attack, but even so I can't help the unease that rushes through me. The memories of my predecessors have revealed that we have done this many times before, but I personally have never fought another person my whole life. How can I possibly know how to engage a well-trained Vigil?

"Uh…maybe we should start with the basics first, then get into the all-out full-body contact?" I say with a shaky smile, all previous joking aside. What's up with everyone here rushing into training? Dev did a similar technique when provoking my powers, except in his version he was throwing rocks and flaming arrows at my head. *Such a sweetheart.*

"We'll definitely do that, but this is a good test to see how much latent ability you've picked up."

With no more warning, he lunges forward, and I instinctively twist my body away, completely shocked to find myself crouching down and sweeping a leg out to trip him. Rae firmly hits the mat, and we're both silent, me wide eyed, staring down at him, and Rae slowly smiling back.

"I'm so sorry!" I attempt to help him up, but he pushes me away.

"No apologies. That was outstanding. It seems the onboarding with Elena went perfectly." He rubs his backside as he stands.

"I still don't understand how I could do that. I've never done anything like that in my life!"

"*You* haven't, but the ones before you have. Each one of you is connected through centuries of duty. All the Dreamers Elena showed today—you didn't only transfer their memories, but you've also inherited their training. Everything they were ever taught for combat, you have now been taught. You might not currently know the extent of it, but that's what this training is for. To awaken it, for you to experience it firsthand and feel comfortable using it again."

This is wild. Could I really be able to do all the things I saw the other Dreamers do? I flex my hands, feeling a weird sense of power in them, like they know exactly what Rae is speaking of even if I—Molly Spero—do not.

"Come on. Let's practice blocks." Rae tucks his head behind his hands, like a boxer getting ready for a punch. "Show me your fighting stance," he says with a nod.

Some part of me knows exactly what he's referring to, and before I have time to think about it, I move my right primary kicking leg back—because now I guess I have a primary kicking leg—and my left leg forward. With my body turned to the side, knowing this makes me a smaller target, I bend my knees slightly for easy movability and raise my hands eye level, making them into fists.

What the...

"Perfect. Now let's begin."

Rae quickly punches out with his right hand, and I easily block it and step to the side. He comes at me with his other fist, and I block that as well. This feels foreign and comfortable all at once. Like I've danced these steps many times before, but it's been a while. My muscles contract and respond with speed and grace I never *ever* associated with myself, and I can't help but laugh.

"This is nuts!" I exclaim excitedly, so caught up in my glee that I miss Rae's other hand, which flashes forward, smacking me palm-out in the chest.

Both the air in my lungs and I get knocked to the ground. I lay there for a moment, coughing and gasping.

"First rule in fighting, never let your guard down." Rae holds out his hand. "Sorry about that, but I'm bound to get one or two in, so might as well do it early."

"God, that hurt," I say, rubbing my chest.

"There are many things that can hurt a lot worse, but hopefully you'll never have to endure it."

"So is this you being the tough teacher?" I ask ruefully, hesitant to show him I'm ready to continue, still smarting from that smackdown.

Rae laughs. "If you think *I'm* tough, just hope you never spar with Dev."

"Really?" I ask, surprised.

"If you ever thought you didn't like Dev now…just wait." He flashes a secretive smile.

Ugh, so not looking forward to that.

"Okay, let's continue. You won't have this much time after getting knocked down by a Metus to catch your breath. You'll need to respond right away. Back into your stance."

And so it goes for the next couple of hours, Rae commenting on some of my form and complimenting me on other crazy moves I seem to inherently know and act upon. With each passing minute, I grow more and more confident in the abilities I've acquired, and I begin to shut down my brain and move instinctually, letting my muscle memory guide my hands, feet, and body to where they need to go to defend myself. At certain points in my training, I lose track of which Dreamer I am and move into the body and mind of the Dreamers from the past. When this happens, I tend to find myself standing above Rae after knocking him to the ground.

This isn't to say that I don't get my fair share of butt being whupped. I know I'll have some colorful, blossoming bruises and more than plenty of sore muscles from the sudden strain of use. But none of it is enough to douse the *all-out, mind-boggling,* holy shit *I can really do all this* euphoria I have pumping in my veins. Screw self-defense classes—everyone just needs some time in the Dreamer Memory Chair.

I'm sweaty and breathing hard as I face off against Rae again, our bodies moving around each other in a large circle. I watch his muscles and eyes for any clue of his next move. I'm not even certain what kind of fighting we're doing. My abilities come from many different techniques and teachings, another hint of the diversity that were my predecessors.

Rae's neck slightly tenses, and I'm more than ready when his arm swings out to catch me right between my ribs. Blocking his hit, I place my other hand on the outside of his forearm, straining his reach and twirling out of his path. I aggressively pin his hand behind him and without losing a beat kick the back of his knee, bringing him to the mat.

Clapping echoes in the room, and I glance up to find Dev casually leaning against the wall next to the door. His eyes are narrowed with appraisal, and his mouth is half-cocked in his signature amused smile. "Impressive," he says as he pushes off the wall and slowly walks toward us. His sudden appearance and graceful saunter rock me out of my fighting mind-set. I take in his broad shoulders and the way his shirt hugs him like a jealous girlfriend.

Letting go of Rae, I tuck strands of hair that fell from my ponytail behind my ear, suddenly aware of how sweaty I am.

"Thanks."

"I'd like to see what you could do against a real opponent," he says with a smirk, crossing his arms. The stance calls attention to his biceps, the same ones I once found myself mortifyingly squeezing.

I leer at him. "And I'm sure you think you're said opponent?"

"There's only one way to find out."

Rae fluidly stands from his fall and drapes an arm around me. "Molly here is a natural."

I snort out a laugh. "And I'm sure retaining past Dreamers' abilities has nothing to do with it."

"Don't be so modest." He squeezes my shoulder.

"Have you practiced with any weapons yet?" Dev moves toward an empty wall in the center of the room. Placing a hand on it, the area drops out, revealing a rack of diverse armament. There's an abundance of blades, and my eyes pause on two hook swords, knowing how they feel in my grip, before traveling on to the axes, clubs, daggers, unusual looking guns, and blunt staffs. Here is where Dev stands, taking out two Bō—a Japanese long staff weapon. Somehow I know all the names and uses of these objects, except for some of the guns. Those remain foreign.

The only difference with these weapons and the ones I'd find at home is the material in which they are made—the same strange gunmetal aluminum as the Arcus. And if my memories from past Dreamers are anything to go by, they can be filled with an altered form of Navitas, making them glow the hot blue-white, and lethal toward any opponent.

"I was saving that part of the training for later," Rae explains soberly.

"Where's the fun in that?" Dev asks, handling the Bō naturally as he walks back to us. "She seems to have grasped her hand-to-hand combat for today. Why not finish with a little sparring?"

"See what I mean about the tough teacher," Rae mutters to me.

"What do you say, Molly? Care to give me a go?" Dev taunts, holding one Bō while twirling the other.

I narrow my eyes and extend a hand. "I know I won't hear the end of it until I do."

He gives me one of his sexy grins while throwing me the staff. I snatch it from the air, immediately knowing I've been trained in the art of bōjutsu.

I smile back.

Oh, it's on.

As if reading my thoughts and without any further warning, Dev sweeps toward me. His intense blue eyes are the last things I register before my mind switches off and I lunge back.

Chapter 5

OUR BŌ CONNECT with a *clank*, and I twirl away gripping my staff in thirds, swinging it around to block another hit. I move like it's an extension of my arm, using my back hand for power and my front for guidance. The memories of the many times I've practiced with this staff swim around me.

Dev drops, sweeping the ground to trip me, but I jump just in time.

We face off again, Dev's amused expression never wavering. I thrust out, and he meets my attack. We go back and forth, hitting and blocking the ends of our Bō from reaching one another. At one point I kick out, but he slaps my leg away. I wince in pain, frustration blossoming.

"Is that all you got, midnight?" he goads.

I'm surprised when a growl escapes me at the sound of his new favorite pet name, and I charge forward, spinning my stick fast and true, waiting for the satisfying *thwak* that will sound when it connects to his shoulder. It never comes. Instead I'm met with a sting to my back and fall forward, Dev moving with lightning speed to deliver the blow.

What the…

Crouching, I thrust backward to where I feel him standing, but my stick meets air. Another smack lashes my arm, followed by a low chuckle. I roll away and stand. Panting hard, my vision goes in and out of focus as Dev dashes from side to side at a dizzying speed.

In all of Terra…how is he doing that?

I barely make him out as he runs toward me. With a flick of his stick, he takes out my legs, and I hit the mat hard, feeling his Bō press against my throat as he pins me to the floor. Cocksure eyes gleam down as Dev's muscular chest rises and falls with his heavy breathing. "I have to admit, I like seeing you under me," he says with a quirk of his mouth.

I lose it. With a yell, and without thinking, I call up my power. Throwing my hand forward, I release a burst of air smack into Dev's chest, sending him flying. He lands with a thump a couple of yards away.

Rae's laughter brings me out of my rage, and I slump back on elbows.

Whoa.

"That was *badass!*" Rae beams. "Oh man. I wish more people were around to see that." He helps Dev up. "I bet you'll think twice about antagonizing our girl again."

Dev's gaze sparks with something that twists my stomach in knots. "On the contrary. I like a woman who fights dirty."

"*Me* fight dirty?" I push up from the floor. "Um, who was the one that suddenly could move, like, superhuman fast? Why didn't you tell me you could do that?" I glance to Rae suspiciously. "Were you holding out on me?" *How come I can't recall the Vigil's speed?*

Dev chuckles smugly.

"Nocturna are generally faster than Vigil," Rae explains. "I can move pretty fast, but not that fast. They are mainly created to protect and guard, so speed is a...requirement of being Nocturna."

"Don't worry. I'll be more than happy to give you another try." Dev leans on his staff. "Who knew you could learn so much in a day. I'd like to see what other"—his gaze lingers up my body—"talents you've acquired."

"*Pfft*. You wish." I eye roll.

There's a blur of movement before Dev's right in front of me. "Is that a challenge?" he asks darkly, and I swallow, keeping myself from taking a startling step back but unable to stop my attention from going to his lips.

Rae clears his throat. "*All right*, that's it for today." He claps his hands together. "Really good work, Molly."

I blink and turn from Dev, pushing aside the unease he so easily evokes.

"We'll pick it up again tomorrow." Rae takes our staffs, placing them back in the rack. "I'm also going to give you a regime to follow when you're back in New York. You'll need to do conditioning both here and when you're awake. It's not going to come *as* easily there, but we'll need you in top shape to maximize your potential. And don't worry. I'll be there for that training too," he says with a wink. "Gotta make sure you're not slacking."

I groan, wondering if I'll have to run as part of my conditioning. I've always hated running. It doesn't seem as cool as learning these talents I've inherited. Rolling my shoulders, I test how strained my muscles are from overuse. They're definitely sore, but in a strangely pleasurable way. I've never felt so physically accomplished before. I would have assumed I'd be passed out on the ground right about now, but I'm surprisingly more awake than ever. Like Rae said earlier, I do feel a bit like a badass.

"I don't know about you guys, but that definitely built up my appetite." Rae pats his stomach.

"Everything builds up your appetite," Dev says dryly.

"Hey, can I help it if I'm a growing Vigil?" Rae walks to the exit. "Come on. Let's show Molly how we eat here in Terra."

⋆⇥⧉ ⧉⇤⋆

After grabbing a quick shower in one of the changing stations, which felt more like a five-star spa—rain forest–style showerheads and side jets, *yes please*—we make it up and out of the Dreamer Containment Center, but not before running into Alec, who said he'd be waiting first thing tomorrow to escort me to my Navitas training. For as starched and folded as he is, I rather enjoy him.

Dev and Rae lead me to the west side of the city, an area they call The Market.

"There's restaurants and stuff like that throughout the city, but if you want to see where it all comes from, eat the freshest of the fresh, you come here." Rae retracts his Arcus and follows Dev down the landing platform.

We hit the sidewalk and are immediately swallowed into the crowd. Nocturna and Vigil mill around, talking and placing orders in front of vendor stands that are like nothing I've ever seen before. Pristine white glowing cubes line either side of the road, their facades illuminated with strange symbols and images of what's being sold. The merchants inside stand behind miniature circular pods that are laid out like a stovetop.

Stopping in front of a vendor that's selling fish, I watch a patron click on a hovering screen in front of him that reflects the menu above. Just as he selects a fish, there's instantly a bright flash of light, and a live flopping salmon appears on one of the empty circles in front of the merchant. He zaps it with some black square device—rendering it still—scoops it up, covers it with glossy silver paper, and hands it to the consumer. It's all quick, painless, and practiced. The next patron steps up to place her order.

"Where are the fish coming from?" I ask as my eyes travel over the endless cubes that fill the street, all selling different things but in a similar fashion. What at first seemed disorganized and chaotic now seems to move like a well-oiled machine, no pushing each other to be heard over the next person, or fighting for a spot up front. The natural behavior in a Manhattan market is nowhere to be found here. I have to say, it's kind of creepy.

"That's where we're headed," Rae explains.

Taking side streets away from the primary market, we cut back onto a main road a few blocks down, and I halt when I take in the structure at the end. Rising higher than any other building is a giant biodome. The round glass-clad ceiling seems to touch the night sky, and the light from within illuminates tall trees of many variants, from northern evergreens at one end all the way to tropical palms at the other. And I don't know if it's my eyes betraying me, but I think I see clouds.

Holy Mother Nature.

I walk forward in a daze, craning my neck farther back the closer we get. "We're going to eat in there?"

"Yup," Rae confirms.

Dev steps beside me. "This is where a large quantity of our food is grown. We have mostly all of Earth's ecosystems contained in here. We call it Anima."

"Anima." I continue to stare at the wonder that is a miniature planet in a glass dome. It's hard to see where the structure ends—it must take up half this section of the city.

A small voice inside my head is asking why it's not familiar to me, given that I just acquired so many past memories. In fact, The Market held no familiarity either. Why am I not getting any flashes of recollection?

"It means life," Dev explains.

"Life, spirit, soul, take your pick," Rae adds.

"Anima," I say again, more to myself.

Dev leans in. "Wait till you see inside."

We walk through one of the many entrances of Anima and have to be zapped clean before breaching the carefully contained environment. Standing with a large group in a subchamber, we wait while a humming noise grows around us. There's a quick flash that's replaced by a gust of wind and followed by a suction of air. The doors in front open with a steamy gasp, and we filter out.

Now, I've been to the Baltimore Aquarium and walked inside its tropical rain forest, but this…this makes that look like a backyard garden. No joke. I feel like I just traveled into the Amazon. The air is thick and humid where we stand, and a variety of fragrances attack my nose as the sound of dozens of creatures buzz.

"Whoa." I tilt my head back and study the canopy of foliage above, unable to see the domed roof.

"Pretty cool, right?" Dev wears a proud smile—which is adorable—and all I can do is nod.

"So what are you in the mood for, Molly?" Rae asks.

"Umm…"

"Well, I feel like Italian," he cuts in. "Nothing like some pasta—some delicious carbs to replenish the body after a workout. What do you say, Dev?" He smacks his friend's shoulder. "Time to pay Elario a visit?"

I follow the guys blindly as we take an elevator to a tram system that runs the perimeter and enter a car that will apparently take us to wherever we can get pasta in this crazy place.

"You'll need to buckle up for the ride," Dev says. "These things move pretty fast."

Without allowing me time to do it myself, he grabs hold of my belt and straps me in. His hands linger on the clasp against my waist longer than, I'm sure, social etiquette allows, and our eyes lock, the brilliant color of his working their magic over my body.

"Thanks." I shift in my seat. "But I understand the basic principles of how a seat belt works."

"Yes, but wasn't it more fun this way?" Teasingly, the corner of his mouth tips up before he moves away, buckling himself in. I would have been annoyed if it weren't for the tram quickly zipping forward, leaving my stomach somewhere on the platform.

Awe quickly replaces my shock as I watch, through the glass windows, the passing scenery. At this height more of Anima's layout is revealed. An oily thin wall, like the surface of a bubble, separates each ecosystem. Glowing colors dance along its length, and though it's transparent, the objects beyond are distorted until we pass into the next area. Some sections are lit like they are in the middle of the day, while others are hued like they are at dusk or the dark of night. We travel through a jungle, into a pine forest, and across a lake with beautiful beaches, until we slow to a stop at a place with rolling green hills in the distance and flat farmland in the center. Wheat and other grain grow tall and golden as they softly sway in a breeze. It's absolutely breathtaking.

"This is one of the drier climate areas," Rae explains as we shuffle out of the car, and I walk to stand in front of the window that separates us from the contained nature. "Good for growing wheat, vegetables, and those grapevines in the distance." He points to the far green hills. "*Excellent* wine. We'd give the French and Italians a run for their money if we could sell our stuff."

"This is amazing," I say as I all but press my face to the glass. "So this is where the food at The Market comes from?"

Rae nods. "Yeah, there are sections in each ecosystem that have newly harvested fruits, vegetables, fish, et cetera. Ready to be portaled to the specific vendors upon request. Everything in Terra is fresh—no preservatives, artificial flavors, any of that nonsense you humans have added to your food over time. We've advanced in many things, but food is not one of them."

I take in the space before me. "I think you could say this is an advancement."

Rae laughs. "Yeah, I guess you could."

"I thought you were hungry?" Dev asks from behind us. "Or was that growling I heard in the tram coming from a different part of your body?"

"*Har-har.* Don't be a Metus turd, Dev. And yeah, let's eat." Rae drapes his big arm around my shoulders, giving them a squeeze. "Elario will love you."

Chapter 6

Elario's restaurant sits a couple of floors below the tramway in a section that's lined with other eateries, a sort of fancy version of a food court. One side of his establishment is completely made of glass, allowing the patrons a view of this particular ecosystem's midafternoon field, giving the impression that we're dining in the middle of a Tuscan countryside. Elario also turns out to be one I love.

"So tell me, Molly." Elario leans in while refilling our water glasses. "What bet did you lose?"

I frown. "Bet?"

His deep-brown eyes crinkle from containing a smile. "To be forced to eat with these two. I can't believe you chose them as your dinner dates of your own volition."

"I think he's trying to offend us." Rae glances to Dev.

Elario *harrumphs* and brushes back a stray lock of gray hair, his black apron stretching across his belly with the movement. "If I haven't yet, then I must be getting rusty."

"We weren't going to mention your rust issue until the end of the meal, but now that you've brought it up…" Dev arcs a brow.

Elario waves away his comment and bends closer to me, which is easily done given that he's only a head taller with me sitting. "I'm serious, dear. How did such a lovely thing end up in the company of two—"

"Devilishly good-looking men?" Dev asks.

"Utterly charming companions?" Rae adds.

"Questionable characters," Elario finishes, his eyes beady as he glares at them from the side.

The guys scoff, and I bite back a grin as I look up into Elario's charming face. "Well, if you must know, I'm their hostage. They've kidnapped me."

He gasps. "I knew it! Would you like me to save you from them?"

"Oh, would you?" I widen my eyes in hope.

"Of course, my dear. As long as you promise to be my dinner companion from here on out."

"If the meals are always at your restaurant, then that's an easy agreement."

"Oh my." Elario fans himself. "I don't think you boys realize the prize you've snagged with this one."

"Trust us." Dev's gaze connects with mine. "We realize."

I fumble with my glass of water before placing it back on the table, and catch Elario's knowing smile. He nods, clearly satisfied, and excuses himself to check on another table.

"Well, I don't think I can eat one more bite." Rae rubs his belly and leans back in his chair.

"Considering you don't have anything left," Dev says and glances at the empty dish in front of his friend, "I'd say you don't have much of a choice."

Rae ignores his comment, suddenly consumed with staring at the last meatball on my plate.

"Yeah, I'm filled to the brim too." I casually push my meal away. "Anyone want this last meatball?"

Rae's eyes light up, and he's about to grab the ball, when it's snatched away by another fork. "Thanks, I thought you'd never ask," Dev mumbles between chews. "Mmm, yup, that definitely hit the spot."

I try hard to keep from laughing as Rae's face morphs into utter despair.

"What?" Dev looks at his friend innocently, and Rae mutters something under his breath about another set of balls going missing, just as Elario walks back to our table.

"So, my friends, any room for desser—"

"Yes!" Rae answers immediately.

⊷⊸⫘ ⫘⊷⊶

After a double order of cannoli—all of which Rae exclusively consumed—we leave Anima. Being inside the biodome made it easy to forget that I'm not back in my world eating a regular meal among friends, but once we're out on the streets of Terra, with the blanket of night and shooting stars, the rush of where I am and what I'm meant to do comes barreling down. It's strange how all at once this place feels so at home and so foreign.

"All right, comrades, it's my time to call it a day. I've got one beautiful redhead waiting for me to take her to a movie." Rae drops his Arcus back into his quiver after we descend a zipline platform that's attached to an office complex close to Dev's apartment.

The mention of my best friend makes me long to pick up my phone and call her. Tell her about everything I've just experienced, something I know I'll never be able to do. I swallow down the lump in my throat.

"What movie are you going to see?" I ask instead.

"I forget the name, but I know it has something to do with time travel and romance."

I smile at Becca's choice. "Well, I'd normally ask you to say hi for me, but I know that would be strange coming from you." I glance at Rae. "It would be, right?"

He grins. "I think I can figure something out."

"Really?" I ask, hopeful.

"Yup, leave it to me. I'll get her a hello from you one way or another."

"Thanks, I really appreciate it."

"Anything for our Dreamer." He brings me in for a bear hug. "I'll see you for our next session." Releasing me, he points a finger at Dev. "Play nice."

"Never have a day in my life," Dev counters.

Rae gives me a shrug. "Well, I tried. You're on your own, Mols." With a salute to his brow, he turns and trots off, disappearing around the corner of a nearby building.

Now alone, Dev and I lock eyes.

"How are you feeling?"

"Fine," I reply automatically.

He studies me, his gaze taking in every detail. "Not tired?"

I contemplate his question. Normally after the day I've had and the delicious meal, I would definitely be crawling into bed to sleep, but for some reason I feel completely fine. Like each activity rejuvenated me rather than slowed me down.

"No, not tired."

He nods, satisfied that I'm telling the truth. "Well then, what would you like to do? The city is our playground." He swings his arm out, showcasing our surroundings. A few Nocturna mill about on the thin sidewalks, which weave themselves between nearby buildings, this part of the city not as heavily populated compared to The Market.

"I don't know. What do you do for fun around here?"

A secret smile grows. "I guess that depends on your definition of 'fun.'"

"I can assure you"—I eye him dubiously—"it's not the same as yours."

"Hmm, perhaps," Dev says before quickly glancing down a side street. His face brightens. "Maybe we can compromise on the subject?" He looks back to me, a flash of a mischievous grin. "I know just the place."

The longer we walk, the more I notice this part of the city getting darker and darker, and along with its dimming light so disappears any signs of life. The street is so quiet and empty that I wouldn't be surprised if a tumbleweed began to roll along beside us.

Since I don't have the added bonus of night vision, I find myself, more than once, tripping on something in my path. I'm not 100 percent certain, but with Dev's constant low chuckling in response to my cursing, I have a feeling he's enjoying my less-than-graceful self.

"If I knew we'd be traveling into a dark cave, I would have brought a flashlight," I bite out. I'm concentrating on the pavement below in order to not trip for the thousandth time, so I don't notice Dev next to me until his hand wraps around my waist.

I freeze.

"Molly, when are you going to realize," he whispers in my ear, "if you want light, all you have to do is make light."

Just as my body leans into his warmth, he's gone. I search the blackness, only discerning a patch of city in the distance where a streetlamp glows blue. Everything else is shrouded in shadows.

"What does that *mean*?" I huff in annoyance. "Where are you?"

His deep chuckle sounds to my left, and I quickly turn, only to jump when his chest is suddenly against my back.

I try shoving him away. "Dev! Stop that." I hate how fast he can move, and his stupid night vision, and his abnormal graceful aging, and I'm sure a lot of other things I can't think of right now. Before I can glimpse his face, he's gone again. Did I mention that I hate how fast he is?

"Make your own light, Molly," his voice echoes out of the darkness.

"Make my own light? What are you talking abou—"

Oh! I almost smack my forehead at my denseness.

Quickly imagining what I desire and gathering energy, I throw out my hand. A ball of pulsing light bounces from my palm and floats in front of me, illuminating my surroundings and the face of one beautiful man. I smile proudly at my new creation and watch Dev walk forward, an appreciative expression painting his features.

"How did you know I could do that?" I ask, taking steps toward him and noticing that the glowing ball follows. It's kind of cute.

"When are *you* going to realize you can do anything, Molly? You just have to believe it," he says and surprises me by gently grazing his thumb against my cheek.

I take in a slow breath, relishing his touch but schooling my features into indifference. "That sounds a bit cheesy, don't you think?"

"Does it?" he replies distractedly while studying my mouth. The hovering light flickers, mimicking the quickening pace of my heart. We both glance at it before I move away, cheeks burning, and clear my throat.

"So where exactly is this place you're taking me? I thought you said it was close?" I ask, moving the subject away from whatever *that* just was.

"You're standing on it."

I step back, exposing a large manhole in the middle of the street.

"You're taking me to the sewers?"

He laughs. "If I said yes, would you still come?"

"Are bananas purple?"

His smile remains as he guides me out of the way. "Don't worry, midnight. This isn't a sewer. It's one of the many entrances to this place."

"And what exactly is *this place*?" I cross my arms over my chest.

Dev bends down and pulls out his Arcus. While still in the baton mode, he fits the device into a space on the top of the manhole, like a key. The rim glows white, and a huff of air releases as the lid shifts to the side, revealing a set of glowing stairs that descend into an unknown depth. A deep reverberating beat is set free and pulses out of the void, beckoning us forward. Dev glances up, a glimmer of the devil in his eye. "There's only one way to find out," he answers before jumping through and disappearing down the stairs.

I turn to my hovering glowing friend. "Yeah, I have a feeling I'll regret this too," I say before extinguishing the light and following Dev below.

Chapter 7

STRIPS OF NAVITAS cord set into concrete walls guide us down a darkened corridor, the low lighting emanating a strange science fiction aura, and I wouldn't be surprised if I saw creatures less than human down here. The air is oddly crisp for being underground, and smells sweet, like sugar. We pass bodies pressed up into shadows, faces lost in one another, and the farther we travel, the louder the music grows.

Dev stops in front of a large tinted turnstile door and guides me to enter first. As I swing around and step out, I'm immediately hit with the noise and heat of the room.

Holy devil's playground.

Bodies cover every inch of the club, moving and swaying in rhythm to the music, which is like nothing I've ever heard before. It's primal and electric, evocative and exotic. It promises to make you forget and give you memories you'll long to remember. My body instantly wants to move to it.

I'm not one that normally goes clubbing in New York. I've only done it once or twice at Becca's incessant requesting, but none of those experiences were anything like this. Here I sense that I could get swept away and never think to leave.

A couple glides in front of me, beckoning with their bodies to join them. I take a step forward, encouraged by the music, which is telling me that's exactly what I want to do, before someone grabs my hand, and I blink up to Dev. He wears a knowing smile and shakes his head. "Careful, midnight. I wouldn't want to lose you in the euphoria just yet." He leans in so I can better hear him, and his unusual fresh scent of spice and night do nothing to clear my suddenly dizzy head. "Try concentrating on one thing and not let all of it overwhelm you. This place, Vex, is meant to hypnotize those who need to escape." I take in his reflective blue eyes and nod. "Follow me. There's a section that's a bit separated from all this."

"Wait." I tug on his hand for him to stop. "I'm not sure it's a good idea for me to be here. Won't someone recognize me?" I ask, remembering Elena's words about my presence here as a Dreamer needing to remain a secret from the Nocturna.

His gaze slides over my form before coming back to lock with mine. "I think the only thing anyone will notice around here is how gorgeous you are," he says before continuing to guide us forward. *Damn*, sometimes he can be one hell of a Casanova.

As we weave through bodies, I study the people who surround us. The patrons' clothes are still black, but there's much less of it. Girls wear outfits cut in crazy geometric designs, and men wear tops that match. Most of the shapes are made from the exposure of skin through absence of fabric. Intense colors of vibrant neon makeup accent people's eyes, making the mass appear like a sea of hovering blinking lights in the dark. There are more than a few clubbers who wear glowing blue-white bands that wrap from their wrist up to their shoulders. Others wear them the length of their necks or sensually down their legs. They remind me of glow sticks, but something about how the liquid swirls inside and the way the owners lovingly stroke the areas in which the bands lie leads me to believe they are something different entirely.

Dev navigates us up steps to a lounge, and I catch glimpses of dark corners with movement. I don't need much of an imagination to know what would materialize if I looked harder.

We pass more bodies that surround a bar where some of the drinks served are familiar, while others are very, very alien. The latter have liquid that gleams and swirls like the bands wrapped around the dancers, but have varying colors like the eye makeup on the patrons. I'm curious what they taste like, but even more curious what they do.

Two large Nocturna block the way of an area beyond. Nodding, they exchange greetings with Dev before stepping aside, allowing us to pass. Dev turns, flashing me a dual cocky and charming smile, and I marvel at the way he can so fluidly combine two opposite personas. The bodyguards give me a fleeting glance, and I wonder how many girls Dev brings to Vex. The thought doesn't sit well.

The music is lower in this less-crowded section, but in a way that's desirable.

"Dev!" A beautiful dark-skinned girl in one of those geometrically cutout ensembles saunters over and wraps her arms around his neck. "You haven't been here in a while." She pouts. "Where have you been hiding? You promised me a dance, remember?"

I stop myself from rolling my eyes at her obvious infatuation, and survey the area. Waiters in white and black outfits walk up to costumers to take orders and serve drinks, reminding me of the bottle service sections you'd find at a club.

Dev gracefully detangles himself from the girl. "Candice, I'd like you to meet a friend. This is Molly."

The mention of another girl's name snaps her out of her fawning, and she slowly rakes her eyes up my body. "And?" She sneers, unimpressed, fixing her attention back on Dev. "Will you dance with me or not?"

Wow, who peed in her Cheerios?

"Yes, Dev, please dance with Candice so she can stop her groveling and I can stop the sensation of wanting to vomit." The words tumble from my mouth before I can stop them.

Candice's head whips around, her jaw dropping. "You little—" She reaches for me just as Dev tugs her back.

"I think it's time for you to leave," he says sternly to her. His worry seems to be more for Candice's safety than mine, and something about that makes me smug, recalling all my training today.

"Are you serious? You're really going to hang with this little *Metus spawn* over me?!" she shrills.

He glances in my direction. "Yeah, I guess I am."

Candice's jaw drops for a second time, and she glares daggers at me. "I'll be watching you." Her words drip with disdain before she saunters away.

"Making friends already?" asks a voice from behind me, and I turn to a small Asian girl with chin-cropped black hair.

"Brenna? What are you doing here?" I smile. Brenna was one of the first Nocturna I met outside of Dev's small family of Aveline and Tim. She was manning one of the landing platforms near City Hall the first time I used the zipline by myself. She's a friend of Aveline's but was very nice to me despite whatever feelings Aveline might have shared with her.

"I could ask you the same thing," she says with a smirk. "Hey, Dev." She looks over my shoulder as he presses a hand on the small of my back. My stomach jumps with the intimacy of the placement.

"Hey, Brenna. Ave here with you?"

"Yeah, she's over there somewhere with Hector."

"Hmm." He searches the semicrowded room with narrowed eyes.

"I was just telling Molly how she's making friends already, from the looks of our retreating Candice," Brenna explains.

"Yes, she was very sweet to her," Dev teases and squeezes my side. "Were you unhappy with something she was doing?" He glances at me innocently, amused.

"Did I or did I not encourage you to dance with her?" I ask flippantly.

His lips twitch from suppressing a smile. "So that's your version of encouragement?" He leans in closer to whisper in my ear. "I must go back and reevaluate all the times I thought you were dismissing me, then."

Despite the heat in the room, a shiver runs the length of me, starting from where his warm breath touched my exposed neck.

Using all my strength, I step away from him. "So, what's good to drink around here?"

Brenna glances between the two of us. "Um, depends what you're in the mood for."

"Something strong."

Her eyes light up, and she grabs my arm. "I know just the thing."

Chapter 8

AFTER A BIT of coaxing from Dev, I'm granted my wish to try one of the glowing drinks. He warns me that they're similar to traditional absinthe liquor, and he's unsure what kind of effect it will have on me, being human. He also tells me I can only have one and to sip it slowly. I concede to his demands but not without pointing out that he is being worse than my father.

"Do I need to show you how much I am not like that?" he asks, his low voice like thick velvet.

Sweet seduction, Batman! Will he not relent?

Silently repeating Jared's name over and over, I create space from Dev by placing Brenna between us at the bar. The patron next to me glares when I knock into her in my haste, but I'll take a disgruntled stranger over Mr. Smooth-Move-McGee any day.

"Is he like this with all the girls?" I ask, sipping my drink and wincing at the burn. The reaction of the concoction quickly rushes through me, turning every cell to liquid heat. *Whoa.*

Brenna glances at my wryly. "Not exactly."

"Loookss like somehawun gave Dev a reprieff from babysitting." Aveline walks up to Dev, throwing a hand on his shoulder.

"Did you make sure she brussshed her teef before you tucked her into bed?" She giggles.

She doesn't take notice of me standing next to Brenna.

"You're drunk." He glares down at his partner. "Who let you get like this?"

"Whud do ya mean *who*?" Aveline pushes at his chest. "I can make my hown decisions. I'm not uh child."

"Your current state proves otherwise," he says, clearly unamused.

"Give it a rest, Devlin." A tall lanky man with white hair tied low in a ponytail steps up behind Aveline, and even in black I know he's a Vigil—something about him just doesn't quite fit with the rest. He looks late twenties but could be well over a century old, for all I know. Again, the Vigil and Nocturna with their annoying graceful aging. His shocking-green eyes dance over me with disinterest before returning to Dev, and I take note of the scar that's slashed across the right. He's attractive in a snobbishly regal way, and everything about him screams villain from a '90's cop drama. The only thing lacking is an Eastern European accent. I have the urge to tell him he should practice one to, you know, complete the package he's going for.

"*Hector.*" Dev spits the name through his clenched teeth. "I should have known this was your doing."

"It might come as a shock to you"—Hector casually leans against the bar—"but Aveline has the ability to order drinks all by herself. She can even tie her own shoes. Oh, and Ave," he says, placing a hand to her back, "why don't you show Devlin here how you can spell your name!" His sarcasm splatters across all of us.

Is this guy for real?

"Enough. I know exactly how capable she is." Dev pins Aveline with a severe stare, obviously sobering her slightly. "I saw it before she even did."

There's a history they relive as they hold each other's gaze. Aveline's eyes soften for a second before they flicker to me, take in my presence, and harden once more.

"You brought *her* here?"

"Aveline." He gently places a hand to her shoulder. "You're not yourself. Let's get you some water."

She shrugs out of his hold. "*Not myself?*" She barks out a laugh. "Look who's calling the Metus smelly!"

"All right, I'm taking you home." He grabs her arm this time.

"No." She loosens herself from his grip once more, and they stand off against one another. When Aveline speaks, her voice is softer but clear. "What are you doing, Dev?" She takes a step closer to him. "Do you really want to go through that again? Because I can promise you, with this one"—she shoots a cold glare my way—"it will end the same."

Dev's body stiffens, and Brenna stands, shocked. "*Aveline.*"

"She's not worth it," Aveline continues, and Dev grows still, too still.

"Be very careful, my friend," he says in a slow, contained voice. "I know these are the drinks talking, so I will let this one pass. But do not talk of things you have no understanding of." He seems his century-old age in this moment.

"I *do* understand," she whispers, her features crumbling with hurt.

"No. You. Do. Not." He punctuates every word, searing them into her, before turning and disappearing into the crowd.

I stare wide eyed, trying to make sense of their exchange. Aveline's bottom lip wobbles like she's holding back tears, and she takes a step closer to me, the gleam in her eyes a mixture of regret, sadness, and complete hatred. I lean away.

"You will *never* be good enough for him," she says vehemently. "You will *never* be her."

I suck in air, and my heart stops. *Her?* My brows pinch in, and my stomach tightens at the deep loss etched in her features.

Hector places a reassuring hand on Aveline's shoulder, but she abruptly steps away, shoving past me. He follows on her heels.

I watch their departing forms get lost in the bodies of the club, the pulse of the music a distant layer. I stand, dumbstruck.

"Well, that sucked." Brenna picks her drink up off the bar, slamming it back.

I open and close my mouth, at a loss for words.

"It's okay. None of that has anything to do with you."

"What happened? What was that about?"

She plays with her empty glass. "It's about something that happened a very long time ago."

"Between Dev and a girl?"

She eyes me apologetically. "It's not my story to tell."

Even though I want to shake her till she spills all her beans and then some, I nod in understanding, respecting whatever loyalty she's holding on to in regards to Dev, Aveline, and their past. And what a past it's turning out to be.

What could have caused such visceral reactions? Or better yet, *who?*

You will never be her.

Aveline's words sound in my ears like a ghostly curse, and I shiver.

Scanning the crowd, I wonder if Dev's still here and if I should seek him out. What would I say? Is this why she hates me so much? She thinks I'm trying to replace someone? And Dev...what was this girl to him? All I know is, she must have been someone important to them both. A hollow feeling erupts in my chest. For whom, I'm not sure.

"I can see your mind running a mile a minute." Brenna nudges me. "He'll be fine, and if there's anything I know about Dev, it's that you'll only find him when he wants to be found." She points to my glass. "Drink up. There's one thing that's a guaranteed fix to this quickly growing melancholy night, and that's to head into that sea of tranced individuals and dance."

Despite myself, I smile, Brenna's attitude reminding me so much of Becca's.

Walking out of the lounge, we make our way toward the pulsating crowd in the center. I don't feel much like dancing, but Brenna's convinced it's just what we need.

After a moment, the beat picks up, and it takes no great effort to give my body over to it. With the finished drink flowing, mixed with the energy coursing through my veins, the music swarms around us like a forbidden siren moving our arms and legs to her desire. I've never felt so primal and, in the midst of the movement of those around me, I easily forget who I am and become one with the mass, hypnotically pushing back on the beat like it pushes on us. The anxiousness and worry that gripped me from the last exchange between Dev and Aveline melts away.

Brenna sways in front, coupled with a girl rocking a glowing band around her arm. The song turns over and becomes hypnotic, turning me into nothing but a reactionary being. Closing my eyes, I block out the flashing lights that skip overhead as a strong hand snakes around my waist, guiding me to a body. The liquid coursing through me loosens the convictions of stopping whoever this stranger is, and I continue to move, tipping my head back against a hard chest. A familiar intoxicating scent lifts my eyelids. Scruff grazes my cheek as another hand snakes around to splay across my thigh, leaving heat trails everywhere it touches. I shift around, heart beating fast, as the bluest eyes grip me with their intensity.

Dev pins me with his beauty, his desire, and—I take note—his anger. Every one of my cells jump with his sudden presence, and in this precarious place, with this hedonistic music spinning around us, the Molly that's telling me I should step away and clear my head, at this point, is a shell of a woman. But the other Molly, the one who wants to push Dev into the shadows, well, she just downed a protein shake and is stronger than ever.

By some miracle, I keep myself from giving in, the need to say something about earlier more pressing. "Dev, about what Aveline sa—" His thumb grazing my bottom lip stops me midsentence.

Leaning in, he commands only one thing, "Dance with me."

And that's the proverbial straw that breaks the stupid camel's back. In that moment I couldn't care less about whatever past is resurrecting between Aveline and Dev. Whatever ghost is coming back to haunt. With his hand skimming the length of me, I close my eyes and let the music in. Let what this place is meant to do take control. Because like all things that feel good in the moment, it clouds the consequences of later. So when Dev positions my back to his front and his lips graze along my neck, I sigh and let go.

We move together as one within a larger mass of one. I imagine this is what it must be like on drugs, the dripping of ecstasy permeating the air, when humans descend to their inner animal.

Dev's strong arms wrap around my front, connecting us further. Mine lock around his neck, again bringing his face precariously close to my exposed skin. I want to turn around and peer into him, see whatever primal expression he wears when moving as he does, because, man, does he know how to move. With his hard torso encompassing my form, I let him explore, knowing this is breaking a thousand boundaries I set in place, yet completely helpless to stop it.

The music shifts into another greedy beat, and I twist to face Dev. My body thrums with heat as his eyes spark in the dimness, devouring me whole. All they see is me. All they want is me. His full lips part invitingly, and his dark features flash in the shifting lights above.

I watch in horror and lust and excitement as my hand reaches up and brushes those lips, the ones I'm trying hard not to kiss. Again. The side of Dev's mouth inches up, and something in his sapphire gaze blazes with satisfaction and sin, like he finally has an answer to a long-standing question. Before I can do anything else, he gently encompasses my outstretched hand and brings the top of it to his mouth. With his lips branding my skin, he presses the small of my back, forcing me closer. I am locked into this man, every inch of me against every inch of him, and it feels wonderful. It feels safe.

He leans in as if to kiss me, and my heart pops in my chest. A million thoughts zip about—the shoulds and should nots of this moment. They all stop, however, when his head moves to my ear instead, his breath caressing my skin.

"This will *not* end the same." His voice is liquid heat as his grip on me tightens.

And then I'm let go, and Dev melts away into the masses as the space he once occupied closes over. The only memory of his presence is the tingling of my hand and the deep thumping of my heart as it replays his words over and over.

This will not end the same.

Chapter 9

I WAKE WITH a start to banging on a door. I look around, confused, my surroundings foreign. I'm in a strange bedroom that I slowly put together is in Dev, Aveline, and Tim's apartment. I'm in Terra.

"Molly? You up? I hope you don't sleep in the nude, because I'm coming in." My door swings open and Rae enters. "Morning!" he says cheerfully.

I groan and glance to the window. "It's still night out." I throw the covers over my head.

"It's always night out." Rae pulls the sheets completely off and away from me. "*Phew*, you don't sleep in the nude. Not that I *really* would have minded."

Ignoring his lewdness, I sit up, rubbing my eyes. "Would I even benefit from asking what time it is?"

"It's time for you to get up." Rae walks back to the door. "We're going for a run before you meet Elena. Come out when you're ready, and by that I mean in fifteen minutes. We'll eat a light snack before we get started." He closes the door behind him.

"Yes, sir." I salute the spot where he stood.

Swinging my feet over the edge of my bed, I stare at my reflection in the mirror across the room. My hair is kinked on one side, and I'm wearing one of my worn college tees with a pair of gray pajama shorts. I vaguely remember bringing to mind this exact outfit before my head hit my pillow and I passed out. I'm still perplexed that I'm able to sleep here.

Shuffling to the connecting bathroom, I wash up, my mind going back to last night. After Dev left me hanging in the middle of Vex's dance floor, I couldn't find him the rest of the night, which honestly kind of irked me. Not only because he vanished after such a cryptic statement and animalistic dance routine, but also because I didn't really know where the apartment was located. Luckily, Brenna did and walked me home.

Tim was the only one there when I got in, comfortably set up on the couch reading a book. We exchanged pleasantries about my first day, and I distinctly remembering trying hard to form coherent words as the effects of my slightly inebriated state wore off. I caught him smiling more than once when I jolted upright on the couch after nodding off in the middle of a couple of sentences. Real classy, Molly.

Though Tim encouraged me to get to bed after that, I was still tempted to stay up and wait for Dev, but my efforts were futile once I realized how exhausted I truly was. Lying between the covers, I replayed the exchange at the club on repeat, between Dev and Aveline, between Dev and me—all of it confusing me further in regards to who this man was and, more importantly, who he was to me. *You will never be her.* Aveline's words spun around and around, filling me with questions I didn't think I had any right to ask. Eventually my lids drooped, and for once, thankfully, like my nights before the accident, I got a break from it all—I dreamt of nothing.

Now donned in Terra garb, I pad down the hall, pulling my hair into a ponytail. I find Rae in the kitchen leaning against the counter, licking remnants of what resembled a granola bar from his fingers and hungrily eyeing the remaining one in front of him.

"Don't even think about it," I say picking up the clear-packaged food.

"If you were a minute later, that thought would have happily been in my stomach."

I roll my eyes and bite into the bar, immediately gagging. "Oh God! What *is* this?"

"It's a *sanus* bar. A sort of protein bar, but highly concentrated. Gives you extra strength. Perfect before a long run."

I force it down. "Um…what is this adjective you're using before the word 'run'?" I glance at him, confused. "I don't understand when you put those two words together like that."

Rae grins coyly. "I think it's better to show you what a long run is instead of explaining it."

"Hmm. Why don't you try explaining first, and then we can decide?"

"Nice try." Rae grabs my arm, ushering me toward the door. "And don't worry. At the end of the *long* run, you'll get another sanus bar as a reward!"

I groan. "Now you're just being cruel."

⇢⟫═◉ ◉═⟪⇠

I lean on my knees, gasping for air. "I hope…that concludes…" I pant, "your definition…of a…long run."

Rae nimbly stretches next to the giant fortified wall that wraps around the metropolis and, like a jerk, is not a smidgen out of breath.

We traveled beyond the city's borders to accomplish his workout routine, or as I titled it, twenty minutes in the *You've Got to Be Friggin' Joking* routine. Rae hardly broke a sweat on his beautiful brown-hued skin, while I, on the other hand, had to switch clothes twice midrun from the indecency of my perspiration. And that wasn't as easy to accomplish as it sounds.

"It's adequate." He leans down, touching his fingers to his toes, which I find extremely impressive given his enormous height. "But you'll definitely have to run in New York. You're terribly unconditioned."

"Thanks." I leer at him. "What's so important about being able to run far anyway? Can't I just use those nice little powers of mine and fighting techniques?"

"You'll find you'll tire easily using both skills if your body isn't properly conditioned. You need to build up your stamina, wake up the muscle memory you've been given. Once this is accomplished, your need to sleep here will also reduce." Rae pops two water canteens from a pack around his back and hands me one. I chug it greedily.

"I hate logic sometimes," I say, wiping my mouth with the back of my hand.

"It does get in the way of laziness," he muses.

"Precisely."

Leaning against the cool metal wall, I rove the peaceful horizon. The tall grass sways in the tepid breeze, and the shooting stars pass over in a constant stream. It's so quiet here, even though there's a massive metropolis lying right behind us. I missed it.

"So I got a message to Becca for you." Rae breaks the silence.

I excitedly push away from the wall. "You did? How?"

"I used your phone and texted her. You left it back at the bookstore, remember?"

"Oh—I forgot. So you texted her?"

He nods and takes another swig from his canteen.

"*Well?*" I widen my eyes impatiently. "What did you say? What did she say? How is she?"

He chuckles. "She's good. Asked how your parents were. I said they were the 'usual.'" He air quotes.

I nod. "Good, sounds like something I'd say."

"I said—well, *you* said—you missed her a lot, but your time at home was the very thing you needed. You asked how New York was and work. You asked her about Rae—"

"*Rae!*" I shove his shoulder. "You can't do that! You can't snoop about you through me!"

"Why not? How else were you going to repay me for this favor?" The corner of his mouth tips up. "Plus, wouldn't you ask her that?"

"Oh. My. God! That's not the point," I scold, but after a moment ask, "What did she say?"

He breaks into a wide grin. "All good things." He rocks back on his heels. "All *very* good things."

I shake my head. "Becca would be *mortified*. Dear Lord, this probably breaks so many friendship codes." I turn on him quickly, poking my finger into his hard chest. "That's the *last* time I will *ever* ask you to give her a message." I walk away, mumbling under my breath, "Can't trust anyone."

Rae catches up to me in three long strides. "Come on, it was all innocent. No harm done. Actually, quite the opposite." There's no hiding the pride in his tone.

I shoot him a glare. "That's still playing dirty."

"Don't you want to know what Jared had to say?"

That stops me in my tracks. "Jared?"

"Yeah, there were quite a lot of texts from him."

Rae quickly recounts what he can remember of his fake conversation as me to Jared. How he misses me and had some big case come up which is keeping him late at work. Some of the more... *colorful* things that Jared divulged make my ears hot, and I want to disappear on the spot hearing them uttered from Rae's mouth.

"All right!" I hold up my hand for him to stop. "I can deduce where the rest of that was going."

Rae merely shrugs, unfazed by my humiliation or the context of the conversation. "You know," he muses, more to himself, "I've never sexted before."

"*Rae!*" My cheeks flame in mortification.

"What? I haven't."

"Ugh." I hide my face in my hands.

"Jared's actually quite funny. I had to text back a lot of LALATs."

I blink up at him. "Don't you mean LOLs?"

"Um, no," he replies, baffled. "Why?"

I stare at him a beat longer. "Rae, what in the world does LALAT mean?"

"Laughing a lot at that," he says like I'm missing a screw.

"Oh my God." I drop my head in my hands once more. "Never again, Rae. Never again."

⋯⟫ ⟪⋯

A while later, Alec guides me down the stark white halls of the Dreamer Containment Center, or as he calls it, the DCC, to a new room where Elena waits. This space replicates the room with the Dreamer Memory Chair, except the walls are alabaster instead of paneled, and a giant ball of churning Navitas rests in the apex of the domed ceiling. My skin prickles and croons at its presence.

"Enjoy your training." Alec says his usual cordial parting words with a slight bow of his head.

"See ya later, Al." I nudge his shoulder and am rewarded with his efforts to hide a tiny smile before turning around. Mission *Get Alec to Lighten Up* has officially begun.

"Did you have a good rest of the day once we parted, Molly?" Elena asks, taking my hands in hers. My power stirs.

"I did, thank you."

She nods knowingly. "The report of your first physical training with Rae was outstanding. You showed remarkable restraint in using your powers."

"Oh? Well, thanks."

"You remember of course that you can also use them while fighting."

I shrug. "Yeah, I guess I didn't really think about it. Since Rae was mainly doing hand to hand, seemed like an unfair advantage." Although I *was* provoked to use it against one particularly annoying individual...

"Excellent. Well, today we're going to work on those skills. We both know you have seen a bit of what you're capable of. So now we'll condition your mind, just like you worked through your muscle memory with Rae." Elena guides us to the center of the room.

"The Navitas above will be your clay." She gestures to the mass churning in the ceiling. "I want you to call it down and contain it. We will work on strengthening your restraint to be joined with it, as that's what all Dreamers desire most when coming here—to be collected into the light, find that space where their dreams can become a reality." She faces me. "I must warn you—this energy is the same that can produce nightmares. You must fight against the path of fear and hate. It can all too easily consume love and joy."

Studying the energy above, I swallow nervously. "How will I know how to fight it?"

"It's in your DNA to know. It's why you were specifically chosen, just like each of your predecessors. As much as this is an exercise, it's also a test. For nightmares are often disguised as dreams—they are a siren's call, alluring and manipulative, but ultimately damning. You must learn your own strength to not give in or be fooled. You must know how you will be when joined." She smiles sympathetically at my concerned expression. "Don't worry. I think you'll do wonderfully. Try and remember how it felt when you experienced the Navitas through other Dreamers. How did they control it? How did they feel? It's all there for you to tap into."

I straighten my shoulders and gaze up at the blue-white energy. How does such power seem so docile? I stare and stare and stare until the pulse of the light matches my own.

"When you're ready Molly, call it down." Elena steps back, giving me room. "You know how."

I fleetingly glance in her direction one last time and know what she said is true—I do know how. I've recently known how to do a lot of things, but to experience it all for the first time, with my own hands and not through another's, has me hesitating. Will I be able to control it like my predecessors? Will I be able to do the things I saw them carry out so fluidly?

Whether I subconsciously conjure them or they really are present, I'm not sure, but the Dreamers that are all at once a part of me and wholly separate stand like phantoms in the room. Riki watches on, her eyes dark, sure, and strong. *I am you.* Her voice resonates in my mind. *You are me.* I meet her gaze before I meet all the others, feeling their energy guiding my instincts, my desires, telling me we've all done this before and I will be able to do it again. Intuitively, I lift my hands, instantly feeling the connection to the Navitas. My body fluctuates between hot and cold, and the hairs on my arms stand on end as I hold the giant form above my head. The blue-white power begins to spin—around and around it turns, condensing into a thick, fiery ball.

Reaching out like a mother calling her child, the Navitas descends, and my heart leaps in my chest. It's so bright, so brilliant, so perfect. The energy cascades down my forearms, the pureness flowing through every fiber, and it's not until a tear slips past my cheek that I realize I'm crying. Even though I've been filled with this energy once before, I'm still moved by the overwhelming sensations. Completeness, and a purity so virginal it aches, warms every nerve ending. A barrage of human emotions and imaginings lap over me one by one, and in this moment I sense how truly powerful I am. I'm not one thing but everything. I'm insignificant and momentous. What I hold can build cities and in an instant destroy them, can birth souls and just as quickly snuff them out. It's the power of a god, and I wet my lips at the temptations, constraining the urge to slip into the shadows that rim with such limitlessness.

"Hold on to it, Molly, but do not let it encompass you. Restrain yourself," says Elena, her voice far away. "Remember, you are its maker."

I am its maker.

Bringing the Navitas closer, the condensed liquid whips around, spinning tendrils of my hair as thin strands of energy lick out toward my forearms. It's so pure, so clean, so empty. Its desire for creation is abounding, and it speaks to me in a thousand voices. *Are you our creator? Are you the one that we will join?*

Riki is at my side along with the Ethiopian boy and the small girl from Croatia—they all are here, all the Dreamers I have collected. *Are you the one that we will join?* they echo.

I watch the cords of human imaginings caress my skin, snake between my fingers. "Yes," I whisper and throw out the energy.

The Navitas explodes, transforming the entirety of the domed ceiling into a brilliant blue sky, the scent of sun and summer passing by. I whip my hands around again, a coldness pricking my mind as the energy that's connected to me shifts into anything and everything I can think of. The room flashes from a sunlit day to a blizzard to heavy rain. From standing on the peak of a mountain to an ocean crashing under our feet, to lightning crackling everywhere, to thousands of butterflies fluttering about as giant flowers grow as tall as trees. With each change, the Navitas sings in happiness, bounds with joy, and I find myself laughing along with it. I build worlds around us and solar systems and creatures that only exist in dreams. I manifest colors that have flavors and darkness that's all encompassing. I go to a place unborn by man, created in a space where the natural law has no reach and the science of reason is washed away, replaced by the basic pure desire to exist, all of it coming from a place I never knew I had.

Marveling at the worlds I create, at the life that springs forth from my mind, and how full my heart feels each time something new is born, I find myself dipping a hand into the ocean that now laps up against my thigh. Cupping the water into my palm, I throw it forward, smiling when the droplets transform into hummingbirds, their colors rare and not from my world. They flutter toward me, encircling my form before shooting up into the azure sky. I laugh and fall back into the water, which gently catches me and rolls me to lie facedown on the belly of a giant furry mammal. It's twice the size of an elephant, and its hide is sunflower yellow and softer than silk. Black unblinking eyes take me in as its wide mouth lets out a soft rumbling mewl. I pet its stomach, knowing it won't hurt me, and grin when it begins to purr. A giant paw slowly shifts me closer so I lay curled against the creature's chest. I look at it with love just as it gazes back at me before I nod a silent good-bye and blink to a new world and then another—floating, flying, and swimming between them all.

Eventually, after a time that can't be quantified, there's a wane in my strength, heaviness in my limbs. My mind aches with a sharpness, and the Navitas pushes on me with pressure I struggle to control. Around the edges of myself dimming is a whisper that will ease the pain, that promises to give me power that will never fade, and I tilt toward it, leaning into the temptation of limitlessness.

And that's when I see it, the creep of the void, a black so dark it calls to me to come closer, to search for something, anything that may be beyond. My mind prickles in warning as my cells shift with longing. Inky forms begin to wriggle free from the emptiness. *Come to us*, they say. Their slick, oily voices murmur my wants and desires—dark secrets kept locked away, buried deep, for no one, not even myself to acknowledge. My breathing grows shallow, and with a hot flash of panic I quickly gather the last remnants of my energy and force them back. There's a howl of anger as the darkness is shut out right before everything goes quiet.

The brightness fades as I contain the Navitas once more into the small twisting ball of an empty canvas, gently returning it to the center of the dome, where it hugs an unknown source, severing my connection.

Breathing heavy, my shoulders sag with a century-long weariness, and for a moment I am bereaved, lonely, unsure where I belong, and then I blink to Elena staring wide eyed, mouth slightly ajar—an expression completely foreign to her.

"Molly, I have never…I mean…that was remarkable."

I flex my hands, ridding them of an ache that has settled deep in the bone, still reveling at all I just did. "Was I supposed to hold on to it longer?"

"No," she breathes, watching me carefully, "you held on to it longer than I thought you'd be able to. What you created…well, normally even after a Dreamer retains predecessors' memories, they need a bit more time to work up to what you accomplished." She peers into my eyes, searching, her scrutiny making me shifty.

"Did I…did I make a mistake?"

She chokes on a bit of laughter, another reaction that seems foreign to her. "No. Quite the opposite," she says. "It seems you are highly advanced in your skills."

"Really?" I ask, shocked, never having been advanced in anything. "Why?"

Elena glances to the Navitas. "I'm not entirely sure, but…"

"But?"

"I have some theories—theories I need to look further into before discussing," she quickly finishes, seeing me about to ask more, and I snap my mouth shut, knowing better than to press her on a subject she deems unready to divulge.

I study the energy above, recalling everything I just did, that I knew I could do, and I remember something from earlier. "Oh, I wanted to ask you—well, I was wondering why some things from past Dreamers I can bring up, while others I can't?"

Elena tilts her head curiously. "What things exactly?"

"The Anima, for starters. I can't remember ever seeing it before or knowing about it."

She nods. "Yes, that's because no past Dreamer *has* seen it before. None have ever walked the city of Terra, seen anything beyond the Containment Center. Besides having to fight the Metus, that is."

"So they never left this underground facility? For all the years they would come here?" Elena nods, and I blink, astonished. "Wow…that must have been…well, really boring." I would go stir crazy if I was only allowed to walk around these halls. Not that I've seen close to the whole Center, but still—to miss out on seeing Terra, with its unique skyscrapers and magic sky, and the Nocturna. To have never met them…Dev…

"It was adequate for what they were sent to do. For one reason or another, they never awoke anywhere but in the Center," Elena explains before turning and narrowing her eyes at the exit. There's a huff as the door opens, and Rae, Dev, and Alec stride in.

This is the first time I've seen Dev since the club, and my stomach scrunches into—well, a scrunchie, when we lock eyes. His face is gorgeously brooding and serious as he breaks our gaze to focus on Elena.

"I'm sorry to interrupt, but we've been notified of a small Metus attack on one of our outpost generators. I wanted to see if the Dreamer should accompany us, though we can handle it if she's occupied." Dev speaks like he barely knows me.

"I can go," I blurt out and then backpedal to compose myself when he shoots me a glare. "I mean…if it's a *small* group, like you say, than this is a perfect time to test my skills."

Dev ignores my response and waits for Elena's. I purse my lips at the brush-off.

"I think Molly's right. With what I've learned from today's session, she's more than ready. "

My chin involuntarily tips up.

"Are you sure?" Dev asks again.

Elena quirks a brow. "I'm not in the habit of making decisions I'm unsure of, Devlin. Ensemble a team that's been briefed on her presence."

He reluctantly inclines his head before pinning me with his sapphire gaze. "You'll need your Arcus."

Chapter 10

THE ENDLESS FIELD whips by in a blur, our speed silent in the hover car. At least that's what I'm calling it, since it's shaped like a car and hovers. It's black inside and out, and its exterior reflects our surroundings like a one-way mirror, a chameleon zooming over the land. The top is completely transparent glass and—because I witnessed it when we climbed in—can fall away, transforming the vehicle into a futuristic sort-of convertible.

Alec drives with Rae in the passenger seat and Dev and I in the back. My eyes flicker over the quickly passing landscape as I anxiously run my palms over my knees, allowing the familiarity of this situation in, the memories of doing something similar before. A hand rests on top of mine, stilling it.

Dev smiles tightly, warily. "Aim for their heads first, and if you can't, then their chests. Navitas spreads the quickest in those areas."

I nod. "Yes, I know."

"Of course," he says softly, squeezing my hand once more before letting go.

There's a loud *beep* right before strange symbols dance across the glass windows—a message.

"So they *were* on their way to the Sea of Dreams." Rae leans forward and types something into the dash. "That means there's at least a pack of them."

"How many is a pack?" I ask.

"Around twenty-five," Alec answers.

Twenty-five. That number might as well be a thousand. Can I really do this? All my instincts say yes, but the part that's still only me, only Molly, is shaking her head vehemently and resisting the urge to pee her pants.

I've got to get a grip.

"What's the Sea of Dreams?" I ask Dev, for distraction.

He smiles warmly for the first time today. "I'll take you there sometime" is his only answer before he turns his attention back to the window.

We only travel for a couple of minutes when I spot a glowing orange mass mixed with blue-white light. A small group of Nocturna and one or two Vigil stand guard around a sleek black building that resembles a half-buried radio tower. A giant antenna juts tall and proud into the sky, where Navitas crackles at the tip, collecting energy from the passing shooting stars.

"Get ready," Rae says, adjusting his sitting position to pounce the moment he's allowed. There's a second of silence, of calm, right before the glass top falls away and the sound of fighting erupts around us.

Dev grabs my arm, his stare unwavering. "Don't leave my side," he says before dragging us both to our feet.

He fluidly retracts his Arcus and, aiming down at the nearby Metus, shoots flaming arrow after arrow into the beasts. A few shriek their inhuman gurgle before bursting apart, while others, now aware of the new threat, dodge in the nick of time.

All four of us jump from the vehicle and run into the chaos, the tall grass whipping against our legs.

Quickly taking in the situation, I push away the urge to vomit from the stench. About sixteen Metus are staggered in groups of four around the outpost building. Their seven-foot-tall burning forms chuck pieces of fiery flesh at their foes, some spewing fire. Alec and Rae join two Nocturna who are fighting a group. One Nocturna, a dark-skinned man named Alexander, whom I met at City Hall, drips with sweat as he goes tête-á-tête with a beast. On the far side, I catch the whipping strawberry-blonde hair of Aurora, still supermodel beautiful, and her partner, whose name Brenna said was Ezekial. They make quick work of the monsters with the help of Aveline. Tim is the last I recognize. He stands closest with one other Nocturna and two Vigil. They push against Metus that have somehow grown their number to six in the span it's taken for us to reach them.

The sounds of howls and grunts fill the air along with the pungency of rot and death. The weapons being used are of a variety—Arcus, whips, flails, and something that looks like a badass shotgun—filled and pulsating with an altered form of Navitas, the kind that will end these nightmares.

Dev reaches Tim's side and with dizzying speed shoves one deadly sharp end of his Arcus into the abdomen of a churning Metus, stopping its forward lunge. The creature belches a scream, attempting to grab the intruding instrument, but Dev quickly twirls again, and my eyes hardly register the slash through the air that decapitates the monster. It melts into a flaming puddle that eventually sinks into the ground, killing the grass below.

I stand stock still, mesmerized, shocked, appalled, and surprisingly giddy. A painful heat slowly registers along my back, along with the oily, thick smell of rotting garbage.

Oh shit.

"Move!" Dev shoves me aside as two of his arrows find a home inside the head of a Metus. The light fills its entirety right before it pops like a mucus-filled balloon and is gone. Burning slime splatters my leg, but I hardly feel it through my protective pants. I can only pant and stare at the place where the creature once was. Where I just was.

"Molly." Dev stares at me angrily. "What are you doing?" He helps me to my feet. "Why aren't you fighting? Did you not see that Metus right behind you?" His tone turns from panic to concern.

"I...I don't know."

"You don't *know*?" he repeats incredulously. "Well, snap out of it! You said you could handle this, so prove it. This isn't training anymore."

His words jolt me into action.

"Yes, yes, not training." I square my shoulders and, ignoring the Arcus strapped to my back, flex my fingers. For some reason I'd rather handle them this way. Letting all that I've seen and learned settle in, I switch off my individuality and open up my pasts. Everything instantly becomes clearer, second nature. Thank God for Dreamer memory osmosis.

A Metus close by sniffs the air before focusing on me. Molten drool drips from an orifice in its head, which I gather could be its mouth, but the thing slides around too much to be certain.

Yuck.

Dev's at my side ready to end the threat, but I step forward as my hand ignites with power. Navitas crackles and swims in my palm, ready to do my bidding.

The Metus tilts its head back, crooning an eerie whine at the sight of what I hold. The sound, filled with longing and desperation, is unsettling.

When it runs straight for me, I'm more than ready. With my mind prickling, I clap my hands together and then part them, turning the energy into a thin blanket of glowing white that quickly shoots forward, engulfing the creature, and collapses in. Right before the Metus vanishes without a trace, erased by the Navitas, a sigh whispers past my mind, a feeling of relief, and I shiver.

"Whoa," Dev says by my side.

My mouth quirks up in an uncharacteristic smirk.

"All right, don't let my praise go to your head or anything."

"You're one to talk."

He merely shoots me a wink before guiding us forward.

We meet up with Aveline, who's heavily attacking a Metus but unable to get a proper kill shot. Dev runs to help, and the two swarm the beast, working in choreographed unison that shines light on their long-standing partnership. With their dual efforts, the monster doesn't stand a chance, and it explodes in a bomb of stink and fire. They share a companionable smile that has me turning away, noticing a rapidly approaching fiery liquid. It heads straight for Aveline, but since it's so low to the ground and approaching from behind, she doesn't see it coming. I run forward just as the creature begins to grow into its form, taking her by surprise. Dev yells her name, too late in realizing the threat, and she turns, horror stricken. But I'm there even if I'm yards away, and when the monster attempts its attack, I will the earth to burst forth, sending it backward. Aveline is rocked to the side, shocked but safe. I throw out my hand, letting cords of Navitas fly forward, and like barbed wire, it clings around the entirety of the Metus, rendering it immobile. Not missing a beat, Dev lets loose an arrow right into the thing's chest. It crackles and fizzes with blue-white light before it bursts apart and is gone.

I'm breathing heavy as my head pinches with the acute pain of having to act so quickly. Dev glances my way and then to Aveline, who's still splayed on the ground, looking shaken. I reach her first and hold out my hand. She stares at it before locking eyes with me, and I give her a small reassuring smile, which she doesn't return. Instead she takes my hand, allowing me to help her up. She holds my gaze a moment longer, a mixture of emotions playing across her features, before she nods ever so slightly and turns away. I'm not positive, but I think that was her version of a thank you.

Eventually the Metus number dwindles, and there's a hopeful levity in the group. I've taken down two more—Dev mostly jumping in front to remove any oncoming beast before I have the chance. I'm beginning to feel a little useless, and I wonder if he'd prefer I wait in the hover car.

It's when I have this lighthearted thought that the worst thing I've ever seen happens. A Nocturna, not fifty feet away, trips trying to dodge a spew of fire from a Metus. Before he can right himself, the monster descends upon him in a wave of lava. Too quickly for me to react, the beast's body dismantles to nothing but liquid for the second it takes to coat the Nocturna.

The man's acid-sharp cry is cut off by the gurgling of pain, bringing me to my knees and bile to my throat. I watch in horror as the Metus literally consumes the form that was once a man. My vision flickers from the world as it is to a world of energy, the once-bright light of the Nocturna now covered by a black sludge. The Metus, desperate and greedy, suffocates the power of dreams into nightmares. When the liquid mass rises, it rises not as one, but as two. The Metus remaking the Nocturna into its own image, into our enemy that now stands seven feet tall and burning orange. The only discernable feature is that its body still partly resembles a man, a tortured shadow of what once was. With my shifting eyesight, I catch a glimpse of a light, barely there, but a light nonetheless, in the center of its chest—all that's left of the once-bright Nocturna's soul.

There's a sickening pop as Dev buries an arrow into the original Metus, breaking it apart in a slimy burst of red and white. The newly formed Metus still remains, and I want to sob when sad, partly human eyes lock with mine. In a strange freezing of time, I sense its plea, the seed of a creature born of dreams still very present, hating what it's become. But then the stopwatch starts again, and its lucidity vanishes, taken over by thirst and greed. It lunges toward me, and I jump to the side, simultaneously knocking away Dev's aim to take it down, postponing the inevitable.

"Molly?"

"Just wait! There has to be another way." I desperately search my memories. How can I fix this? I have to be able to fix this.

"This *is* the only way." Dev pulls me to him right before a dripping claw can swipe me.

I shift back to the other plane of sight, suddenly finding it easy to do, and dig further into the beast's chest to the tiny pebble of light, trying to figure out how to bring him back. But then I'm momentarily blinded by a slash of bright Navitas, and I blink to Dev twirling out with an Arcus that now glows white, slicing the creature's head clear off. Its body crumbles in on itself, melting into the ground, and is gone.

"No!" I reach forward only to be held back by Dev. "No," I say again, but it comes out in a whisper.

"It had to be done," Dev says softly. "Do you understand? It had to be done."

I sag in his arms, barely registering the sounds of the other Nocturna and Vigil eradicating the remaining beasts, leaving only the residual stench of nightmares.

Glancing at the singed dirt in front of me, knowing a life was taken there, I step away from Dev, and he hesitantly lets me. The image of a writhing, melting form is forever in my memory, the first memory of a loss in battle that's all my own.

"Are you okay?" Dev peers down in worry.

"What was his name?" I ask.

"Cree." It's Tim's voice that answers, coming to my side.

"What does it mean?"

His sorrowful gaze takes in the darkened grass. "Warrior."

I nod.

"He lived up to his creation. That's all any of us can hope for."

"His creation was to be brutally devoured into a Metus?" It comes out more biting than intended.

"That's not what Tim meant," Dev says. "He fought bravely, honored his name."

These answers for some reason anger me, and I walk away. Even with their remorseful tones, their single-minded sense of duty for Terra currently annoys me. I know deep down they're probably right, but I'm still only surface level, wishing there was more I could have done. Walking among the remaining Nocturna and Vigil, I try not to stare too long at the injured, even though their presence reminds me further of my current uselessness to help them. *There has to be more to my power here than to kill Metus.*

"You did good, Dreamer." As if on cue, Aurora, all exotic eyed and perfectly coiffed hair—yes, even after a fight—steps in front of me. "I saw you take one down. It was impressive."

It's odd to receive a compliment as if I just made a goal or a basket or a touch down instead of killing something, but I merely nod my thanks because I don't know what else to say, too in my own head and too tempted in my anger and sadness to mess up her hair.

I wait by the car while they check the outpost generator and discuss what just transpired. For the first time, I don't feel much like talking or asking questions.

I receive curious glances from the group now and again, and I wonder if it's because of how angry I was earlier or because of the small handful of new Nocturna who have been briefed on who I am.

Dev steps in front of me, blocking my view. "Hey," he says softly.

"Hey."

"How you holding up?"

"Fine."

"Mmm."

"Really. I am."

Again, "Mmm."

"*What?*" I glare up at him.

"You didn't seem like you were fine earlier." He moves to my side and leans against the car.

"Well...I wasn't, but now I am."

"Okay." He keeps staring at me.

"Is there another reason why you came over here?" I ask, watching Rae, Alec, and a few others guide glowing devices over the charred areas; black and still-sizzling orange goo gets sucked up, the grass once again green.

"Is wanting to see how you are not a good enough reason?"

I don't answer, wishing I were still angry with him for the other night at the club, because that's a silly, foolish thing to be angry at, and I'm starting to really miss silly, foolish things. Instead I'm standing in another dimension trying to come to terms with the reality of my past memories, my supposed destiny, and wondering exactly what sort of good I can really do here.

"You know, in the end we only have our duty to fall back on," Dev says after a moment.

I glance his way.

"When someone is taken from us, whether it be in a battle or not, if we didn't have our duty, our belief to keep fighting for, working for, none of us would last very long. This"—he gestures to our surroundings—"is what we've done for centuries, what we've fought for, and what we'll keep fighting for. Because if we stop, if we do that, then *they* win and what Cree, what any fallen Nocturna or Vigil died for, would be in vain.

"Cree died doing what he was born to do, what he lived to do, and we can't take that away from him. If we keep moving forward and living, then he keeps living too."

I study his profile, sensing he's not saying this just so I can hear it.

"But don't mistake that to mean we aren't angry," he continues, "or upset or wish any of us could have changed the outcome. Because we have...some of us have wished a different ending more than our next breath." His brows pinch in as he stares into the distance. "But if there's one thing I've learned in all my time here, it's that we can't change the past. We can only try and guide the future." His eyes rest on mine, a shadow of sadness still lingering.

"I—"

He holds up a hand to stop me. "I'm not telling you this to make you feel bad. I'm telling you this so you understand. When any of us go, because eventually we all do, we merely hope, if it's not peacefully, then it's for what we were given life to do." He watches me a moment, a small smile inching across his lips. "Because, I mean, how much would it suck to go out tripping on your shoelace?"

I shake my head, fighting a grin at his lame attempt at levity after such a speech. "Yeah, that would suck pretty hard."

"And you know what else I think?" he asks, his face suddenly close to mine. Always close to mine.

My pulse quickens. "What's that?"

"I think, when loss is a possible everyday occurrence, you should live fuller in the moments you have." His gaze bounces from my eyes to my lips and then back up again. "Food for thought," he whispers before stepping away and, without a backward glance, returns to the group.

I press my lips together, spinning around the words he deliberately left hanging. Again. In the distance, Aveline watches Dev walk away before her gaze pierces mine, and the thought of things being left hanging takes on a whole new meaning.

Chapter 11

THE RIDE BACK is silent. The walk back to the apartment is even quieter. Everyone seems to be in a mood, and I'm sure most of it has to do with Cree. I know there will be no funeral, no wake to say good-bye. There will only be a carving of his name onto a wall in City Hall. Joining a million others that have been carved before.

With each step, my muscles wince in pain, my first physical fight leaving me more shocked and wary than I would have thought. Even with my ability to remember worse things than a single Nocturna being killed, much, *much* worse things, those memories are like recalling a brutal scene in a gory movie—a bit removed. They felt extremely real and all my own when I was given them, but once I fell back into my body, their severity dulled a bit. I'm now realizing it must be a coping mechanism, one that I'm extremely thankful for. Because to be so openly raw to the collective brutality that all the past Dreamers experienced would leave me in an extremely disturbed vegetable state.

Walking into their apartment, Aveline immediately goes to her room while the rest of us enter the kitchen. Tim fetches Dev and me a glass of water.

"So...the group of Nocturna tonight are aware of what I am?" I take a sip of the cool liquid, ridding the taste of bile that clung to me since the fight.

Dev leans against the counter next to me. "Yeah, the ones with us were debriefed. We found it necessary to inform a few select priority people before you arrived."

"Aurora's priority people?" The question tumbles out before I can stop it, and I want to immediately punch my own face, uncomfortable with the bit of jealousy I have toward her and knowing this isn't the time or place for such emotions.

"Some think so." Dev hides a smile that I'm sure would be wolfish.

I bite down on inquiring if *he* thinks so and instead ask, "What was that building they were going after?"

"A Navitas generator," Tim says, pulling food from the fridge. "We have a few scattered around the outskirts of the city. It's one of the ways we collect energy."

I nod, vaguely remembering something about the generators, but my recent acquired Dreamers seem to hail from a distant past where such inventions weren't yet constructed.

"A few decades ago, the Metus learned they could use it to produce more of themselves," Dev explains. "We've created barriers, making it more difficult for them to get at the energy, but it seems they've learned a way around them."

"So what can we do?" I ask.

"That's what I'm going to meet with my Security board about."

"I'll go with you." I reach for my quiver, but Dev stops me.

"I think it's best if you took it easy the rest of the day." He roams my appearance, and whatever he sees softens his features. "You've done a lot, and if you don't feel it now, you will soon."

I frown. "But I think it's important for me to attend these meetings. I need to learn more about fighting these things, and I can help. Maybe there's something I can do to protect the generators."

"Yes, but for now I'd like you to get some rest. Let what you experienced today settle a bit."

"What do you mean, settle? I'm fine." I glance to them both. "I'm fine."

Dev looks at me as if to ask, *are you?*

"You know, Molly," Tim says, holding up a head of lettuce, "I could use some help making dinner. Maybe we can play around with your Dreamer skills in the kitchen, yeah?" He lifts his brows in excitement.

Glancing back to Dev and his careful appraisal, I find myself letting out a resigned sigh. "Okay, sure."

Dev flashes me a grateful smile. "Thank you."

"Yeah, whatever." I brush him off. "Next time, I'm coming with."

He playfully tugs my earlobe. "Deal."

I hate that that gesture has me softly grinning up to him rather than scowling.

"I'll be back soon," Dev says, wrapping his quiver across his chest. "And Molly"—he pins me with a look of pride and something else that has my stomach somersaulting—"you were breathtaking out there."

A blush gathers on my cheeks as his compliment fills me with warmth. "Thanks."

He winks and then leaves me with a humming Tim, who's already filling my hands with tasks.

"And that's how you make proper garlic bread." Tim sprinkles on a bit of cheese with a flourish.

He's been making me laugh for the past hour with his cooking enthusiasm, seeming to channel what he believes is an Italian cook, but I think he sounds more like the Swedish Chef from *The Muppet Show*.

"Do you cook at home, Molly?" He places the bread to the side, checking on the sauce.

"Not like this. My kitchen barely fits me, let alone enough room to make a proper meal."

"That's a shame." He frowns, unknowingly wiping a bit of food into his grizzly beard. "Well, you're welcome to cook here all you'd like. I find the ritual of it to be therapeutic. Raises the spirits."

"I can see that."

His grin is sheepish. "Yes, I'm a bit much, aren't I?"

"No, you're perfect. It's always nice being around someone when they're doing something they love."

He chuckles and shrugs away the compliment. "Tell that to Aveline and Dev. They tend to conveniently step away when I cook." He gestures to the empty apartment. "As you can see."

Just then Aveline stomps into the living room, Arcus and duffel bag in tow. "I'm going to the roof," she says, swinging open the front door and, without a backward glance, slams it shut behind her.

Tim flashes me a halfhearted smile. "Sorry about her. She might not say it, but she really is grateful for your help out there. We all are. Aveline's just not used to sharing our space."

I snort out a laugh. "I appreciate the cover-up, Tim, but it's pretty obvious she hates me, and not because we share the same roof."

"She doesn't *hate* you. She just…well, she can be a bit overprotective of the people in her life."

"Meaning, Dev."

The side of his mouth quirks up knowingly. "Why don't you go clean up before we eat. I'm sure you'd like to wash off."

I glance down and wrinkle my nose, forgetting for a moment that I was still in my grimy clothes from the fight. "What about you?"

"I will in a bit, but for now I've got the rest of this covered." As if to demonstrate, he tastes a spoonful of sauce, makes a face, and grabs for more seasonings.

"All right, if you're sure…"

"More than sure." He waves me off.

I'm halfway to the hall when he calls my name. "Yeah?" I turn back around.

"Can you do me a favor?" he asks. "Can you grab Aveline when you're done?"

I quirk a brow at him as if to say, *are you serious?*

His responsive grin is a bit too bright and coy for his intentions to be innocent.

⊷⟩⟩ ⟨⟨⊶

The air is crisp with the accompanying wind as I walk onto the roof. The night sky's clear and bright with the passing stars, and the surrounding city sprawls out in a peaceful wave.

The rhythmic sound of *thwacking* comes from my right, and I step around the elevator building, spotting Aveline in a section that's set up as a practice area. Keeping in the shadows, I watch her aim down small targets in the distance. Her technique is fluid, as if the Arcus is merely another appendage, and with her moon-pale hair pulled away from her face, I can make out the delicate pinch of her brows, the mark of concentration. With her features void of her usual scowl, I'm allowed a glimpse at the likeable Aveline, reminding me of the first time I heard her laugh genuinely and how infectious it was.

"Are you here for something other than being a stalker and watching me in the shadows?"

I stiffen when she addresses me, thinking my presence had gone unnoticed. *Great, add* Molly is a creep *to her reasons for hating me.* Swallowing my embarrassment, I walk forward. "You're good at that."

"We're all good at this." She validates her statement by methodically shooting arrow after arrow at the targets, each finding their way to the intended marks. I wonder if it's my face she's imagining on them that gives her such precision.

"Okay…well, Tim sent me up to tell you dinner was ready."

"Fine."

"*Fine.*" I match her curt tone and turn to leave. Why I even try with this one, I have no idea.

"Molly, wait," she calls, stopping me.

Turning back, I catch her studying the end of the practice field, the silence between us stretching on for an awkwardly long time. I'm about to continue to the elevator, when she finally speaks. "I…I owe you an apology," she says, forcing the words out like food turned bad.

I blink, confused, and then glance around, searching for the other person that statement was surely meant for, but when I look back, her attention's on me.

"Um…okay?"

"What I said to you…and to Dev the other day…well, I wasn't myself and…and I just wanted to say that I'm sorry." The two of us are having a hard time holding each other's gaze.

"It's all right," I surprisingly hear myself saying.

"I also wanted to thank you for earlier, at the generator."

Is this for real? The sickly and rather pained expression she wears makes me think so. Eating her pride must not agree with her.

"Aveline, you don't need to thank me for that. You'd do the same for me." As soon as I say it, I hear the uncertainty there. We lock eyes, and I know she's thinking the same thing, but eventually she nods.

"I'm not usually this…rude."

"Mean." We say the last words simultaneously, and the side of her mouth tips up.

"Yeah, I guess mean is also accurate."

"More like generous," I mumble.

"All right, don't push it."

I raise my hands in peace, and she seems mollified, if only temporarily. "So why are you?" I ask, walking forward. "Mean to me?"

She fiddles with her Arcus. "There's a lot you don't know. A lot of history that makes your presence…complicated."

"Complicated? Complicated for whom?"

She looks at me pointedly.

"Dev?" I ask with raised brows.

"Did he ever tell you how we became partners?"

I shake my head, and she regards me silently for a moment before placing the remainder of her arrows into a case. Closing it with a click, she stands by the roof's edge, looking out.

"I was brought into this world unfit for most positions. Too small to lead, too weak to fight, too shy for politics. They were quick to christen me a waste of a dream, a girl that probably wouldn't see life past the Nursery—the place where we're raised until we come of age. They thought it cruel that my name summoning would give me Aveline—life—when it was so obvious I wouldn't have one." Her eyes catch mine, a yellow fire burning bright as they bring up memories. "I didn't accept that fate, of course. I knew I would prove them all wrong, if only given the chance, and Dev gave me just that.

"He came looking for a partner. The infamous General Devlin, stepping down from his esteemed position to return to guard duty." Aveline's tone is laced with fond mockery. "The Nursery was in a fluster gathering all the potential candidates. They were to try out in front of him, and he would choose. No one had heard of something like this before. A warrior such as he removing himself from office to take on a position far beneath him, especially to consider the Nursery, of all places, to find that particular partner was, well…shocking. But leave it to Dev to challenge the norm." Her eyes shine with pride. "All Nocturna and Vigil are given basic combat training in the beginning, but I was always forced to sit out for fear of my health. Obviously, I found a way around this and would practice on my own and in secret. Surprisingly, the exertion improved my health, and I grew strong, finally tasting what comes from such things—freedom. Never again would I sit idly by and let someone else tell me my capabilities, or in this case, lack thereof. I knew then that I would be a Nocturna guard no matter what anyone said."

Aveline takes in a deep breath, calming the quake in her voice. "I snuck into the tryouts that day and rushed the line, taking my position to start my turn. You can imagine the scene that caused." She twinkles a laugh. "They swarmed to take me away, mortified at my behavior and pitying what I'm sure they thought was a delusional dream. That was the first time I bit someone." Her mouth curves to one side. "Dev was the one that called them to stop. I remember what happened next like it was yesterday." She glances up at the passing stars. "He walked up to me, and I thought he was the most beautiful thing in the world. I was also terrified. I had heard the stories of his accomplishments, his quick rise in ranks, and of…other things, things that happened more recently. He asked me my name, and I'm not sure what he saw when I answered, but he announced that I would be given a chance to try out. I nearly passed out right there." She tips her head back to laugh again.

"Well, how'd you do?"

Her smile is crooked. "You don't see someone else partnered to Dev, do you?"

As I take in her playful expression, I'm simply floored by this other side of Aveline.

"So you see," she continues, "he was there, believing in me when no one else would. He's guarded and guided me through this life to be more than even I thought I could be. I owe him everything, Molly. Do you understand? *Everything.*"

"Yes, I can see why your loyalty would be strong," I say, studying her sharp features, "but what does that have to do with not liking me?"

"I don't want Dev to get hurt."

"And you think I'd hurt him?"

She shakes her head, a sad smile appearing. "I think you'd kill him."

Chapter 12

THERE'S AN OLD parlor trick that has always astonished me. A trick that no matter how many times I've seen it done has always left me a bit baffled. The trick where someone rips a tablecloth off a table, leaving all the delicately placed dishes and glasses in place. How on earth do they remain upright when the very thing they were resting on was just unexpectedly torn from beneath them? As I stare, stunned, at Aveline, I realize it's probably the same miracle that's keeping me standing now.

"*Kill him*? What are you talking about?"

"There was a reason he stepped down from his position to be a guard. He…he lost someone."

Having an idea where this is headed, my stomach tightens. "A girl?"

Aveline nods. "Her name was Anebel. She was the love of his life."

And like a sixty-mile-an-hour tractor-trailer to my gut, there it is, the missing puzzle piece that clicks it all into place. The remorseful cryptic comments, the haunting gazes, the desperate declarations that he would keep me safe. All remnants of a lost love.

I'm not sure what my reaction should be upon hearing this. He's not mine to feel the sting of jealousy or the desire to run and console him, which is why it sucks that I feel all those things and then some.

An image of Jared's smiling face flashes before me, lying with him in bed as the morning light plays through his honey-colored hair. I hold back a cringe of guilt, knowing whom my emotional loyalty should remain with. Pushing away my confused thoughts, I focus back on Aveline. "What happened?" I ask.

"She was killed by Metus."

Unwillingly, I find myself sifting through all the memories I have of these monsters taking a life, each brutal, each undeserved. Were any of them her? I swallow back the rage and despair that creeps up my throat.

"The worst of it was that it wasn't even during a big battle," Aveline continues. "We tend to prepare for loss then. But she was ambushed on a standard patrol. Aaron, Anebel's partner, said the numbers came out of nowhere and that he had no idea how he even survived it." Aveline frowns. "Terra knows, he wished he hadn't."

"What do you mean?"

She studies me, seeming to weigh her options on how much to divulge, but with a heavy sigh she goes on. "Aaron loved Anebel. And I don't mean in a brotherly way—he wanted to *be* with her, be her mate, and from what I've been told about Anabel, no one can blame him. She's said to have been very beautiful and kind, passionate beyond belief. Tim says that she burned as bright as the stars." Instinctively Aveline and I both glance up to the brilliance of the passing lights. "Dev never resented Aaron for his feelings for her. He seemed to understand the draw Anebel had, but when she died, both men lost themselves. Aaron completely vanished. One moment he was there, and the next he just wandered off to die in his final fight against the Metus. Maybe to find penance for the blame he put on himself for her death." She shrugs, unsure. "But Dev... well, I was told he became a shadow, also disappearing for a time. When he returned, he looked like he went through hell and back, and in a way I think he had. He doesn't really speak of it, the time he was gone. I just know he sought whatever retribution he could find. That's when he resigned his high-titled position and went back to guard duty."

"To honor her memory."

"Yes," Aveline says softly. "When I became partners with Dev, he had a very single-minded drive to find Metus. Normally we're meant to patrol the surrounding area and make sure none come too close, but Dev, well, Dev took it upon himself to seek them out. I was terrified those first years, thinking each patrol was a suicide mission, but I never said anything. In a way it forced me to learn faster, made me almost as good as him." She glances at the targets in the distance. "I only really knew him as hollow in the beginning. Like he was merely a vessel carrying out his duty and nothing more. But eventually, slowly, a spark flickered on again, and I realized how much of Dev was missing for all those years, what withered for a time after Anebel."

I rub my chest, attempting to subdue the ache that's growing there.

"Tim was the one that was around before and after. He stayed with Dev at the apartment, watching over him, and when I moved in, he decided to stay. It's been the three of us ever since. It took a while for Dev to open up to me, but we've been partnered for a long time, and I've seen his eyes slowly resume their vibrancy, their will to live." Her gaze bores into mine. "I won't see that spark go out of him again. And I'm sorry to point this out, but with what you're meant to do here, it doesn't exactly put you in the safest of situations."

"Gee, thanks for the reminder."

"Molly, I'm serious."

"Yeah, so am I. I get it. Dreamer, battles, will probably die, yadda yadda. Trust me—I get it," I say, using sarcasm to mask my very real fear of the future. "I just...I don't know what to say to all this."

"You don't need to say anything. I merely want you to hear, to understand. Dev can't take a loss like that again, and I see the way he looks at you. I see—" She cuts herself off.

"So what are you asking me, exactly? To be extra careful? To have Dev not like me?" I laugh humorously. "First off, I don't have much choice in my activities around here, do I? And secondly, I have a boyfriend. Dev and I can't be like that. We *aren't* like that. So there's nothing to worry about."

"Molly, don't be dense." She glares at me, and I'd take offense if I didn't notice the desperation in her eyes. "It's only too obvious how you two feel toward each other. And that's good you have a boyfriend. Hold on to that. Because Dev...well, it nearly destroyed him the first time. He won't survive it a second."

"I think that's enough storytelling for tonight," a deep voice says from behind us, and we both jump.

Shit.

Dev stands, arms tightly crossed, wearing an unreadable expression. His gaze is piercing, and in that moment, I pity Aveline for being on the receiving end of it.

"Hey," she says with surprising calm, "we didn't hear you come up."

"Yes, it seems I interrupted a rather engrossing conversation."

Aveline and I lock eyes.

"We were making amends," she says.

"Really?" He regards us both. "Best friends now? Good. Terra knows, it will make my life easier. I am curious though as to what caused such quick kinship...no? Not going to tell me," he says when we both remain silent. "That's fine. We all have secrets we'd rather *keep* secret. Know what I mean, Aveline?" There's no mistaking the undertone of his contained fury. "Well, the reason I came up, besides to disrupt you and your new best friend, is to tell you that dinner is ready. A task I believe was given to Molly, but she obviously got distracted."

"Uh, great, thanks." Aveline picks up her supplies, ignoring all his barbed comments. "Come on, Molly. I'll tell you the best way to look like you've drank the wine Tim insists on making. He can cook like a god, but his fermenting skills, well...he has no fermenting skills."

She tries brushing past Dev, but he snags her arm. "We'll be talking later," he says in an ominously low voice, his stare unforgiving. She nods without comment, and he releases her, allowing for her quick retreat. He turns to me, his gaze like a thousand pounds of pressure bearing down. For the first time, I feel ashamed in his presence, and even with our eyes locked, he seems miles away, the carefree Dev nowhere to be found. A wall has gone up, and I'm unsure which one of us erected it. So I break away from his stare and shuffle past him.

And he lets me.

Chapter 13

DINNER IS A strange test of wills. Aveline does her best to pretend that everything is perfectly fine and she wasn't just caught gossiping about an obviously delicate subject, while Tim artfully refrains from asking what's going on. And it's only too obvious that something's going on.

Dev sits at the head of the table, calmly cutting into his dinner and methodically chewing each piece. As if he needs all his movements to be slow, purposeful, or the rolling storm that seems to be coiling around his taut muscles will explode and collapse the foundation of the building.

I push around the food on my plate, feeling utterly and completely out of place. I've never swum in these waters before. What do you do in a situation like this? Do you discuss the elephant in the room? Or keep letting it take giant, mammal-sized dumps everywhere and merely walk around it? Personally, I'd rather not deal with the smell.

Dev pours himself more wine, his fourth glass, and when he brings it to his lips, we catch eyes. Immediately I look away and then feel dumb for suddenly becoming gun shy around him. Glancing back, I find him still staring at me, and he keeps staring, daring me to look away again, to show my discomfort, and in that moment I grow achingly sad for him. Seeing the change in my expression, his jaw flexes, and he tears his gaze from mine.

"That's good the Defense Department has a solution to the generator issue." Tim cuts into the quiet. "Will it take very long to carry out?"

Dev glares into his glass. "No."

"Wonderful! Elena will be pleased to hear it," Tim says with way more exuberance than necessary, and Aveline animatedly nods in agreement.

Ignoring the elephant it is.

"So, Molly, will you do more onboarding tomorrow before you leave?" Tim asks.

"Uh, yeah. I have another session with Elena before more physical training with Rae."

"Excellent. It's really amazing how all that works, isn't it? The ability to transfer memories into actual tangible skills. Simply fascinating. I wonder what other things the Vigil have kept secret all these years." There's a slight edge to his last statement, and I shift in my chair, really not ready to handle any more tension in the room.

"Tim," Aveline says, "I forgot to mention it earlier, but this meal is friggin' awesome. Thanks again for cooking."

"Yes, thank you." I sneak an appreciative smile at Aveline before raising my glass to toast. Being on the same side of Dev's anger is a quick bonding mechanism, it seems.

"Oh," Tim beams. "It's no problem at all." He lifts his wine. "To hopefully many more family dinners."

The sound of metal scraping across the floor brings our attention to Dev standing. "Sorry to cut this nice moment short, but

I've got to get back to City Hall. Tim, thank you for cooking. I'll see the rest of you later." He grabs his Arcus and quickly exits the apartment.

Tim turns to us. "Okay, will someone please now tell me what the Metus is going on?"

Aveline and I share a look before I stand to follow Dev.

"I'd let him go," she says.

"No, this is ridiculous. I at least want to talk about what he overheard."

"Not a good idea!" she calls out right before I shut the front door behind me.

"Dev!" I run to catch up to him before he enters the elevator. "Don't you dare get in!"

He turns around, quirking a brow. "Since when did you become so demanding?"

"Since always," I say, out of breath. Running with a full belly of pasta—bad idea.

"So." He crosses his arms over his broad chest. "To what do I owe the pleasure of seeing you chase after me?" His gaze dances over my body like it always does, and I wonder if he's even conscious of it anymore. Terra knows, I certainly am.

"We should talk."

"Whatever about?"

I purse my lips. "About what you heard Aveline and me discussing on the roof."

"And what exactly was that?"

"*Dev*," I say, slightly exasperated. "Can we drop the act for a second? You're making me regret coming out here."

"Than that will make two of us." He calls the elevator again.

"Please. I just want to talk. I know this…is a sensitive subject, but—"

"That's just it—you don't know anything about it. So don't throw your pity party my way."

I flinch. "That's not what I'm doing."

"No? Your sad puppy-dog eyes say differently."

"First of all, my eyes naturally glisten with emotion on the account of them being so big. So you'll just have to get used to that. Think of me as an anime character."

"A what?"

"Never mind, not important." I wave my hand dismissively. "You're right though. I don't know anything about your past, but… I'd like to."

"And why's that?"

"Because I consider you a friend."

"A friend." He seems to flip the word around in his mouth. "A friend," he says again as his eyes travel the length of me once more, the energy in the hall suddenly shifting. "Is that what I am to you?" He takes slow, predatory steps toward me. "A platonic entity in your life?" Closer he stalks. "Someone to go shopping with? To confide in about your *boyfriend*?" My back hits up against the wall, and he rests his hands on either side of my head, trapping me in with his body. I feel consumed by his mass—small, and his nearness confuses my thoughts, jumbles my nerves. The sound of heavy breathing reaches my ears, and I realize it's my own erratic intake of air. "Is that what this feels like to you, Molly?" His voice is thick and smooth, his blue gaze like a gathering storm. "*Friendly*?"

The small space between us cracks and fissures, and I'm suddenly hot, too hot. Glancing up, I notice a light sheen of sweat gathering on Dev's skin. The temperature around us shifts and rises, and I become embarrassingly aware it's my own doing, but I'm helpless in stopping it. The side of his mouth curls up. "No, this doesn't feel friendly at all."

"I…"

"Yes?" He dares to bring his body even closer, the sweet scent of wine wafting from his lips. "You what?"

"I…I need some space."

He doesn't move an inch. Instead his eyes follow a bead of my sweat as it slides down my neck and between my breasts, which peak out from my shirt.

The temperature spikes.

"Dev, please," I whisper, ignoring the flickering illumination of the hallway that matches my racing heart.

He stays silent, letting the space grow hotter and hotter, the lights to pulse more erratically. I want to scream at my powers for betraying me in this moment.

"Let's make a deal," he finally says. "I'll tell you all my secrets, the truth of my sins, and regrets, losses and desires"—his gaze lingers on my lips—"when you finally tell yourself the truth."

"About what?"

"About what I really am to you. And let me give you a hint," he continues when he sees me about to respond. "It's not a friend." He pushes off from the wall and calls the elevator. I stay pressed against the solid structure as the doors open. "I'd get some air if I were you. From the feel of it, you seem a little hot and bothered."

My cheeks flame as I glare at his smug face, instinctively willing the elevator to shake with him inside. I gain satisfaction when his eyes widen in shock. "And I'd be more careful who you piss off," I bite out, making the doors slide shut, but not before catching his delighted grin.

I think I actually growl.

Wiping the sweat from my brow, I replay Dev's "not a friend" point he rather dramatically made very clear, and one my body oh-too-obviously agreed with.

Shit.

Using my powers, I change the air to icy and try pushing away my instinct to analyze. *When you finally tell yourself the truth about what I really am to you.* The truth. What is the truth? No, don't go there! There's Jared, god damn it. Sweet, wonderful, not-an-ounce-aggravating Jared. Dragging my hands over my face, I groan. *This couldn't be just a* little *easy for me, could it?*

Taking a deep breath, I head back to the apartment. Aveline was certainly right about one thing, chasing after Dev—absolutely terrible idea. Leaving to go home tomorrow couldn't have come at a better time.

Chapter 14

I RUB MY eyes, trying to rid them of the sting that I'm slowly growing accustomed to feeling after receiving Dreamers' memories.

"That last one was a bit intense." I slowly sit up.

"Yes, that battle was one of our biggest here in Terra." Elena returns the containers of memories to their designated places in the wall.

"I can't imagine being a Dreamer during a World War...to have to live such despair while sleeping *and* being awake. How do they not go insane?"

"You're a very brave group and were chosen for a reason."

"I really don't know if I'm *that* brave. I've definitely jumped onto a chair when I thought I saw a mouse in my apartment."

Elena smiles. "Brave when it matters most." She unhooks the heart-rate monitor from my finger. "Plus, we have ways of calming Dreamers down if absolutely necessary."

"What do you mean? Like a sedative?"

"Something like that."

"What would make you want to do that?"

She steals a glance my way, waiting a beat before answering. "Sometimes the limitless power of the imagination can be a bit much for certain individuals to control. It can bring out a…dangerous aspect in a person."

I swallow. "So…meaning they went power hungry and got a little too *Pinky and The Brain*, 'let's take over the world,' on everything?"

"I don't know what this *Pinky and The Brain* is, but yes, you could say that's how they got."

"Well, that's not terrifying or anything." I rub my palm over my thigh as I think about my powers. "But in a way…in a way I can see how it could happen. The Navitas, well, it can be very seductive."

"Yes," Elena agrees. "That's one of its tools in pulling out one's deepest desires. It seduces out the very core of an idea to bring it life. That's why the Dreamers who come to us are meant to have a balance of both light and dark. Having too much in either direction can cause catastrophic consequences when connected with the Navitas here."

"Interesting." The idea that I have a balanced inner consciousness seems rather comical. Becca would certainly be rolling around on the floor right about now if she heard this, considering she thinks I have a few screws loose, since I have habit of stubbing out others' discarded cigarettes thrown on the street, yet have no issue spitting my gum out the window while driving.

"Speaking of Navitas"—I swing my legs around to dangle off the chair—"when will I be shown the Dreamers that have dealt with seeing it in people."

Elena stops typing. "What do you mean?"

"The Navitas in people. You know, the energy I can see flowing in all of you."

She grows very still. "You can see our life's energy?"

"Um, yeah."

"Right now? You can see mine right now?"

I flip my eyesight to the other plane, something I've easily been able to do since the day I saw a Metus consume the Nocturna, Cree. Elena's life energy, as she called it, is surprisingly bright, brighter than Dev's and Rae's. It's also thicker in her veins, the blue-white strands more protective around each of her organs, like armor. No matter how many times I shift to this plane, the beauty of it always mesmerizes me, the life it represents, the soul of the person in front of me. I switch back to my normal vision.

"Yes, I can see yours, and it's actually brighter than the others. Why is that?"

She's silent.

"Elena?" I ask, growing concerned. "Is something wrong? Why are you looking at me like that?"

"We have to end our session early today." She abruptly turns off all the equipment, and I have to jump up from the chair to keep from falling onto the floor with it.

"What? Why?"

"There's something I have to look into."

"About me seeing the Navitas in people? Is that bad?" Okay, panic definitely setting in. She walks to the exit without answering, and I follow. "Elena, you're freaking me out. What am I supposed to do now?"

"Start your next session with Rae," she instructs as Alec steps into the doorframe right as it opens.

"But what about meditating? Don't I need to do that first?"

"Yes, yes, do that," she says distractedly as her guards surround her and quickly usher her to wherever she's in a hurry to go.

Well, crap. I glance to Alec. "What just happened?"

He shrugs as if to say my guess is as good as his.

"I think I said something wrong." I head back into the giant domed room. "Do you think I said something wrong?"

"I don't think you could ever say anything wrong," Alec replies neutrally.

"Oh, you smooth man, you. Don't you know flattery will get you everywhere?"

His smile almost peeks through at that one. *Damn, so close.* I take a seat on the floor and cross my legs. Looking at Alec standing stoically on guard by the wall, I pat the space beside me. "Why don't you join me?"

"In meditating?" He seems rather taken aback by my offer.

"Yes, do you meditate?"

"All Vigil are meant to meditate for two to three hours a day."

"And have you done yours yet?"

He shifts uncomfortably. "No."

I pat the space again. "Then this is the perfect time for you to do it."

"But I'm meant to guard you."

"Does that door lock?"

He glances at it. "Yes."

"Then there you go."

He sucks in his cheeks, looking uncertain.

"Alec, as your Dreamer, I command you to sit and meditate with me." I know it's not fair to pull that card on him, but come on, he deserves to take a load off. Plus, I'm pretty sure I wouldn't be able to get in the zone with him standing and staring at me the whole time.

He hesitates a moment more before coming to sit beside me, his thick legs impressively folding into a pretzel shape. I smile, pleased. Taking a deep breath, I close my eyes, ready to channel my inner Riki and let her put me in the chi mode. She's much better at this than I am, and currently I need all the help I can get. Elena's reaction has left me a bit mentally preoccupied. Not that having a new handful of memories swimming in my brain helps either.

"Thank you, Molly."

I pry open one eye to see Alec looking at me with such reverence and gratitude that I frown. "For what?"

"You honor me by asking me to sit with you and share your meditation."

"Oh, Alec," I say, reaching over and placing my hand on top of his large one, "I'm the one who's honored."

The small grin and blush that spreads across his face is enough to make me burst into tears. He's such a young boy in this moment, despite his extra-large form, and I suddenly feel extremely protective of him. Clearing my throat, I sit up straighter. "Okay, my young deshi, let's do this thing."

And with that we both shut our eyes and go to that space of emptiness, allowing our bodies to be deconstructed and then put back together again—to become reborn.

Who knew meditating could be so cool?

⇥⊜ ⊜⇤

A while later, feeling a lot better, I walk with Alec to the training room. His dark complexion shines, almost glowing, reminding me of how Elena looked after she meditated. I wonder if that's due to the fact that they're Vigil. If so, it's a nice benefit of being from their race, well...one of many, I guess, given their long lives and ability to easily travel between dimensions.

Studying Alec's profile—his crooked nose that has become such an endearing quality to his features, and the small speckle of gray near his temple—I wonder about his actual age.

"Alec, did you know the last Dreamer?"

He glances down to me. "Yes, I did."

"Really? What was she, or he, like?"

He thinks for a moment as we continue forward. "He was very passionate and noble, an exemplary fighter—"

"Not to sound unimpressed or anything, but most of the Dreamers I've seen have all been like that. I want to know what he was *like* like—his personality."

Alec's brows furrow. "Okay, well...he had a strange obsession for practical jokes, most of which we Vigil were the butt of." Despite his dismissive tone, I catch a lightness in his eyes, and I laugh.

"Sounds like I would have liked him."

He grins ever so slightly. "Yes, I think you would have too."

I try to imagine who this man was, what he was feeling and if he enjoyed that he was the Dreamer.

"So what happened to him?"

Alec's features quickly shut down. "He stopped coming" is his simple reply, and with that I know the topic has closed. *For now.* I'll definitely be asking Elena for this particular Dreamer's memories. I purse my lips. I only hope she'll oblige.

Once Alec drops me off at the training room. I walk in to find it empty. Deciding to do some stretching while I wait for Rae,

I multitask by poking around my memories for any hints of past Dreamers' deaths. It's all blank though, like that part was cut out, redacted, omitted. Is Alec telling the truth, that they merely stopped coming, just like that? The fact that I can't even find a specific cutoff time makes me believe otherwise. It all just grows fuzzy, dissipating into a fog. But why hide information for any other reason than because it's worth hiding? Flashes of all the violent and abrupt endings of Vigil and Nocturna flicker before me, and I swallow. Was that also the fate of every Dreamer? Is it my own?

"Cool it, Molly," I pep talk myself. "Don't go spiraling out of control just yet." It's not lost on me that by talking in the third person—and out loud—I might already have.

Shaking my head and feeling as stretched out as a medieval prisoner on the rack, I lie back, watching the swirling Navitas in the lights above. *Where in all of Terra is Rae?* I smile at my new use of vernacular. Man, how has so much changed in such a short amount of time? Have I really only been here for two days? It feels like months. What will it be like to return to my world later today, to see Becca and Jared? My job? *My job!* I groan. It will be *so* mind numbing. As if it wasn't already.

Spreading my arms out to the side, I mimic making a snow angel on the padded floor. What I am excited for is the sun. *Ah, sun, how I've missed you.* Closing my eyes, I imagine lying in the bright-green grass of Central Park, the morning light filtering between the leaves of the trees above. How beautiful the lit-up canopy is. I can almost feel the warmth, smell the sweet spring air.

The sound of someone walking into the room has me turning my head to find Dev standing in the doorway. He glances around, an odd expression on his face. And that's when I notice the thousands of green leaves fluttering and falling from the ceiling, filling the room with their vibrancy. I hadn't even realized I called upon my power to manifest them, so stuck in my daydream. My abilities seem to be getting more fluid with each Dreamer's memories that I receive.

Dev plucks an errant leaf from the air and rubs it between his fingers. Embarrassed, I make them all disappear. He looks up just as the one in his palm vanishes, and his eyes hold me still. His gaze is searing and seems to reach into me, searching, exploring, and filled with such reverence that I can't help the warmth that spreads through me.

"What are you doing here?" I sit up, tucking one side of my hair behind my ear.

Dev blinks, removing any visible remnants of emotion from his face. "I'm to train you today," he says, walking forward, his black T-shirt stretching against his muscles with the movement.

"You?" I ask as my stomach drops, thinking about our last encounter in the hallway and how much I still don't know about him and Anebel. Looking at him looking at me, I would never have guessed he suffered such a loss. But if there's one thing I know about Dev, it's that, if he wants to, he's an Oscar winner at hiding his true feelings.

"Isn't that what I just said?" He steps past me.

"All right, no need for the 'tude." I push myself up from the floor. "Didn't realize Rae wouldn't be coming, is all…or will he later?"

"Nope. It's just you and me." The way he draws out the last few words causes me to shift on my feet.

"Um, okay."

"The change in teachers was unplanned." Dev goes to the wall that houses the weapons. "But I thought it would benefit for you to overcome my speed advantage."

"Is that even possible?" None of my memories bring up this skill.

"At this point, I wouldn't limit you to anything."

Well, if he's going to talk like that…

"Here." Dev throws me a Bō.

I catch it and internally groan, remembering the last time we sparred with these.

"As a warning, I won't be going easy on you."

"Have you ever?" I murmur.

He doesn't respond, merely scrutinizes the way I hold my staff as he begins to circle me, our usual easy banter seemingly lost in the quicksand of his awakened past. Taking a deep breath, I push aside those thoughts for now and start flipping my Bō around as well, keeping an equal distance from him. We both stalk one another, waiting and watching.

There's a quick flash in Dev's gaze right before he's nothing but a blur and I'm knocked to the ground. I don't even have the chance to put the air back in my lungs when he's helping me to my feet.

"Again," he says.

I narrow my eyes and step back, trying to figure out how to track his movements, but it's like one moment he's twenty feet away and the next I'm on the mat, my backside smarting.

"Well, this is super fun." I ignore Dev's outreached hand and stand on my own.

"Again," he repeats.

"Okay, let's hold up there, Mr. Miyagi. How 'bout you provide a little instruction before we continue down this path where my ass ends up in a cast."

He arcs a brow. "Can that happen?"

"I'd rather not find out. Now, tell me what to do."

Dev leans on his staff. "Well, normally, if you were Nocturna, you'd be able to visually break down my speed and react accordingly."

"*Riiight*. But here's the thing…I'm *not* a Nocturna."

"Yes, I can see that," he says dryly.

"Okay, then what's a normal person like me supposed to do?"

"Realizing you're not a normal person would probably help."

I roll my eyes. "Fine. What's a normal *Dreamer* like me supposed to do?"

"Well, I think that's *your* area of expertise, don't you?"

"Dev! Are you serious right now? How is this helping in any way?"

He shrugs. "It's helping to keep me entertained."

Motherfu—I rush him with a growl, twirling my Bō, and smile when I hear and feel the satisfying *thwak* as it makes contact. I move to strike a second time, but Dev's gone, spinning around behind me and with breathless speed swipes at my feet. I go down with a grunt.

Bending over me, his face is infuriatingly passive as he simply says one word. "Again."

Chapter 15

I HAVE NO idea how long we repeat this pathetic dance of me standing up only to get knocked back down, but one thing's for certain—I. Hate. Dev. But, *for real*, I do. I've had to constantly rein in my...rather disturbing...vengeful thoughts in fear that they might actually manifest. And I'm pretty certain Dev would rather keep his arms attached to where they are and not shoved up a certain...uncomfortably small place. As I roll over with a groan from my most recent fall, I begin to question if he really deserves my mental restraint anymore.

"This isn't helping." I remain lying on the ground. I'll be down here in a few seconds anyway.

"You need to tap into your power, Molly. Figure out how to use it to overcome my speed."

"Oh, is that all?"

"There has to be something you're not using," he says, not a speck of remorse in his voice.

"Trust me, there's a lot I'm holding back right now." I think about my creative revenge again.

"Come on." Dev pokes me with his stick. I hate that stick. "Get up. We're not stopping until you've figured this out."

I actually whimper.

"You'll benefit from this, trust me."

I slowly sit up. "Why? The Metus aren't as fast as you."

"They could be now. We don't know all of their new abilities, and I have a feeling them changing into liquid isn't their deadliest new addition."

"Why do you say that?"

"They're growing smarter. I don't think they would show all their cards so soon."

"Why do you think they're getting smarter?"

Dev rubs his hand against the back of his neck. "I think it has to do with the advancements in your world. The new breed of evil on Earth is rather sickening. Terrorism, cyberterrorism, nuclear and biological warfare, the amount of negativity and fear that spawns from those groups are a Metus's dream."

Using my Bō to help me stand, and ignoring all my protesting muscles, I replay his words. "Dev, do you think that if the new evil in my world can affect things here, that the new good could as well?"

He twirls his staff, thinking. "I guess it's possible. Why?"

"Well, when I was with Elena earlier, I mentioned some things about my abilities that she found surprising."

"Like what?"

I hesitate in answering, not wanting him to freak out like she did. "Um, well, I can see the Navitas in you guys."

His Bō stills. "What?"

"Elena called it your life's energy."

Dev's eyes widen. "You can see that in us? But how?"

I shrug. "I'm not sure. I just can. Ever since what happened with Cree, I can kind of flip my vision back and forth between this plane and that. Like right now, I can see these blue-white strands moving through your veins, wrapping around your body."

"Molly, that's incredible!"

"Elena seemed worried."

Dev waves his hand, unconcerned. "She has a tendency to take things too seriously."

"Where you have a tendency to take nothing seriously."

"On the contrary, I can name one thing that I never joke about." His gaze darkens as it rests on me, and I resist the urge to squirm. "Wait—" Dev says, blinking back to clarity as a new thought comes to him. "Try using that sight when fighting me. See if it makes a difference."

"I don't know…"

"Why not?"

"I'm scared I'd hurt you or something. I'm not sure what I'm looking for, and I have a feeling that if I touch any part of the energy in you, it would be really, really bad."

"Well, maybe it's not about messing with my energy, but keeping tabs on it."

"I have absolutely no idea what that means."

"*Molly*," he says with slight exasperation. "Listen, I can't see what you can to assess it properly, but humor me for a second. Try fighting me while focusing on my life's energy."

I frown, still unsure when Dev quickly smacks a blow to either side of my arms.

"Ouch! What was that for?"

"Don't you want to keep me from being able to do this?" He hits my legs this time.

"Stop it!"

"Make me," he goads suddenly from behind, and my ear gets flicked. I spin around as he retreats with a small grin.

"And here I was thinking you couldn't get any more annoying," I say through clenched teeth as I follow his movements, switching to the sight that illuminates his essence.

He wants me to humor him? Oh, I'll humor him all right. All the way to the infirmary where they'll have to remove my stick from his—

I pause, stunned, noticing the Navitas in Dev reach out to the left a second before he moves there. *No way.* And then there's a *whoosh* through the air as my legs are knocked out from beneath me, but this time as I hit the ground, I'm smiling instead of cursing.

I jump up, my heart racing in excitement. "Again."

Dev clucks his tongue. "And I thought you hated that word."

I don't respond, but instead I pay closer attention to how his energy pulses and flows through him. Seeing through this plane reminds me a little of when Dev made the protective wall of Navitas and it channeled into me. It's like being submerged in water—my body feels weightless, things around me move slower, and everything is a bit blurry, except where there's Navitas—that remains like a beacon, solidifying what it surrounds.

This time when Dev rushes me, I see the trail of blue-white light shoot out in front of him, as if that's his conscious thought leading him forward, marking his path.

Unfrickenbelievable.

I easily step to the side, and he runs right past me. Turning around, his brows pinch in with confusion, but he only hesitates for a second before twirling toward me again. And again I see it all before it happens, my movements seeming more fluid than his as I block his Bō with my own. One. Two. Three. I meet him attack for attack, and a giddy laugh bubbles up.

"Whatever you're doing"—he knocks his staff against mine—"keep doing it."

My mind tingles with the exertion to focus on his energy, and sweat slides down my face as I work on finding the upper hand. I'd think after having the training of more than a dozen past Dreamers I'd be the one with the advantage, but Dev's extremely skilled. Even with the ability to predict his moves, I'm still only able to defend.

With the strain of pushing myself in two directions—physically and mentally—my head grows thicker and thicker with tension right before it explodes in white-hot pain and I drop to the floor, groaning.

"Molly, are you okay?" Dev asks in a panic.

"Ah!" I put pressure on my temples and squeeze my eyes shut. It feels like I'm having a massive brain freeze.

"What can I do? Should I get help?" He brings me to lean against him.

I shake my head while taking in calming breaths and slowly open my eyes. I blink, finding my vision has returned to normal, and with it the pain dissipates.

"Wow," I say, relaxing. "That sucked."

"Are you all right?"

"Yeah, I think so."

"What happened?" Dev reassuringly strokes my arm, making me very aware of his embrace, but I don't move away, telling myself I need the comfort.

"I think using that sight has a time limit. I get a similar pain if I use my power too fast or for too long. My brain tends to freeze up, but this time it came quicker than normal. Watching you like that must suck my power up more rapidly."

"Okay, we'll be careful next time then. Won't push you longer than necessary," he says as his hand absently moves to play with a strand of hair near my neck. If I were a cat I'd be purring, which means I should definitely move, should definitely be standing up, shouldn't be considering holding off for a couple more seconds...

"You were incredible though." He leans back to find my gaze. "You were moving just as fast as me. Did you know that?"

I shake my head. "No. When I was in the other plane, it seemed like you slowed down and I could see where your movements were going before you took them. Like the energy in you was highlighting the path you had in your mind."

"Incredible," he says again.

"It *was* pretty cool," I admit with a grin.

He chuckles, the first sign of his old self, before his attention flickers to my mouth and then back to my eyes. Instantly the size of the room shrinks to just the two of us. Him and me and the intimacy of our position. *Okay, this is probably my cue to move away. Why am I not moving away?*

"We'll need to figure out all the advantages of using that sight," he says after a moment, his voice rough, like he needs a drink of water, his gaze telling me I'm that drink of water.

"Won't be satisfied till I have the upper hand?" I laugh nervously, searching for a way to lighten things up a little.

"Molly," he says softly as his attention drops to my mouth again. "That you already have."

My lips part on a shallow gasp, and my heart jackrabbits when Dev slowly inches toward them. *Patter, patter, patter,* it counts down the seconds till his lips collide with mine. *Patter, patter, patter.* Only one more *patter* till—

"There you are." Rae's voice booms through the room, and I practically hit the ceiling, jumping away from Dev's arms.

Holy ghost scares!

"Jesus, Rae!" I clench my chest. "Startle people much?"

His grin widens as his look shifts between Dev and me. "Sorry?"

Dev mumbles something under his breath, which sounds kind of like *you will be*, but I'm not certain.

"I didn't think you'd still be in here. You were supposed to be done an hour ago." He flickers a glance toward Dev. "It's time for you to head home."

My posture straightens. "To New York?"

"Yup, it's time to wake up."

"What? Like now? Like right now?"

"Like right now," he confirms.

"Oh." I glance to Dev, who's studying the ground, a frown in place. "Okay. Do I...do I need to bring anything?"

"Just you." He walks back to the door. "I'll be waiting out here, to, uh, give you two a moment."

Once Rae is out of sight, I turn to Dev, suddenly finding it hard to look him in the eyes, especially when he's staring at me so intensely. "Well, I guess this is it...thanks for, um, letting me stay at your place and training me today."

He nods. "Of course."

"And I'll see you a little later?"

"Unfortunately, I won't be able to meet you tonight. You have training with another Vigil."

"Oh." I frown. "Okay. Then I guess this is good-bye for a bit."

"I guess so."

I can see him shutting down again, outside thoughts clouding his usually light temperament, and I want to ask him what he's thinking, what's causing these mood shifts he's been falling into as of late, if it's all due to an old memory of a ghost that's newly awoken? But I ask none of these things. Instead, I manage a small smile and head for the exit, hoping he'll tell me when he's ready and that I'll be able to handle it when he is.

Chapter 16

THERE ARE THOSE massive, ridiculous-looking sunglasses they give out after a trip to the eye doctor, the ones that haven't been redesigned in about fifty years that protect the eyes from the sun after they've been dilated to the size of saucers. Well, I never thought I'd find myself wishing I had those facial fashion atrocities more than I do in this moment. When did the sun become so *bright*?! I feel like my face has morphed into a prune from how hard I'm squinting. And since when did New York City smell so bad? My God, how it smells. And the noise! Don't even get me started on the noise. Isn't it only ten in the morning? How are people already honking?

"Are you going to complain the whole way to your apartment?" Rae asks as we stop at an intersection.

"Oh, I didn't realize I was saying that out loud."

"Yes, ever since we stepped out of the shop."

I grimace. "Sorry, just getting used to it all again, I guess."

"You've only been gone two days." He raises a brow. "This can't possibly be that shocking to come back to?"

I shrug. "For some reason it is. Even though Terra's a city, it's different from here."

"Yes, it certainly—"

"Oo! Coffee!" I skip across the street, zeroing in on one of my favorite cafés. "Now this is something Terra could use. How do you guys go without coffee?" I ask as I press my face up to the glass, ignoring the patrons sitting by the window who give me the stink eye.

"We don't need the pick-me-up, remember?" Rae says from behind me.

"Yes, but what about the taste? We *all* need that."

Rae laughs. "Come on. Let's get you a cup before you freak those people out even more."

Stepping into the café, I pause as I'm hit with the glorious scent of roasted coffee beans. Okay, get reacclimated with New York—done.

After practically chugging my cup of joe—sorry, tongue, for the burn, but it was necessary—Rae and I part ways, allowing me to take a leisurely stroll back to my apartment. The air is warmer than I remembered, and I smile as I compare the differences between my two worlds and the strange ways in which they are very similar but at the same time completely different. One of the contrasts being the garbage. New York could definitely do with less litter. Terra seems a lot more self-efficient, a contained well-oiled machine, taking care of its people the way they take care of it.

Pausing on the sidewalk, I bend down to retie my shoelace, noticing it's come undone. While partly kneeling, a strange feeling of being watched creeps up my spine, and I peer over my shoulder. Besides an old lady walking her dog and a couple talking on their stoop, the street is empty. I frown and stand, taking another glance around, but nothing seems out of place. I must still be a bit discombobulated from being back from Terra. That, or I'm starting to show signs of the paranoid schizophrenia Elena mentioned. *Awesome.* Turning around, I walk a little faster to my building, never completely shaking the feeling that I was followed the whole way there. *Paranoia it is.*

⟶══◉ ◉══⟵

"Hey, you," Jared says, stepping through my door a little later that night and sweeping me into his arms. He's in his dark jeans and a light-gray sweater that smells deliciously like him—fresh laundry and cologne.

"Hey," I mumble with a smile against his lips.

His hazel eyes regard me with warmth. "I've missed you. How was home?"

"Um, it was great. Just what I needed." *Liar, liar, pants on fire.*

"Good." He leans down to kiss me again before placing the food he brought on my kitchen counter.

"How was your weekend?" I ask.

"Uneventful. Like I texted you, I had to work the whole time."

"Oh yeah." I try remembering the conversation Rae had with Jared. I still can't help but blush when recalling certain parts of the back and forth. Friggin' Rae.

"Have you seen Becca yet?" Jared asks, taking off his shoes and sliding onto my bed.

"No, not yet. I actually just got off the phone with her before you came over. I'll be seeing her tomorrow at work. She's already planned a *long* out-of-the-office lunch to celebrate my return. Because, you know, I've been working way too hard as it is."

He laughs and pulls me down next to him. "Good. I say take all the time you need before going back to work, but I know how you like to stay busy."

He doesn't even know the half of how busy I actually am.

"Home was definitely a good decision." He tucks a strand of my hair behind my ear.

"What do you mean?"

"You just sound more relaxed, not as shaken up."

"Yeah, I guess I am in a better place than I was last week," I say, thinking what a difference learning the truth about my dreams and then having two days to get acclimated to that truth will do for a gal.

"Well, then I guess it was worth putting me through the torture of not seeing you."

I snort. "Jared, I don't think it was really that bad for you."

He trails his fingers down my side. "Then you think wrong."

My stomach does a flip-flop when his hand inches under my shirt to glide up my back. His gaze darkens when he sees my lips part, and he leans in to claim them. The kiss starts off slow, each of us reexploring the other, and my fingers tighten in his thick blond hair when he presses himself into me.

"Don't tell me you didn't at least miss this part of me." His voice is deep and lust filled as he moves his weight against me. I groan in response, and he smiles, satisfied. Licking and kissing his way down my body, he slowly removes my jeans and then my shirt.

As he kneels fully clothed above me, he frowns.

"What?" I ask, suddenly self-conscious.

"Have you lost weight?"

I glance down, surprised to find I do look a little skinnier, my stomach a bit more toned, my legs a little muscular. *Hunh?* Is it possible that all that training in Terra affected my body here?

"I didn't realize I had," I say awkwardly, not really knowing how else to explain it.

"I don't like it."

I blink at him stunned. "What?"

"You don't need to lose weight. Are you sure you're okay?"

"Jared." I laugh and his frown deepens. "You are the sweetest man in the world for saying that. I honestly didn't realize I lost any. I started running while I was home. I guess my body reacted strangely fast to it."

He eyes me skeptically.

"Come here." I pull on the waistband of his jeans. "You're way too dressed compared to me. I need to remedy that." As I help him out of his shirt, a small grin inches across his lips again. "There, much better," I say, taking in his gloriously defined chest and tan skin. Skin that reflects living life under the sun, something that another man's pallor doesn't, another man that I'm surprised to be thinking about at all in this moment.

I shake away those thoughts as Jared rids himself of his jeans and climbs back over me. Pressing sweet kisses to my neck, his hand slides over every dip of my body, every curve of my frame, and I sigh with pleasure. Kneading my fingers into his muscular back, I remind myself this is the man I should be with, the man who grounds me. This is Jared. My boyfriend. And as I drink in his love-filled eyes as he slips on a condom and then into me, I pray it's enough.

Chapter 17

A PIECE OF bread bounces off my forehead, and I glance up startled.

"Are you going to talk to me at all during this lunch or keep ignoring me to read that thing?" Becca's green eyes narrow at the newspaper in my hands. "I mean, I know I can be tiring, but I seriously can't be worse than the daily news."

"Sorry." I fold the paper, placing it back on the chair where I found it. "I just hadn't heard about those shootings."

Becca leans back with a frown, an errant red curl springing free from her tightly styled bun. "For real? It was all over the news. I'm surprised your dad didn't mention it when you were home. Doesn't he religiously watch that stuff?"

"Yeah, but he never said anything." I glance back to the headline that still glares up at me. "Eight Civilians Shot Dead in Park." My stomach turns over, and I know I won't be able to finish the other half of my sandwich.

"Yeah, it was horrible. People can be fucking monsters," Becca says, scrunching her napkin. "Seriously, what's wrong with the world?"

Under the table my hand tightens on my thigh.

What's wrong with the world?

I shake my head, not only in disgust but also because the answer I want to give her...I can't. A strange wave of guilt fills my chest. Is this because of me? Could I have prevented this? Am I not doing enough in Terra? And maybe more importantly, can I stop anything like this from happening in the future?

A waiter drops a rag on a nearby table to wipe it clean, the movement breaking my quickly spiraling thoughts. The café we're eating at is pleasantly quiet for a New York City lunch hour, and the front doors are thrown open, letting in a warm breeze. I look up to see a little boy at a booth across the room trying to feed his baby sister, his mom smiling when most of the food ends up on the little girl's bib.

So much love living next to so much hate.

"Not to belittle what happened, but can we change the subject?" Becca asks. "I'd like to not go back to work in a worse mood than when we left."

"Yeah, that's probably a good idea." I pick up my iced tea, washing away the acidic taste that was beginning to coat my tongue. "How was your weekend with Rae?"

Becca's cheeks suddenly redden, and I blink, thinking I'm seeing things. "Becca...are you...are you blushing?"

She presses her lips together, her eyes dancing away from me.

"Oh my God, you are! What in the world could cause Ms. Unshockable to get tongue tied?"

She throws a hand over her face. "This is so embarrassing."

"*What*? You're embarrassed too? Are pigs flying right now?" I quickly peer out the windows. "This has to be a new record. Wait! Let me get my phone so I can take a picture."

"Molly!" She snatches my cell away when I pull it from my bag. "You're *not* getting proof of this."

I harrumph and drop my shoulders. "Not fair. This never happens to you. I need a souvenir from the moment."

"It's called your memory."

"Fine, but that means I'm just going to have to bring it up *a lot* so as to never forget." I smile cheekily.

She rolls her eyes.

"So what happened?" I push. "What's so embarrassing? Is it Rae? Did he do something? Oh man, did he finally fart in front of you?"

Becca bursts out laughing, and a couple of patrons glance our way. "I wish that's what happened," she says after containing herself. "No, I'm afraid it's rather worse."

"*Worse?*" My eyes widen. "Oh man, now I'm scared to ask."

"Yeah, well, don't say I didn't warn you." She wets her lips. "So Rae...he started to..."

"My God, woman, spit it out."

"He started to sext me," she says quickly, and I stare at her, deadpan, my fears swallowing a smile from forming because if I know Rae as well as I'm starting to, this isn't the end of the story. "And normally I'm all for a little verbal foreplay," she continues. "It is *me* after all. But..." Becca looks up, apprehension in her eyes.

"He's not very good at it?" I ask with a fearful grimace.

"Oh, Molly, he's *horrible!*" She deflates, placing both hands on the table. "I don't know where he's getting any of his innuendos from. They make zero sense! I spend half the conversation trying to figure out what he's saying while becoming the complete opposite of turned on. I mean, what in the world does 'I'm going to put grill marks on you' mean?"

That's when I lose it. I lean forward and laugh so hard I start to cry.

"It's really not funny," Becca says with a whine.

"It's actually the definition of funny." I pat my eyes with my napkin. "And I think he was trying to say that he'll burn you with his touch, or something like that." I start chuckling again. "Oh, poor Rae."

"Ugh, still no better! How do I tell him to stop?"

"I don't know, maybe by telling him to stop?" I raise a brow.

Becca purses her lips. "It's not that easy. He seems so into it, like he's proud of himself or something. He even asked me when we met up what I thought of our 'conversation.'" She air quotes.

I hold back another laugh. "Is it just me, or is his failure at sexting kind of adorable?"

Becca sighs. "No, it's not just you. It is adorable. Extremely cute, in fact." She rubs her eyes. "I guess that's the positive way to spin all this."

I start giggling again, that is until I abruptly stop, because with a blood-freezing realization I remember that Rae had my phone this weekend, and he mentioned something about sexting with Jared. *Oh no. Please, no!* I glance to my cellphone that rests next to Becca, it now looking more like a viper waiting to fill me with poison. *I can't. I can't check it.* If his responses were as bad as Becca's example and the—let's not even go there—LALAT acronym, Jared would have mentioned something, right?

Right?!

"Molly, are you okay?" Becca asks, and I blink up to her. "You look pale. Was it the tuna fish?"

"Can you do me a favor?" I sit up straight.

"Sure, what is it?"

"Can you go to my text conversation with Jared." I nudge my phone closer to her. "Right now, while I'm sitting here."

"Uh, okay." She glances to me once it's in her hands. "Now what?"

"Delete the thread."

"What? Why?"

"Just do it! Before I change my mind."

She frowns. "You are so weird." Tapping her fingers a few times on the screen, she places it back down. "There, all deleted. Feel better?"

"Not really."

"Did you text him something you don't want to remember?"

I swallow. "I really hope not."

She snorts and picks up her water. "You make no sense sometimes."

I try not to think about how little sense I might have made to Jared over the weekend. Elena's words of knowledge being power come back to me, but as my phone now sits clean of any possible mental contamination, I know in this moment that ignorance is a way more blissful option.

Chapter 18

TIME SEEMS TO pass in a blur of waking up to go to work and waking up to train for Terra. And when I say train, I mean in both my worlds. Rae, in addition to now being semi-difficult to look at with a straight face, mysteriously retains a copy of my apartment key, something I think Becca was the unknowing culprit of providing, and takes it upon himself to sporadically get me up at the butt crack of dawn for runs. I've never been less pleased about something in all my life. I think it even trumps the time I learned I needed to keep my braces on for my freshman year of high school. Hell, I'll put braces *back* on if it means no more Raes before sunrise, which yes, I realize is also an amazing name for a band. Nevertheless, the actuality of it sucks something awful. So I naturally attempted to booby trap my door to keep him out, but besides making him now hate one of America's greatest holiday movies ever made and the inspiration for most of my ideas—thank you, Kevin McCallister—I got myself stuck with an extra mile on those particularly creative mornings. *Gross.*

Surprisingly, what I thought would be the hardest part of all this—lying to Becca and Jared—has turned out to be quite easy. I'm not proud of this fact or really sure what that says about me, but I'm beginning to learn when not to overanalyze. Terra knows, I've got enough on my mind already.

Because when I fall asleep, I am once again reminded of my responsibility and a certain man that confuses me at every turn.

I don't see Dev as often as I'd like, given that I'm usually training most nights with Rae—again, feelings I'd rather not overanalyze—but when I do see him, he keeps our encounters friendly and professional. No more inappropriate comments or situations that have him slowly leaning in to kiss me and, maybe more importantly, a certain name hasn't been uttered since Aveline last spoke it. Because of all this, I've begun to wonder if our past stolen kisses are exactly that, the past, and if that little speech about *not being my friend* while pressing me up against the wall was just a wine-induced slip of the tongue. As I stand in the same room as him looking over a map of Terra with a few council members, I'm left to believe that it was. Besides a quick hello when I entered with Rae, he hasn't glanced at me once. Even though it stings, I know it's probably for the best.

"Patrols say that a larger group of Metus have moved into the Lost City to the northwest of here." Alexander, who I've learned is one of the heads of Security, points to an area on the screen. Alex typically ignores me at these things or acts as if my presence is the equivalent to finding a bug in his morning wheatgrass shake.

Standing around a table, we study a digital projection of Terra Somniorum that floats in the middle. Most of it makes no sense to me because the areas are all marked with the strange Latin lettering, something I still haven't been taught and I suspect is intentional. What I can tell from the map, however, is that this world is massive, endless, and I know we're only looking at a very small area of it.

"That means they're advancing from Terra Diavolo." Dev scratches his stubble-filled chin.

"Yes, but what I want to know is, why? What are they planning?" Alexander leans on the table.

"Until we can learn more, we mainly need to act on that fact alone—that they are." Dev turns to two Nocturna behind him. "Put together a scouting mission to find out exactly how many we're dealing with and what part of the Lost City they're inhabiting. We can plan to engage from the other angles."

With a nod, the man and woman leave.

The meeting continues in a similar fashion, and I tune in and out as I lean over the map, studying it again. I hone in on the pulsing orange mass that represents the group of Metus being discussed. While the violence on Earth has gotten a little worse, it's been nothing like here. Almost every night there's something that needs to be taken care of or planned or double fortified. On Earth there's definitely been horrific acts of random violence, but only an above-average amount of terrorist threats, and I say *only* because while, yes, this is making everyone a bit on edge, there hasn't yet been any actual action. Something I'm determined to hold off as long as possible. Thankfully, I've been allowed access into a few of these security meetings, helping me learn way more than my predecessors ever had about the land of Terra and the movement of the Metus. I have a feeling my admittance is mainly due to Dev and the weight he's able to pull around this place.

Though these meetings have occasionally acted as detours in my training, I've still managed to keep up in both my physical and energy teachings. The only thing I haven't done more of is collect Dreamers' memories. After asking Elena about this and if I could get the memory from my most recent predecessor, she simply explained it was too dangerous to receive any of them unless I was induced back into sleep. When I asked if I should then prepare for another visit like that, her evasive response was merely, "Soon."

"Molly, did you hear what I said?" Rae asks beside me.

I blink, realizing that the meeting has ended and most of the people have left. Dev stands in the corner, talking to Alex.

"Uh, no, sorry, I missed it."

Rae studies me a moment and then follows my flickering glance that seems to always rest on Dev, a Dev who's doing a fine job of not returning the gesture.

"Penny for your thoughts?" Rae nudges my side, returning my attention to him.

"How much longer do I have until I wake up?" I ask.

"I'd say about an hour or so, why?"

"Want to go to Anima?"

"You hungry?"

"Not particularly, but I'm sure you are."

He grins. "That goes without saying."

"Great." I head for the door. "Then let's go." It takes all my effort not to look back.

I absently watch Rae devour a plate of fried calamari as we sit at Elario's restaurant. I've been relatively quiet for the meal, too busy brooding on the reasons for Dev's change in attitude. Trying to figure out what made him go from the all hot-and-heavy *Molly, I want you* to acting like I'm last week's gossip rag.

"You shouldn't let it bother you."

I glance to Rae. "Let what bother me?"

He wipes his mouth with his napkin. "Dev acting the way he is."

"So you've noticed it too?"

He snorts out a laugh. "Who hasn't?"

"What's up with him then? Did I do something wrong?"

"I think he's trying to respect the fact that you have feelings for someone else."

My brows rise. "Jared?"

"Who else is there?"

"Well, he doesn't need to completely avoid me to respect that."

"I think he does." My confused expression causes Rae to smile. "What I'm trying to say is that I don't think he knows how to *just* be friends with you."

"Funny, he once said something similar." I push around the food on my plate.

"Give it time, Molly." Rae pats my hand. "I'm sure you two can work up to being friends eventually."

"Yeah," I say halfheartedly, wondering if that's in fact what I really want. But what other relationship could we have? We're not from the same world. Plus there's Jared, who's been so good to me, good *for* me. And I do have feelings for him. Even if they might not be on the same level as his, don't we still deserve a chance for me to get there? Through all these thoughts, Aveline's words about not hurting Dev resurface. Would that really be our fate, me inevitably causing him pain? I know deep down it's probably best for all parties if I don't attempt to find out.

Rae and I end up walking through a small park in Anima as my time before I wake up winds down. Becca's birthday is coming up in a month, and I've been helping him with a few ideas of what to get her. As he tells me some of the options he's thought of, I can't help but feel a tad bit jealous of them. Even though Becca has no idea about who or what Rae really is, their relationship seems so simple. That he can travel to my world and be with her for as long as he wants seems unfair compared to the limited time I get in Terra, not to mention that Dev can't leave at—*Stop it*!

I shake my head.

Stay focused. Dev and I are *not* a thing.

"I was thinking that renting a sailboat for the day might be the best way to go, then maybe a nice dinner somewhere downtown." Rae continues to mull over ideas as we pass under an ivy-covered bridge and enter a more secluded section of the park. Couples are nestled here and there in certain nooks, and I'm about to tell him we should probably turn around, when I catch sight of a familiar figure near a column in the corner.

One of his hands rests on the marble structure where a girl leans, smiling up at him. His fingers play with one of her earrings, and he says something that causes her to laugh and then blush.

In that moment the world teeters, and a wave of nausea collides with my gut. I take a staggering step back, bumping into Rae.

"Whoa, you okay there?" He steadies me. "What's wrong? Did the food not agree with…" Rae trails off as his eyes find what I'm staring at. "*Collö*," he says under his breath and lightly tugs on my arm. I barely hear him say we should leave as a *whooshing* sound fills my ears and I'm locked into watching the girl slowly lean into the man, and the man lets her. The moment their lips touch, my heart cracks, and I'm choking, choking, and then falling. Falling into an explosion of white that recedes into my apartment. I lie paralyzed in my bed, and even though I'm now awake, I don't have to close my eyes to see the vision that has left me shattered. The vision of a girl kissing Dev and of Dev kissing a girl.

As a tear rolls down my cheek, I realize that Aveline's wrong. Either way, pain is inevitable.

Chapter 19

I'M GRANTED A reprieve from seeing Dev after that night. Rae has consumed most of my Terra visits and, if not him, then Elena. I think Rae's purposely planned it this way, and I'm eternally grateful. I know I'll eventually need to be around Dev and face the emotions that came from seeing him with a girl, but I'm not exactly in a rush to do so. I never thought it would hurt as bad as it did to find him with someone, given that I'm with Jared and Dev and I owe each other nothing in that regard, but I'd be lying to say it didn't leave me clamoring to remove the knife that seems to have found its way into my heart.

I feel like a zombie for the next two days and unfairly snap at Becca at work when she asks me what's wrong.

But now as I wait for Jared outside of his office, I find the strength to lock away those particular melancholy thoughts, just like I do after many hard nights in Terra. It also doesn't hurt to catch sight of Jared pushing through the doors of his building, head thrown back, laughing with a coworker. I can't help the sides of my mouth from curling up as I watch him talk to his friend, his grin infectious. As if sensing an onlooker, he turns, clear hazel eyes finding mine and warming. Patting his peer on the shoulder, he makes his way toward me, his three-piece gray suit showcasing his lean body with each step.

"Hi, beautiful." He bends down for a kiss. "Did I keep you waiting long?"

"Nope, got here a few minutes ago."

"Good." He wraps an arm around my shoulder. "As much as I love you in those heels, I know they have a countdown for comfort. Wouldn't want you wasting any time in them."

I breathe out a laugh. "How thoughtful of you, but don't worry. The timer still has a few hours left."

"Perfect, then maybe we should skip dinner and use up the rest of those heel hours at my place." His gaze is every bit trouble and every bit serious.

I shake my head while fighting a grin. "As much as Becca would normally pardon such a reason for cancelling our double date, unfortunately tonight is not one of those times. She and Rae have been waiting for weeks to get into this restaurant."

"How are they both not a thousand pounds?" Jared intertwines our fingers as he walks us to the curb to hail a cab. "They always want to go to places with twelve-course meals."

"I think the more important question is, how are *we* not a thousand pounds for being forced to go with them?"

"Oh, well, that's because I always shove some of my food onto Rae's plate when no one's looking."

My mouth pops open. "No you don't!" The mischievous gleam that grows in his eyes causes me to bark out a laugh. "Oh my God, Jared! That's hilarious. And genius."

"Thanks." He puffs out his chest with pride just as a cab pulls up. "And don't worry, young grasshopper." He opens the door for me. "I'll teach you the ways of the dinner ninja on the ride there."

I clap my hands together before slipping into the backseat. "Tonight is going to be awesome."

And just as predicted, it is. Not only was dinner amazing, with the food being delicious, but also because Jared and I left without needing to be rolled out in wheelbarrows. His stealth with a spoon and misdirecting people's line of sight was honestly next level. He somehow managed to take care of both of our excessive meals with no Becca or Rae the wiser. If anyone had threatened our cover, it would have been me, since I caught myself more than once about to applaud in exhilaration after his extra-sly food drops. It was truly one of the best dinner shows I've been to. Not only did it distract me from my usual constant thoughts of Terra, but as I now sit down in the movie theater, part two of our double date, I can lean back in comfort rather than misery from overeating. I need to remember to high-five Jared later.

"Okay, I was able to convince the boys to get snacks." Becca plops down beside me, impatiently pushing back her curly apricot hair.

I groan. "Seriously, Bec? We just had dinner. We do *not* need snacks."

She waves away my comment. "Whatever. I needed some girl-on-girl time with you."

"Oh, well, I'm flattered, but you know I don't roll that way."

"Please, you only wish you were so lucky to get some of this." She wiggles her hips in her seat.

I snort out a laugh. "Oh *yeah*, I'm definitely missing out."

She flashes a crooked grin before growing serious. "I really do need to ask you something, though."

"Okay, shoot."

She takes a deep breath. "I think something's wrong with Rae."

My hands inadvertently tighten in my lap. "What do you mean?"

"I think he might have insomnia or something."

"Insomnia?"

"Yeah. I've never seen him sleep."

My burst of laughter draws annoyed glances from nearby moviegoers.

Becca smacks my arm. "Molly, I'm serious!"

"Yeah, and apparently also violent." I rub my bicep.

"You're absolutely no help." She turns forward with a pout.

"Okay, okay." I tuck away my smile. "Sorry, it just sounds a bit ridiculous. What do you mean you've never seen him sleep? And why on earth would you want to?"

"Well, I didn't at first, because who looks out for stuff like that?"

"Apparently you."

She narrows her gaze at me before continuing. "But *then* I started noticing that when he sleeps over, I'm always the first to fall asleep, and in the morning he's the first to be awake."

"That hardly means he's an insomniac," I say while making a mental note to tell Rae about this slipup.

She huffs. "You just have to be there, I guess. I'm telling you, something's going on. I've also been hinting that we should go away one weekend, but he always dodges it. Says he can't because of work, but he *never* works the weekend, so I don't know what he's talking about."

I do. Right now Rae needs constant access to get back to Terra in case something happens, and he's also been assigned to look after me. A trip like that, though short, would never be allowed. And even if they went on vacation to another place that had a portal, how would he explain his absence if he needed to leave? Yeah, it just wouldn't work.

"Well, maybe he's on standby or something." I glance behind us, hoping the boys come back soon.

"Then why doesn't he just say that? No, I think something's up."

"Like what?"

She frowns. "I don't know…just…something."

I place my hand on top of hers. "Bec, even if there is—which I highly doubt—I know *one hundred percent* that it has nothing to do with how he feels toward you. I've never seen someone as smitten as Rae."

She smiles, a bit of her worry melting away. "Yeah, I've got him tied around my finger a little, don't I?"

"More like tattooed." I nudge her side and she laughs.

"What's so funny?" Jared asks as he and Rae make their way into their seats beside us. *Thank you, timing gods.*

"Nothing," Becca quips as she takes the popcorn from Rae. "Good, you got the tub. I'm starving."

"We just ate dinner." Jared eyes her with disbelief.

"That was like, thirty minutes ago," she scoffs and begins to shovel handfuls into her mouth.

Rae wraps his arm around her with pride while Jared and I share a look of fear. Both, I'm sure, wondering if we should make a run for it now or wait until the lights dim. Either won't save us from the future of eating with these food Hoovers. But the way I see it, as long as I still have Jared to hocus-pocus part of my meal away, I should be fine.

Chapter 20

THERE NEEDS BE a way to retrieve brain cells once you've been robbed of them after a particularly mind-numbing day at work. Or at least a note of apology.

> *Dear Molly,*
>
> *Sorry to have taken up extremely useful brain storage to make room for that electric keyboard hold song that was playing while you waited two hours for IT to pick it up. It will most likely happen again tomorrow.*
>
> *Always thinking of new ways to torture you.*
>
> *Yours never truly,*
>
> *Work Day*

At least that would be a start.

It's times like these where I find myself growing a bit resentful toward my world and what I'm doing in it. My life in Terra has so much more meaning and importance, and it seems horribly selfish that none of us have any idea that Terra's unknowing hard work allows us the frivolities of our lives. Lives that most of us take for granted. I know there was a time when we were aware of it, of them. Riki lived in that era, but that was many, many centuries ago, and for one reason or another, the secrets of this other dimension have been lost over time. So while I sit here in Jared's apartment, both of us sipping wine, I can't help brooding over the fact that at this very moment, Metus could be attacking another generator, killing another Nocturna. It's enough to make me want to pull out my hair with the anxiety to get back there later tonight.

"Do you know what you just agreed to?" Jared pokes me with his fork, bringing me out of my thoughts.

"Uh, yeah…" I say and then frown. "Okay, no, sorry. I was someplace else."

"You don't say?" He flashes me a wry grin. "Want to talk about it?"

"No, no, just work stuff." I take a bite of food. "Sorry, what were you saying?"

"I was telling you that my parents are coming into town next week."

"Oh, that's nice."

"And I want them to meet you."

"Oh."

Jared leans back in his chair and brushes his fingers through his blond hair. "Not exactly the response you gave a few seconds ago."

"Sorry…it's just…isn't it a little soon?"

"Soon?" He snorts. "Molly, we've been dating for months now, and I've already met your parents."

"Yes, but that was due to very unusual circumstances."

"Maybe, but the when and where doesn't really matter in the end."

"What do you mean?"

He sighs and reaches for my hand. Placing it on top of mine, he scans my face with slight nervousness. "Molly...I love you."

I'm frozen while everything else in me speeds up.

I love you.

I knew this was coming. I could see it in the way he's been looking at me for weeks. I just thought by the time it was verbalized, I'd have caught up, would be right there with him. I mean, everything's been going so well with us, I should be there. I should.

But...I'm not.

Fuck. Fuck. Fuck.

"And by your silence, I gather you don't feel the same way." He removes his hand.

"No." I reach out and twine my fingers with his. "It's just... I'm just...you caught me off guard."

His eyes fill with a tinge of hope, and I want to kick myself. "So then...you do feel the same?"

I worry my bottom lip, desperately trying to figure out the best way to handle this. "I think that I can get there after some more time." He tries to pull his hand back again, but I hold firm. "Jared, I care about you. A lot. I love when I'm with you. I love what we have together."

"You just don't love me." His eyes narrow with hurt before looking away.

"I..."

"Molly, it's okay." He suddenly stands and begins to clear the table. "It's okay," he says again.

"Jared, stop for a second." I follow him to his kitchen, where he drops the dishes in the sink and grabs the edge, his knuckles turning white.

"I knew I was taking a chance by saying it first," he mumbles absently. "There always has to be one person to say it first." He abruptly steps back and opens one of his cabinets. Grabbing a bottle of scotch, he pours himself a generous glass and then turns to me. "Want one?"

I shake my head.

"Of course you don't." He laughs without humor. "You're not the one that just put their heart on the table to get skewered."

"Jared, I didn't mean to—"

"No, you never do, Molly." He tips back the amber liquid.

I raise my brows. "What does *that* mean?"

"Nothing." He studies his glass. "It means nothing."

"Well, it obviously means *something*, or you wouldn't have said it."

He eyes me for a second, a flash of cold in his gaze before it changes back to sadness, and my heart breaks for a second time tonight even though I know it's all my own doing.

"I shouldn't have said anything. None of it." He takes another swig. "Actually, you know what? No." He puts down his glass and turns to me. "I'm glad I did. It's all out in the open now. I always knew I felt more for you than you did for me anyway."

"That's not fair. I care for you, Jared. You can't say that I don't. Plus, this isn't a competition. You can't race to something that's supposed to grow naturally. Just because I'm not in love with you right now doesn't mean I won't be eventually."

"Exactly!" he yells, and I jump. "*Eventually*!" He takes a step toward me, and I can't help but take one back. "I want to be with someone that doesn't need *eventually*," he says with forced calm. "Or more time, or maybe. Molly, I knew I was going to fall in love you the first time we met."

My breath hitches, and I open and close my mouth, lost for words.

"I knew the moment I saw you at that party that you were the one, my one," he says with more softness as he comes to stand directly in front of me, and my chest aches from the emotions on his face—the anguish, the hurt, the hope. He moves to touch my cheek, but hesitates, so with shaky fingers I reach up and press his hand to my skin.

He closes his eyes briefly, as if in pain. "I felt your reluctance in the beginning. I was never blind to that. I saw that you were scared of relying on someone so heavily, but I thought if I was patient enough, we'd move past that.

"We have," I say, digging my fingers into his T-shirt.

"Maybe, but it's not enough for you to love me."

"Please," I whisper, my throat growing tight, "just give me a little more time."

"And what happens when time's not enough?" He shakes his head and looks down. "No, you either know or you don't. It's that simple."

Is it? Deep down I know he's right. I know because it felt that simple with someone else, and yet I still want to scream.

"And honestly, you've been distant lately. I should have taken it as a sign."

"Distant? We hang out almost every night."

"You've been mentally someplace else for weeks."

My heart begins to work in overtime. "What are you talking about?"

"Well, like earlier." He motions to the table. "You tune out like that all the time now. Even though you're with me physically, I feel like you're mentally somewhere else. That you *want* to be somewhere else."

"I...I don't mean to be." I'm out of my depths with this one. How do I explain myself without telling the truth? The truth that he 100 percent won't believe.

"Is there someone else?" he asks.

"Of course not!" I quickly counter, ignoring the sudden guilt clawing at me.

He nods, the tension in his body relaxing slightly.

"Jared, I can try harder. I didn't know you felt this way. I can be better—"

"I know," he says softly. "But maybe...maybe given what was said earlier—or wasn't—it's for the best."

The food in my stomach turns sour. "What does that mean? What are you saying?"

His features pinch in with pain. "I'm saying this isn't working. I can't wait for someone to make up their mind when it was never a decision for me in the first place."

"But—"

"Molly, let's be honest for once. We're really good together. Jesus, we really are, and I wish that were enough for you to get there, for you to see..." He swallows as if the words tasted bad coming out. "But something's holding you back, because it shouldn't be this hard to know about me, to know if I'm your one."

"I..." My throat has gone dry, my words stuck.

He briefly glances to the floor. "This isn't working," he says, his eyes returning to me. "And you know it."

I take in a shaky breath, count to five, and then five again before I crack. I crack wide open and tumble. Leaning into his chest, I cry. I cry for us. I cry for knowing he's right, for having known for a while but being too scared to act on it. I cry for not being able to love someone so perfect, just merely not my perfect, and I cry from the way Jared still holds me even though I just broke his heart, broke our hearts.

"Is this really happening right now?" I ask, burying my face further into his now-damp shirt. He presses his lips to the top of my head, and I wrap myself tighter around him. "Are you sure you can't give me more time?"

"Oh, Molly." He tips my head up to look at him. "If only that were all that was needed." Slow tears track down his cheeks, and my lips wobble, teetering on another sob.

"*Stop.*" I push my face in his chest again, not wanting to see my own sorrow reflected in his eyes. "Why are you doing this?"

"I'm doing it for the both of us."

"No." I mumble into him.

"Trust me. I wish the outcome of what I said earlier was different, *very* different, but it wasn't. We both need more. I see that now, and I know you do too."

I hold my eyes shut for a moment before glancing up. "Can you at least be a *little* bit of a jerk to make this easier?"

"Sorry to disappoint."

"I'm the one that's a disappointment."

"Maybe." He attempts a playful grin, but it comes out more pained.

"I'm so sorry, Jared." I hesitantly take a step back from him. "I'm sorry that I...that I..."

"I know," he says softly. "Me too." His sad hazel gaze meets mine, and now that we're not touching, I suddenly become very cold. The space between us, though small, feels a canyon's distance, and I realize neither of us can cross it now. This is it. This is the end. It's horrible how quickly a person can go from being an intimate part of your life to a stranger.

"I guess...I guess I should go then?"

He doesn't say yes, but more importantly he doesn't say no, so wordlessly I retrieve my coat and purse, feeling the presence of him everywhere, like a blanket. The emotion in the room is suffocating, strangling, and I itch to run from it, all the while not wanting to leave. Slowly I head to the door, swallowing back the new tears that threaten to fall.

That's where we meet, each of us wearing a mask. A once-normal night turns into a disaster. *How did this happen?* I open my mouth to say something, anything, when Jared sweeps me into his arms and kisses me like it's the last time. Because it is the last time. With my fingers digging into his hair and his strong hands wrapped tightly around my waist, I taste the salt from both our tears, and I take it in, all of it. I let it seep into my bones, my blood. *Feel this. Feel all of this.* Then all too soon he's lowering me away, our only connection maintained from our touching foreheads. It's in this position that we whisper the final words that need to be spoken. The apologies, the could haves, the well wishes, the things that will never be forgotten. We say all of it, empty it all out. And then gently, after a time I can't quantify, he lets me go.

And with slow steps forward, I let him go.

Chapter 21

PUNCH, PUNCH, KICK. Breathe in. Breathe out.

Punch, punch, kick. Breathe in. Breathe out.

Repeat. Repeat. Repeat.

Sweat drips into my eyes. I ignore it.

My throat claws for hydration. I ignore it.

My heart sags. I ignore it.

Thoughts of Jared. Thoughts of Dev. Thoughts of what I'm doing here.

Ignore it. Ignore it. Ignore it.

"Okay, I think that's enough for today." Rae steps back, lowering his sparring gloves.

"I can go a little longer." I pant, readying myself to continue.

"Maybe, but it's enough for today."

I frown, dropping my hands. "Fine."

Walking to the edge of the training room, I grab my towel and wipe myself down.

Two days after Jared and I broke up, Elena informed me that I needed to plan another extended stay in Terra. I nearly ran to the

Village Portal bookstore the next night to meet Rae. Even though this city isn't much of an emotional reprieve from New York, it's a step up from wallowing in my apartment with Becca.

She was the first call after leaving Jared's. Always my first call. I only managed to choke out "I need you," but that's all she had to hear. With my head in her lap, she listened when I told her what happened, didn't ask questions when I said it was for the best, held me when I broke down in tears again, and understood when I said I was going home for the weekend. I know a part of her thinks I'm completely mad for letting Jared go, or more accurately letting him dump me, but she'll never tell me that. She just kept repeating that she wants me to do whatever will make me happy. If Jared's not that, then he's not that. My only fear is that the person who might be *the one* isn't that much better of a choice, if he's still a choice at all.

"You doing all right?" Rae asks from behind me.

"Just peachy, why?"

"Becca told me what happened."

Of course she did. I take a swig of water.

"I'm sorry. I know you liked him a lot."

"Yeah, well apparently liking him a lot wasn't enough." I press one of the panels in the wall and throw my towel into a compartment for cleaning.

Rae runs his fingers through his hair, not sure what else to say.

I let out a sigh. "Sorry. I'm being a jerk. I'm just dealing with a lot…emotionally right now."

"It probably wasn't the best timing, huh?"

"Actually, it probably was. I don't need the extra distraction right now." I've had this reasoning on repeat since getting here.

Rae nods, at a loss for words again, but that's fine with me because I don't feel much like talking.

"I'm going to shower and meet Elena for our session," I say, walking to the exit. Even though I can easily imagine myself clean, nothing beats actually standing under steaming hot water. Alec is already there to accompany me, a small smile in place, and for once his lack of natural inquisitiveness is a blessing.

"And then how about you come back and we can train a little more?" Rae calls after me.

I turn around, confused. "I thought you said that was enough for today."

"What? You tired already?"

I know what he's doing. I know, and I completely love him for it. "Not in the least." I flash him an appreciative grin. Keeping busy won't fix things, but it certainly will help.

⋅⊷⊨⊙ ⊙⊨⊶⋅

Sandbags, thousands of them. All tied to my body weighing me down as I walk into the elevator to Tim, Aveline, and Dev's building—and, strangely, mine too now. A day and a half of nonstop training. A day and a half of concentrating on not getting knocked down, not letting the power of the Navitas slip from my grasp or the memories of past Dreamers overwhelm me. A day and a half of blissful, beautiful mental distractions.

The elevator doors shut.

A moment of silent ascent.

God damn it. I let out an audible moan as it all comes crashing down, in, and around. The thoughts I left in New York invade like Vikings in Normandy.

Jared and I are over. One less string holding me to my other life. But who am I kidding? I knew this was coming. Knew I was asking for it, and honestly, how could I have done anything differently? I thought I was doing a good job of maintaining a balance of both worlds, but everything happening in Terra is too demanding, both mentally and physically. It's impossible for them not to take up my thoughts when I'm awake. How do you shut down something that has been fused to your very soul? How do you hide that in a relationship when you're meant to share everything?

Stepping out of the elevator, I wipe an idle tear that tracks down my cheek, feeling so selfish to have held on to Jared when I knew deep down I would never truly love him the way I was supposed to, the way he deserves.

A girl's laughter interrupts my thoughts, and I stop outside the apartment door. The light joyous sound filters through again, but this time it's accompanied by a man's. My stomach twists into a sour grape knowing who's connected to the other end of that deep rumble. Who the girl is? I have no idea. The image of the last woman I saw Dev with flashes before me, and I swallow.

I was going to have to deal with this eventually. Why not just pile it on top of everything else? *They don't call it a shit sandwich for nothing.* Taking a deep breath, I open the door.

The girl sitting next to Dev isn't the one from Anima. No, she's someone much, *much* worse.

Aurora and Dev glance up from their close positioning on the couch.

"Hey, Molly," Aurora says with a smile, placing the tablet she and Dev were sharing onto his lap. Her eyes glide over my form, and I self-consciously have the urge to take out my ponytail and fluff my hair to meet her approval. *Ugh.*

"Hey," I mumble, shuffling toward the kitchen. Dev's gaze follows me the whole way, which a month ago wouldn't be weird, but now after practically being ignored by him for weeks is kind of disconcerting. It takes all my strength not to look back in his direction as I grab a glass of water.

"How was training?" Dev asks.

I almost choke midsip. *For real?* Days of silent treatment, and the first thing he says to me is *how was training?* Not responding, I place my glass in the sink and walk toward my room.

"Molly?" he calls out to my retreating form, which keeps retreating until I'm safely behind my closed door, where I sag against it.

I'm so tired, and not just because of my recent nonstop training. How can I keep all this up? Especially when the hardest part hasn't even happened yet. I'm still somehow supposed to save mankind from being mentally infected by demons. Or something like that.

I rub my eyes. Maybe I'll conjure up a hot tub on the roof and soak in that for a while.

A light knock raps on my door, and I jump.

"Molly? It's me," Dev says from the other side.

I chew my bottom lip, wondering how I should handle this. "What do you want?"

There's a moment of silence, and then my doorknob begins to turn.

Shit. I didn't lock it.

Dev steps in and stops, surprised at finding me right there.

"Are you okay?" he asks, coming all the way in and closing the door behind him. We haven't stood this close in a while. I forgot how tall he was, and his scent wraps around me like a desire-filled embrace. I switch to breathing out of my mouth, which only makes it sound like I'm panting. *Great.*

"I don't remember saying you could come in." I scowl.

"And I don't remember you saying I couldn't."

I let out a sigh and turn away because a small part of me wants to smile at that, but there's a larger part that really, *really* doesn't. "What do you want, Dev?"

"To talk. We haven't seen each other in a while."

"And whose fault is that?" I glance over my shoulder to see him casually inspecting the row of random knickknacks on my dresser—a chipped piece of marble from the stairs at City Hall, a dimming wristband from my night at Vex, a discarded boot string, the list goes on. I've unintentionally started to gather things from places I've been in Terra. *Maybe I'm a hoarder after all.*

"I wouldn't say it's any *one* person's fault," Dev says while picking up a wooden utensil I took from Elario's. *Okay, maybe klepto is a more accurate diagnosis.* He grins before placing it back. "We've both had pretty packed schedules."

"That never seemed to be an excuse before."

Blue eyes find mine. "I didn't realize it was bothering you so much."

"I—it's not bothering me."

"Then why are you mad?" He slowly walks toward me, my room shrinking with each step.

"I'm not...that's not what I'm...isn't Aurora waiting for you?"

"She left." His gaze never leaves mine.

"Your date over so soon?" *What am I even saying right now?!*

He stops a few inches away, and I realize I've forgotten how hypnotizing it is to be on the receiving end of his attention. I hate that I like it, hate that I've grown to need it.

"Is that what you're mad about? Aurora being here?" He tilts his head to the side.

"No." *Yes. Maybe. I don't know!*

"But why would that bother you?" he muses, more to himself, ignoring my answer. "Why would you be jealous of a friend hanging out with a girl?"

I snort. "Dev, I am *not* jealous."

"I mean, you have a boyfriend," he continues. "So what's there to be jealous about?"

"I said I *wasn't* and I...I..." I swallow, my heart doing butterfly kicks as I search for a way to answer him. Knowing it's fear that's keeping me from telling him the truth. Fear of how much more intense this thing between us would become if we let it happen. If he even still wants me.

I don't think you'd hurt him. I think you'd kill him.

Would I? Would he? After all, we all know what happened to Icarus.

"What are you trying to say, Molly?" Dev pushes.

I take in a deep breath. "That I don't."

"You don't *what?*"

"I don't have a boyfriend. Not anymore."

His eyes spark like flint being hit, and my chest rises and falls, rises and falls as I watch the side of his mouth slowly tip up, a king about to conquer a land.

"I know," he says.

And then he's on me.

Chapter 22

WE'RE FREE-FALLING. DOWN, down, down we plummet. The only thing that matters in our descent is his lips, his hands, his body. We hit my mattress, and my eyes briefly open to see the Navitas in the fixtures above sparking like lightning, churning like a storm. It feels what I feel, somersaults the way my blood rushes through me.

I gasp as Dev's hands search, explore—his lips never leaving mine. His touch is searing, branding, my soul nothing but pure euphoria as I give in, allow myself to finally have what I've wanted since the moment I saw him, all without the restraints, without the guilt.

Thud, thud, thud. My heart pounds in my chest, in my ears, in the room as his body surrounds me, covers me, presses down with a claim. With every kiss he's telling me I'm his now. With every touch, he's saying forever. And my body answers him. Yes, yes, yes. Forever.

It's all a blur, a whirlwind of months of desperation. He's removing my boots, my shirt, my pants. With every layer, he also takes a part of my reserve, a piece of armor I fortified against him. Against this.

"In all of Terra…" His gaze devours me from where he stands at the edge of the bed. "You're so beautiful."

I feel bold under his praise, and I smile. Sitting up, I help remove his shirt, his pants, and smooth my hands over his abs, up his broad chest, taking in every perfect piece of him. "So are you."

With a growl he's on me again, worshiping every inch of me. "Molly," he says over and over. *Molly.* I bask in it. Lose myself in it until he's hovering above me, a silent question in his gaze, one that I silently answer. Slowly, gently, we remove our individuality and on a gasp, we're nothing but a tangle of cells, a melting of atoms moving together. Every time I breathe out, he breathes in. With each moan there's a sigh. With each ask for more there's a give. He lifts me up like I'm made of air and holds me against him, never stopping as he fills me over and over. He's all consuming, his bright-blue eyes dominating as his fingers knead into my skin. His teeth run along my collarbone as he grabs my breast, and I forget my name, my purpose, forget which dimension I'm floating in. There's only here, this, us, now. Skin gliding over skin. Sweat mingling with sweat. Until, with fingers intertwined and both our names on one another's lips, we collide and then burst apart.

The room shimmers with the stars that take up space in my head, and I watch them with a lazy smile. Dev's still smothering me with his body, and I marvel at how natural it all feels—his labored breath against my neck, my hands running patterns on his back, the way our chests rise and fall together.

My eyes catch on something in the room, and I begin to giggle, taking a better look around.

"That's not exactly a sound that feeds a man's confidence after what we just did." Dev's head lifts up.

"Like you have a problem with your self-esteem."

"Well...actually, some people tend to think it's *too* big a problem." He smiles wickedly.

"*Ugh*." I smack his shoulder. "Don't ruin the moment."

"Oh, are we having one of those? Sorry, let me get back into it."

He places his hands on either side of my head and stares into my eyes, his slowly widening with each second till he looks like a crazy person.

"Dev!" I push his shoulders with a laugh. "You're so weird!"

He chuckles with me and then cuts us both off with a kiss.

"Is that what made you laugh before? Realizing too late how weird I am?" he asks.

"No, I was laughing because I kind of made a mess of the room."

He tilts his head to look where I am. Along with the shimmering orbs filling the space, all the furniture is thrown about, and somehow our bed got moved to the center of the space.

"Well, I knew I had skills, but—"

"Careful, don't give me reason not to do this again."

His eyes meet mine, their color so clear, so happy, that I have to take in a deep breath. "Oh, trust me. We'll be doing this again." He kisses me. "And again"...another kiss..."and again." I smile against his lips. "You have no idea how long I've been waiting for you."

I swallow the emotions crawling their way up my throat. "But I thought you just wanted to be friends?"

His features flash to incredulous so fast that I laugh so hard, I snort. With a grumble, Dev rolls us to the side. "You made me *insane* with the 'just friends' thing."

"Well, now we're even on the making-each-other-insane camp."

His eyes glint amused, and he holds out his hand for me to shake. "Truce?"

I bite back a grin. "Truce."

⊷⊜ ⊜⊷

Peering through a clear glass window, I take in the new terrain as Dev maneuvers the hover car over a barren sea of sand. We've only been driving for twenty minutes, but at this speed I know we've covered a large distance.

"Where are we going?" I ask.

"Patience," he says, pulling my hand into his, and I glance down, grinning at the connection. I know it's probably wrong to be so happy so soon after Jared and I ended things, but I try not to dwell on that. Instead I allow myself to feel all the joy in this moment, all the peace.

"What are you thinking about?" Dev asks.

I turn my gaze from the window and take in his sharp profile and the majestic quality of his blue eyes as they flicker my way.

"How happy I am."

His genuine smile is radiating, never ceasing to take my breath away. He kisses the top of my hand. "Good, you deserve to always be happy."

"Why Dev, you secret romantic you."

He shoots me a wink. "I have my moments."

I chuckle and tip my head back, watching the zipping stars through the glass, the gentle rocking comforting. The sky is night for miles and miles.

"Dev?"

"Mmm?"

"Have you ever seen a sunrise?"

He glances my way. "Once in a video, a long time ago. Why?"

"Just wondering."

We continue to drive in companionable silence, the car dipping and gliding over the sand dunes, and I keep my gaze straight, watching the dark horizon.

Softly, slowly, an orange glow begins to peek through at the farthest hill.

Dev's breath catches, and I watch him from the corner of my eye as his face is gently bathed in yellow, warmed with light. His eyes grow wide, full of wonder as the car slows to a stop.

With his hand in mine, we watch the sunrise. Watch as it grows and expands, painting the land with colors it's never seen before—he's never seen before.

When it reaches its full ascent, I comb my fingers through the back of Dev's hair, turning his face toward mine. His eyes shimmer with unshed tears as he regards me like I'm a greater wonder than the sun in front of us. "Thank you." His voice is rough with emotion.

I smile. "I can be romantic too."

His responding laughter is soft and rumbling. "You're much better at it," he says before taking me in his arms and kissing me.

We stay locked like this long after the sun sets.

Chapter 23

DEV SPEEDS AROUND giant boulders that now cover the desert landscape. I still don't know where we're going, but the Navitas in me started to thrum a couple of miles back.

"It's right around this bend," he says.

I lean forward in anticipation, wondering what was so important that he dragged me all the way out here. As we draw nearer to the rocks' end, my breathing grows quick, like my body knows what's coming even if I don't. Blue waves of color peek out from the boulder's edge, and as soon as we round it, we're washed in light.

I squint at the sudden accosting, and then my eyes grow wide as my mouth falls open. "What in all of Terra…"

Before us is a giant ocean floating above the land. It emanates bright blues and whites and rainbows of color. The miles-wide liquid shifts like an amoeba, and I crane my neck, taking in its colossal height—it has to be at least thirty floors high. With my head tilted back I notice all the stars above falling. Like a meteor shower they rain down and crash into the mass, two magnets colliding.

"Welcome to the Sea of Dreams," Dev says, stopping the car and pushing a button so the glass around us falls away.

With the hit of fresh air, the energy coming off the Sea wraps around my cells, and I become momentarily lightheaded. *Whoa.*

"You okay?"

"Yeah, I'm just...taking it all in." My eyes remain locked onto the majestic mass. "Can we get out?"

"Of course."

Jumping from the car, we make our way forward, and I marvel at how the Sea floats above the sand, never truly touching the ground. It's almost like a ginormous bubble of Navitas jelly. I feel so tiny in front of it, and I smile knowing no other Dreamer I've received so far has experienced this.

"You like?" Dev asks.

I turn to him. "Are you kidding? I *love.*"

His proud grin beams. "This is where you all go to dream." He points to the endless falling stars. "Your unconscious minds seeking the Sea of Dreams."

"It's so beautiful." I walk closer to it, and the Navitas in me jumps again, a constant internal buzzing at being so close to such a power. "So it just floats like this?"

He nods. "It has a tendency to move around and is always shifting in size. No ground would be able to contain its constantly adjusting form."

A flashing light along the perimeter of where we stand catches my eye. "What's that?"

Dev squints at where I'm pointing and then reaches behind to his Arcus holder. A small round object pops out, and with a twist it starts to blink like the light in the distance. Dev raises it above his head. "That's a Nocturna guard," he says. "They're set up all along the border in small moveable camps."

"Protection against the Metus?"

"Yeah, they stay out here for longer rotations than those around the city. Normally the Sea would devour any Metus that tried to harness Navitas straight from it, considering how highly concentrated it is. But now with all the signs of the Metus evolving, we'd rather be safe than sorry and guard it, for the time being."

"Good plan." I take a step away from the potent energy.

Dev settles himself on the ground behind me, gesturing for me to join.

Taking a seat, I cup a pile of sand in my hand, letting the grains sift through my fingers as I watch the mesmerizing colors dance inside the Sea. Every few second there's a sparking of light within, matching when stars collide.

"I can't believe this place exists," I say, not really sure if I'm talking about the Sea or Terra itself.

"It is pretty amazing." Dev leans back.

We sit silently for a while, taking in the sound of each Dreamer making contact with the mass, a sigh on the wind.

After a time, I glance at Dev. "Can I ask you something, about earlier?"

"Of course."

"Did Rae tell you? About…"

His gaze finds mine. "Yes."

"How long did you know?"

"The night it happened."

My brows shoot up. "And you didn't say anything?"

"I don't recall you rushing to tell me yourself."

I press my lips together, conceding to his point.

"I wanted to give you the time you needed," he continues. "If you were truly going through a heartbreak, I wasn't about to be a rebound. Though"—he slowly peruses my body—"I don't think I'd put up much of a fight if you came to me begging for a release."

"How very chivalrous and...crass of you." I purse my lips, and his responding smile is crooked.

Lifting a hand, he brushes my cheek. "Are you though?" he asks, serious once more.

"Am I what?"

"Experiencing heartbreak?" His eyes hold a wariness, waiting for my answer.

I think about his question, think about what exactly the pain in my chest is from when I think of Jared. "No," I say, and his muscles relax ever so slightly. "I realized that most of my sadness is from guilt. I was holding on to that relationship for selfish reasons. I needed some semblance of normalcy." I breathe out a humorless laugh. "The irony of which isn't lost on me given how long I hated how 'normal'"—I air quote—"everything in my life was." Studying the ground, I play with the sand by my side. "I did care for him though, and hate any pain I've caused him."

"I'm sorry," Dev says, lacing his fingers in mine, grains falling into the crevices.

"For what?"

"That you're experiencing any sort of sadness."

"Since when did you become so understanding?"

A small smile plays on his lips. "I have my moments," he says, and I can't help but grin at the line he used earlier tonight.

The two of us fall into a companionable silence again, Dev tracing the outline of my hand, over and over, as if this is how we've always been—years of togetherness to create such a comfortable pocket of time. Eventually new thoughts enter my mind, and I bite the side of my cheek, unsure if I really want to bring this up now, but it's been nagging me too much to ignore.

"Can I ask you something else?"

He nods, still mesmerized with drawing patterns around my fingers.

"Are you…seeing someone?"

His gaze whips to me, brows pinching in. "Why would you think that?"

I swallow. "Well, I, uh, saw you with a girl. In Anima."

"A girl…" He glances off in the distance, connecting the dots. "You saw that?"

I nod, the memory still spurning a sweep of jealousy I'm not proud of. I just don't want any more uncertainties when it comes to him and me. It's a waste of time, considering it's already taken us so long to get to this particular moment.

"She…was a distraction," he says after a moment. "If you wanted to truly stay friends, I was trying to respect that. I thought that if I was with someone too, it might help things." He rubs his chin and studies the ground intently.

"Did it?"

He smiles, as if I said something funny, before meeting my gaze. "No, Molly. It only made me angry with you."

I frown. "What? Why?"

"Because we *can't* just be friends." He breathes out a laugh. "And you know it. No one else would have changed that, and I was angry that you were making me try."

I press my hands into the sand. "Sorry."

"It's fine. None of that matters anymore." He brings his arm around me, scooting me closer. "This is real now, me and you. You're my irreplaceable midnight." He places a kiss to my temple.

My heart flutters from his words, and I can feel the deep blush creep across my cheeks. "But what about Aurora?"

"What about her?"

"Weren't you on a date tonight?"

He stills, a beat of quiet before he's tipping his head back and laughing.

"Dev!" I push his shoulder. "I'm not joking."

He takes a little longer to compose himself, but when he does he turns to me with an amused grin. "Let's just say that Aurora would be more into *your* company than mine."

"What do you mean?"

One of his brows quirks up. "Do I really need me to spell it out for you?"

My eyes widen. "Oh. *Oh!*"

"Yeah, exactly. *Oh.* And that's probably a sound she'd love to hear you to make too."

"Oh my God!"

"And that."

"Dev!" I kick sand at him. "*Real* mature. Are you sure you're not twelve?"

He smiles, pleased with himself. "Pretty sure."

"But I thought you two…ya know." I incline my head.

"We what?"

"Ya know. *Did* it," I whisper.

"Did it?" He leans back, laughing again. "Who's the twelve-year-old now?"

"Ugh, never mind." I turn away.

Dev stifles a chuckle before reaching over and brushing back my hair. "Do you really want to talk about me and Aurora?"

"No, but I want to know your past, Dev, even if it might suck to hear." I'm leading him, corralling him into possibly sharing more than just Aurora.

His eyes study mine. Whatever he searches for he seems to find, because on a sigh he says, "Okay."

Okay? My chest flutters in anticipation, and I sit up.

"Yes, Aurora and I have been intimate in the past."

I swallow, unsure how I feel about this. "But she likes girls?"

"Yes, but also enjoys a male's company once in a while."

"Meaning yours?" I ask dryly.

"Not *just* mine, but as you know"—he leans with a crude grin—"I *am* hard to resist."

I roll my eyes. "Right."

"Yes, I am. But in all seriousness, we were intimate for a short period of time, which was a very long time ago and only because of...certain circumstances."

"What do you mean? What circumstances?" I try to keep my voice calm.

Dev glances my way, hesitancy in his eyes—a shadow from the past flickering through them, and I'm about to tell him never mind when he speaks. "I don't know if you noticed, but Aurora's a Vigil."

I always thought there was something different about her. Now it makes sense. "Then why is she a Nocturna guard?"

"I have to start farther back to answer that." Dev focuses on the Sea in front of us. The light emanating from it basks his face in a soft blue. "Aurora's unique in many ways, the first being that she's a twin. Now you have to understand something to get why that's a big deal. We're not born like humans. We can't conceive like you can. We're a very balanced population only created when there's a need. A death causes a life, or Terra senses a growth of Metus, et cetera. Our world is a scale always meant to remain still, balanced."

I blink, astonished. "Then how are you guys made?"

"There's a place called the Nursery, but that's a whole other conversation that we'll have to save for later."

"Okay." I nod, remembering Aveline mentioning her time at the Nursery, but not realizing its greater importance.

"Because of the sensitive way our population is controlled, we're normally created as individuals. There have been twins in the past, but it's very rare, and when it happens, the bond between the two, be it Nocturna or Vigil, is extremely strong."

"Like siblings," I say.

"Yes, I suppose like that."

"So wait, do you have parents?"

"No, not in the traditional sense, at least."

"What do you mean?"

"Some of us find parent-type figures—Tim, for example. I've known him for practically my entire life, and he's grown into a guardian role for Aveline and I, though we never asked him to." Dev grins to himself. "I imagine the love I have for him is similar to the love you have for your parents."

"Yes." I intertwine my fingers with his. "I imagine it is." Even though I'm extremely happy that these three found each other, I can't help feeling a bit sad knowing he'll never get to experience fatherhood in the biological sense, that no one here will. I also try not to think about what this might mean for our future, if there indeed is one.

"Because of this bond," Dev continues, "it's hard for twins to be away from each other for long periods of time. I'm not sure what exactly causes this, maybe because they're created from the same energy, but twins in Terra need to be close to one another."

"Is Ezekial Aurora's brother?" Thinking about her partner, I frown. They look nothing alike. He's all dark curly hair and tan skin.

"No." Dev looks down before meeting my gaze. "Aurora's brother was Aaron."

I balk. "*Aaron*? As in Anebel's partner, Aaron? The one who disappeared?" I snap my mouth shut, not meaning to say that out loud—*her* name out loud. *Shit.*

Dev flinches ever so slightly. "I see that Aveline left no rock unturned."

"Sorry." I grimace.

He turns to me, his stare intense. "Listen, I was going to tell you eventually, about…my past. I just didn't think it would be the same day we started this." He gestures between the two of us.

"You don't have to if you don't want. I'll understand," I say, even though I *really*, really want him to.

"No, I want to…I just…I can't tell you everything right now."

"That's all right." I squeeze his hand reassuringly, and he squeezes back.

"But yes, Aurora's brother was Aaron and…" He hesitates. "Anebel's partner. Nocturna and Vigil are both raised in the Nursery. That's where Anebel and Aaron first met and became friends. She was training to be a Nocturna guard, and I think that's what made him want to be one too. He never took to the lessons that were meant for Vigil, insisting a Nocturna guard was all he was going to be or he'd be nothing at all. I'm not exactly sure what went down politically, but because they were twins, I think certain…liberties were given for both of them to try out."

"Both? Aurora wanted to be a guard too?"

"No, not really, but she couldn't be without her brother. Like I said, the bond is extremely strong. If she weren't a Nocturna guard, they would have spent large amounts of time separated from one another. It wasn't an option."

"Wow." I can't imagine what it must be like to have a bond that powerful, not to mention what happened to her when she lost him. "So they both passed?"

"Yes." Dev nods. "And it caused quite a stir. No other Nocturna wanted to be paired with him. They were angry that a Vigil was given a chance at our duty when it's pretty much impossible for a Nocturna to guard the Dreamers when they're awake. Aaron specifically was ridiculed, cast as an outsider. Anebel—" Dev's words catch in his throat, and he turns toward the Sea. My stomach twists hearing the love still in his voice when he says her name. "She defended Aaron, and to prove that the naysayers were being a bunch of Metus heads, partnered with him."

A heavy silence settles in, Dev obviously replaying his past and me trying to imagine it.

"Were you in the Nursery at the same time as them?"

"For a period, but I'm older and graduated to the city a few years before. We were all close though, the four of us. And after what happened—" Dev swallows, and I want to hug away his sorrow. "After what happened, Aurora and I found solace in each other for a time, made sure the other kept breathing. There were moments where I didn't think either of us would make it. She's definitely grown weaker by the separation, but luckily she was strong to begin with," he says with a small smile.

I suddenly feel silly sitting next to Dev, holding his hand. How is our bond anything like what he had with Anebel or even still has with Aurora? I know I shouldn't be comparing, shouldn't be feeling insecure, but I can't help it. The stupid, lame, immature part of me is crying in the corner, feeling rather worthless. Dev and I barely know each other compared to his past relationships.

"Don't." Dev tugs on my arm.

I frown. "Don't what?"

"I see what's turning in your head. That was my past, Molly. It will always be a part of who I am, and I'm glad for that. But you"—his blue eyes dance with the reflected colors of the Sea—"you're my future."

I take a deep breath, at a loss for words, which luckily isn't a problem, because at that moment Dev leans down and kisses me.

I wrap my arms around his neck and pull myself closer, loving how his scruff grazes my skin and the possessiveness of his hands as they roam along my body.

A low humming interrupts our moment, and we break apart to see a vehicle zooming across the sand to meet us. We stand, watching it approach.

"Alec?" I walk up to the car as he jumps down. "What are you doing here?"

His close to seven-foot form thumps toward us, his heavy footfall puffing up sand with each step. "I tried beeping you guys, but the Sea must be messing up the connection."

Dev walks to our car and fiddles with the console screen. "Yeah, the signal is all screwy. Sorry about that." He turns back to Alec. "But what's so important that it couldn't wait?"

"Elena wants to see Molly."

"I already did my lesson with her today," I say, confused.

"She wants another Memory session before you leave tomorrow. She seemed rather insistent upon it actually, so we need to head back."

"Okay, okay." I hold up a hand. "Don't need to be pushy. We get the hint."

"But I wasn't hinting at anything." Alec frowns. "I'm saying we need to get going."

Dev and I share a look.

"Okay, big boy." Dev slaps Alec on the shoulder. "We hear you loud and clear. Lead the way."

We all turn to our cars and stop short. My blood freezes as the wretched stench of death floods the air.

"Where are they?" I glance around at the maze of giant boulders in front of us. All is still, but they could be hiding anywhere in there.

"They're close, wherever they are." Dev already has his Arcus out, Alec a double-barreled shotgun that pulses blue. *Whoa.*

"Should we get to the cars?" As soon as I ask, burning orange forms blink on in the distance, surrounding our exit.

"Collö," Dev curses, and both he and Alec step in front of me. Peeking through them, my mouth goes dry as I watch Metus— dozens of them—popping up from the rocks and tumbling down. None pause as they run straight for us.

Chapter 24

THEY BARREL FORWARD in the distance, and with every step closer their stink grows stronger and stronger—an attempt to blot out our hope for survival.

"We have enough time to get to the cars," I say, backpedaling.

"There's too many." Dev notches three arrows at once. "They'd overtake us."

"So what? We're better *out here*?"

Dev glances my way, his mouth tilting up at the side. "We've got this, Dreamer."

"Stay behind us," Alec instructs, his massive form seeming to get even bigger.

"Um, yeah, screw that." I wedge my way between them. "It's you two that should be getting behind me."

"Confident little one, isn't she?" Dev says to Alec, who merely grunts his displeasure.

Ignoring them both, I concentrate on the football field length of sand separating us from the monsters. Taking in a deep breath, I lift my hands, allowing the Navitas within me to spread and expand, taking over every cell. Then quickly I suction it back in, forming it into a concentrated ball. At the precipice of the gathered energy, I sharply exhale, dropping my arms. The ground rubbles, and a large fissure opens beneath the first wave of Metus, swallowing a handful. The chasm expands, separating us from them.

"Whoa," Dev breathes. "Definitely glad I'm on your side."

My confident smile is short lived when the remaining Metus merely jump over the gap, continuing their charge.

"Shit," I say, counting at least eighteen heading our way.

Dev lets loose his arrows, dropping a handful with a sickening wet explosion, and that's the last thing I register before chaos collides.

Breathing out of my mouth—so as not to gag on the stench—I hold off two creatures. Working hard to conserve my strength, I strike only when there's an easy opening, dancing around their dripping claws and spewing fire.

Alec's gun goes off in patterned bursts behind me, each time echoing a wet hit, and it's like music to my ears knowing he's okay.

Dev is a blur of movement in my periphery, seeming to have moved on to the decapitating way of fighting. I've come to realize he prefers this method, and I'm not really sure what that says about him. An oncoming Metus refocuses my attention as it starts chucking pieces of flesh at me. I meet it head on with my own flaming balls of Navitas. Shooting them from my hands, I hit it square in the chest and don't stop until it's burning blue and white and bursting apart.

The three of us repeat this exhausting dance until I realize our numbers are now five. Two more Nocturna have entered the fight, the closest ones guarding the Sea of Dreams.

"Thank God," I breathe, finally allowing myself to feel hopeful, yet still the Metus come. A few drop to their lava forms, and I jump back, surprised when one of the new Nocturna sprays them with bright liquid from a holster strapped to her back. By the almost blindingly bright energy being shot out, I realize it's Navitas straight from the Sea. My cells scream in yearning. As soon as the Metus puddles are hit, they cry out in a sharp wail and quickly bubble away, cells being devoured by acid. *Holy third-degree burns.* Remind me to stay clear of that stuff.

Turning around, I run toward Alec, who's now fighting three alone. I'm breathing heavy knowing I'm reaching my limit but refusing to acknowledge it. Ignoring the pain gathering in my head, I shoot out a wall of energy, barely registering the one Metus being wiped away by it, since I've already moved on to another. Alec reaches for more ammo as I engage, giving him time to recharge, and as I push to simultaneously hold off the second beast, my mind suddenly bursts in white-hot agony.

With a scream, I collapse to the ground, momentarily blinded by pain. Another gurgling cry surrounds me, and it takes me a moment to realize it's not my own. Stomach in my throat, I look up, seeing one of the Metus holding Alec in a death grip, its mouth suctioned to the side of his neck. Alec's dark skin has turned ghostly, and his eyes blaze with agony as he continues to scream and scream and scream.

"NO!" I shuffle to my feet, wobbling slightly, and attempt to use what little power I have left to separate them. With a grunt, I push a burst at the monster's head. The hit manages to release its feeding but not its grip. "GET OFF HIM!" I desperately shoot out more, knife-sharp torture splintering my skull. The creature's burning liquid form has almost completely covered Alec, and the pain must be too much. He's gone unconscious in its grasp. Something deep and dark sparks on in my chest, seeing him like this, and with newfound strength I call forth a rod of lightning. With it floating in my palm, I run up to the Metus and stab it in the head. With a yell, I keep jabbing long after it bursts apart, bits of lava burning my skin, my clothes—the stench bringing tears to my eyes. I keep stabbing even when there's nothing left in my hand.

"Molly." Dev lifts me into his arms. "It's gone. You killed it."

I blink and push away from him. "Alec! We have to help Alec!"

I'm pulled back again, but I fight his grip. "Molly, stop! Alec is—we can't help him."

I refuse to hear his words. *No no no no no.* It's my fault. My fault!

A glowing mass slowly stands in my periphery, and I turn to see a newly formed Metus, one that still partly resembles a man.

"*No,*" I whisper, and Dev tries to keep me back as I move forward. "Get off of me!" I shove him away and stand before the beast.

The creature growls, moving awkwardly in its new body.

"I'm so sorry," I say on a sob, tears blurring my vision. "I'm so sorry, Alec."

It takes a step toward me, a hunger in its eyes, and I raise the ground by its feet, tripping it. Splayed on the sand, I hold it down by shooting cords of Navitas to wrap around its appendages. The Metus, once Vigil, howls in frustration and spits fire.

"Let me do it." Dev says by my side, and I shake my head. "Don't touch him."

"Please, Molly, let me do this for you."

"No!" I push at him. "Just—just let me try." Tears keep streaming down my face, and I wipe at them roughly. Staring at the Metus—at Alec, because I know he's in there somewhere—I change to the sight of energy, slowing time. The thing grunts, claws, and wriggles before me, but I see it—I see the once-bright soul of a Vigil buried beneath the sludge. Holding out my hand, I dare to do what I was terrified of before. I touch its energy, *his* energy—the seed of Navitas still connecting this thing to the world.

When my power locks with the beast's, I experience something that I know no other Dreamer has ever felt for a Metus before—pity. Pity because I can feel the torture of existing as one of these things, the nightmare within a nightmare and the sense of relief when it knows it's almost over. Is this the small part still left of Alec, or is it in every Metus? Either way, I have empathy, empathy and a desperation to find the light that I know is hiding somewhere deep inside, the soul that has to still belong to my friend. On a large intake of air, I transfer the energy found in my own body to his, and with mine weakening, I notice his light getting stronger.

"What are you doing?" Dev's worried voice filters through the barrier of fog. "Molly, stop! You're hurting yourself." But I don't stop. I can't. I keep going until bits of burning orange flesh fall away from him and I can see a glimpse of Alec underneath. My chest flutters in hope, and even though I'm sagging, my body tapping out, I push forward. *Almost, almost—*

I'm thrown to the side, my vision blinking back to normal. Dev is on top of me, severing my connection. "What've you done?!" I frantically try sitting up, but I'm too weak.

"You were killing yourself!" Dev's eyes are panicked. He's about to say something else, when a new Metus charges toward us. I forgot we were still surrounded. With an impatient growl, Dev presses a button on his Arcus, shifting it around to be a double-ended sword, and in a blur of lethal blue-white movement, decapitates the creature. He turns back, our gazes locking before his slides to something next to me.

I shift around to see a half-charred body lying in the sand. Parts are still covered with glowing orange mucus, while others—the more human parts—are singed black and smoking.

I crawl toward it, bile rising in my throat, terrified of what I'll find.

A disfigured face stares up at me. Its ears are missing, part of its lips are burned away revealing skeleton teeth, and the entirety of its skin is charred black, cracking on each of its labored, shallow breathes. The only thing recognizable is its eyes, its deep-caramel eyes.

"Alec." My voice sounds distant, like I'm floating above myself. "Alec, I'm so sorry." I want to press my hand to his face, but I'm scared it will cause him more pain. "It's my fault," I say on a sob. "I left you open. It's my fault." He tries to move his mouth, but only a gurgle comes out. His gaze flashes in agony. "I tried." I keep talking like that will make things better. "I tried. I'm so sorry."

A sound filters out of him—words, barely a whisper. I lean in to make them out, and what I hear sends a knife straight to my heart.

"*Kill…me,*" he wheezes. "*Kill me.*"

Chapter 25

THERE MUST BE a circuit malfunction that happens in the human body right at the moment of trauma. Some synapse that doesn't fire, doesn't connect, allowing the person to be momentarily suspended in a void of nothing. No feelings. No thoughts. No reality. Nothing. But then, like a marionette's strings being cut, the bad, the horrible, the nightmares—they all come crashing back, and you fall. You fall and you never get up.

I barely register Dev gently sticking Alec in the chest with one of his arrows. Barely hear Alec taking his last gasp, one filled with relief, before he bursts apart. And I barely feel Dev lifting me into his arms, holding me like a child.

The sound of fighting still wraps around us, and with dead eyes, I take in the scene. Five Metus remain, and the two Nocturna guards continue to hold them off.

I'm so over it. The fighting, the Nocturna turning into our enemy, having to kill them once they do. I need it to stop. I need *them* to stop! *Stop, stop, STOP!*

Without meaning to, an ear-shattering wail channels out of me, and I'm momentarily consumed by a dark, powerful force that seeps out of my remaining energy.

I blink to time frozen. Dev, the beasts, the Sea, and sky—all of it—stopped. Looking out of eyes that are not my own, I step out of Dev's embrace. My past Dreamers are with me now, and they guide me forward—us forward—closer to the monsters. I see through them, feel their hate and anger toward the creatures that only live to destroy, my empathy long gone. With new vengefulness churning inside me, I sense the power of it as well as the warning of what it can do to me, but at this moment none of us care. We raise my arms—our arms—and let it out and the slick satisfaction of retribution in. Too easy now, we lock on to the small speck of light within each creature, and our lips curl into a smile as we watch the remaining Metus get blown apart, one by one, like patterned timers going off. Until they're gone and I'm alone and finally, with great relief, I collapse.

⊷⟫═⊙ ⊙═⟪⊶

"How long has she been like this?"

My body is being carried, my limbs deadweight in someone's arms.

"The whole ride here. What's wrong with her? Is she okay?" Dev's voice—panicked.

A light touch to my wrist. A slight tug in my core. "Yes, but her power is extremely low. She's drained herself."

"What do we do?"

"Follow me."

We run. Wind passes over my skin, and my head bounces back and forth, back and forth. Then I fall away again, into the place where nothing matters.

⊷⟫═⊙ ⊙═⟪⊶

I blink my eyes open to emptiness, a white ceiling so blank and stark that I know I'm in the Dreamer Containment Center. I stay like this, staring. Pretending that I'm just a head without a body, because if I have no body, then I have no heart, and if I have no heart, then I have no pain. But unfortunately I know the reality— I'm whole even if I'm Swiss cheese. And pain, it occupies every drilled-out cavern in me.

"She's up!" I hear a man's voice call, and then a hand is in mine. "Molly." I turn to Dev standing beside the bed I'm in, his brows pinched, face stretched with exhaustion.

"You look tired." My voice comes out hoarse, broken. "Are you sure you don't need sleep?"

His relieved smile puts youth back in his eyes, if only momentarily. "You gave us a scare. How are you feeling?"

I really wish he didn't ask me that. When people ask how you're feeling, you have to then think about why they needed to ask in the first place. More holes, more pain.

"He's gone," I whisper, "and it's my fault." Tears gather in my eyes again. "I told him I had it and then left him wide open."

"Shhh." Dev sits on the edge of my bed, stroking my hair. "That's not true. Each of us did everything we could. We were outnumbered."

The image of Alec's disfigured face flashes before me, and I know it will never dim. "I tried to help him, Dev. I tried, but I...I made it worse." I bunch my hands into fists. "What's the point of having me here if I can't even protect my friends? What's the point of learning any of this?!"

"Life's the point." Elena enters my room.

"*Life?*" I ask incredulously. "How is life the point when there's only been death?"

"To live is to sacrifice, Molly. We all must do our duties in our universes."

"Why? Who makes these rules? Can't we just live to *live?*"

"Some can, but not you. Not any of us." She glances at Dev before looking back at me. "Some of us have roles that need to be earned with the gifts that are given."

"*Gifts?!*" I choke out. "I never asked for any of this! Never asked to have these powers!"

"Didn't you?" Elena's eyes lock with mine, and my heart patters in my chest—a rabbit's foot gone crazy. How many times had I thought about wanting to be more, about doing something that really mattered? Her gaze tells me she knows the secrets I barely tell myself, and I hold back a shiver before looking away.

"Alec will be missed," she says in a softer tone. "He served Terra bravely. His duty was always one of risk, but he carried it out loyally. He was a Vigil to aspire to and will be remembered by us all with honor."

"It's not fair," I say more to myself. "He didn't deserve this end."

"It's not how you die that's important, Molly. It's about what you did in the time that you lived."

I stay quiet, too tired to fight any more. Even though I wish they would have a wake or a service for those lost, I'm relieved to hear that Elena genuinely feels sadness for Alec's death. Sometimes I wonder if she's not filled entirely with apathy.

I track her movements as she crosses the room to sit. Her bodyguards trail behind, remora fish following their shark. "We must discuss what happened," she says, smoothing the fabric of her white dress.

"We were ambushed." Dev stands. "Dozens came out of nowhere. I have no idea why scouts on the way to the Sea didn't see them coming. I haven't had a chance to talk with the ones at the outpost yet."

Elena nods. "Yes, it's disconcerting that so many could have moved such a great distance undetected. Their advancement in cognitive thought seems to be greater than we predicted."

Something in her tone makes me think there's more that she's keeping at bay. I sit up straighter, ignoring every screaming muscle as I do. "You have another theory to this, don't you?"

"Yes, but..." Elena's brows pinch in slightly. "It's too uncertain to entertain at the moment. Something's definitely off though." Her eyes grow unfocused for a moment. "I can feel it."

We're all quiet, wrapping our heads around this new development of Metus movement. The idea that their advancement could all be caused because of the new breed of sickos on Earth makes me even more depressed than I currently am. It also makes me angry, really angry. Don't we have enough problems to deal with? People living in starvation, trying to fight terminal diseases, natural disasters leaving humans homeless. Do we really need to be fighting each other on top of that? Killing one another? The thought makes me see red. All of these actions leading up to tonight and...Alec. A simmering heat swirls in my belly.

"Careful." Dev places a calming hand to my cheek, and I blink up to him. "You were making the lights tweak out. You only do that when you're feeling one of two things, and since I'm not lying in that bed with you, I can only assume which one it was."

"*Dev.*" I flicker a glance at Elena as I redden.

A hint of a smile plays across his lips. "I was worried I'd never see color in those cheeks again."

I clear my throat, ignoring the flustering state Dev still manages to put me in, and during a moment like this, *for Terra's sake.* "So what can we do?" I ask.

"A lot," Elena says. "But that's not what we're going to discuss right now. There's something else we need to take care of first." She stands. "I know you've been through much today, but I'm going to ask for a little more."

"A little more of what?" Dev moves closer to me.

"You tried doing something to Alec tonight, didn't you Molly?" Elena asks. "Tried to get him back?"

I swallow and nod.

"No other Dreamer has attempted to do that before. Has ever known they could."

"So?"

"So, you're more powerful than any Dreamer we've ever had."

The world tilts. "H...how?"

"My theory to this is why I called you back for another Memory session. There's something you need t—"

"She can't do a session right now," Dev interjects. "She's barely able to lift her head, let alone mentally take on someone else's thoughts. She needs more time to rest."

"Unfortunately, more time isn't a luxury we have at the moment. She'll be woken up soon, and then we won't get another chance until she's locked in again."

"Then we'll wait."

"Dev." I grab for his hand, but he pulls it away.

"No, Molly. It's too dangerous. You've been through too much. Do you have no sense of self-preservation?" He turns to Elena. "Can't you tell us your theory? Why all the dramatics of her needing to get another memory?"

"Because this is something she deserves to see firsthand."

Deserves? My heartbeat quickens. "Which Dreamer is it?"

Elena meets my gaze. "The last one who was here."

Chapter 26

ALEC'S ABSENCE IS a consistent punch to my heart as we walk down the halls. I keep expecting him to be waiting around every corner we turn, but the hall remains empty, a void not even his ghost can fill. Besides my grandmother passing, I haven't experienced many deaths of the people closest to me, which I know means I'm extremely lucky, but as I lay my head against the soft material of the Dreamer Memory Chair, I have a sinking feeling that's all about to change.

"I still think this is a bad idea." Dev frowns, watching Elena set up. After an intense debate that, I'll be honest, was more of a fight, Dev conceded to me receiving the memory, but only on the condition that he could be there, which, if I am to be honest again, I prefer.

"She'll be perfectly fine." Elena connects the floating box filled with my predecessors' memories into the screen that wraps around my head. "We are monitoring her vitals and can bring her back in a second."

I interlock my fingers with Dev's, and he looks down at me—worry and frustration evident in his features. "And you're here," I say. "I'm always okay when you're here."

"You heard that, right?" He glances up at Elena. "Because I'll be using you as a witness when she denies it later."

I tug on his arm. "Well, don't make me deny it so soon after saying it."

He grins. "I wish your face wasn't covered."

"Why?"

"Because I want to kiss you."

I can't help it. I smile, and it momentarily dulls the pain.

Elena clears her throat and looks between the two of us and then down at our connected hands. *Whoops, I guess that cat's out of the bag.* She doesn't say anything, but glances back to Dev, a silent conversation passing. His brows furrow and he nods, to which Elena quirks up the side of her mouth, seemingly pleased.

I'm about to ask what exactly just happened, when she lays a gentle touch to my arm, testing my energy. Every cell jumps, my body indicating it's restored. "We're ready," she says. "Dev, I'll need you to stand back."

He doesn't look happy about this but moves away nonetheless. My attention is pulled from him and refocused toward the Navitas now seeping across my gridded screen. Two swirling blue points drip down directly above my eyes, and I hold perfectly still as they latch on to my pupils, locking me in and sending me away.

Most of these memories start out the same. I learn my name—Robert. Learn the year—1926, and that I'm a very young American boy not yet introduced to Terra, my life still normal. Then there's the storm, and everything changes. I find out what I am, experience the shock, and then quickly accept it, as I have no other choice.

Time passes, my nights consumed only with the Vigil and training and the stark white walls of the DCC.

Robert never experiences Terra like I do, never sees the outside until he has to, until there's something in need of protecting.

Time leaps forward again, and we're no longer a boy. We follow two Vigil guards down a dark hallway, the only illumination coming from strips of Navitas that run its length. We stop in front of wide chrome doors with a glowing lightning bolt in the center—the symbol indicating that whatever lies beyond we cannot access on our own. Our curiosity piques. After one Vigil verifies our identities, the giant door huffs open in the middle, and we're immediately hit with the euphoria that only comes with an excess amount of Navitas. Walking forward, both Robert and I take in a scene that neither of us has ever laid eyes on before. Standing on a second-floor railing, we look down upon a massive dark expanse. Rows upon rows of glowing Navitas orbs are evenly patterned throughout the space and seem to go on for an immeasurable distance. Some pulse blue-white in color, while others are a sickly, swirling sludge of red and black. Each is double the height of the average human and has a monitoring Nocturna circling its perimeter, rapidly touching the liquid surface in random patterns. *I* know them as Nocturna, but Robert sees them merely as Vigil dressed in black. To him, they are no different than the man and woman leading us. Descending stairs, we're guided between the mazes of orbs, enabling us to take a closer look. Dozens of images float across their expanse, and the longer we watch we come to realize these are people's dreams. Some scenes seem like everyday life, others are beautiful and bright, while the ones in the slow-churning black and red are mutated and strange—nightmares. The monitoring Nocturna pay us no mind, completely consumed with tapping on certain images they find of interest. When their hands make contact, the selected scenes glow brighter for a moment before vanishing, being replaced by something new. Glancing from blue-white mass to blue-white mass, our jaw grows slack with awe taking in the vastness of the things imagined, the energy in our core humming to join.

We travel deeper into the heart of the cluster before our guides stop. Looking away from an image of a little girl with butterfly wings, we glance forward, and our breath catches. There before us, surrounded by a ring of thick pulsing Navitas, is Elena. She floats several feet above the ground, golden hair moving as if in a gentle breeze, eyes unfocused and glowing white as thousands of tendrils of energy connect from the circle around her to every part of her body. Robert has no idea who she is other than the most freakishly beautiful thing he's ever seen, and I—Molly—am completely mind blown. *Holy cosmic goddess*! This is what Elena is? And I was just yelling at her! We stand there for several minutes, watching Elena frozen as if in a trance, and it doesn't take a rocket scientist...or, uh, a Navitas scientist...to understand that she's taking in every single image the Nocturna are tapping. *What does she do with all those dreams?*

Eventually the circle of energy surrounding her begins to spin faster and faster, sending off a gust of wind and a low hum. Slowly Elena floats down until we can no longer see her behind the swirling ring of Navitas, and Robert cranes his neck in an attempt to keep her in his sight. We jump back in surprise when the energy suddenly suctions in like an implosion and filters straight into Elena. She glows inhumanly bright for a moment before the light in her eyes fades to a startling blue, and she stands staring at us. We hide a shiver at the connection, and Robert uses all his strength to remain still as she walks forward. She seems younger than I, Molly, know her to be now, but only slightly.

"Robert," she says in her breathy authoritative tone, and goose bumps erupt on our skin. "I'm Elena." She extends her hand for us to take, and when we're connected, our power jumps in our chest. Robert pulls his arm back, startled.

With a blank expression, she tilts her head in an assessing manner. "You're not how I imagined you to be."

"How did you imagine me?"

A hint of a smile. "Not as tall."

By the way Robert's heart—our heart—thumps wildly in our chest, I can tell he's attracted to her, and I squirm awkwardly.

"Let me show you around." She leads us forward, explaining the purpose of this facility, that it's where they monitor dreams and select those with potential, check the status of nightmares on Earth and the general mental well-being of our population. Robert and I already know most of this because all Dreamers were briefed on Terra's purpose, but we never realized that such a specific facility existed or that Elena, a single person, provided a central role in the monitoring process. But what we really can't wrap our head around is why we're only being shown it now. Thankfully, Robert asks.

"Dreamers are only given access to this facility when our findings forecast an abnormally high amount of nightmares," Elena says.

"Can you explain that in layman's terms please?"

She glances over her shoulder. "I thought I did."

"Uh," Robert falters to reply.

"I'll try again." Elena's eyes spark, amused. "We believe a war is coming that's bigger than the ones that normally constitute receiving a Dreamer in Terra."

We stop, our blood running cold. "Like a World War?"

She nods.

"But Earth just went through one of those."

"So did we."

"But...but how can—are you sure?"

"Unfortunately, yes. The rapidity of human minds filling with nightmares is staggering. You needed to see this facility—see for yourself what we're dealing with in order to prepare."

We glance around, now noting that a majority of the orbs are pulsing the sickly red-black. Robert takes in a deep breath, a million thoughts about what would happen if he fails consuming his mind. I wish I were able to let him know I understand his fear, that he's not alone, but I can only watch as we continue to walk forward again, Elena resuming her tour.

"What do you do here?" Robert asks after traveling down several more rows.

"I'm the closest mortal connection Terra has to all of this." Her delicate hand gestures to our surroundings. "And all of you."

"So you are mortal, not a god?"

She studies us, a curiosity alight in her eyes. "I'm mortal in Terra's standards, yes."

"And in Earth's?"

The quirk of her mouth is answer enough, and we swallow.

"Come." She surprises us by threading her cool fingers in ours. "We have more to see." I want to flinch away at the odd intimacy, but Robert's a mass of barely contained male hormones, excited by the gesture and internally marveling at the silkiness of her skin. *Really, dude?*

"Were you seeing all the dreams?" Robert asks. "Earlier when I arrived?"

"The ones deemed of interest."

"What do you do with them?"

"You already know the answer to that."

Robert tugs her to a stop, a bold move in my opinion, and she glances up with a raised brow. "No, what I meant was, what do *you* do with them, Elena?"

She blinks, momentarily stunned by his question, and then slowly, with a look of intrigue, her lips curve up. "I dream."

The scene suddenly skips away, the orb-filled room replaced by more memories, more time. The year is now 1941, and we're angrily pacing in a white room. The door huffs open, and four Vigil file in followed by a lady in white. Our heart jumps at the sight of her.

"Elena, you can't keep me in here. I need to be woken up!" Robert barks out while stalking toward her. The guards move between us. "I'm not going to hurt her, you fools!"

Elena lays her hand on one of the male Vigil's shoulders, and a jealous spike runs through us. "It's fine. Let us speak." The men and women hesitate for a moment before filing out.

When we're alone, the energy in the room shifts, and I wiggle uncomfortably in this body again, feeling the attraction it has for the woman in front of us.

"Hector told me what's happening on Earth. What happened yesterday with the bombings. America is in this war now. I need to get back."

Elena begins to circle us, and we stand rigid, focusing on a nondescript point in front. "You will in two days' time," she says.

We aren't happy with this answer. "This is ridiculous! You can't keep me locked in here."

"Actually, I can."

Anger sparks within us, and our Navitas pushes out, but does nothing. We growl in frustration that this room's equipped to strip our power.

"I don't enjoy keeping you in here, Robert. I need you to help us just as you want to help your people. But I fear if I let you out, you'll do something foolish again to try to return." She stops in front of us. "Did you *really* think you'd survive one of our portals?" Her intense cerulean gaze collides with ours.

We ignore her question. "Then don't hold me in here like a prisoner. Help me."

"I'm trying to."

"How is shoving me in a depowering cell helping?"

"What if we didn't find you when we did? What if you actually tried to cross through to your dimension like that? Did you even stop to think what that action could have meant for your body there?"

We're silent, taking in her words.

"No, just like the hothead you are, you were all action before you thought of the consequences." She looks away disappointed, and for me—Molly—the first time I've ever seen her angry. "You're only your conscious self here. Don't ever forget that. If you went through that portal from our side, your mind would have been eviscerated. You would have left your body back on Earth an empty vessel, mindless and in a coma you'd never wake up from. Do you understand?!"

I shrink back at her uncharacteristic rage, but Robert merely steps forward, wrapping her in our arms. "I'm sorry," he whispers. "You're right. I didn't think."

Elena nuzzles closer, and as her sunflower fragrance encircles us, I hit up against all the walls of Robert's body, trying to extract myself. *What are you doing*?! This is Elena! Alien, creepily omniscient, I-am-in-no-way-capable-of-having-romantic-feelings Elena!

"You have no idea how terrified I was when Hector told me what he thought you were going to do. I was afraid…afraid I'd be too late."

"I'm sorry," he says again as we run our hands along her back. "I didn't mean to worry you, but I have responsibilities at home as well as here. You know this."

She tilts her head to look at us. "Yes, but you also know you can help Earth by helping here, more so in fact. Stop the monsters in Terra, and you'll stop them everywhere."

"It's not always that black and white. You don't know what it's like to have two homes. Two places you care about," he says softly as we gaze at her with love. I want to run away from the desire I have to touch her hair and feel how soft her skin is. I retreat further into Robert's body when we move in to do so. *Stop*! I scream. *We're not allowed to touch her*! But Elena doesn't seem to mind when we tuck a lock behind her ear. Her smile is radiating, and our lips break into joy upon seeing it. Then we're moving in, closer and closer, and she's letting us. My heart rattles around frantically when our lips touch, and my soul seems to sigh at the connection. I'm at home with her in my arms. I'm safe with her by my side. *Oh, dear lord in heaven.* Talk about a mind fuck.

Time shoots forward again, to which I am eternally grateful, except now there's been death, destruction, and lost hope in both our worlds. World War II rages on just as the battles do in Terra. We're exhausted, never able to rest, as we're a soldier both awake and asleep. It's too much, too tasking, and we fear we won't survive it. How can this possibly end with us still alive?

Slumping on the bed that's in our DCC quarters, we look into the mirror across the room, and I take in this Dreamer's face for the first time.

What I see shatters me into a million pieces.

It's not the hollowness of Robert's cheekbones or the despair written across his features that is the shock. It's that I know him, though a very different version.

My Robert is fifteen pounds heavier, with thick-rimmed glasses, wrinkles, and hair that is no longer brown, but white.

We roam our appearance in the reflection. Him exhausted, me obliterated, and then we look up again, and I stare into my eyes, eyes that are my grandfather's.

Chapter 27

I GASP, MY chest arching forward as I'm unlocked. Once again myself, I squint at the sudden brightness.

Holy shit. My grandfather was a Dreamer. Hector knew him, Elena...

Finding her beside me, I flinch back and scramble to figure out which emotions are mine and which belong to Robert. I'm completely discombobulated. They had a *relationship*, were in love. What does this mean? I study her blank face, the way her cerulean gaze shrouds—an arctic sea hiding what lurks below. There's a look of warning, however, telling me not to broach a particular topic dealing with the heart.

"Are you okay?" Dev asks.

"You knew," I whisper, unable to look away from Elena. "You knew who he was to me."

She barely blinks. "Yes."

"Why didn't you say anything?" My reality is once again warping, once again making me feel like I know nothing of who I really am.

"It wasn't of consequence before."

I bulk. "Wasn't of consequence? He's my *grandfather*!"

"Who is? What's going on?" Dev places a hand on my shoulder.

"The last Dreamer was my grandfather." I glance to him before returning to Elena.

"*What?* How? What does this mean?"

"It means Molly is the first direct descendent from a past Dreamer."

Dev and I are silent for a moment, and then we're talking at once—Dev asking how this is possible again and me repeating my question of why she never said anything before.

Elena briefly closes her eyes while taking in a deep breath. It's the first I've seen her need to find her bearings. *Welcome to my world, sister.*

"I don't know how this is possible," she begins. "I also don't know if this means we're about to get hit harder than we ever have before."

The room grows out of focus for a second before it slams back. *Oh God.* "Because Terra wouldn't need someone as strong as me otherwise?" As if he knows I need something grounding me, Dev finds my hand and holds tight.

"That would be my theory," Elena says. "But I also have another."

"Is it happier? I only want to hear it if it's happier."

"It is."

I let out a breath.

"Remember how I told you that all Dreamers leave some impression behind in Terra, some influence that changes us?"

I nod. "You think this could be what I leave behind? Something to do with my lineage?"

"I researched in every one of our history books and found nothing like this. No other Dreamer has ever come from such a direct bloodline before. I can only hope the purpose is a positive one."

"Hope, huh?" I worry my bottom lip. "I don't know if *hope* will help me sleep at night."

"No, but I'll be here," Dev says, his hand tightening in mine. "And I can protect you a lot better than hope."

⋅►═◓ ◑═◄⋅

The streets are quiet as Rae and I make our way to my apartment from the bookstore. It's barely five in the morning, and Manhattan is still a slumbering giant, this small pocket of early morning its snore before the city rolls out of bed.

"Your grandfather?" Rae asks for the tenth time.

"Yeah, my grandfather."

"In all of Terra…" He runs his hand through his hair. "So what are we supposed to do?"

"I don't know about *we*, but I need to go see him. Elena didn't explain why he never told any of us."

"Um…probably for the same reasons you haven't told anyone."

"Good point."

"Especially back then," Rae continues. "He would have been lobotomized for sure."

I frown, wondering if this is why my parents think he's losing it. After all these years, is he no longer able to hold in such a secret? Is Terra actually the "nonsense" my mother says he's spouting on about? My impatience grows to get home and find out.

"There's one positive thing that's come out of this though. He's the first Dreamer I've gotten solid evidence of living past Terra." I glance to Rae. "Do you know what happened to the rest of them?"

Rae's about respond, when he suddenly stills. Every muscle in him is strung tight as he grabs my shoulder and forces me to stop. "What the—" I snap my mouth closed when he brings his finger to his lips. He swivels so I'm behind him, and he peers into the alley we stand in front of.

"What is it?" I whisper, trying to peek around him into the darkness.

He takes a step forward and almost seems to sniff the air. After a moment more of standing like a statue, his shoulders relax and he nudges me forward, still glancing around with alertness.

"You're scaring me. Did you see something?"

"More like sensed."

The hairs on the back of my neck rise. "What kind of sense?"

"The *we're being followed* kind."

I look behind us, but the street is empty. "Funny, I felt the same way a couple of weeks ago."

"What?" Rae whips around me. "When was this? Did you see anyone?"

"No, no one. It was just a feeling. Nobody was there. Relax."

"Molly, you need to tell me when things like that happen."

"Sorry, *yeesh*, I didn't know. But it's not like I'm in danger here, from the Metus anyway. What? You going to protect me from being pick-pocketed?"

He doesn't appreciate my attempt at levity. "Yeah, that's *exactly* what I'm going to protect you from. My job is to make sure you don't so much as get a splinter."

"What about a paper cut? I'd rather you make sure I never get one of those. They are *way* worse."

Again, no laugh. *Man, is this mic on?*

"One thing's for certain." Rae shuffles us forward at a quicker pace. "You'll need to invite Becca to stay this weekend."

"Why would I do that?"

"Because there is no way I'm letting you out of my sight right now, and it would be a little weird for me to stay at your parents without her there. I'd rather us avoid lying to Becca when we can."

"I agree with you there, but isn't this why you have other trained Vigil? To trust for things like this?"

"Oh, it's not them I don't trust."

I balk. "Wha—*me?* You don't trust me? I'm not going to run out looking for danger, Rae. I get enough of that when I'm asleep."

"It's not only the trouble I'm worried about." He eyes me from the side. "Let's just say, I don't think my guards would make it past some of your booby traps when they try waking you up for your runs."

I purse my lips. *Damn.* I thought I'd get a break this weekend, and by the knowing look on Rae's face, he knew what I thought. These are the moments when I wish I were back in Terra so I could whip up a storm cloud to follow him around all day. *Poop on Earth and its nonmagic ways.*

⋆⇒ ⇐⋆

"Road trip!"

"Bec, we've been driving for an hour and a half. That declaration can't be said with the same enthusiasm after an hour and a half."

"Sure it can. Road trip! See, same enthusiasm."

I roll my eyes and glance to Rae in the rearview mirror. He's hiding a smile while looking out the window. We just got back in the rental car after a pit stop to fill up on junk food. The week at work dragged to get to this point, and at night, even though Dev helped in taking away some of my sadness, every time I was greeted by Alec's replacement, I was hit with a wave of pain, a wave of regret. I practically burned rubber tearing out of the Holland Tunnel to leave New York, impatient to talk with my grandfather and desperate to find some hope in what's quickly feeling like a hopeless cause.

"This was a great idea." Becca opens a bag of chips. "I haven't come home with you in a while. It's long overdue."

"Yeah, my parents were excited to hear you were coming and that you were bringing your *boyfriend*," I tease. Becca and Rae just titled themselves a few weeks ago, and one would have thought he asked her to marry him, by her reaction. But I guess being someone as independent as her, it kind of was like that.

Becca flashes me a coy smile. "So your gramps has moved in with your parents for a while?"

I nod. "He's been there for the past couple of weeks. They thought it made sense since they were basically driving over to see him every other day. My mom says he seems to be better since the move."

"I'm sure. Who wouldn't want to be around their family when they're his age?"

"When's the last time you saw him?" Rae asks from the back.

"It's been a while, maybe since before my birthday."

"But you were home last weekend." Becca's forehead wrinkles in confusion.

Crap! Rae and I lock eyes in the mirror.

"Oh, yeah…well, um, he was back and forth at the doctor's the whole time. We weren't really on the same schedules. So I didn't get any solid quality time with him, ya know? He probably doesn't even remember I was there." My heart tumbles in my chest as I try to remember all the lies I've told Becca. There's too many to keep track. I only hope she doesn't bring up my recent visit to my parents. I didn't even think about that! I grind my teeth in frustration and glare at Rae. He shoots me a meek grin, apology written all over his face. *Couldn't trust me, my butt.* This weekend just got a lot more complicated.

Chapter 28

"YOU GUYS MADE great time." My dad takes my bag from my shoulder as we walk into the house. "We're just about to sit down for dinner."

My parents live in one of those stucco cookie-cutter houses in a gated community in Pennsylvania. If it wasn't for my mom's obsession with flamingos, I would have mistaken any of the identical facades as my home as a kid. But luckily, the bright-pink birds stuck in our front flowerbed were the perfect homing device when coming back from playing at a neighbor's.

"Molly!" My mom brings me in for a hug. "Oh, you feel too skinny. Have you been eating?"

"Nice to see you too, Mom." I step back as she practically jumps into Becca's arms.

"You're even taller than I remember. Ack, and that hair!" My mom fluffs Becca's already-voluminous mane.

"Kathy, I want to introduce you to my boyfriend, Rae." Becca smiles up to him, and my mom practically falls over, taking in his height and build.

"Oh my..."

"Hi, Mrs. Spero." Rae holds out his hand. "I've heard a lot about you."

"Kathy, please, and I hope it's been from Becca and not Molly," she says wryly, shooting me a glance. "We also only give hugs in this house, not handshakes."

He chuckles and leans down to wrap his arms around her.

"Charles, look! I disappeared!" Mom mumbles to my dad as she indeed vanishes within Rae's large embrace. Becca and I crack up.

"Sorry about that, Rae." My dad shakes his head. "She doesn't get out much."

My mom *tsks*, stepping back. "And whose fault is that?"

"I leave the door wide open for you all the time."

She smacks his arm. "Come on, you three. Let's leave before he starts to think he has an audience for his jokes."

"So easily she forgets," my Dad faux whispers to Rae, "that I have legs and can follow."

After leaving the comic parade to put my bag in my room, I head back downstairs to look for my grandfather. I find him in the living room, his glasses at the edge of his nose as he reads a book and twirls a pen in his hand, ready for the moment when he sees something worth underlining. Even at ninety years old he's maintained a youthful aura, never really falling into the typical grandparent routine. His flannel shirt is tucked into his dark-blue jeans, and he rocks rather stylish sneakers. Taking in his peaceful presence, I marvel that this is the same person I saw brutally and fluidly destroying Metus, that he's a Dreamer just like me.

"Hey, Grandpa."

He glances up from his text, his face breaking into a grin. "Molly! Your dad told me you were coming home for the weekend."

I lean down to give him a hug. "How are you feeling today?"

"Good, good. Selma leaves me alone more now that I'm here, so I can't complain."

"She's only trying to help," I say, talking about his part-time nurse.

"Help annoy me."

"Grandpa." I laugh. "Don't be a curmudgeonly old man. You're better than to fall into a stereotype."

"I'm in my nineties. I can be however I want to be."

"Fair enough." I hold up my hands in submission and take a seat on the ottoman next to him. "I know better than to argue with that."

"Yes you do." He closes his book. "So, how have you been feeling, sweetheart? I haven't seen you since before the accident. You look well enough."

I glance around to make sure Becca wasn't around to hear that. "I'm fine, but actually...I, uh, wanted to ask you something about that."

"Oh?"

"Yeah. Well, my dad said you got hit too, when you were a child?"

My grandfather's eyes go out of focus for a moment. "Yes, I was thirteen. I've never felt that kind of pain. It's enough to kill a man."

I nod in agreement. "It's weird, isn't it? That we've both gotten struck by lightning."

"Extremely."

"Did you…did you ever have strange dreams after?"

His eyes lock with mine. "Dreams?"

"Yeah, problems sleeping?"

"Did your mom put you up to this?" He leans back in his chair.
"No." I frown. "Why?"

He studies me. "Are *you* having strange dreams, Molly?"

My pulse quickens. *Time to go out on the ledge.* "Yes, very. Lifelike
strange."

We sit there, staring at one another, a million questions spinning through my mind of what my next move should be. Do I just
tell him? Does he even remember? If he doesn't, will he think I'm
crazy? And if he does, will the overwhelming knowledge that I'm
also a Dreamer send him into cardiac arrest?

My grandfather opens his mouth to say something, when my
mom walks in. "There you two are. Molly, come help me set the
table. Robert, we'll be eating in five."

I remain watching him, waiting for him to say whatever he was
about to say, but he doesn't. Instead he looks over my shoulder to
my mom and tells her he'll be right in. I slump in disappointment.

"Are you coming, Molly?" Mom persists.

"Yeah." I stand, taking one more glance at my grandfather. For
the briefest of moments, our gazes collide, but then he looks away,
staring off at nothing and making me doubt he remembers anything at all.

⊷⊷ ⊶⊶

"So why didn't Jared tag along?" Mom asks as we sit down for dinner.

Becca glances at me, brows pinched in.

"Um, because we broke up."

My mom blinks wide. "Oh, well, that's just...I'm sorry to hear that. When did this happen?"

"Last week."

Becca turns to my mom. "She didn't tell you when she c—"

"I had a lot going on." I cut Becca off. "I'm sorry I didn't mention anything before. It's been...hard."

I catch a curious glance from my grandfather, and I wish desperately that we weren't eating right now so we could talk. *He has to know. He has to remember.*

"Of course, sweetie." My mom covers my hand. "But what happened? You two seemed so good together."

"We wanted different things."

"Like what?" She frowns.

"Just different things."

"Yes, you said that, but what *kind*?"

"Oh, leave the poor girl alone," my grandfather pipes in. "Not everyone is so pleated and ironed out like you and Charles."

"Well." My mom picks up her wine. "I'll take that as a compliment."

"You can take it as a to-go bag if you like—just let Molly share when she wants to share."

My dad chuckles under his breath, and my mom purses her lips at him before turning to me. "Sorry, I didn't mean to pry. Just want to see you happy."

"I know, Mom, but don't worry. I am."

She nods, seemingly mollified, and I look at my grandfather, but he's now preoccupied with trying to stab a cherry tomato.

"And how is everything else? Have you needed to see Dr. Marshall?" Mom asks, referring to the doctor who saw me at the hospital after I got struck.

"No, after my last check-in, I haven't needed to go back."

"That's good." She cuts into her meal. "Though…maybe you should make an appointment to see him again."

My brows crease. "Why? I feel fine."

"Yes, but now that you're single…"

Becca's eyes go wide across from me.

"Oh my *God*, Mom, are you telling me I should go back to the hospital to see if I can score with the doctor?"

"What?" She glances at me innocently. "He was young and good looking and a *doctor*."

"Unbelievable." I shake my head.

"You never told me he was good looking." Becca leans in, mirth in her gaze.

"Gee, I wonder why that skipped my attention? Oh, that's right…because I just got hit by lightning."

Rae laughs next to me and then presses his lips together when he meets my glare.

"Still, that's an important detail to leave out," Becca continues.

"Why?" I cross my arms.

"Because then I would have definitely gone with you for your checkup."

"I think I should be offended right now." Rae raises his brows at her.

"Oh no, there's nothing to worry about, babe." Becca slides him a grin. "I'm just an appreciator of fine-looking gentlemen. I can't pass up a chance to see one in the wild."

"Here, here." My mom raises her glass and takes a sip.

"I don't know why women always say men are the pigs." My dad casually shakes pepper onto his potatoes. "From the sound of you two, women are way worse."

"No." My mom peers at him over the rim her glass. "We just have more finesse when it comes to observing the opposite sex. While you brutes resort to catcalls."

"Really? Well, if my memory's still intact, I remember a certain individual whistling at me the other night when—"

"La la la, daughter in the room! Daughter in the room!" I desperately cover my ears while Becca and Rae try to control their laughter. My parents stop their banter, *thank God*, but still eye each other across the table. *Gross.* My grandfather merely looks around, confused, seeming to have missed the whole conversation. *Lucky bastard.*

Dinner continues with the usual Spero chatter, but, wonderfully, with no more sexual innuendos. Even with the almost-suffocating desire to speak with my grandfather, I begin to relax for the first time in a while and actually allow myself to enjoy my time with my family. That is until we have one or two more close calls with Becca almost mentioning my trip home last weekend. When she eventually excuses herself to go to the bathroom, and with the advantage of my parents indulged with their own discussion, I lean over to Rae next to me. "You *cannot* let her be alone with them at any point this weekend."

He nods in agreement.

"This is turning into a total shit show," I mumble.

"What did you say, sweetheart?" my mom asks.

"Oh, um, I was just asking Rae if he likes Shih Tzus."

"Shih Tzus?" My dad frowns. "Furry rats, if you ask me."

"Well, luckily, no one did, dear."

"I love side shows," says my grandfather.

"What was that, Dad?"

"Side shows." My grandfather points his fork at Rae. "What Molly just asked her friend about. I love 'em."

"No, *Shih Tzus*," my father says slowly.

"A what?"

"It's a type of dog," Mom clarifies. "Shih Tzu."

My grandfather frowns. "Why the hell would anyone name a dog Shit?"

On a choked laugh, Rae spits out some of his wine, and I pat him on the back. *Yup, total Shih Tzu of a weekend.*

⋘ ⋙

"Where's Grandpa?" I ask my dad, who's laid out on the couch with Rae, watching—no shocker here—*Die Hard.*

"He went to sleep."

My heart sinks. "Already?"

"Yeah, said he wasn't feeling well. He usually goes to bed earlier than this, but wanted to stay up to have dinner with all of us."

"Oh."

Rae looks to me, a silent question in his gaze. I shake my head, and he gives me an encouraging *there's always tomorrow* smile.

Walking out to the back patio, I find my mom and Becca lounging around the fire pit, drinking wine. *Awesome.* Nice job, Rae, making sure Becca wasn't alone with one of them.

"Here, Pop-Tart, we poured you one." Becca hands me a glass.

"Thanks." I take a seat in one of the cushiony chairs.

"Becca was just telling me about how she met Rae"—my mom smiles—"and that it's all because of you."

"Me?"

"Yeah." Becca nods. "If you never went up to get us drinks that night, I might never have met him."

"That's true." I burrow into the pillows around me. "So, I guess this means you have to name your firstborn after me."

"How about my first goldfish?"

"You hate fish. You'll never get one of those."

"Exactly." She smiles wide, and I shake my head.

"So ungrateful."

"Fine. How about our first car?"

"Deal." We raise our glasses in an agreement.

"You two are so strange." My mom refills her wine, even though I'm pretty sure she doesn't need to.

"So Grandpa seems like he's doing better. He was extremely lucid at dinner," I say to my mom.

"Oh, lucidity was never the issue. During the day, he's always as sharp as a tack. It's the night terrors that make us think he's suffering from dementia."

"Night terrors?"

"Yeah, you know, waking up in a fright and declaring all sorts of crazy things."

I work hard to control my breathing. "What kinds of things?"

My mom thinks about it for a second. "Well, like the other night, he woke up screaming someone's name and how he needed to get back. He was all out of sorts. Wouldn't listen when we told him it was just a dream."

My heart wants to leap from my chest. "Whose name?"

My mom wiggles her hand dismissively. "No one your dad or I have ever heard of. But," she says, lowering her voice, "if you ask me, I think he had an affair."

"While he was with Grandma?" My brows rise.

"Mhmm." She takes a sip of her wine.

"Why would you think that?"

"Because the name he's always yelling is a woman's, and it's not hers."

My surroundings fall away for a second, taking in this news.

"Oh wow." Becca's eyes grow wide. "Do you really think so?"

"Charles doesn't, of course, being that they're his parents, but why else would a man in his nineties suddenly be calling out for a woman that's not his wife, while he's asleep?"

"Ain't that the question of the year." Becca lifts her glass in a salute, and my mom giggles before doing the same. I zone out to the rest of their conversation as my eyes find the outside of my grandfather's bedroom. As I stare at the darkened window, I can't help wondering if the man sleeping inside is a preview of my future.

Chapter 29

The air is colder than normal, and I wrap my arms around my legs as I gaze out to the lit-up city in the distance, watching as a form slowly approaches. The stars zip by in a constant stream overhead, and the field sways in a gentle breeze. I rest my head against the trunk of my tree.

"Why didn't you meet me on the platform?" Dev takes a seat beside me.

"I needed the silence."

"Your family that overwhelming?" He smiles.

"I haven't been able to talk with my grandfather yet."

"You'll find time."

I close my eyes and lean into him as his fingers brush back my hair. "I think he knows about me though. I tried hinting at it without overwhelming him."

"How did he respond?"

"That's the confusing thing. He didn't. Not really anyway, not the way I would have expected him to." Dev stays silent, letting me talk it out. "I just don't understand why Elena wouldn't tell me what happened to him, what happened to any of them. I mean, my grandfather's alive, so they couldn't *all* have died, right? Well, I know the rest are dead because of time, that they aren't like walking around hundreds of years old or anything." I pull at the grass by my feet. "But I guess that's the thing—they could be. Maybe being a chosen Dreamer gives you immortality or something. I wouldn't know though, because Elena doesn't tell me crap." I turn to him. "I just don't get why there's still all these secrets? I thought I was past that with this place."

"Who knows why Elena or any of the elders do the things they do. I mean, look at the Nocturna. We had no clue that Dreamers existed in Terra until recently, and the majority of us still don't. And we've worked closely with the Vigil for hundreds and hundreds of years."

"Yeah, that's dumb."

"Well, let's hope your grandfather can shed some light to all this."

I sigh. "Yeah."

"Come on." Dev nudges my side before standing. "Help me do my rounds."

"Where's Aveline?"

"With Hector."

"Oh, I wanted to talk to him."

"Why?" He turns to me with a glower.

"Easy there, I just want to ask him about my grandfather. Because they knew each other, and all that." I follow his still-tense back as he begins to patrol the perimeter. "Why do you hate him so much anyway?"

"I don't hate him."

"*Dev.*" I give him a *don't bullshit me* look.

"I don't. I'm just…not particularly fond of him."

"Okay, so why are you not particularly *fond* of him?"

"He hangs with a crowd I don't find to be the best influence for Aveline." He kneels down to inspect a chunk of simmering lava in the grass—Metus droppings. *Yum.* I glance around to see if there are any nearby, but the night is dark and calm, the air clear of the scent of decay.

"What kind of people?"

We continue to walk forward. "Remember when we were at that nightclub?"

My body instantly warms recalling the night that he and I danced together. *How could I forget?* "Um, yes."

"Well, there were glowing bands people wore that made them act—"

"Like they were in heat? Yeah, I remember."

As if that were an invitation, Dev's eyes light with mischief, and he takes a step closer. I hold up a to hand stop him. "Dev. Concentrate."

He smirks at my attempt to keep us on task, but stays put. "Hector deals in those."

My brows rise. "He's a drug dealer?"

"They aren't illegal, so not a drug dealer in the mobster sense, but the business can be just as dangerous. Like anything to do with an addictive substance."

"So that's his main purpose in Terra? To get people high?"

"It wasn't always. He once was a very respected Vigil."

"What happened?"

"You know that scar across his face?"

I nod.

"Well, he got it when he was guarding a Dreamer on Earth."

"What?" I stop walking.

"Yeah, he used to be sent out to guard certain Dreamers of interest and—" Dev pauses, his brows creasing with thought.

"What is it?" I ask.

"In all Terra…it makes sense now."

"What? What does?"

Dev turns to me. "I think Hector was your grandfather's Vigil guard?"

My mouth drops open. "Why would you think that?"

"He got the scar in your World War II. And he was a high-profile Vigil. He wouldn't have been sent out to guard just anyone. By the Navitas…now I understand his self-torment."

"Dev, *please* stop talking to yourself and explain."

"I don't know too many details, considering I didn't know too much about his particular Dreamer, but what I do know is that Hector went to war with the one he was protecting. Acted as a soldier in the American army, in the same platoon. They got caught in a firefight while abroad in Europe. The Dreamer he was protecting very nearly died, and when Hector came back, he had a vicious scar across his face that he wouldn't let any of our healers fix. He barely talked about what happened, save for saying how he failed in his duty, quitting his position and never portaling back to Earth again."

I try and think about the war stories my grandfather's shared with us, about one particular time he always seems to gloss over. I also search his memories that I was given. Many have Hector in them, but none outright title him as my grandfather's guardian. For some reason, the memories of my grandfather that Elena gave are piecemeal. Not as full or fluid as the other Dreamers, and I have a feeling it's because most were redacted that had her and him together. The amount missing speaks volumes. "Wow. Do you really—"

There's a bright burst of light, and Dev suddenly throws us to the ground right as something grazes past my cheek. An explosion rocks the night, and my ears ring as I blink, trying to clear my head. *What the hell?* Dev is off of me in a flash and running in the opposite direction we were headed. I sit up, still trying to get my bearings, only to see a dark form in front of him. *Is he chasing someone?* The person jumps on what looks like a slick black hovering motorcycle, except it only has one large wheel, and without making a sound, it speeds off. Even with Dev's lightning-fast abilities, he would never be able to catch up with whomever that was. I hear him curse as he lets fly Navitas-filled arrow after arrow. The bike swerves left and then right, easily dodging his attack, and then, just as quickly as their arrival, they're gone.

"What the hell was that?" I ask Dev as he comes running back. He holds my shoulders and inspects my every inch, turning me around, lifting up my arms. "Dev, Dev." I stop him. "I'm fine, just some bruising from the fall." His eyes are wild as they find mine, and then he's kissing me just as crazily. His fingers weave into my hair, holding my head firm, almost painfully. His other hand presses me to his body, and I'm lost for a moment in his desperation.

"Thank Terra you didn't wake up," he says, pressing his forehead against mine. "I would have gone crazy not knowing if you were okay."

"I'm fine. I promise."

His shoulders sag with relief.

"What was that?" I step back.

"Someone attacked us." With my hand securely in his, we walk to the blast area. In the center of a simmering and glowing blue-white circle, where the grass is blown-back, protrudes a sleek silver arrow.

"Attacked us? But why?!" I glance to our surroundings again, finding nothing.

"I don't know." Dev's whole body is a coil ready to spring. "But one thing's for certain." He stares at the weapon sticking out of the ground. "It wasn't a Metus."

⭿⊨◉ ◉⊨⭿

Elena glances from the arrow in Dev's hand up to us, shock written all over her face. "Someone shot at you with this?"

"I think they were mainly trying to hit Molly. I couldn't get a good look at them. They were head to toe in black and had a Tacet bike." He looks to me. "That's why we didn't hear them approach. Tacet bikes are used for stealth missions."

Elena gingerly picks up the arrow from Dev's palm and carefully inspects it before turning to one of her guards. "Inform the Vigil elders that we need to convene."

The guard nods and quickly exits.

"Elena, what's going on?" Dev's tone is low, a warning of his barely contained rage.

"We should sit." She gestures to her two couches that reside in front of a window spanning one whole side of her office. The view looks out to City Hall Square.

"We're fine." Dev crosses his arms.

Elena nods but takes a seat anyway, seeming to need it more for herself. *Crap.* This so isn't good.

"This is a Conscious arrow." She places it carefully on her white coffee table, the silver blending in with the surface. "They are made to protect Terra against Dreamers, in case they end up abusing their power."

"What does it do?" I ask.

"It cuts you off."

My body stills. "Um, what do you mean, exactly, when you say it cuts me off?"

"Precisely that. It severs your connection to Terra. You would no longer be transported here through your dreams."

The blood drains from my face. "You were right. We should sit." I practically fall onto the couch. "So basically...I was almost locked out of Terra tonight?"

She nods.

Holy Mother of—

"What Vigil have access to these?" Dev grabs the back of the sofa, his knuckles turning white. "We know it couldn't have been a Nocturna, because the majority of us have no idea about Dreamers here, about Molly or these weapons. It has to be one of your people."

Elena shakes her head, almost in a daze, and I have to say that her present bewilderment with our situation is in no way comforting. *She's supposed to have all the answers!* Where are her omniscient powers when we need them? "There's only a very select few who have access—who know about these, but none of them would want to use this against the Dreamer. It makes no sense."

"Well, someone in Terra wants her gone. Because it definitely wasn't a Metus, and they definitely weren't aiming to miss."

I suddenly grow extremely pissed, and the lights in the room wink in and out with my palpable rage. Dev glances to me. "Mol—"

"Why would someone want me gone? Don't they know I'm trying to help?!" I stand. "I risk my life every time I come here, and this is how they repay me? So what? Now I need to be scared of the very people I'm trying to protect? Well, fuck that." I turn to Elena. "You need to tell me everything. Every little detail about what you guys have made that could possibly be used against me. No more half briefings. If you want me to help, then start talking."

She's nodding but still says nothing.

"*Elena.*"

She blinks up to me, the faraway look in her eyes clearing. "Yes, you're right. Tomorrow night. You'll come with me when I talk with the Vigil elders, and then I'll explain what's been created to inhibit your powers."

"Why tomorrow? Tell me now."

She shakes her head. "We've run out of time. You're waking up."

I frown. "No I'm not. I feel fine. I'm not—" There's a sudden tug to my body, and my legs become trapped around a soft material. Great, *now* she uses her omniscient powers. I glance to Dev, slight panic washing over me for leaving when there's still so much to know.

He reaches out. "Tomorrow," he says, his words coming out blanketed, and our fingertips barely brush before I'm swept away.

I open my eyes to the early morning light filtering into my childhood bedroom. Lying still, I study the glow-in-the-dark stars on my ceiling and replay everything that happened tonight. Who would want to cut me off? Dev seemed pretty certain it was a Vigil, but it doesn't make any sense. They treat me like I'm practically royalty. No, it can't be them. Maybe a Nocturna who knows about me? I flip through the list of potentials. Even though I've always been a bit sour to Aurora, she's been nothing but nice to me. And she's Vigil too. Brenna? *No way in Metus dung would she do that.* I drum my fingers on the mattress when my thoughts stop on a certain individual. *Aveline.* If this happened a month ago, I might think she was capable, but now...no. She knows what that would do to Dev, to me. She would never...right? With a frustrated sigh, I roll to my side and then bolt upright, seeing someone sitting at my desk chair near my bed.

"Grandpa?"

He tilts his head, studying me.

"Grandpa, what are you doing? You scared me." I pull the covers closer to my chest.

"Did you see her?" he asks, his eyes growing wide, desperate.

"Who?"

He leans forward. "Elena."

Chapter 30

ONE TIME I fell asleep in the middle of my college psych class. It was during one of those periods near the end of the day, just weeks before school let out for the summer. I happened to take a seat closest to the window and got bathed with the warmth of the afternoon sun, the exact hour in which it's the coziest. So it was no surprise that with the extra warmth, combined with a beautiful food coma from my earlier lunch, I winked out. And I have to say, there's nothing more discombobulating than being woken up mere minutes into a catnap to find a roomful of people staring at the drool sliding down your face and your professor demanding you give the answer to a question you very obviously didn't hear. Nope, nothing as flustering...that is, until this moment.

"You remember?" I sit up straighter, my heart a jackhammer in my chest.

My grandfather nods. "And you know who I'm talking about." It's not a question.

My turn to nod.

He takes in a deep breath and leans back. "I thought I was losing my mind."

"No." I slide forward on the bed. "It's real. Terra's real."

"Terra." He says the name on a whisper, his eyes growing unfocused for a moment. "So you must be…" He turns back. "You're our Dreamer?"

"Yes."

"By all that's holy…"

"But, Grandpa, you were too."

His gaze meets mine, tears suddenly collecting in his eyes. "Oh, Molly," he chokes out and then covers his face as he begins to cry.

"Shh, it's okay." I kneel on my carpet, soothingly rubbing his arm. We've been sitting like this for a couple of minutes, and I glance to my closed door, wondering if my parents are up.

"I can't believe this." He tries to compose himself, and my heart breaks, seeing him in any way upset. "You're a Dreamer. You're seeing everything I did. It's all real." He grabs both my hands. "You've met Elena."

"Yes. Actually, I was just with her."

A smile filled with fond memories breaks across his face.

"I know about you two, by the way."

His brows rise. "Did she tell you?"

"Not exactly. She let me see some of your memories."

He's silent for a moment. "I never thought she'd let anyone… Well, that must have been awkward for you."

"Yeah…only when I found out whose memories they were. But, Grandpa, seriously, *Elena*?"

He laughs. "She's a lot more than what she allows people to see."

"Yeah, I learned that. Kind of the hard way."

He hides a smile before throwing his hands in the air. "This is amazing. I feel like my adolescent self again. You have to tell me everything that's going on. Is it bad there? Will there be another World War? I've been watching the news. The temperature isn't the greatest, but it's nothing like how it was when I was a Dreamer."

I've never seen him so animated before...well, not when I knew him only as my grandfather. "Yeah, you had it bad. I've only collected one or two Dreamers that have seen war as intense as you."

"Riki?"

"You remember her?" My ears perk up.

He nods. "She was the fiercest Dreamer I was ever given."

I grin. "Yeah, she's a total badass. She actually pops up the most out of any of the Dreamers when I need to tap into more energy."

My grandfather pats my hand. "I bet this is weird for you. Talking to me...about all this."

"Weird for *me*? What about you? Grandpa, we're both Dreamers! This is so crazy!"

He shakes his head. "I never thought anything like this was possible. That my own granddaughter..."

"Neither did Elena."

"She didn't?" His eyes widen. "How?"

I sit back on my bed and tell him everything. That Elena couldn't find anything in their history books about Terra ever having a direct bloodline Dreamer, that my powers are supposedly stronger because of it. I tell him her theories on why this might have happened and about what I've done so far, the Metus I've fought and the people I've lost. He nods in understanding and shares some of his own stories, stories that I didn't experience through his eyes. I greedily take in his every word, and when he's done, I tell him about the Nocturna, to which he falls deeply transfixed. He makes me explain, in painful detail, the city of Terra and what the

Nocturna are like. He catches my tone when I mention Dev, and his eyes alight with compassion, but thankfully he doesn't pry. He lets me go on and on about everything I've ever wanted to share with someone from my world. That it's with family—well, that's the superrich, sprinkle-covered cherry on top.

"So who's your Vigil guard?" he asks as I step out of my bathroom after putting on running clothes. Yeah, even after all this, I know I'm still going to be forced to run. We've been talking for the past hour, but because I woke up early, we haven't yet been disturbed.

"This is the part you'll find amusing. It's Rae."

"Becca's boyfriend, Rae?" He shakes his head. "I should've known. Look at the size of him! And that hair color. Why are they always so good looking?"

"*Right?*" I laugh while putting on my sneakers. When I'm done, I glance up to him. "Can I ask you something?"

"Of course, anything."

"Was Hector yours?"

"Hector—" His breath hitches. "Dear Lord, is he still alive?"

I nod, and my heart skips in excitement to tell Dev what he suspected was true.

"I never knew what happened to him. He was my closest friend for many years, and then..." He looks away, brows creased. "I woke up in a hospital at the end of the war, and he was just... gone."

I want to ask him more about this, about what happened, but I'm momentarily rendered speechless by all the information, and I instead find myself asking, "How have you been able to handle it for all these years, keeping Terra a secret? Did Grandma know?"

He snorts out a laugh. "Goodness no. I met her at the very end, around your age actually, so it wasn't that big of a problem. And I hadn't started remembering Terra again until very recently. I don't think they planned for me to live this long."

I frown. "What do you mean?"

"Because I chose Earth," he says like that explains everything. "Have you decided yet? It has to be much harder for you, since you've actually spent time in the city and met these Nocturna folks. I'm not sure what I would have chosen if I were able to see more than war and those white walls of the Center. But, it's probably best that I—" He stops when he catches my blank stare. "Oh, Molly." A sad realization washes across his face. "You don't know, do you?"

My chest tightens. "Don't know what?"

"This is terrible." He glances away, his jaw tight. "I shouldn't be the one to tell you this. I thought you knew. You're *twenty-four*—you should've already known. What is Elena thinking?"

"Grandpa, you're freaking me out."

"I'm sorry." He leans forward, taking my hands in his, seeming to think over how to explain. "Have you ever wondered why I stopped coming to Terra?"

"Of course. That was my next question."

He nods. "So you must have known…even a little…that you wouldn't be able to live like this forever."

My stomach plummets, and I stay very still as he says his next words.

"You will have to choose, Molly. On your twenty-fifth birthday, you will have to choose which world you will call home."

Chapter 31

I'M FLOATING OUTSIDE my body, barely listening to my grandfather as he continues spewing words that hold no meaning to me. It's just loud clunky sounds coming out of his mouth. I walk around myself, taking in the way my chest rises and falls, wondering how that's possible when I can't seem to breathe. I study my dry eyes, not understanding why they aren't red and puffy from the sobbing that's taking place inside.

My grandfather says my name. I remain separate. He says it again, this time with a tug to my arm, and I'm slammed back together.

"Are you okay?" he asks, his question coming out clear.

My mouth opens, but nothing's said.

"I'm so sorry you had to learn this way. I was told a few years before the cutoff, but maybe because you've only had access to Terra recently, Elena, for some reason, thought to hold off explaining."

"But I don't understand…" I'm nothing but a hollow vessel, a robot now gathering information. "Why?"

He shrugs. "They say it's always been this way, a chance to give us a normal life. And it's not like we could keep fighting the Metus our whole lives. That's what the next Dreamers are for."

"But...I just got to Terra," I say in a small voice and watch as his eyes fill with sorrow. He squeezes my hand.

"I know, sweetheart."

None of this makes sense. How can I have less than a year left? The big battle hasn't even begun yet. My mind is rejecting any of this from seeping in, protecting me as long as it can. "How does the choice work?"

He sits back, contemplatively. "From what I remember, you're able to travel to Terra in your full human form for only that day. I honestly forget most of the specifics—it was so long ago, but something about our molecular makeup aligning then. This gives you the choice—portal to Terra and wait for the door to close to Earth, or stay in Earth and let go of Terra."

"And you chose Earth?"

He nods. "I had just met your grandmother. I wanted a normal life. I was sick of war and, like I said before, I only experienced a very select portion of Terra, from the sounds of what you've seen."

"So...what happened after?"

"Well, all of it, the dreams, the memories of Terra, the next day, it was just"—he snaps his fingers—"gone."

⇢═◉ ◉═⇠

My throat burns, a dragon about to spit fire, and I run faster and faster. My destination—does it really matter anymore?

I quickly left my grandfather back in my room after reaching my limit for what I could hear. I finally felt the tears, the overwhelming hopelessness and confusion that was threatening to devour me whole, and I needed to get the hell out there before I let the waterworks free.

I'm so over crying. It gets you nowhere. Doesn't bring back Alec, doesn't win this war, and doesn't stop the ticking clock now counting down the seconds I have left in one of my worlds.

What I do let out is rage. Deep, mind-consuming rage. Toward Elena for keeping me in the dark, toward fate for letting Dev into my heart, and toward the injustice of getting thrust into a life, forced to accept a completely new home, only to have it ripped from my fingers.

Thud. Thud. Thud.

My sneakers hit the asphalt at the pace of my pounding heart.

Thud. Thud. Thud.

What am I going to do? How can I give up Terra, have my memories wiped clean of Dev? Could I really live with never seeing my family, or Becca? An unbearable pressure builds in my lungs.

Thud. Thud. Thud.

I quicken my pace and turn off the road onto a forest path. The air is cooler under the canopy of leaves, and I breathe in the crispness, trying to force a calm. When running became therapeutic is beyond me. All I know is that I have no idea what to do once I stop.

I round one of the trail's bends and slow, when I suddenly sense a presence behind me. Turning, I expect to find Rae, but the path is clear. I come to a complete stop when I catch sight of something nearby darting behind a close cluster of trees.

"Hello?" I call out, trying to even my heavy breathing.

Silence.

"Rae?"

A snap of twigs has me spinning to the other side. I squint, thinking I see a form vanish behind a boulder, but it disappears so fast, I'm uncertain. My heart works in overtime.

"Hello?" I call again and begin to backpedal. Birds caw, there's a shuffling of squirrels, but no one else makes his or her presence known. *You're being paranoid. There's no one there.* Just to be on the safe side, I turn back and make my way home, my steps somehow even faster than before.

I pull my internal wall up as I jog into my neighborhood and see Rae running toward me. "What the Metus? Why didn't you wait for me?"

"I couldn't." I keep moving past him, and he turns to catch up.

"Are you okay? What happened?"

"I don't want to talk about it."

"Are you sure? You look like you're out for murder."

"I kind of am."

He grabs my arm, tugging me to a stop. "Tell me."

I pull out of his grasp and keep walking.

"Mol—"

"Did you know about the cutoff?" I spin around.

He frowns. "The what?"

"The cutoff. On my twenty-fifth birthday I have to choose either Earth"—I swing my arms widely to our surroundings—"or Terra. Losing one permanently."

"Oh, that."

Everything disappears…the houses, the sun, the ground beneath me. There's just me and Rae and his complete and utter betrayal. "*What?!*" I scream.

He flinches, shocked at my quick anger. "Yeah, I thought you knew?"

"How in all of Terra would I have *known*?! None of you Vigil tell me shit!"

"Molly." Rae glances around. "Can you lower your voice? It's eight in the morning."

"*No I will not*!" I take purposeful strides toward him, and he backs up, his eyes wide. "Why haven't you mentioned this before?! How could this not have been in your briefing? What's wrong with you? What's wrong with *all of you*?! Were you not going to give me the chance to decide myself? Were you just going to let me turn twenty-five and then forget everything?!"

"Molly, Molly, please calm down." He raises his hands to ward me off. "I thought Elena told you. I swear. She's the one who's meant to tell you."

I'm a panting bull ready to charge. I want to scream, scream and destroy something. *What's happening to me?* I have a twisted desire to see something more torn apart than myself. I swivel away with a growl. I don't know what to believe anymore, what to think about any of this. Every moment I think I've got a hold on what I'm doing, what Terra is, the sands shift, and I get covered, suffocated.

"Did you tell Dev?" I force myself to ask, not knowing if I can take the news.

"No." He shakes his head. "I haven't said anything to him. I didn't think it was my place."

It's impossible now, impossible to think clearly about any of this. It's too much. I look up and know my eyes hold nothing but desperation and sorrow. "Rae, what am I going to do?"

Chapter 32

THE REST OF the day passes in a surreal blur. I walk around projecting the image of normalcy. I smile when I'm meant to smile. I answer questions when they're directed at me, and most importantly, I tell my grandfather I'm fine when he asks how I'm doing, not wanting to upset him any more for being the one to have told me. I see how his worry wears on him, and at his age he doesn't need the extra stress. The last thing I could handle is for him to get sick.

The one thing I can't fake though is my anger toward Rae, so I ignore him as best I can. I still have a hard time believing that he thought I knew—if he did, why wouldn't he warn me before getting involved with Dev? At least mention it *once*. Watching him and Becca cuddle on the floor gives me my answer. If he thinks they have a future, I'm sure in his twisted optimistic brain he believes Dev and I do too. But the only future in which that's possible is if I give up this one.

My surroundings suddenly shift in depth, and I feel like I'm standing outside a window display looking in. I study my mother, lazily thumbing through her magazine, her feet resting in my father's lap as he absently rubs them while reading work papers. My grandfather sits in his corner chair, talking with Rae and Becca, who are cozied up on the carpet next to him. My gaze bounces around the room, taking in the pictures on the wall filled with my parents and me, to my framed childhood drawings. What would happen to them if I chose Terra? What would my parents think of my sudden disappearance? Could I live a life where I never stepped foot in this house again? Would I forget about this life like I would forget about Terra? It seemed like such an easy choice for my grandfather. But for me, it's not a choice at all. No, for me it feels like a death sentence. I merely need to pick which life I want to kill.

"Molly, what're you doing over there?" Becca asks with a laugh. "You've been holding our drinks for the past ten minutes like a zombie."

I blink back into the room. "Sorry." I walk to everybody and hand them their drinks off the tray.

"I wish you all could stay longer." My mom pouts, putting down her magazine and sitting up. "It feels like you guys just got here."

"Trust us." Becca takes a sip of her beer. "We all wish we could stay too. I could totally have a few more days, or *years*, off work."

"Work hard now—play hard later." Rae pulls on one of her curls.

"Precisely." My dad nods. "Keep this one around, Becca. He's wise beyond his years."

My grandfather and I share a look as if to say, *if he only knew.*

Even though I've kept my distance from Rae, I know that he and my grandfather have been able to talk. While my mood has only plummeted into the pits of hell since this morning, my grandfather's seems to have done nothing but risen, and who can blame him? I practically exploded with relief after learning Terra was real, so I can only imagine the sense of reprieve and accompanying nostalgia that he's experiencing upon learning that all his sudden resurfacing memories are true.

Taking a long pull from my drink, I let my own personal dread in about going back to New York. Not only is work the last thing on my list of priorities, but I now have a desperate need to be around my family as much as I can. The months I have left before my choice feel like nothing but seconds for such a large decision. How will I be able to live every day without being consumed by these thoughts? Terra knows I already have enough on my mind. I swallow back the lump that forms in my throat. None of this is fair, but I guess no one ever said life is.

⋅⇥═◉ ◉═⇤⋅

Later that night, I drift in the darkness longer than normal, my mind restless and unsure of where to travel. Eventually the scent of night filters through the void, a touch of cool, and I open my eyes to the spinning sky, the edge of my tree's canopy partly masking the view. I lie there for a moment, replaying the first time I awoke here and the two people who greeted me. How long ago that feels...how much has changed since that night. I keep still, studying the passing stars above. Even after I change my clothes to the Terra uniform, I stay frozen. I don't move when I sense a form walk to my side.

My new companion watches me for a moment before lying down beside me. A familiar scent caresses, surrounds, and I close my eyes, not realizing until now just how much I've grown to associate it with safety, with calm.

"Hi," I eventually say.

"Hi," he returns.

"I've missed you."

He's suddenly above me, two cerulean jewels gazing down. "I'm never far."

I manage a small smile and rest my hand against his stubble-filled cheek. "I know."

His lips find mine, and my worry momentarily slinks away. His touch is gentle, lingering, at opposites with what I currently need, and with a moan I pull him closer. I want more. I want everything. My fingers dig into his back, glide under his shirt, and rake along his skin. He groans and gathers me into his arms, pressing down so heat blossoms between my legs. My heart races as he slips off my top and then his, our mouths colliding again. He moves to my throat, and I glance up to the sky on a gasp, feeling us spinning just as the stars shoot by. We stay locked in this dance, each second tumbling further into each other's arms, falling deeper into obscurity. This man has quickly grown to be my everything, and as we become connected, I desperately push away the thoughts that might force us apart.

"We need to get you to Elena." Dev traces the outline of my face.

"I know."

"That usually involves moving."

"I know that too."

He smiles. "So why aren't we?"

"Because I need to press Pause for a second."

His brows crease. "Everything okay? Did you talk with your grandfather?" My hesitation causes Dev to sit up. "Molly, what's happened?"

Even though his concerned gaze has me wanting to spill everything, I can't seem to tell him right now. I know it's unfair to him, but I need more time with this on my own. "Nothing." I interweave my fingers with his. "We talked. It was nice to hear about his experience here and to share with someone from my world about it all. Someone who's been through it before."

"So he remembers?"

I nod. "And you were right about Hector."

"Really?" Dev asks, astonished. "Did he say what happened?"

"No, we didn't have time to get into specifics. There was so much to talk about. I asked him about the Conscious arrow."

"And?"

"And he had no idea about them either. He knew the Vigil had some things that stave off our powers. From what I gathered from his memories and a few other Dreamers', I think I know what some of those countermeasures are," I say and explain the depowering cells and the lightning-bolt symbols that cover certain doors and armbands of the Nocturna and Vigil guards. How it keeps me from using my powers on them.

He looks off to the glowing city. "They updated the guards' uniforms to include them a few decades ago. They said those bolts indicated certain security forces. I had no idea they were also an armor."

"Why don't you wear one?"

He shrugs. "Patrolling Nocturna never acquired them, for some reason, but maybe I should request one." He turns to me with a side smile.

"Just don't piss me off, and you'll be perfectly fine." I bop him on the nose with my finger, and he grabs my hand, bringing it to his lips.

"Noted," he says and kisses my open palm. My body instantly warms, starting from where his soft mouth presses against my skin. "As much as I'd love to sit here with you all night, we should go." He helps me to stand. "Elena and the Vigil elders won't be pleased to have been kept waiting."

"Then I'll just remind them who was shot at with one of their weapons. We'll see who deserves to be the most *unpleased* then."

The corner of Dev's mouth quirks up. "I like when you're feisty."

"Then you should see me when I'm irate."

"Oh, I have." He leans in close, his warm breath caressing the side of my neck. "And we'd need more than tonight for me to show you what that does to me." For the second time in so many minutes, Dev momentarily allows me to forget my worries, distracting me by the flash of wickedness in his eyes. I only wish the distraction could last a while longer.

⌁⊷⊶⌁

"How was it?" Dev greets me outside the chambers of the Vigil elders.

"Actually, extremely boring. They talked in circles and had so much political protocol, I almost nodded off."

His brows rise. "And that's coming from someone who's already asleep."

"Exactly."

"So was there *any* development on who could have attacked us, or was the meeting a total wash?"

"Well, they gathered a list of the Vigil scientist who developed it, who they'll question, but nobody thinks it could be one of them. There's nothing for them to gain by cutting me off." One Vigil elder was like a broken record on this particular point, and it took all my effort not to lash out with the fact that I might be getting cut off anyway, Conscious arrow or not. I haven't had the proper moment to confront Elena about this yet, but with my snippy attitude toward her tonight, it doesn't take an omniscient semigoddess to understand something's bothering me. And speaking of...

"Dev." Elena nods to him in greeting before turning to me. "We need to head to the Center. You'll be waking up in a couple of hours, and I need to show you some of the Dreamer inventions."

"You don't need to be so PC about it, Elena. I know what they are. You can call them weapons."

"Actually, I can't," she says, ignoring my tone, "because they aren't all weapons."

"They aren't?"

"No. Some have been developed to help you."

"Oh." *Talk about taking the piss out of you.*

She turns to Dev. "I'm sorry, but you won't be able to join for this."

His brows pinch in. "Why?"

"Because of the recent events, security is even tighter around these devices."

Dev laughs. "You don't actually think I'd use them against Molly, do you?"

"I'm sorry, but she'll meet you after."

"Elena—"

"It's not open for discussion."

The level of tension between the three of us just skyrocketed. *Oh boy.* Touching Dev's shoulder, I give him a reassuring smile. "It's okay. If I don't wake up, I'll come find you after."

He stares at me for a second, and then he's tugging me into his arms, his lips pressing firmly to mine. We stay locked like this, him kissing me in front of everyone, kissing me *very* inappropriately in front of everyone, before he's gently setting me down, my legs left unsteady—a melted gummy worm found inside a kid's pocket.

"Was that really necessary?" Elena purses her lips as she glances around to our silent audience of Vigil elders.

Without turning his gaze from mine, Dev says, "Yes."

Even though I'm smiling as I walk away, internally I'm growing into a panicked mess. Every moment longer I spend with Dev is another cord tethered tight, another connection I can't imagine living through if it ends up getting cut.

Chapter 33

My nose crinkles from the sweet metallic scent of energy mixing with a cleaning product. The white room we stand in is blanketed with rows upon rows of alien sleek contraptions floating inside hologram boxes. Following Elena, I study the devices while an accompanying Vigil scientist explains their various purposes. Not only are there arrows made to contain the Conscious serum, but also guns, syringes, knives, and creepy spiderlike robots that can squeeze into any sort of crack to get at their victim—basically, any weapon that can cleanly and efficiently inject the concentrated liquid into my chest.

"Is the altered Navitas in these the same that's in those glowing lightning bolts? The ones that prevent my powers from working on the things they cover?" I ask, tapping the side of the hologram box that contains the mechanical spiders. They rapidly spring to life and start clambering all over each other. *Whoops.* I step back.

"It's similar in that it acts as a repellent, but not quite the same mixture of energy."

I nod, not needing any more detail than that. It's not a secret that chemistry was never my strong suit.

"Here, let me show you some of the things we've developed to help you." The Vigil excitedly walks to another row, and I follow, taking in the new equipment. Some of it is familiar—having experienced past Dreamers using them—while others hold no recollection. One of those things being a crisscross-strapped black vest. The scientist holds it up for me to take.

"We just put the finishing touches on this."

I expect it to be heavy, given its durability, but it's like holding a silk scarf. "What is it?"

"It's a replenishing vest. Almost like a power-up for your energy. It can also convert any Metus hits you take into Navitas you can use."

"Whoa," I say with wide eyes. "Can I try it on?"

"Of course." He fumbles, placing down another contraption he was going to show me. "You can test it out too. We haven't been able to see the vest at its full potential yet because it needs, well, it needs you to operate it properly. We have a testing room right through here." He leads us into a circular white chamber where an orb of Navitas rests in its dome, similar to the space where Elena and I do my energy training. I'm helped into the vest and given instructions on how I can absorb some of the prefilled Navitas in the material and gather more from the nearby energy floating above me. And if I'm hit with any Metus sludge to the chest, it can break down its energy and transfer it to be used to my advantage. Elena watches from the side as I walk to the center of the room, targets already popping up in the distance.

"Can you feel the Navitas in the vest?" The Vigil asks, and I nod, sensing the pulsing energy that swims in the fabric covering my back and front. "Good, good. Now all you have to do, in theory, is channel it into yourself and use it however you like to take out the targets."

"In theory?" I turn to him with an arched brow.

"Well...yes." He blushes slightly. "Like I said, none of us could test it fully to see if it works when worn by someone like you."

Awesome. I glance to Elena, silently asking her what my next move should be.

"Go ahead, Molly. Raymond is one of our very best Navitas engineers." Raymond's chest puffs out so far it threatens to pop his top shirt buttons.

Facing forward, I shake away the nervousness that I could blow myself up instead of my targets and concentrate on the energy encircling me. It's similar to when I'm around any concentrated Navitas—the pull to be connected, used—but what's different is I can sense the material acting as a sifter, allowing me to carefully monitor how much energy I take in or hold back.

The objects in the distance continue to appear and disappear in random order, and I call up my own energy first. Raising my hand, I twirl around to take down target after target, sensing when each approaches. After loosening up, I test taking from the well of Navitas strapped to my chest. Holding out two hands, I'm almost knocked back by the force of energy that shoots forth. *Holy death beams.*

Taking a steadying step, I glance over to Elena and Raymond. "That was awesome!"

Raymond's smile nearly splits his face in two. Elena merely nods her approval. Facing forward again, I continue to take bits of excess energy, easily evaporating every threat that comes at me. The headache that normally comes from using so much Navitas at once never arrives, and my breathing's not as labored. I grin like a kid on Christmas morning. After a couple more hits, Raymond announces that he's turning on the Metus simulator to test the rebound capabilities.

"You're going to have to go against your basic instincts to attack with this one. Let them hit you. You'll see how it will reverse the impact."

I nod and ready myself. A very realistic version of a Metus materializes before me, sans the garbage can of stink—thank goodness—and charges. It rips some of its flesh free and lobs it straight at me. I clamp down on my jaw, preparing myself for the sting, but it never comes. Instead, like a magnet, the vest pulls the flaming ball toward my chest and swallows it completely, as if it was thrown into a black hole. My vest grows warm and glows bright white before I'm suddenly jolted with an excess of energy, every one of my cells filling to their capacity. Unprepared for such a large collection of power, my back arcs and out shoots a burst of Navitas right from the spot I was hit. It collides straight into the Metus's head, quickly blowing it apart.

The room falls quiet as we all take in what just happened.

"*Well*," I say on an outtake of air, turning to my two wide-eyed companions, "I'm not gonna lie. I kind of feel like a superhero."

⋆⇒◉ ◉⇐⋆

After finishing up with Raymond, who immediately starting bragging to all his peers about what he just witnessed, Elena and I walk the halls of the engineers' lab. The area is laid out in a complicated network of glass partitions and invisible doors separating each experiment with an air-controlled, soundproofed barrier. Around the perimeter are the giant domed spaces for testing equipment, along with smaller rooms that house various contraptions.

Peeking into each door we pass, I'm slowly drumming up the necessary energy to finally confront Elena about what my grandfather told me, when I see something that causes me to stop. In one of the smaller chambers with the lights turned off—the area seemingly forgotten—are two white pods. They're similar to the white coffin I lay in back at the Village Portal Bookstore, but these are connected to one another by thousands of small wires and have two domed glass coverings.

"What's in there?"

She glances to where I'm looking, before walking on. "A closed experiment."

I take one more look at the pods before double-stepping to catch up. "What kind?"

"One that went on for too long and should never have started in the first place."

I roll my eyes. "I thought the point of bringing me here was to stop with the evasive answers?"

She stays silent.

"Would you have even agreed to show me all this if I had never gotten attacked by that Conscious arrow? I mean, past Dreamers knew about some of these things, so why hide it from me?"

"I'm not hiding anything. You needed to properly pass your energy trainings to get to this point. It all takes time, Molly."

"Yeah, time I recently found out I don't have much left of."

"You'll be back tomorrow night, and we can continue with your training then."

"I'm not talking about waking up, Elena." I stop, forcing her to look at me. "I'm talking about the lovely present I'll be receiving on my twenty-fifth birthday." Elena's features grow marble-still. "Yeah, I know about the cutoff," I say, feeling my suppressed rage slowly boil up again. "But what I don't understand is why the *hell* you never told me about it."

She blinks at me before grabbing my arm and pulling me into a side room, closing the door behind her. "You spoke with Robert." It's not a question.

"He said you should have told me by now."

She scoffs in a very un-Elena like way. "He doesn't know anything about what I should or should not be doing."

My eyebrows creep up my face. *Um...*

"I didn't want to add anything else to your plate." She goes on. "You came to us very late for a Dreamer. Most have years here before this subject is even broached. You've had to rapidly take in and adapt much quicker than any Dreamer before. I didn't want your attention to be sidetracked by this."

"So it's true. There's a cutoff?" My stomach threatens to release its contents when she nods. One of the reasons I was postponing this conversation was because until Elena confirmed my worst fear, I could still pretend it was all a mistake, an old man's mix-up. But now it's real, set in stone, the law, and I have absolutely no idea what to do. "There has to be a way to push it," I say, stepping back. "I can't be cut off in less than a year! What if the war doesn't even start until after? Why was I brought on so late?!"

She places a hand on my shoulder, steadying me, and a wave of calm passes from her touch throughout my body. I frown. "That's only a temporary fix, Elena."

"Yes, but your anxiety was about to wake you up."

I relax my shoulders, giving in to her momentary sedative. "My grandfather said that my Terra memories would be erased if I choose Earth."

"It's to preserve our anonymity, and really, your sanity. Giving you a chance to live normally in the world you've chosen."

"But what happens if I choose Terra?"

Elena's gaze locks with mine. "Is that something you're considering?"

"I don't...I don't know what I'm considering. I just want to know my options for each situation."

She studies me a moment longer before speaking. "I'm not completely sure what will happen to your memories of Earth. No Dreamer has ever chosen Terra for us to know."

"Why?"

"That's not really my place to say for certain, but I'm sure it has something to do with only being confined to our facilities and battles with the Metus. Like I mentioned when you first got here, none were sent to us as you were."

"So is the reason why none of the Dreamer memories you've give me go into old age because they were cut off from here before then?" She nods, and I exhale a relieving sigh. At least they didn't all die here... Or—"Have any of the Dreamers been killed in Terra?"

Elena presses her lips together—a contemplative gesture.

"Tell me."

"There have been some known tragedies."

"*Some known*—Elena." I let out a huff and shake my head. "Stop sugarcoating everything. Say that they *died* if that's what happened—could happen to me. This piecemeal briefing procedure of yours really sucks."

"By your constant reactions to each piece, I would have to disagree."

I shoot her a glare.

"Molly, you have to trust that I've been going about this because of my centuries of experience in dealing with your kind." My mind trips up when she says centuries. "You are not the first Dreamer to have reacted this way. Even when I've told them years before their cutoff, none took it very well."

"But they still all chose Earth?"

"When it came down to it, yes. Like I said, all they knew here was training and war."

I turn away, rubbing my forehead. None of this is really helping.

"But you," she continues, "you have seen so much more. Everything about you here is unique. Waking beyond the Containment Center, your heritage, the strength of your power—"

"You want me to stay."

"I want you to consider all your options."

"*Options*? How is robbing my parents of their only child an option?"

"We would fill their memory of you with something else, so they wouldn't even realize they had a child to lose. Everyone's memory of you would be altered, in fact, if that's what you wished."

I snort an incredulous laugh. "God, you're lucky I'm still on this calming high, because I'm pretty sure I'd be losing my shit right about now."

She stands unfazed. "It's a lot to take in, I know. It also might not seem so, but you still have time before this decision. Much can happen."

I shift on my feet, annoyed at the numbness that still rings along my skin from Elena's touch. Yet without my anxiety clouding my thoughts, a seed of deep-buried desire surfaces, and as I stare out at nothing, it slowly grows into something bigger, something that I know once I have my feelings back will terrify me. Because there's a part of me that's actually considering this place. This place as my forever.

Chapter 34

WE LEAVE MY parents early on Sunday for the long drive back to the city. My hugs were held extra-long from not knowing when I'd be back to visit, but promising it would be soon. My grandfather and I were able to talk briefly in the morning about what happened in Terra that night, about Elena confirming the cutoff, and the equipment I was shown by the Vigil engineers. He asked me to call him whenever I needed to talk, which I assured him would be often. He also told me that whatever I ended up deciding in the end, it would be the right choice. Unfortunately, that unconditional support helps me zero percent. In a twisted way, I wish I wasn't allowed a choice. That someone would just tell me I'd be either cut out or made to stay in. Then I could at least figure out how to come to terms with either. Now I feel like I'm floating in purgatory, and purgatory kind of sucks.

"Thanks for inviting us, Mols." Becca adjusts her seat to recline, giving her better access to Rae, who sits behind us. "I love your family."

"Of course," I say. "And it's a little too obvious how they feel about you."

"Yeah, that's because I'm the only one that can keep up with your mom when she's in wine mode." Rae chuckles, causing her to turn around. "What did you think of the Speros? You and Charles were palling it up watching movies together."

"We share an affinity when it comes to action films."

"Well then, you and Molly probably get on really well. She's a fiend for them. You'd never know though, because she's such a gentle little bumble bee." Becca tugs on my ponytail.

"Bees sting, you know." I glance at her from the side.

"Yeah, but it's only when they're forced. They don't inherently *want* to be violent."

"Oh yeah? Why's that?"

"Because then they die."

Rae and I lock eyes in the rearview mirror. Clearing his throat, he leans forward, draping an arm over her seat. "So, babe, you excited for your birthday this week?"

"Um, duh."

He chuckles. "And you're sure you just want to do the bar thing?"

"On my actual birthday, yeah. But I, *of course*, won't mind something one-on-one later that weekend." She flashes him a flirty smile, and I make a gagging sound. "Oh stop." She smacks my arm. "Just because you're humdrum single now doesn't mean you can poo on my shmoop parade."

"Shmoop parade?" I quirk a brow at her, and she rolls her eyes.

"Rae, please explain to Molly what a shmoop parade is."

"Uh, yeah, pass." He sits back. "I'll leave the education to you, babe."

She sighs, feigning annoyance. "I always have to do everything around here."

"It's okay. I think I'm fine never knowing what that is."

"Don't be so sure." She creepily walks her fingers up my shoulder. "Everyone likes a good shmoop."

"Ick." I shake her hand off. "Rae, when we stop for food, you two are so switching seats."

⋆⇥◉ ◉⇤⋆

The following week of work moves at a snail's pace, per usual, while my nights continue to be filled with constant Metus attacks. None are as large as when we got ambushed at the Sea of Dreams, but all popping up just as unannounced in major areas around Terra—larger outpost generators, small Vigil towns outside the walls. Dev and the security team rack their brains on how none of the stations caught the Metus approaching, some whispering that this is a new ability of the Metus—being able to cloak themselves in shadow. I pray to any and all the gods residing in this universe that this isn't the case. I also convince myself this is the reason I still haven't mentioned anything to Dev about the cutoff—there just hasn't been the proper moment. Not that there really *is* ever a good time to tell the person you're most assuredly falling in love with that he may never see you again, and there's nothing he can do. It all still feels so unreal, too sudden. I need more time with it. The bitter irony of which is all too apparent.

By Wednesday I'm exhausted. Becca's birthday drinks are the following night, and if I don't get somewhat of a relaxing sleep, I might be caught passed out on the bar, and not for fun reasons.

I meet Dev at our usual zipline platform along the wall and immediately fall into his embrace. As his strong arms hold me to him, I breathe in his unique scent, wondering if there will ever be a time where it doesn't coat my cells with calm and tingle my nerves with the desire for his touch.

"You look tired," he says, smoothing back my hair.

"Because I am."

He kisses the top of my head. "Follow me." Taking my hand, he leads me to the zipline.

"Don't you need to do rounds?"

"Aveline and I did them earlier." He adjusts the cables. "And I got you out of training tonight. If all goes well, I have something else planned."

"What?"

He gives me a lazy smile. "You'll see" is his only response before he jumps onto the line and zips off. No longer needing to raise the platform, it only takes me a moment to follow.

Careening past buildings that are unfamiliar, never having traveled to this part of the city, we dip and swerve on the cable as other Terra inhabitants cross our path. The line takes us high above the city, where a majority of skyscrapers stretch to the sky. My form is reflected back as I speed past seamless glass windows, and people are mere specks on the ground below. I close my eyes, taking in the air weaving through my hair, rushing across my skin. It's moments like this, suspended above the world, that I truly feel free. No worries touch me up here, and I wonder if this is how birds feel when they take flight. For a splash in time I think...I think perhaps I'd like to let my hands go and see if I could set my own course for once. There's a rush in my belly, a heat that swirls to my head, cooling, provoking. Do I dare? Could I wake in time if it didn't work? Tentatively, with the desire ever present in my mind, I loosen my grip one finger at a time, my throat dry in anticipation. I have no idea what has caused such recklessness, why I test this now versus the hundreds of times I've taken the zipline, but something about the recent trying days and all that I've come to learn has set a wild card free. I want to live as fully as I can in this world, this place that seems limitless to my abilities, and if I am the most powerful, why not see?

I let go.

And…nothing happens. I stay afloat, my Arcus *whooshing* way from me. With wide eyes, a sound of pure astonishment barks from my throat, and instinctually I pump my arms, sending me higher. As I shoot above all the lines, away from anyone's sight, the air is weightless, filtering through my fingers, like swimming in silk. *Holy gods.* I'm flying! I move around, growing accustomed to the sensation before looking for Dev. He's but a dot in the distance, and I tip my body to catch up to him. I have no idea how long I can maintain this, but so far, my mind's undisturbed by this use of energy. I glide through the air, twirling like a plane with my arms out, and then tuck them to my side, shooting forward. My eyes tear from the speed, my stomach dropping away, and I can't stop smiling. I've never felt so happy in my whole existence, and something in my core swells, giving me more power. I laugh crazily, euphorically, unable to stop—I might even die from it.

Dev lands on top of a high-rise building and turns to search me out. As I come into view, he takes staggering steps back, almost tripping over his own feet, his mouth opening in a silent yell.

"Look!" I glide to a stop above him and spin in place. "I can fly!" I giggle like an idiot again, but not caring because, *hello*, I'm an idiot who can fly!

He says nothing, just watches me—eyes wide, face white.

"Isn't this awesome." I float nearer.

"Molly..." My name's barely a whisper on his lips. "How..."

"I don't really know. I was just up there"—I point behind me—"holding on to my Arcus, feeling like a bird, and thought, how much could I *really* be like them?"

Dev is silent again, looking at me in a way that seems pained. I come down, settling my feet on the roof. "What's wrong?" I walk to him. "I'm okay, see." I lift my arms and turn. "Not a scratch."

"I...I actually think I might be...I might be jealous," he says, stunned, and then equally so by his own admission.

I'm right there with him. "Really?"

He nods. "I've always wanted to fly."

"Well"—I cock my head to the side—"do you want to try?"

His mouth pops open again. "Can you do that?"

I shrug. "I don't know, but," I say, my lips curving up at the side, "there's only one way to find out."

"Stop fidgeting. It's hard to concentrate."

"What if you drop me?"

"Then you'll die."

His eyes narrow.

"Dev." I breathe out a laugh. "For someone who's so keen on flying, you sure are nervous about it."

"I'm only nervous because it's contingent on *you*."

I cluck my tongue. "Ye of so little faith. Where's all that *you can do anything you put your mind to* attitude?"

"*Molly.*"

"Oh hush. I'm just joking. Now stand still. I think I know what I need to do. It might feel weird though."

"Why?"

"I said *hush.*" Taking a steadying breath, I change to the sight of energy. Following the glowing Navitas flowing through him, I pinpoint where it's the brightest—his chest. Resting my hand on my own chest, I allow some of my power to collect there before I gently throw it out, a line being released from a fishing rod. The blue-white cord unspools until it latches on to my desired target, Dev, and goes taut.

We both gasp at the connection, a deep warmth running through us, for now I can feel all of his sensations, his excitement, nervousness, desires—

"Molly, what's happening?"

I swallow, pushing down the overwhelming sensations. "I'm connecting my energy to yours. Think of it as sharing."

"Is that safe for you?"

"Is anything here? Now quiet. I'm almost done." Biting my lip, I secure the Navitas between us as best I can before I blink back to regular sight. The cord of energy disappears, but I still feel the tug. "Okay, you ready?"

He nods once, squaring his shoulders.

Gently I test this experiment. *Up*, I think. *Weightless.*

Dev flails slightly when his feet lift off the ground, and I smile as I collectively raise us higher and higher. My mind prickles now that there are two of us. I won't be able to do this forever, but all we really need is a moment.

"This is...look at us!" Dev throws his arms wide as a heart-melting grin breaks across his face. My chest swells with his elation. "Can I move around?"

"Yes, but we have to stay close to one another. I'm basically feeding you a part of my abilities, and I don't know how far the connection can go."

"Okay." Dev floats left, then right. "So I just think what I want to do? Where I want to go?"

"Basically."

With eyes as bright as reflected topaz, Dev shoots up into the night sky, and I go with him.

The stars whip past us, burning orbs flying to their destination, and I can just barely make out the human forms cocooned inside. They slumber, wrapped in their personal spool of blinding Navitas, unaware of their minds traveling through another universe to reach their dreams. Dev and I swim among them—a school of fish. We haven't said a word to each other, but with the connection, neither of us need to. I can feel everything he feels, and we share face-splitting grins. I'm pretty certain he can sense my emotions too, which is equally terrifying and relieving. Terrifying in that what's bursting in my heart is consuming, fierce, with a promise to overwhelm. But relieving because it's equally shared, equally felt, and I gaze at Dev soaring beside me, eyes briefly closed, taking in the sensations. I know there's absolutely no way I can live without him. The realization momentarily stops my pulse, and we drop.

"Molly!" Dev calls out just as I right us.

I don't look at him. I can't, even though he can feel my anxiety—there's nowhere to hide it. He says my name again, but I keep pressing forward, tipping my head to watch the miniature land below. Suddenly there's a tug to my core, and I'm thrown back, an invisible source pulling me into his arms. He holds me to him, paused and floating above the world. Dev's gaze is scalding as it seeps into mine, not letting me go. "I think I finally know what dreaming's like," he says as his hand brushes my cheek. "You. Whenever I'm with you, it must be a dream."

I take in a shaky breath, the emotions in my chest overflowing until it spills out my mouth. "Dev," I whisper, but he cuts me off, first with his thumb tracing my lip and then with a kiss.

The air around us shifts as our mouths dance together. My heart, his heart beat as one, faster and faster as his hands wrap tighter around my waist, dig through my hair. My mind is momentarily enflamed with only him, only his touch, his warmth. I have no idea how we're still floating, what's keeping us up, but our collected Navitas crackles and sparks between us, lassoing us together.

Dev is the one who severs the connection just as I hunger for more. He leans back, still holding me, and looks into my eyes. The blue that circles his pupils is on fire, the hottest part of a flame. "Molly." His voice is gruff. "I love you."

The sky rumbles, the shooting stars burn brighter, but the wind roaring past us stills. "I love you too," I say, and the words easily flow from my lips as if they've been waiting all this time to be set free.

Our shared energy buzzes, electric, and I'm pulled to him again, my tears coating his skin as his mouth finds mine. I don't know how long we stay like this, desperate to somehow get closer to one another, but eventually we tip forward, continuing our flight. The heat from the zooming orbs laps across our skin as we spin between them, and my emotion soars higher than the atmosphere that contains us. Up and up it floats, untouchable by gravity, but just as it takes its last giant leap, there's a falter, a wane that threatens to plummet, for even though I know I've just gained something monumental, I can't shake the feeling that I may have lost something equally important in the process.

Chapter 35

TOUCHING DOWN ONTO the roof, I lightly unhook my energy from Dev, and both our shoulders visibly sag. The air seems colder now, my chest less full, but our gazes momentarily lock, a secret smile shared.

With an effortless tug, Dev brings me into his arms. "Thank you. That was…" He shakes his head, at a loss.

"I know." I peek up at him, suddenly feeling vulnerable after… everything.

He searches my eyes like he can't believe I'm real. "Every day I thank Terra that I was the one to have found you that night. I don't know what my life would have been like if I hadn't—"

I stop him with a quick kiss, not wanting to hear anything else that will make my mind whirl with the decision that lies ahead. "We're both lucky."

His gaze lights up before flickering behind me. "The thing I had originally planned seems a bit lame now."

"What was it?" I try peering over my shoulder.

Taking my hand, he guides us around the roof's elevator bay to reveal a very simple picnic set up on the other side. A blanket is spread across the hard concrete with a few pillows and a chrome cooler resting in the center.

"Did *you* do this?" I turn to him, a smile on my lips.

He nods shyly.

"That is absolutely adorable." I lean up, chastely kissing his cheek before skipping to the blanket. "I've never had a picnic on the top of a skyscraper before."

With a look of relief and a bit of pride, he joins me. Placing his hand on top of the metal box, it falls open, unfolding itself to present us with matching dishware, beautifully arranged cheeses, fruits, and breads along with a bottle of what I assume is alcohol.

"I can't take all the credit. Elario helped me with the food."

"Then maybe I should be on a picnic with him."

One of Dev's brows arch. "I can easily arrange that for next time. Terra knows it took a great deal of effort to keep him from coming tonight."

I chuckle. "Tell him I miss him too."

"I think the sentiment would be better received coming straight from you."

"Well then, I'll be sure to visit him the next chance I get."

He shoots me a coy glance. "If I didn't know better, I might actually think I had something to worry about."

"Don't be so sure that you don't. He may like men, but we have a bond that goes beyond cannoli."

Dev chokes on his own breath before cracking a smile. "I think you've been hanging around me too much."

"What, scared my innuendos will surpass yours?"

"Let's not get ahead of ourselves. We all know my innuendo is the biggest around."

I let out a grumbling sigh, raking my hand down my face. "*Aaand* there it is."

"Game. Point. Match." He smugly gestures to himself.

I snort. "Whatever gets you through the day."

"Winning always does." He winks before continuing to unpack our meal. I watch him while biting back a smile. Taking in his handsome features, the way the cords in his arms wrap around his muscles until they disappear beneath his shirt, I'm still not used to the fact that he's mine and I'm his. Besides our gentle banter, there's an intensity to all this now, a growing force that wasn't there before. I feel desperate for every moment together, every touch, every look. This place that started out as only one half of my life has quickly become way, way more. I have a sudden desperate desire to tell Dev everything, share in the burden of my impending fate, but I can't bring myself to. It's so rare we get a quiet night together, and after what was spoken…I can't ruin it with this news. I'm also terrified of his reaction, not only because he might beg me to stay, but on the small chance he'll tell me not to.

He catches me studying him and smirks. "You know, some people consider staring to be rude."

I purse my lips from him using one of my lines from the first time we met. "Cute."

"I am, aren't I?"

My eyes pull a muscle from how fast they roll.

"Here." He hands me a glass of something bubbly before raising his own. "To a night without Metus decapitations."

I thrum my fingers on my thigh. "So that's what you're summing up this night as?"

"Well, among other things." He flashes a devious grin.

"Okay." I laugh and lift my drink. "Then to other things."

After eating most of the food and finishing half of the bottle, Dev settles us down on the blanket. Tucking me into his side, we gaze up and watch the Dreamers shoot across the sky, taking in the quiet, the only sound the subtle *whooshing* of people passing on the lines close by. Dev plays with a strand of my hair, and I draw patterns on his chest. Thoughts begin to swirl in my mind again, but I push them away, far away. *Tomorrow.* I'll tell him tomorrow. As I twine my fingers with his, I wonder how many more tomorrows I can have.

Chapter 36

THE SCENT OF hairspray wafts from my bathroom as Becca primps herself in the mirror. Standing next to my bed, I hold up one of two dresses, debating which one to wear tonight.

"The cobalt," Becca yells, and I smile, hanging the black one back in my closet. Draping the form-hugging dress over my body, I begin to sift through my shoes.

"What do you think?" I glance up to Becca standing by the door. She does a little twirl, and her emerald-green dress flows out at the waist before it hugs around her hips, falling fluidly to her thighs. Her apricot hair is relaxed in waves past her shoulders, and her freckles brighten her complexion to a lively glow.

"You look stunning! Rae won't know how to behave properly at all tonight."

She giggles and claps her hands together. "My plan exactly."

"Here, now I can give you your birthday present." I walk to my dresser and remove two small boxes from a drawer.

"You didn't need to get me anything," she says as I hand her one.

"Don't play the demure card, Bec. You know as well as I do that you love getting gifts."

Her grin is devilish. "I don't know *what* you're talking about."

"These are actually for both of us." I peek in my box to make sure I have the right one, and Becca's eyes alight with curiosity. "Okay, you can open yours." Without waiting a beat, she pops off the top and gasps.

"It's part of a set," I say, showing her mine. "I got them specially made and have the other half."

"Oh my gosh." She holds her fingers to her mouth as her eyes get misty. "Molly, these are...these are perfect."

I smile and take mine out of the box. In the middle of a simple gold necklace, in beautiful cursive, is the word *Turtle*. Becca holds hers up, revealing the word *Dove*.

"You *are* my little turtle." She wraps her arms around me.

"And you're my dove." I hug her back.

"Turtle doves. Oh God! We are too cute! We have to always wear them when we're together." Her grin is wide as she clasps the necklace on. "Rae is going to puke from how adorable we are. I love it! Thank you. Thank you!" She squeezes me again. "I don't know what I'd do without you."

Swallowing back the sudden barrage of emotions, I swat her butt. "Okay, birthday girl, let's finish getting you ready for the ball."

Rae, in his consistent romantic gestures, rented out The Wicker Horse for the entire night—the bar where they first met—and it's packed with Becca's many friends. The lady of the hour floats about, saying hi to everyone and enthusiastically taking each drink handed to her. I've been mentally devising when those will be traded out for waters.

Stephanie, Becca's older sister, is here with her husband, Kelly, and they've been keeping me company most of the night. While the two sisters share the same fiery mane and willowy form, that's as far as the similarities go. Steph, while very nice, is more comfortable discussing the weather than anything truly personal. That's why her next words catch me off guard.

"I was sorry to hear about you and Jared," she says while playing with the small straw in her drink. Coworkers at the same law firm, she's the one who introduced Jared to me.

"Oh...yeah." I glance to Kelly, whose brown eyes are magnified by his thick-rimmed glasses. He pushes them up the bridge of his nose. "I'm sorry it didn't work out too," he says.

"Have you guys spoken since?"

I shift on my feet. "No." And I haven't thought much of him in these past few days either. What's more surprising is, I don't feel guilty about it. Recent worries and losses take up enough room in that bag.

She nods and shares a look with Kelly.

"Why? Has he—how is he doing?" I ask.

"Better." She attempts a smile.

"*Now.*" Kelly adds, and I frown.

"You left on civil terms though, right?" Steph glides over her husband's remark.

"Yes, I think so." I gaze out to the crowd, focusing on nothing before turning back to them. "You guys *do* know that he's the one that ended things."

Steph's brows rise, acknowledging that she didn't.

"Why would he do that?" Kelly asks, clearly confused.

"*Kelly.*" Steph lightly taps his arm. "That's not our business."

"But—" A quick glare from her shuts his mouth.

Steph leans toward me. "We're sorry to be so nosey. We just wanted to make sure things wouldn't be awkward tonight."

I tilt my head. "Tonight—what do you mean?"

"Uh…Becca didn't tell you?" Steph and her husband share another glance while I start piecing the puzzle together. *Oh no, she didn't.*

Excusing myself, I search for the girl whom, if it weren't for her current celebration of being born, I'd murder. Finding her as she just finishes taking a shot with a group, I tug her into a corner.

"*Hey.*" She pulls her arm from my grasp and works to steady herself on her four-inch heels. "What's wrong with you?"

"*Jared's* invited tonight?!"

"Oh." She pushes a pocket of air into one of her cheeks before expelling it. "That."

"What the hell, Bec?"

"Listen." She places a hand on my shoulder, and I'd shrug it off if it didn't seem like she needed it there to stabilize herself. "I didn't purposefully invite him. It sorta just happened."

"How on *earth* does inviting my recent ex-boyfriend *sorta* just happen? And why didn't you tell me?!"

"Mols, it's gonna be okay. He's probably not even going to show. I went to have dinner at my sister's, and he was there too. They were talking about my birthday drinks, and I felt rude not inviting him. There was nothing I could do!"

"Um, there were plenty of things you could have done. Like— oh, I don't know. *Not* invite him." I drag my fingers through my hair. "This is going to be so awkward."

"Mols, it won't. Trust me. You're both adults. Plus, you seemed to have moved on. *Rather quickly,*" she adds with a mutter, and I glower. "Which is great!" she continues. "But like I said, he probably won't come. I mean, it is *my* birthday. The best friend of his ex-girlfriend. He knows you'd be here. And the invite was one of those 'oh yeah, you should *totally* come, but please *don't*' kind of thing. He's an idiot if he didn't get that."

"Well, then I guess he's an idiot." My gaze falls to the front of the bar as my stomach drops. "Because he just walked in."

Chapter 37

WHEN I WAS a kid, I used to think that if I shut my eyes, I would become invisible. Close my eyes—disappear. Open my eyes—reappear. If I couldn't see other people, then they couldn't see me. Terra would have a field day with the magic of a nine-year-old's brain. Now watching Jared slowly walk around the bar, and waiting for the moment when his gaze collides with mine, I wish desperately for my powers to function here so I can squeeze my lids shut and vanish.

"Just breathe," Becca says from my side. "He hasn't seen you yet, so we can just—" We both stiffen as he makes eye contact, lone gazelles spotted by the lion, and my heart thumps loudly in my head.

"Don't you dare." I grab Becca's arm, sensing her about to flee. She mumbles a curse.

"Hi." He stands before us, blond hair a little longer than I remember but just as tousled and attractive. His heather-green T-shirt shows off a deep tan and…other aspects of his body that I move my gaze away from. His grin is unsure but friendly.

"Hi," I say back.

"Jared! So glad you came. I *really* didn't think you would." Becca smiles overgenuinely, and I keep myself from elbowing her in the ribs.

"Yeah, I thought I'd stop by for a second and wish you a Happy Birthday."

"Aw, thank you. That's so sweet. Oh look." She waves to nobody behind Jared. "Some old friends just walked in that I have to go say hi to." She grabs both of our shoulders. "You guys be civil now." And then she skips away.

I mentally imagine a redheaded voodoo doll stuck with thousands of pins before returning my attention to Jared. We blink at one another.

"So." He scratches the back of his neck. "This is awkward, huh?"

I let out a relieving laugh. "Yeah, just a bit."

"I didn't mean to ruin your night. I really did want to wish her a Happy Birthday, but I'll admit, I wanted to see you more."

What to do? What to say?

"You look beautiful, by the way."

"Oh." I gaze down at my dress. "Thank you."

"How have you been?" His honey-colored eyes roam my face.

"I've been…okay."

"Yeah." He nods like he understands. "Me too."

I comb over his appearance again, taking in his freshly shaven face and sun-kissed skin. He actually looks more than okay—he looks…well rested. "Did you just go on a vacation?"

His eyes widen. "How'd you know?"

"Well, you seem…" I gesture to his body. "Like you were lying on a beach with cucumbers on your eyes while being fanned by island girls."

His familiar laugh causes an easy smile to escape me. "I wish about the island girls, and though I did have cucumbers, they were in my drinks rather than on my eyes. I went to Saint Lucia with a few friends." His gaze momentarily flickers away from mine. "Needed to get out of the city for a while."

"I understand."

"Yeah, I suppose you do."

A bit of an awkward silence settles in, and we both watch the partygoers around us, even though I know neither of us is seeing much of anything.

"Can I ask you something?" I take a sip of my drink, still facing away.

"Sure."

"Do you regret ending things?" Feeling his heavy gaze, I finally turn toward him. His expression is pained, and I immediately wish I could take back my words, but I selfishly want to know that he is as okay with all this as I am.

"At first...at first I did." He shoves a hand into his front pocket. "Those days right after, I felt like the biggest idiot. My finger hovered over your name, wanting to call so bad, but I never pressed it... and neither did you. But it was a good thing," he adds quickly, seeing me frown. "After some time, I realized I really did mean what I said about needing more from someone. And I don't regret telling you I loved you. I'll never regret that."

I swirl my drink, studying the reflective colors in the liquid before looking back at him. "I don't regret it either. I'm sorry that I—"

"I know." He flashes a small smile. "I'm just glad we can still be civil. Maybe the next time we bump into one another, it will be even less awkward."

"If Becca's there, I highly doubt it."

He chuckles, allowing his tense shoulders to finally fall. "Speaking of, I should go say hi to Steph and Kelly." He glances out to the crowd for a moment before returning his attention to me, his eyes now holding a new warmth. "It was really great seeing you, Molly."

"You too," I say, and I mean it.

Gently touching my elbow, he leans in and kisses my cheek, and I'm momentarily surrounded by his familiar scent. But this time it stirs nothing but an old ache of what once was. Giving me a final friendly grin, one that I return, he walks away.

Saddled at the bar, I push around the melting ice in my untouched drink. Jared only stayed for a little longer before I saw him duck out and make his final exit. As much as I didn't have seeing him tonight on the top of my favorite-surprises list, I am glad we were able to talk peacefully. It seems there was more closure with this interaction than the last, and I'm a bit relieved to be able to shut that chapter for good. Now to just deal with what lies ahead. I snort. Yeah, *only* that.

"What did those ice cubes ever do to you?" Rae takes a seat next to me, and I stop stabbing at my cocktail.

"How's the birthday girl holding up?" I ask.

"Look behind you."

Glancing over my shoulder, I find Becca leading half the bar in a game of flip cup. Her team yells in excitement, the sound vibrating through the floor. I shake my head, smiling. "You can take the girl out of college…" I turn back around after a moment more of watching. Rae stares at me as if waiting for something. "What?"

He blinks. "Are you going to finish that sentence? You can take a girl out of college…and what?"

My brows lift. "Uh, it's a saying. Don't you know it?"

"What kind of saying is that? It goes nowhere."

"No, I mean—yes, it goes somewhere. I didn't think I needed to finish it because—oh, never mind." I shake my head. "Just forget about it. Let's move on. How's your night been?"

"I could ask you the same thing. I saw you and Jared talking earlier."

"Yeah. It was…fine, actually. Maybe a little awkward in the beginning, but it was good to see him."

He nods. "I caught him before he left. Looked like he was doing okay."

"Tan, right?"

Rae smiles. "Very."

I laugh and place my elbows back on the bar, swirling my drink again.

"So…" Rae plays with the label on his beer. "Have you told Dev yet?"

I bite the inside of my cheek. "No. Not yet."

"You will though?"

I glance at him from the side. "I should."

He inclines his head. "You should."

Taking in a deep breath, I slump my shoulders. "I still don't know what I'm going to do."

"We'll figure something out."

I turn to him. "We will?"

Rae twirls his now-empty bottle on the table. When it stops, the lip points at me. "Yeah," he says, meeting my gaze, "I think we will."

⊶⊫⊜ ⊜⊨⊰⊷

The giggles haven't ceased for the past five minutes.

"Are you sure you don't want us to drop you off at your apartment?" Rae says while trying to keep Becca's legs from making their way back out of the cab. Her laughter grows louder as he vise-grips her feet in the crook of his arm.

"Yeeeah, no thanks. Are *you* sure you don't want to tell the driver her address and take a separate one?"

He scowls. "Funny."

"Oh, I'm being one hundred percent serious."

Suddenly Becca's kicking stops, and she grows quiet. We glance at one another.

"Babe?" Rae tips his head into the backseat. Light snoring emanates out, and I press my lips together to keep from cracking up.

"Thank Terra," he mutters, detangling himself and standing.

"Good thing she took off work tomorrow."

He grunts his agreement. "She'll be feeling this all the way till next week."

"And you'll be there the *whole* time to nurse her back to health." I smile sweetly, and he groans.

Running fingers through his blond hair, he looks back at the cab. "She had fun though, which was the plan."

"You did good." I slap his large shoulder. "You make her very happy."

He worries his bottom lip for a moment. "You think?"

I laugh. "Rae, I'm not even going to entertain that uncertainty. You guys are like peanut butter and jelly, spaghetti and sauce, chocolate chips in cookie dough—"

"Okay, okay." He holds up his hands. "I get it. But now you just made me really hungry."

"Shocker."

He rolls his eyes. "All right, I think it's time we got you a cab."

"I'm going to walk, actually."

"No."

"Uh, yeah."

"Molly, please don't give me something else to worry about tonight. Since I can't drop you at home, please just take a cab."

"Where's one of your men? Can't they walk with me?"

"I didn't think I needed them tonight because I thought *someone* wouldn't be a hard-ass. I should've known better."

There's a moan from inside the car, and the cabby sticks his head out the window. "If she gets sick in here, you're paying for this whole thing to be washed."

Rae sighs, and I give him a sympathetic smile. "Get her home. I'll be fine. It's only a couple blocks, and I'll even text you when I get to my apartment."

He glances between me and the now-consistent groaning coming from the car. "*Right* when you get home." He climbs into the backseat.

"Not a second later." I salute.

"I won't be in Terra tonight," he says while closing the door and placing an elbow out of the window. "I'll need to look after this one, but Dev will be waiting, and I'll see you tomorrow."

"No worries."

"And Mols?"

"Yeah?"

"Tell him." He tucks his arm in. "Tonight."

I frown, but nod and watch as the yellow cab pulls away.

Chapter 38

THE AIR IS humid for early summer, and I twist my hair up and off my shoulders as I walk the busy sidewalks of the West Village. Thursday nights more often play out like Fridays in the city, and I smile as rowdy groups pass by, still on a mission to find their next watering hole.

Finding a clean-ish looking stoop, I momentarily stop to rub my feet and attempt to gather my wits on how best to tell Dev this seriously crappy news. Rae says we'll figure it out, but which "it" exactly? How to let Terra go, or how to leave all my friends and family? Unless there's a third option, I don't see how either of those can be "figured out." Forced to accept, sure. Unwillingly chosen, no problem. But figured out? I don't think so. Maybe he knows something I don't.

I snort.

Well, he *obviously* knows things I don't. I bet there are still millions of secrets the Vigil are keeping from me. I rub my temples. This seriously sucks.

Slipping my heels back on, I begin my stroll again, my mind continuing to flip over. Telling Dev might actually be relieving. Ever since learning of the cutoff, I've felt like a giant vise has been pressing down on my chest. Like I've been stuck at the bottom of crystal-clear water, able to see the surface but unable to get there or knowing if I should even try. What will Dev say to all this? How will he rea—

A large form walks in front of my path, and my heart jumps, but besides clipping the side of my arm when passing, the figure pays me no mind. I let out a breath. *Man, paranoid much?* Still, I find myself glancing around. Rae's making me so jumpy. Isn't it bad enough that I'm constantly looking over my shoulder in Terra? Do I *really* need to be worried here too? Shaking off the feeling of unease, I quickly cover the last three blocks home.

⋅⊷═◉ ◉═⊷⋅

"Oh, pajamas, have I told you how much I love you?" Jumping into my bed, I nestle into the covers. As soon as I stepped into my apartment, I went straight for my comfy clothes, that is, only *after* shooting Rae a quick text letting him know I got kidnapped and am currently being chopped into tiny bits. His response was merely to ask which culinary school the murdering chef went to. Cheeky bastard.

Sighing, I close my eyes, more than ready to pass out. Using the technique Elena taught me for calming my thoughts, I count down from fifty in my head. Around twenty-three, my mind slips into silence. Blissfully it floats in the void of nothing, every part of me relaxed, calm, a gentle breeze carried through clouds. A minute goes by, then three, four—time disappears and glides in forever. Then there's a familiar jolt, the nerve endings across my skin hum, and in a burst of white light I open my eyes to a vast sky covered with shooting stars. Grass brushes along my legs as a light breeze filters through the stalks, the quiet melody of a field dancing. Without moving, I know he's there.

"How was Becca's birthday?" His deep voice settles in and around me.

Rolling to my stomach and propping my head in my hands, I find Dev leaning against the trunk of my tree. His entirety is in shadow, except his long fingers, which peek out into the soft light. They rhythmically twirl a piece of grass.

"It was good. She was loaded by the end of it." His deep chuckle warms my skin, and I crawl to his side, settling beside him. "What's been going on here?"

"So far it's quiet." He tucks strands of my hair behind my ear, his gaze roaming my face before resting on my lips, the corner of which tips up.

"Well, are you going to kiss them or just keep staring?"

Amused eyes find mine. "I'm definitely rubbing off on you."

"I have a super-inappropriate and cheesy line in response to that, but to disprove your theory, I'm not going to say it."

He tilts his head back and laughs. "Oh, now I've *got* to hear it."

"Nope." I sit up straight. "Opportunity lost. It goes with me to the grave."

"Then it's a good thing I'm the original mastermind behind super-inappropriate lines. Because I can certainly entertain myself with a few possibilities."

"You forgot cheesy," I say. "Inappropriate and *cheesy* lines."

"Oh, I didn't forget it." His grin is sly.

"You're ridiculous."

In a flash of movement that has me letting out a surprised squeak, I'm suddenly straddling his lap. His hands run up and under my pajama shirt. "You not wearing a bra." One of his eyebrows arc. "Now *that* can make me a lot of things. None of which are ridiculous."

"Dev—"

He cuts me off with a kiss, his mouth gentle and slow—teasing, and I press myself further into him, wrapping my hands around his neck. All rational thought fizzles away as his thumb skims my breast, his fingers moving to encircle my waist. I let out a soft moan.

"I wish you were locked in tonight," he whispers against my mouth. "I hate only having a few hours with you. They're never quiet like this. I want more of this." He kisses me again, and my heart squeezes, hearing his words. The vise presses down.

"Dev." I lean back. His blue eyes, like a cool dip in water, regard me softly.

"Yes?" With his finger, he smooths the crease that's formed between my brows. "What's wrong?"

"We need to talk."

His arms tense around me. "I already don't like it."

I worry my bottom lip and glance off into the distance.

"Okay…now I really don't like it. Molly." He tips my chin so I look at him again. "What's going on?"

I take in a giant breath. Here goes everything. "Elena recently informed me about something. Actually, my grandfather did first, but he thought I already knew, which I most *definitely* did not. Because if I did…well, I probably would have freaked out just as much, but it for *sure* would have been better to have known this earlier. I'm still mega pissed at Elena—"

"Midnight." Dev brushes my arm, attempting to calm me. "Whatever it is, it'll be all right. We'll figure it out."

I play with the T-shirt material covering his chest. "That's what Rae said."

"Because we will."

I shake my head, hiding my face in my hands. "But, Dev, I don't know how that's possible." *I will not cry. I will not cry.*

"Well, why don't you tell me what you learned, and we can go from there."

"I'm scared to."

"Molly." He pries my fingers apart.

"Okay, okay. Like a Band-Aid, right?" My stomach is in my mouth. *Breathe. Just breathe.* "I learned...I learned that Dreamers have cutoffs—*I* have a cutoff. On my twenty-fifth birthday, I'll have to choose either Earth or Terra, locking myself out of one permanently."

The leaves in the tree rustle above us. Stars streak by. Dev blinks. "What?"

I swallow. "Eventually I won't be able to come to Terra anymore. That, or I'll never be able to go home."

He shakes his head. "No." Popping up, he causes me to tumble from his lap. I watch from the ground as he begins to pace. "No."

"I didn't believe it at first either, but Elena confirmed—"

"*No!*" Dev presses his palms against his forehead, his breathing labored. "This can't be happening." I stay silent, letting it sink in as much as something like this can. He glances to the city and grows quiet, contemplative, before looking back at me. "Did she say why? Is it always this way?"

I nod, my throat working. "Always. It happened to my grandfather and every Dreamer before him. They say it's to give us a chance at a normal life. But, Dev, if I...if I choose Earth, I'll lose all my memories of this place." *And of you.* The words burn as they leave my mouth.

Horror fills his gaze before it grows dark, deadly. He kneels in front of me, grabbing my hands. "I won't lose you, Molly. I...I can't. There has to be another way. Something else that can be done."

"I know." The anguish in my voice is evident. "But I can't think of what. I've been going over it for days—"

"Days?" His brows knit. "How long have you known this?"

"Uh, since last weekend."

"Since last..." He drops my hands. "Why didn't you tell me right away?!" Hurt is worn in every crease on his face.

"I'm sorry. I just...I couldn't yet. I know I should have, but I needed time with it. It was a huge thing to learn."

He looks away from me, a lost expression in his features. "This can't be happening." The words come out so softly that I barely hear them. My heart breaks and then breaks again. Do I tell him that I've been thinking of choosing Terra? Do I give him that hope when I'm not completely certain myself? I've never seen Dev cry before, but watching him now, his chest heaving, his hands in white-knuckled fists, and his eyes torturously pained, I think he might. And I can't see that. If I do...I won't be able to keep it together anymore, because then that truly means there's no hope.

I reach for him, and he quickly takes me into his arms, hugging me so tight I might bruise. But I don't care. I need this. This is a good discomfort, a necessary one. Unlike the agony going on in my throat to try keeping my own tears at bay.

"I love you," I say as I press my face into the crook of his neck. His grip on me strengthens as a shaky breath releases.

"You are my everything," he says.

We stay wrapped like this. Time, for the first time, is of no consequence. As long as we're here, like this, together, everything's all right. Everything makes sense.

Gently, he pulls back and studies me, committing everything to memory. "You know I can't ask you to give up your family," he says, and I nod solemnly. "But I also can't let you disappear from my life." Cupping my cheeks in his hands, he stares into my eyes with a new resolve. "Rae's right. We're going to figure this out. I promise you. We'll figure it out." I try shaking my head and looking away, but he won't let me. "Molly, do you trust me?"

I bite the inside of my cheek as his steady gaze is just that—steady. "Yes, I trust you."

"Then trust that I'll figure this out."

I inhale a calming breath. "Okay."

And then he's kissing me. Claiming my soul again. Reminding me over and over why he's the man worth fighting fate for. Momentarily, my worry drops away, and I truly believe we might actually have a chance, that we can find a solution to this divide. Hope bubbles. But then all too quickly, like a Metus invading, I'm reminded of something.

We must all wake up from dreams.

Chapter 39

MAKING OUR WAY to the wall, Dev is in the middle of explaining where he's going to look first for answers, when a hover car bursts from a hole that opens in the fortification. It races toward us, and Dev removes his Arcus as I switch into to the Terra uniform, knowing what the sudden arrival of this vehicle means.

"Sir." Michael, a Nocturna guard who has been cleared of my purpose here, nods to Dev. The number of Nocturna aware of my presence has done nothing but grow, and I know it's only a matter of days till the whole city is buzzing with the knowledge of a Dreamer in their midst. Elena has already prepared a plan to address the population and introduce the Dreamers' history and me. There will most certainly be an uprising of some sort, since not everyone will be pleased to learn there's a human walking among them, let alone one that carries limitless abilities. But Elena merely reminded me about how every Dreamer has caused a change in Terra, and this one seems to be mine—letting their world see the very thing they live to protect and unlocking a history centuries kept secret. Because of the special bands that can be worn to ward off my abilities, she seems confident the news will be more inspiring than hostile. I'm happy to help in any way I can, but I can't stop the unease that twists in my gut thinking about the kind of unwanted attention this will garner and even more security. I've definitely been taking traveling under the radar here for granted.

"Michael," Dev greets his cadet. "What's going on now?"

"Sir, it's the Nursery." He glances between the both of us, his gray eyes a powerful contrast to his dark skin

"Again?"

"Yes, sir, and it's bad. There are three or four packs."

"Jesus." My eyebrows shoot to my hairline. Almost one hundred Metus.

Dev is already climbing into the car. "Take us, and put on all thrusters."

My stomach is plastered to the back of my spine. We've traveled for less than a minute at a cosmic speed, the surrounding glass lit up with thermal energy surveillance as Dev communicates with the city for backup. The area where the Metus are attacking glows an angry orange-red. "How long ago did this start?" He zooms in and rotates the image along the glass.

"Not long. The guards on the Nursery wall saw them approaching and called it in."

Dev frowns. "That's not consistent to their recent behavior. Why so openly reveal themselves now?"

"What's that?" I point to a hot blue-white blob on the map that's close to the Nursery's fortification, where the Metus seemed to have gathered.

"It's a new Navitas generator. There was a recent shift in atmospheric energy, and we've needed to construct towers in new areas for mining. Not an ideal location obviously, but it's not like we can tell you Dreamers to fly in more convenient places. It's always changing."

Huh, I didn't know that.

"We're here." Michael presses a button on the control panel, slowing the vehicle. I'm finally able to take a deep breath, but it hitches when the opaque glass becomes clear and I take in the scene. They're everywhere. A field of glowing lava forms, surrounding a sleek jutting radio tower, the tip of which crackles with blue-white energy that's being collected from the sky. The tall metal walls to the Nursery are only three football fields in length away, and I can imagine the terrified children on the other side, their carefully created population so close to a threat. My gaze moves back to the tower, running upward along its smooth black sides. A handful of Metus have already begun climbing to the top. Their bodies shift between liquid and solid as they suction themselves forward, a sludge coating the building like a stain. A few are shot with arrows and burst apart, but just as one is destroyed, another comes, each desperate to get to their prize at the tip.

"There's so few of us," I whisper, sweeping my gaze over the chaotic tumbling of glowing blues to oranges, only spotting two dozen or so Vigil and Nocturna. Though our car is soundproof, the angry roar of battle is apparent everywhere I look.

"More are on their way." Dev turns to me. "Ready?"

I flex my fingers and nod.

"Michael, tell the Nursery to engage the wall units and shoot when they have a clear target. Molly and I will try to clear the tower until more backup comes."

"Yes, sir." Michael quickly types instructions into his monitor as the glass top opens with a whoosh. I'm almost knocked back into my seat from the wave of stink that crashes into me, the vibrating howl of nightmares setting my follicles on end.

Dev squats when he hits the ground, and I'm right beside him. "We'll take the wide route and clear a path as best we can. Most of us are between the generator and the Nursery." He points to where a cluster of men and women fight. "We're too concentrated. We need to spread out, or we'll be easily surrounded." He turns to me, eyes flashing like reflected steel. "I'll need you to watch our sides and back as I aim for the tower. Whatever happens, they *cannot* reach the top."

I shiver, knowing the horror of such consequences only from another's memory. A flash of a bloated, engorged Metus, immeasurable power spewing from every orifice. Nocturna screams, and death. I push the images aside. "Okay, but Dev"—I grab his arm as he's about to make a run for it—"what happens if my brain freezes up again like…" I swallow.

He places his hand atop mine and squeezes. "It won't. Listen to me. It won't. Just don't push yourself too much. If you need to use your Arcus, use it. That's what it's there for."

"I wish I had that vest," I mutter, glancing out to the battle. But there's no way I can imagine that here. The energy inside is too complicated and unknown for me try and replicate it properly.

"What vest?" Dev asks.

I shake my head. "Nothing. Never mind." Squaring my shoulders, I try the best I can to set my nerves to stone. "Okay, let's go."

With a quick flash of his encouraging smile, Dev turns and moves forward. I follow close behind as we run crouched in the tall grass, staying out of sight as long as we can. Gently I begin to ball my energy into my chest, preparing to use it whenever needed.

The first one is easy to take down, a straggler, and I ease Navitas out and forward, coating his burning form and dissolving him silently. The next two I attack at once. Shooting thick balls from either palm, I aim straight for their heads, and they barely get a scream out before bursting apart.

Dev glances over his shoulder, a proud smile momentarily overtaking his lips before continuing forward. My breathing is steady but labored, and adrenaline dances in every vein as we come to a stop. We settle ourselves low, blending into the night.

"Okay, it's going to be a bit tougher from here." Dev nods to our left, where two Nocturna engage three Metus. "Can you help them while I start taking down the climbers? I'll be next to you, but we need more bodies so we can start creating a ring around the base."

"Got it." I slowly approach the tangle of unaware fighters, eyeing the three monsters as a plan materializes in my head. Lying flat on the ground, I extend my arms, imagining what I need to grow out of each finger, and smile when ten identical Navitas snakes wriggle free, quickly slithering unseen to their targets. I watch as they pair off and combine from ten to three, growing their bodies bigger and bigger. I whisper instructions in my mind, telling them where to go, what to destroy.

A fighting Nocturna yelps in shock and jumps back as one of the glowing serpents travels over its foot. The group momentarily freezes, each mesmerized by the new shining intrusions that now curl around the base of each Metus. The nightmares do nothing to stop them, for they too are transfixed by these creatures that wind around and around, curling up and up, the Metus' liquid skin solidifying where they roam. When the energy snakes reach the monsters' heads, they quickly wrap around the base of their necks in one identical movement. Finally realizing what's happening, the Metus howl in panic and dig their claws into the now vise-tight cords, trying to dislodge them. But the attempt is futile as I hold them locked in my mind. *Tighter,* my thoughts whisper as sweat drips down my forehead. *Tighter.* A dark feeling edges out from a crack in my chest—how much easier it is to use my powers to destroy. The hate I let loose after Alec's death effortlessly accessible, like evil muscle memory in my heart. I wet my lips as gurgles emanate from the Metus, my power keeping them from turning to liquid. How many will I need to kill for this to stop? How many will it take for me to start liking it? The black smoke begins to grow inside me. *Molly.* A girl's voice sounds in my head, and I tense. *No.* It's barely a whisper, barely a breath, but I can sense it screaming at me. *Riki?* My mind searches for her, but she evades. *Do not give in.* Her words are louder now. *You are not them. You are strong. Stop this.* I blink to lucidity, watching as I continue to hold the Metus as choking prisoners. The realization of what I'm doing, what I was starting to enjoy, slaps me hard, and my clarity sends the internal darkness scattering. I focus back on my task and wait for the moment when the beasts open their mouths, emanating a bleat of pain. Just as they do, each snake dives inside, filling their heads instantly with blinding blue-white light. Like an overfilled water balloon, they burst apart, leaving nothing but simmering bits of glowing lava. Taking in a shaky breath, I stand, ignoring the twisted place my energy momentarily took me. Three slack-jawed Nocturna stare at me.

"Pretty frightening, isn't she?" Dev smirks, stepping to my side.

I glance to him. "I thought you were supposed to be taking down the climbers."

"Oh, I am." He lifts his Arcus and, without removing his gaze from mine, lets free an arrow. There's a piercing wail as it hits its target right before the sound of a goopy pop.

I roll my eyes. "Show off."

"Someone's calling the kettle black, Queen Cleopatra." He turns to our new added reinforcements and gestures for them to follow. As I step behind them, I shiver away the thought of comparing myself to that woman's fated demise.

Creating a half circle around the base of the tower, we hold back any Metus that attempt to climb it. Like Dev promised, more backup guards begin to make their way from Terra, and collectively we're able to engage the monsters at a steady pace. Even so, no matter how many we take down, more come, like they are appearing out of a hole in the ground. I tangle them up with my powers, take off limbs before removing heads, throw protective walls over certain fighters as Metus attempt to douse them with spewing fire. Over and over it goes, until my arms ache and my mind begins its familiar icy burn of exhaustion.

Tim is now here with Aveline as well as Aurora and Ezekial, and they spread out to my right. "Guys," I call over my shoulder as another knife pricks my brain. "I need to rest for a second."

Tim nods and moves in front, wedging me between his back and the generator's wall as he pumps out balls of energy from a complicated-looking gun. I pant, massaging my temples. *Not now. Don't do this now.*

"Over there!" A Nocturna points to a mass of new Metus in the distance beginning to attack the Nursery's wall. The Nocturna on the platforms above shoot down at the beasts, keeping them from getting too close.

"Where are they all coming from?!" Aveline growls as she lets loose an arrow into an approaching monster.

"It's like they're popping up from the ground." I shake out my arms, getting ready to engage again. I'm not nearly rested enough, but the Metus don't seem to care about that.

"The ground…" Tim's head lifts, his eyes going round. "Why didn't we think of that before?"

"Think of what?" I ask.

"Dev!" Tim waves his hand to get his attention. He's a few yards away, a blur of movement as he dances around two monsters. He decapitates one and then glances over just as the second's fiery paw swipes at his abdomen. I gasp, but he twists away in the nick of time, twirling his Arcus fluidly through the air to lodge in the top of the Metus's head. He pulls it out with a sickening wet pop. Dev raises his hands to guard off most of the splatter.

"Really, Tim?" He jogs over, flicking an errant glob off his shoulder. "Couldn't you see I was busy?"

"The tunnels!" Tim says, brushing away Dev's words. "That's where they must be coming from. Why we haven't seen them approach."

"What tunnels?" Aveline and I both ask.

"But they were supposed to have collapsed and been closed off." Dev frowns, glancing to where the new Nocturna reinforcements are speeding to defend the wall.

"Some of them must not be." Tim searches the area. "Terra, this is bad. They have pathways to *everything*."

My mind quickly flickers through all the memories I've gathered, and I suck in air, locking on to one of Riki's. Caverns everywhere, underneath us, stretching out like a complicated web. They were used to travel between outposts and areas around Terra before they had the safety of the hover cars and other vehicles. I never thought to connect them with this recent problem. "You're right, Dev," I say, my gaze unfocused. "They were destroyed. One of the Dreamers saw to it when they were breached just like this."

"See, then it can't be that." Dev quickly whips up his Arcus and shoots down a charging Metus. I push out a shield of Navitas to keep spewed lava from hitting us.

Tim shakes his head. "No, it has to still be—see there!" He points to a small grove of trees in the distance, an area directly between the tower and the wall. As if blinking into existence, a few orange masses leap up from their liquid forms close by. "There must be an entrance in there. I'm sure of it. They've been using their nonsolid forms to hide in the grass for as long as they can, so as not to give away where they're coming from."

"*Collö*." Dev aggressively runs his hand over his short-cropped hair.

"Here." Aveline throws him a small black bracelet.

Bringing it to his mouth, Dev rattles off instructions to someone on the other end, informing them of the security breach. Turning around, I take in the state of things. The Nocturna and few Vigil in our area have thinned, most moving to engage the new threat at the wall. There's maybe a handful left guarding the tower, most of which are now distracted and looking at the small grove of trees where a tunnel entrance supposedly is. They stand ready to aim down any new monster that shows itself. My stomach drops, and my spine tingles with the feeling that we just got played.

Turning, I see that my fear has become a reality. "Um, guys." No one acknowledges me. "Guys." I blindly swat at the nearest form.

"*What?*" Aveline turns to me.

"I think we fell for the classic bait and switch."

"What do you—" Aveline stumbles back as she follows my gaze and takes in the Metus gathering in front of us. I count twenty of them to the eight of us.

"Molly, get behind me." Dev pushes me back.

"Dev, stop. I can—" There's a tug around my feet. *Oh no.* "Dev!"

"Molly, stop. We need to pro—"

"No, I'm waking up!" He turns to me. "I can't wake up now!"

"Shh, try and stay calm." He places his hands on my shoulder while maintaining a visual on our threat. "It happens faster when you get too excited."

"I need to stay! I need to help you. You're outnumbered!"

"It's going to be okay. We've been outnumbered before."

That does nothing to reassure me given what happened the last... *No no no.* Glancing from him to what lies beyond, I let out a frustrated groan as another tug of consciousness fills my body. "You better be here when I get back." I kiss him hard on the mouth and then, with my last breath, let out as much of my reserved Navitas as I can straight into the nearest group of Metus. When the final drop leaves my body, my mind is punched forward, and I'm gone.

Chapter 40

THE MORNING IS too bright as I open my eyes, my jaw sore from clenching it in my sleep, my heart still pumping wildly. There's a waking chirp from a bird and a chime from a bicycle riding by on the street below. I curse. This is ridiculous! How am I here right now, bathed in this cheery daylight, when my friends could be dying at this very moment?

This isn't the first time I woke up in the middle of an attack, but it's surely one of the most threatening. I scrub at my face with my hands and sit up. The tunnels. Why didn't I ever think about the tunnels?! Because they weren't supposed to be accessible anymore, that's why. My alarm blares and I jump, a last reminding middle finger that my life, literally, couldn't be any more night and day. Quickly reaching for my phone, I switch off the buzzer and dial the only person who can calm me at this moment.

It rings and rings and rings, and then Rae's lame attempt at a funny voicemail comes on. Growling, I restrain myself from throwing my cell across the room. Now is not the time to be without communication. Please let this mean he's back in Terra. I try Becca.

It rings twice, and then there's a sound like whoever is on the other end is dragging her phone through sand. "Gullo?" asks a raspy voice.

"Becca! Are you awake?"

There's a pause filled with heavy breathing. "Is this a joke?"

"Is Rae with you?"

The sound of shuffling again and then a muttered groan. "Molly, it's *seven in the morning*. Do you know who you just called? Do you remember what event took place last night? Do you want to remain my friend? Then *never* make the mistake of doing this to me again."

The line goes dead.

Shit.

I wring my hands and stare at nothing. What should I do? What *can* I do? I glance at my work clothes draped over my desk chair. My shoulders droop. *Oh yeah*, I guess there's that.

⇥⟫⟪⇤

If there was ever a time to hate my job, it's right now. Standing over our shoddy copier, I jam random buttons, hoping it will fix whatever is causing its malfunction. I'm supposed to be getting papers ready for a meeting in five minutes, but I couldn't give two flying monkey butts about it. This whole day is a joke. Every minute of every hour a farce, the universe laughing at me, and I really don't know what I did to deserve it. All I can think about is what's happening at this very moment in a place very far away, and who will be left to greet me tonight. My teeth grind together, and I slam my hands down on the copier again.

"I don't think breaking the printer will get it working." Tony, a creative director here and one of Becca's old crushes—seriously, thank God that's over—walks up to grab some paper from a cabinet.

"No, but if it's going to give me a splitting headache, then I'm going to return the favor." I kick the machine to demonstrate my point.

The side of his mouth rises along with his eyebrows. "Wow, violent much? I didn't realize you were such a fighter." He chuckles before dipping out of the room.

I stare down at the flashing red Error button. It winks on and off, on and off. A taunt, a warning, a truth. This life isn't right. This life is wrong. *Error. Error. Error.* Balling my hand into a fist, I land one last plastic-crunching punch to the screen. The light doesn't come on again. A satisfying grin slips across my lips. "Tony, you have no idea."

Tap. Tap. Tap. My legs bounce restlessly as I listen to my boss, Jim, go over our team's next project, his voice sounding more and more like the teacher from the *Peanuts* cartoon as the minutes tick by. Under the desk, I spin my cell phone between my fingers, praying for it to buzz but terrified for the moment when it does.

I've called and left messages for Rae so many times that I'm surprised his phone provider hasn't tried to block my number on its own. My continued hope for his silence is that he's in a place that doesn't get service. I need him to be able to tell me what's going on in Terra, because I can't shake the feeling that it's something bad—more than the usual bad. It could be because the TVs pocketed around the office are playing nothing but the recent bombings that all simultaneously happened overnight—a few in Europe, one in Asia, and two in small towns in the United States. World leaders have been trying to figure out if it was any of the handfuls of new terrorist groups that have popped up, but I know the truth. I know the root of the problem isn't anything they can see. Isn't anything they can fix. That's my job, my responsibility, and here I am listening to Q3 and Q4 client demands. I hiss as my bottom lip splits open from my incessant tic of biting it with worry.

"Molly, are you okay?" Jim's question brings the entire room's attention to me.

I stop, dabbing at my mouth. "Uh, yeah, sorry. Just bit my lip."

His gaze stays on me an extra beat before continuing. I wonder how long it will be until I'm called into his office and fired. Would I even care at this point? Rae mentioned once about some kind of Swiss fund the Vigil have created for Dreamers. I could always tap into that. I frown, wondering if that's also something that gets cut off after my twenty-fifth birthday. I try not counting how many months I have left until I need to make that decision. Nine. *Goddammit, brain.*

My hands falter when they feel a vibration. Glancing down, my heart stops, and I jump up from my seat. "Excuse me. I...ah, I have to take this." Ignoring the alarmed faces of my colleagues and a pissed-off one from Jim, I quickly exit the conference room.

"What's going on? Did they stop them? Is Dev okay?" My words fall all over themselves as I speed-walk to my desk, the echo of my heels on the tiled floor like the beat of a war drum.

"He's fine. We're holding them off for now, but...but it's bad." Rae sounds winded, as if he's still in the middle of running. "Molly, I need you to get to the bookstore. Now. Meet me there as soon as you can."

I don't even have a chance to respond before he hangs up. The viselike grip on my chest eases, knowing Dev isn't hurt, but the panic in Rae's voice still sets my nerves on edge. Glancing around my desk and then to the open floor plan of my office, I take in the hum of clicking keyboards, colleagues' voices, and the occasional laugh. No one here has the smidgen of awareness of what's happening in another dimension to keep them all safe, oblivious. No one knows of the centuries of lives lost at their expense, ones that could be ending this very second. Without another moment of hesitation, I grab my purse and run.

Chapter 41

EVEN THOUGH IT'S the middle of the day, the bookstore is closed when I get there, and for a moment I fear that Rae left without me. But then his form fills the doorframe from the other side, and there's a chime as he lets me in. The pungent fragrance of recently lit incense is still strong, and if I weren't burning to learn about Terra, I'd ask how he got them to close the shop so early.

"What's going on? Is this it?" I follow tight on his heels as we make our way to the back room.

"No, but it's still not good." He opens one of the two closet doors and walks inside. "They were able to remove the threat from the Nursery when I was contacted, but it's like we plugged one hole just for water to burst out of three more. There have been heavy losses on both sides."

My mouth runs dry. "Tim, Aveline?"

"Both okay…at least when I left, they were." Lifting back a switch panel on the far side of the room, he pushes a button, and we step back as a huff of air announces the decline of the wall. I never thought seeing the stark white room on the other side would be a relief, but as I take in the space, the tightness in my muscles loosen.

Rae moves around like a man on a mission, because that's exactly what he is, and I feel useless waiting for him to set up. "Most of the units are gathering in the Armory on the southwest part of the city for deployment, so that's where I'll program us to arrive. A pack is attacking a Vigil town close by, and another two or three are concentrated on an area of Terra's wall." He types quickly over a hovering keyboard, arranging boxes and apparatuses to come out of the floor and walls, while my coffin floats and docks in the center. The blue-white circular portal in the corner glows on.

"Why that town? Why that part of the fortification?" My brain searches for any importance with those areas, but I'm so overstimulated that I feel as if I'm short-circuiting, my brain unable to logically sift through another's borrowed memories.

"There's a major underground Navitas line that runs from that section of Terra to the Vigil city."

"Underground? But I thought Terra switched to free-range energy transferring." I take off my shoes and place them into a walled compartment, along with my purse.

"We did, but we still rely on a few underground channels to send higher concentrated amounts of energy from area to area. Okay"—he steps up to the white bed—"we're ready."

Climbing nimbly into my coffin, I nestle into the material and allow it to hug my body like a security blanket. "So, what area am I needed?"

"I left to get you before that was decided. I'm sure they will inform us when we get to the Armory."

I let out a deep breath, the white in the room suddenly blindingly bright. There's not an ounce of me that's able to fall asleep right now. "Rae, my mind's all over the place. I think you'll need to give me something. Like whatever that was you stuck me with the first time. That worked really well."

"Are you sure?"

"Yeah, yeah." I wave my hand impatiently.

Rae ducks out of view, and I try to steady my breathing as I clench and unclench my fists. My foot wants to tap to dispel my excess restless energy, but the material surrounding it holds it still.

"Extend your arm." He's back hovering above me, and I wince when the needle pricks my skin. Cool liquid swims in my veins, and almost instantaneously my body relaxes, limbs like paperweights. "How do you feel?"

"Better." The word seems to come out in slo-mo. I blink, and it's like lifting a rusted-shut window. *Geez, is this really the same stuff?*

"Okay, good, because I made the dosage higher," Rae says, and I'd scowl at him, but I don't think my facial nerves are capable. He presses his fingers to my pulse and stares at something out of my view. "You should fall asleep any minute n—"

Darkness. Like a bag being thrown over my head, there's suddenly only darkness.

My mind tumbles through space, no body constraining or confining it to a shape. It stretches forward and back, reaches up and over, like a dancing liquid blob without gravity. And then slowly a hum grows out of the void, the sound becoming loud, chaotic, and my conscious wants to shrink away from it, return back to the comfort of silence. But something doesn't allow this. Something gives me a forceful shove forward. The noise transforms into light, a bright-white light. And then...

My eyes open, and I gasp, my back stiffening on a hard, cool surface.

"I've got you." Dev is suddenly beside me. "You're in Terra. It's all right." His hand brushes back my hair.

My gaze finds his, and my heart skips. "Given what I've been told of the state of things here, that's not very relieving."

His smile brings crinkles to the corners of his eyes, eyes that—despite his grin—hold exhaustion. Slowly he helps me to sit up, and I glance around the empty room. The familiar noise that invaded my sleep comes from the open glass doors to my left. I look through the wall of windows and take in a giant military hangar on the other side. More white mixed with tall chrome support beams. Nocturna and Vigil briskly run about, from hover vehicles to the multiple weapons depots. My memories recall being here once before, but in another's body—my grandfather's.

I turn back to Dev and intertwine my fingers with his. "I'm so glad you're okay. I was a crazy mess all day."

He looks affronted. "I can't believe you ever doubted I would be. I'm a legend on the battlefield, remember?"

I roll my eyes with a shake of my head. "Really?"

"Yes, *really*. Just ask anyone." He glances over his shoulder and calls out to a passing Nocturna. "Hey, Bernard, can you please tell this young lady how much of a—"

I shove Dev in the shoulder. "No, Bernard, keep doing what you were doing." I wave away the confused man. "You don't have an off switch, do you?" Standing, I stretch out my limbs, making sure everything is working properly, and then change out of my crumpled work clothes to the usual black uniform. Walking to the glass partition, I take in the buzz of energy. "Now tell me what's been happening."

Rae meets up with Dev and I as we walk past row upon row of hover cars mixed with lines of sleek pointed airships. The ships are new to me, and I run my gaze from sharp-tipped end to sharp-tipped end, taking in the three-pointed dorsal fins that jut out from either of their sides and tops. I assume they help in guiding the aerodynamic forms. Their underbellies are covered in long strips of thrusters, rather than the circular ones I'm used to seeing in sci-fi films. While each is identical in appearance, the sizes range from a two-manned ship to what could possibly hold dozens. Walking under the nose of a larger one, I study the seamless material making up the body. It's the same used on the hover cars, and I wonder if they have the same chameleon capability when flying through Terra's surroundings.

"These are new," I say.

Dev turns from his conversation with Rae and glances to what I'm referencing. "Maybe a couple of decades new."

I frown. Man, even with my predecessor's memories, there's still so much to learn.

An organized group of Nocturna men and women march past us, and we step aside, their identical austere expressions fluttering by. I glance to the array of handheld weapons, noting that the fighters are wearing the glowing lightning-bolt bands around their biceps. Curious, I reach out with my power and hit up against a shield surrounding them. I'm unable to affect these soldiers, and I recall a similar feeling when I tried to physically manipulate guards in

City Hall, but failed, not realizing they were protected by the same Dreamer-resistant energy. The thought that anyone would need to be protected from me does weird things to my psyche.

Continuing on, we weave through the hangar's energy of people all maneuvering to their assigned locales. The air is tense, but there's a sense of order to the chaos. The military units of Terra run like a well-oiled machine, and it's both sad and relieving how comfortable they are working under such constant threats.

I spot Alexander standing with Elena and Raymond, the Vigil engineer, by a circular command post in the center of the room. A few other military personnel linger close by as a map of Terra spins in the middle, coordinates and alerts flashing and popping up along the side.

"Molly." Elena inclines her head in a bow of greeting as we approach. Her companions do the same, though Alex doesn't seem thrilled at having to show me any sign of respect. I'm still not sure what about me bothers him so much.

A nearby ship's thrusters come on with a whirl, and a cool wind whips against us as the large pointed machine lifts up and out of the open hangar ceiling. It momentarily blots out the shooting stars above before careening forward with a burst of blue-white light from its rear engines.

I glance back at the awaiting group. "Dev said you wanted to see me?"

"Yes." Elena folds her hands together. "I assume you've been somewhat briefed on the state of things?"

I nod. "A significant number of packs are attacking two main areas that expose an underground Navitas line."

"Correct." Alex swirls his hand over the hovering map, zooming in on the southwest portion of Terra's fortification. "The greater worry at the moment is the threat here." The image shows a large mass of red pressed up against the wall. "There's an energy dock that *should* have been removed by now," he says and glances to Raymond, whose lips thin, "and the Metus have a chance of breaking it open and getting to the Navitas flowing through."

"How many packs do we have there now? Still two?" Dev studies the image.

"The numbers along the wall have doubled."

Dev's jaw flexes, and his eyes grow steely. "The tunnels?"

Alex frowns. "Yes, we've located an opening close by. Though a few of our airships have just been sent to deal with it."

Dev slams his hand down on the tabletop. The map flickers. "How did we not see this? We don't even have an estimate of how many are living in those hovels, how many they've been able to create." He glances to Alex. "That's why the number in Terra Diablo never increased. They've been hiding underneath us this whole time."

"Yes, we're all in agreement that this turn of events is most inconvenient, but let's try to stick with eradicating our current threat before overwhelming ourselves with having to deal with the rest of this." Alex rubs at the bridge of his nose.

"Fine, but get a team on locating where those tunnels connect within the city. Even if they're still blocked, we need guards at every possible entrance. The last thing we need right now is to send all our forces out only to be attacked from within."

"Agreed." Alex turns to a waiting guard and tells her to start gathering peers to be deployed for this mission.

"Thank Terra!" Aveline runs up with Tim, her blonde ponytail whipping back and forth, her cheeks flushed red from exertion. "I never thought I'd ever be so happy to see you, Molly."

"Uh, thanks?"

"We just got back from the Vigil port," Tim says, his appearance askew and eyes bright from the action, a small part of him seeming to enjoy this. "The lake surrounding the city has kept the civilians unharmed, and we've been able to reduce the pack's number significantly. The threat on the line there should be removed soon."

"Well, that's the first good news all day." Alex turns to Elena. "Why don't you tell our Dreamer here what you have planned for her assignment."

I resist biting my already-sore bottom lip as all eyes flicker from me to our Vigil elder. "Usually we station the Dreamer to fight a distance away for these bigger battles, not only for your protection but largely to keep you out of sight of the Nocturna," Elena explains while Tim shifts uncomfortably beside me. "But since a handful have already been briefed on your existence, I think now is the moment to introduce you to *all* of them. It's time for your debut, Molly. We'll show your capabilities tonight and win the respect of the Nocturna guards, then helping win the favor of the people."

I blink. Not sure I heard her right. "So...so your big battle plan for me is a *political* move?"

"We must seize opportunity in every circumstance."

I barely contain an incredulous snort. "Well then, how lucky that this attack should coincide with your Dreamer rollout plan."

Tim clears his throat with a cough, and Alex narrows his eyes. Elena remains unfazed by my sarcasm—per usual. "Lucky indeed," she says and turns to the engineer. "Now Raymond, why don't you help our Dreamer into her vest?"

Chapter 42

"We should've taken one of the ships." Aveline pouts behind me as Dev maneuvers our hover car through a narrow tunnel that leads from the Armory to the outside wall.

"Where's the point in that?" Rae asks, attaching canisters of Navitas to his four-cylinder shotgun. Seeing the weapon brings up memories of Alec, and I lean back in my seat, pushing away the flash of sadness. That was one of his favorites.

"The *point* would be that we could have attacked from the sky."

"But we have units on the ground, Aveline," Tim says next to her, the three of them sharing the backseat. "Closely engaging with the Metus. It would be too risky."

She grunts, displeased, and I don't have to see her to imagine the scowl overtaking her features.

I absently run my hands over the material of my vest, feeling the flexible ridges of the material, and gently push around the renewable energy inside. Knowing it's there lessens the fluttering of nerves that dance in my abdomen. Dev places his hand on my thigh, and I glance over to him. "We've got this." The corner of his mouth tips up, his blue eyes unnaturally bright in the dim light.

I wet my lips. "I know."

"Just remember the plan." He twines our fingers together and then brings my hand to his mouth.

"Ugh, can you guys not?" Aveline says from the back.

I try pulling away, embarrassed, but Dev holds tight. With a quick wicked gleam, he presses his lips to my skin again, and in an exaggerated gesture starts slobbering kisses all over it.

There's a high-pitched squeal of disgust accompanied by deep laughs from Rae and Tim. Finally, I pry my fingers free, but am unable to keep the smile from my face. "Thanks for that." I wipe my hand on my pants. "I knew I forgot to wash that one today."

"What I'm here for." Dev throws me a wink.

Aveline makes another barf sound. "In all of Terra, I've never wished to be in the company of Metus more in my life."

"Well, you won't have to wish for too long, because we're coming up on the exit now." A wash of light fills the tunnel as a hole opens up at the far end. Our car passes through soundlessly, and Dev immediately angles us to the right, hugging the wall. We suddenly face what can only be described as a field of parasitic orange globs surrounding a large titanium tube that juts five stories high from the ground and connects with Terra's fortification. Other hover cars have encircled themselves around the pipe at a distance, shooting where they can without causing casualties to any of the grounded Nocturna and Vigil who take on the monsters head to head.

"*Good demons everywhere*, there's hundreds of them!" Tim grabs the back of Dev's chair and leans forward. We're all momentarily stunned by the sight.

"Maybe we should call everyone off and bomb them," Aveline says.

Dev shakes his head. "We'd destroy the energy dock and only help the Metus by letting loose the Navitas."

Aveline mutters a curse and twirls her Arcus baton between our seats.

"I think the original plan stands," Rae says while powering on his gun, the thrum of energy reaching out to me.

"Agreed. Let me get closer." Dev glides forward. "Remember, don't leave the hover until I either run out of ammo or we're forced to."

I flex my fingers as the anticipation builds.

"Opening the top," Dev announces and presses a button on the console. Our glass encasing falls away.

"Dear Metus dung." Aveline scrunches up her face as the overwhelming stench of our enemies coat our every pore.

"Still wishing for their company?" Rae stands and immediately aims down two unaware targets. With a high-pitched whirl, Dev engages the weaponry of our vehicle and starts shooting at the mass of nightmares, their sickening wet pops a sweet lullaby to my ears. The rest of us stand with Rae and take any clear shot we can get. I yell for a nearby Nocturna to duck just as I push out a stream of Navitas from my palm straight at a Metus sneaking up behind her. With the threat removed, the woman blinks up at me in shock. Her face quickly transforms from questioning to gracious, and she jumps to her feet, joining our positioned attack. As we free up more guards, we grow the number of soldiers encircling us, allowing us, inch by inch, to fight our way through the thick field of monsters and gain closer ground to the energy dock.

"We need to get at the ones at the seam," Dev yells. "We can't let them crack so much as a hairline, or they can start sucking at the energy."

Shots begin to fire up at where the Metus climb. Grunts and shouts roar from both sides as I maintain the force field I've willed around us—keeping us safe from the spews of fire and lobbed lava chunks. The vest pumps my veins full of energy whenever I call for more, and so far my mind is clear from even the slightest prick of exhaustion. I only hope it remains that way.

"They're still crawling up!" Rae presses a button on his gun, and the front and back extend out like a bazooka. "But don't you worry. I'll take care of it." He positions it over one shoulder and tilts his head to aim down the barrel. With a loud *thunk thunk*, his body jerks back as two massive balls of altered Navitas fly high, colliding into a mangle of Metus suctioning their way along the energy dock. A spew of glowing disembodied parts rain down. Tim shifts his Arcus into a long-range bow and pulls back the string, now fitted with four flaming arrows. They find their marks with terrifying precision.

"They're all moving to the other side!" A Nocturna guard points to where the monsters are repositioning themselves out of our range.

"Run, little mucus droppings, run." Rae grins as he adds more energy canisters to his gun and then drapes a pulsing ammo belt over his chest. "I think it might be time to spread out our dance here, Dev."

Looking displeased by the idea, but taking in the new arrangement of the Metus, he nods. "I think you're right."

I study the orange glow emanating from the other side of the tube, where Metus hide from our concentrated aim. "You know how Elena mentioned this being my chance to introduce myself to everyone?" I glance to Dev. "I think I know just how to make my debut."

He opens his mouth to say something, but I'm already sucking in a deep breath of air, bunching up my energy. In one large exhale, I expel a ring of Navitas to burst from the epicenter that is our hover. The wave of power barrels through any nearby threats, winking out six or seven from existence, and I shake away a headache that's begun to form from using such a large dose of energy at once. The closest Nocturna all look up at me in surprise, searching for whatever weapon I must be holding to cause such efficient destruction. But I don't hang around to explain. Instead, I push up off of the car and go flying into the air. Rae's voice reaches me from below. "Since when did our birdie get wings?"

I zoom above the battle, taking in the situation. Most of us are gathered to the right of the tube, where the fewest Metus remain. Dev and the rest of the team jump from the car, fighting their way to the other side. Following their projected path, my eyes narrow at what will greet them. At least two packs wait at the ready, already a dozen climbing up the pipe, close to reaching the weakest part— where the wall and seam meet.

I glide down to be in front of the three still-manned vehicles. "Two of you stay on the right side and make sure no other Metus come that way. We need to push them back and hold them in one area. You." I point to the last hover. "Come with me. We'll help engage on the left." None of the guards move. They merely stare wide eyed up at me and then exchange confused glances. I let out a frustrated sigh. "Listen, I don't have time to explain what's going on with"—I gesture to my floating form—"this, but trust that I'm on your side and I can really, *seriously*, help you." As if to aid in my demonstration, an errant Metus separates from its pack and on a howl charges the unengaged vehicles. With a quick whip of my hand, the ground under its feet lifts up and throws it back. Punching out with my other hand, a ball of energy flies out of my palm and collides into the creature's chest, engulfing its body with blue-white light before it gushes apart.

"See." I look back at my rapt companions with a smile that's most definitely at odds with the destruction just accomplished. Their mouths hang open. "Now let's move." I slap my hands together, and that seems to momentarily waken them from their daze. I turn and fly forward, relieved when I see one of the hovers following.

This side of the wall is a mess. Nocturna and Vigil spar tightly together against an onslaught of monsters. There's three or four Metus to every two guards, and I almost falter in flight when I glance, too late, to see a group of Nocturna being overtaken with orange sludge. Their piercing cries of pain cut off with a gurgle as they get devoured, red lava coating them. I wonder for a moment if I can try and help them, try and reverse the process like I tried to do with Alec, but when the newly formed nightmares rise on their own, nothing human left in their appearance, I know my powers are useless to them. With a shout of rage, I spit pulse after pulse of altered Navitas into any threat that gets in my path, and make my way up the tube. I can hardly see the titanium surface under the angry red globs that now coat it. They've managed to suction themselves along the seam like leeches, and even though one spot opens when I try to spray them off, it merely grows back over with a new body.

The dozens of individual creatures have morphed into one large one, blanketing everything.

"Molly, what's happening up there?" Dev's voice reaches me through my earpiece, and I quickly glance down to find him fighting back to back with Aveline.

"They've made it to the seam," I yell. "I can't seem to get them off. It's…it's as if they are coating it like a second skin." There's a sudden hiss, and my cells scream as a burst of Navitas shoots out of a dislodged tap along the pipe. "Oh fuck."

The Metus go crazy, all of them, even the ones on the ground, howl and rush the tube.

"They broke open a valve or something!" I pump wave after wave of repellent, creating a bright wall around the break, but that only manages to hold them off for now. The raw energy from the tube still gushes out of the hole. *This isn't good. This isn't good.* My vest tingles along my chest, the first signs of it reaching its limit. *No no no.* It needs to be charged somehow. I glance around desperately, at a loss. How do I do that while holding the field around the break?

A brave monster, frantic to get at the power on the other side, tries to jump through the walled shield but instantly explodes upon impact. My hands shake to hold it in place while the rest now stay cautiously back, wailing their inhuman curdles of displeasure. *Good, stay sad, you creepos.* My power wanes again, and so does the brightness of the field, the warning flicker of a dying bulb. *Shit. Shit. Shit.*

I look to Dev, who's shooting continuous lines of arrows at oncoming beasts. An idea swims forward. "Dev!" I call down. "Shoot me!"

He falters, the only shot he misses. "What?" He gazes up at me like I've sprouted six heads.

"My vest, it needs to be recharged! You can do that with one of your arrows. It'll transfer the energy to ten times the strength...or something." I forget the exact numbers Raymond told me.

"I'm not shooting you."

"You have to! I can't keep the field up much longer and stay flying."

"No." His brows knit with his final decision.

"For the love of Terra." Aveline's voices filters through, and she pushes him aside. "I'll do it." Before he can knock off her aim, she lets loose an arrow, and I brace myself for the impact. But just like before, it never comes. Instead, the vest swallows it whole, and my body instantly gets a bump of adrenaline, a wave of power, and my manifested wall shoots higher. *Sweet caffeine highs.* Smiling, now with the renewed strength, I slowly extend the force field out, edging the creatures back and away from the broken valve. They hiss and roar with each retreating step.

"Take them as they come down!" Tim yells from somewhere below, but I don't remove my gaze from the cracked opening where bright blue-white light endlessly dances out of it. Little by little, I send out bits of strength, imagining the fissure closing, the titanium knitting itself back together. My head is dizzy from the multitasking. *Push Metus away. Fix hole. Stay flying.* My body is covered in sweat, strands of loose hair are plastered to my neck, and my mind sends out prickles of warning as I silently chant over and over my desires, till finally, the ever-flowing energy suddenly shuts off, the area quickly growing dark—the crack fixed. My shoulders sag, and I drop my arms. The shield falls away.

I hear a whoop from the ground. "That's our Dreamer!" Rae pumps a fist up at me as he pulls the trigger of his shotgun with the other, blowing apart a nearby monster. "You hear that, everyone? She's the Dreamer sent to save all our behinds."

I land next to him, my legs threatening to give way upon impact.

A few guards stand around astonished at what they just witnessed—a close one even takes a step back, but most are still too busy eradicating the enemy to gawk.

"All right." Tim fights nearby. "Let's celebrate after we clear out the rest of these—" He falls back, tripping over a mound of what's left of a Metus's carcass.

"Careful there, old man." Rae reaches down to help him up and then pauses, eyes flying wide. I follow his gaze to see a large portion of the orange-red goo beginning to inch its way up Tim's arm. As if it's still alive, it clings to him, growing brighter with the climb. He screams in pain and tries brushing the stuff off, but that only makes it worse by spreading it to his other hand.

"Tim!" Aveline rushes over, putting down a Metus that tries to make its way forward. "Get it off him!" She glances to me in a panic. "Molly, get it off him!"

But all I can do is stand there, paralyzed. Watching, stomach in my throat, Tim fall to his knees in agony. The burning mucus expands with each second, and the only thought screaming through my mind is that it's happening again. It's happening all over again.

Chapter 43

MY HEAD WHIPS to the side as a vicious sting swells along my cheek. I blink to Aveline's angry and desperate eyes, her hand hovering close by. "*Snap out of it*!" She tugs me forward. "You can help him!"

Tim lies on the ground, skin pale, lips blue, and his hair seeming to grow grayer by the second as the parasite eats at his energy. His chest heaves up and down, up and down, and his gaze is glazed over as both his arms, and now part of his chest, are covered with the burning lava. Slowly he is becoming one of them—even in death they can still destroy.

"*Molly.*" It's not Aveline's slap that brings me back, but her heartbreaking plea. I shake out of my panicked haze and push away my biggest fear. *We will not lose you. I refuse to lose you.*

"Yes, yes. I can help." Quickly, I kneel by his side. "Guard us," I say, and switch to the sight of energy. Tim's abdomen glows blue-white, but the areas where the Metus mucus slides forth devours every Navitas cell it crosses, growing stronger and covering it with a black sludge. Taking in a deep breath, I have another second of hesitation, when images of doing this before flash in front of me—a barely discernable face staring up at me, agony in his eyes, and a last desperate gurgled plea to end his life. I push back a sob. *This will not end the same. It is not too late.* Holding my hands over his body, I gather my personal supply of power, knowing it's more potent than what's trapped in my vest. Searching out, I find what I'm looking for—the seed of his soul flutters erratically beneath his ribcage, like a caged bird aware of its impending death. This time without hesitation, I lock on to it and gasp. Every ounce of Tim's emotions radiates into me—terror, hopelessness, excruciating endless pain, the tortuous sensation of thousands of knives raking along my arms, working their way up and over every nerve. It takes all my strength not to vomit from the agony and break the connection. With a desperate burst of will, I swallow down the bile edging up my throat and stay concentrated on pouring my Navitas into Tim, refilling the empty-ing canister. I push the brightness onto the dark, feeling the night-mares trying to fight back, their whispers of how I will fail, that there's nothing that can be done, I'm a loser, a nobody, a fake. I plug my mind from the hate, separate its words of defeat from my deter-mination to succeed. *I can do this. I* will *do this. I am powerful. I can make a difference.* Like a slug dusted with salt, the darkness squirms and begins to curl away. Repelled by my thoughts, my good intentions.

The noise of battle is a far-off layer of reality as I remain hold-ing tight, pouring and pouring. *Goodness, love, heal, hope.* The power of light eats away the emptiness of hate. My skin grows cold, my mouth dries, but I don't stop until the last black drop of evil and death is gone. And when it is, I blink back to the world as it is. The heightened plane of energy fades, and I sway on my knees.

"I've got you." Dev allows me to fall into his side as my mind pounds, every inch of my skin moaning with exhaustion.

"Is he...did I?" I can hardly keep my eyes open.

"Yes, you saved him. You were amazing." His lips press to my temple. "But we need to go. He needs to get to the infirmary."

I saved him... My heart swells with disbelief, and I manage a glance down. Tim's eyes are closed, but his chest rises and falls. While he's no longer covered in the parasitic lava, he hardly looks any better with his angry red skin that's swollen and bubbling with blisters. Parts of his black uniform have melted into his flesh like a plastic toy left in the sun.

"Oh God." I lean forward. "Tim, Tim! Oh God, his arms! His chest!"

"It looks worse than it is. Trust me, but we need to get him out of here. The sooner he's with the doctors, the better. Can you stand?"

I nod and push up onto shaky feet. All I really want to do is collapse into a puddle and sleep, sleep for days, sleep an eternity, but I notice all the remaining Nocturna and Vigil watching me now. The last Metus must have either retreated or were all destroyed, but I can't currently bring myself to care about the specifics. All I know is that we've won, for now, and the only thing important is getting Tim back, and fast. "Dev, I can make a portal...one to the outside of the hospital."

His brows knit. "Are you sure? You seem like you're about to faint."

"Yeah, I just need..." I glance to the nearest Nocturna. "Can I have that?"

He numbly glances down to the flaming arrow that's uselessly hanging from his fingers and then raises it up to me, a question in his gaze.

"Thanks." I take it and angle the burning head straight at my heart. He shouts a warning just as I stab myself with the implement, the vest suctioning it in. My body jolts with energy, and my eyes momentarily go wide. *Holy wake-up calls.*

"Let's hope you don't start doing that recreationally." Rae is holding up one end of a shiny white gurney, Tim lying in the center. Aveline has an oxygen mask to his face, and everyone acts fast to utilize the first-aid kits located in the nearby hover cars. Taking a wider glance around, I notice more injured Nocturna and Vigil being held up and helped by their comrades.

With no time to react, I breathe in a settling breath and imagine the place we need, the place I've walked by dozens of times. Almost instantly, the space in front of us opens, the scene on the other side the entrance to the hospital that's in City Hall Square. The Nocturna around us gasp and mutter between themselves as Rae, Aveline, and another Vigil hurry through.

"Take all the injured." I nod at the doorway. "I'll hold it until then."

The group doesn't move, still wondering who and what I am, but then Dev barks a command, and they jump into action.

It doesn't take long for the last hurt soldier to hobble across the portal's threshold, and even though we suffered a number of losses, thankfully our casualties aren't as high as I had originally thought.

Dev touches my elbow. "Our turn."

Relieved by the prospect of finally leaving this field, whose odor only holds the memories of death, I step forward, Dev following on my heels. The fresh air that greets us almost brings tears to my eyes.

"You can close it," he says as we stand at the base of the hospital's steps. "The rest are staying to take care of the damages, and another team is on their way to help."

I drop the visual from my mind, and the door puckers out of existence. I sigh, the first real breath I've taken tonight. Stepping back, I watch as doctors and nurses rush from the sleek entrance of the building, taking in the new arrival of patients. Their eyes widen with shock at our sudden appearance, but they dutifully wait to ask questions.

A few turn to us, but Dev waves them off, telling them to concentrate on the others. A crowd has started to grow from the square, asking what's going on. A line of city soldiers march onto the scene, keeping the onlookers from interfering with the hospital staff attending the wounded and carrying them inside. One guard addresses the people, explaining a simplified—and less threatening, I might add—version of the recent Metus attacks. While I want to scream at him that, no, it wasn't only a *few*, I understand his reasoning for not wanting to scare a mob of worried onlookers.

I hear whispers of "they just appeared out of nowhere" along with mutters of the possibility of a war with the Metus. I lower my head as I catch eyes with a few civilians, not knowing if they suspect me to be any different from them, but not wanting to stick around to find out. Thankfully, Dev places his hand on my back and guides us toward the hospital. The glass doors silently slide apart as we enter. "We need to find Aveline and Rae, see where they took Tim."

I work hard to keep up with his brisk pace. Even with the renewed energy from the recent arrow, my body is well aware that was merely a temporary fix for what only proper rest can give. But I stay silent on the subject of exhaustion and try to ignore the dull throb that's growing at the base of my skull, for I know what the imperative is in this moment—Tim.

The hospital's sterile scent digs into my nose, and the endless white of the floors, ceiling, and walls is discombobulating. Dev stops at one of a dozen tablets hovering nearby, and his fingers dance across the screen, quickly bringing up the crazy Latin lettering and foreign symbols. Deep grooves etch between his brows as he searches for whatever he's looking for, his hard gaze revealing his desperation in learning the fate of his friend. "This way." He grabs my hand, and we enter an elevator and ascend a few flights until a woman's voice announces, "You have arrived at the Corpus Regen level."

"What's the—"

"It's where Tim is." Dev cuts me off and breaks into a jog. We weave through doctors and patients who don't seem surprised at all by two people quickly moving down the hall. Turning a corner, we spot them, Aveline and Rae standing transfixed outside one of the many rooms lining this area, looking through a glass partition.

Aveline glances up as we arrive and grabs for Dev's hand as he approaches, her eyes red from crying. For a moment, I fear the worst. My heart jumps into my throat, and my nerves stand on end, but then she smiles, a huge relieving grin, and I nearly collapse anyway. "He's going to be okay," she says, her voice croaking. "They're able to regenerate what's been damaged. They're doing it now."

We turn to peer through the window. In the center of an all-white room is a large, thick alabaster ring standing on end. In the center floats Tim, his body positioned toward us like Da Vinci's

Vitruvian Man, eyes closed as millions of blue-white lasers criss-cross over his bare body, concentrating on his arms and chest. Two technicians in full hazard suits walk around him, checking on the readouts displaying along the far wall, and every so often reposition the circle that holds Tim hovering in space.

"They're growing his skin back?" I ask, mesmerized by the strange rhythm of the equipment.

"Regenerating," Rae says from behind me. "Earth will have this ability soon."

"That's amazing." I step closer. "So he'll really be...he's going to be okay?"

A delicate hand touches my arm, and I turn to Aveline, her gaze shimmering with barely contained emotion. "Molly...I—" Suddenly, I'm wrapped in her arms. "We owe you everything. I don't know how to ever repay you for saving him. I can't...I can't..." She hiccups on a sob, and I bring my hands around her small body, returning the hug.

"There's nothing to repay. I love him too." Aveline grips me tighter. "Plus, I think it's me that needs to be thanking you." She leans back, confusion puckering her brows. "If I ever needed a slap in the face, that was the moment."

Relieving laughter twinkles out of her, and she shakes her head. "Yeah, sorry about that."

I'm momentarily thrown off balance when Rae's large arm corrals me into his side. "You did good, kid." He squeezes my shoulder. "Real good."

"There were still losses." I frown.

"Yes, but you kept there from being a lot more."

"What are we going to do about the tunnels?" I ask, not wanting to be praised anymore for what is still a tragedy for any who knew the lost.

Dev presses his fingertips to the lip of the windowsill, his expression grave as he stares into Tim's room. "I don't know yet, but we'll need to figure it out soon. A lot of those routes have been lost over the centuries, and if the Metus have been clearing them on their own, they could have made new paths. Ones that are unmapped."

The thought of all that still needs to be done suddenly drops an extra layer of weight onto my already-exhausted shoulders. Rae catches the droop in my body. "Has no one attended to you yet?"

"*Terra*, I'm sorry, Molly." Dev spins to face me. "I was so worried about Tim—"

I wave away his concern. "I'm fine. I just...need a little rest, that's all. Tim's priority right now."

He glances back through the glass before returning his attention to me. "Tim's with the best people he can be with at the moment. There's nothing more we can do for him until his procedure is done." He steps forward and traces his fingertips across my cheek and then behind my ear, my body instantly easing from the touch. "Let's find you a Vigil doctor who can check on your vitals."

I look to Aveline and Rae, who both nod that I should go. "We'll be here," Rae says. "We'll make sure he signs a thank you card when he wakes up, for you saving his clumsy butt." We blink at him, and Aveline purses her lips. "What?" He glances between each of us. "Too soon?" Aveline smacks the side of his arm. "*Ow.*" He rubs the sting. "You could have just said yes. Haven't we had enough violence tonight?"

The echo of their bickering reaches us even after Dev and I turn the corner away from their hallway. And despite all the destruction, all the nightmares we had to fight against and the recent terror of possibly losing someone close to me, again, I allow myself to smile. I only hope it's not in vain.

Chapter 44

DRIP. DRIP. DRIP. The healing bag of Navitas slowly eases into my veins through an IV, and I shiver for maybe the tenth time. The energy is freezing as it enters my bloodstream, but turns to liquid heat as it mixes. The sensation gives me the willies, and I try not to look down at the needle inserted into the top of my hand.

"That's it. I'm getting you that blanket." Dev walks to the door to flag down a nurse.

"No, I'm fine. I swear."

"Your teeth are chattering. You are *not* fine."

"It's all the adrenaline and this stuff." I flick the glowing blue-white bag that hangs from a nearby hook. "How much longer do I need to be pumped with this stuff? I feel a lot better."

Dev thanks a medical assistant who hands him a fluffy gray blanket, and walks back to me. "Until it's gone."

We were quick to find a Vigil doctor who knew of me and could help with the right medicine. She actually seemed flustered with the honor to treat the Dreamer and would probably have stayed hovering in our room if it weren't for the many other new patients demanding the hospital staff stay busy.

Dev drapes the soft material around me where I sit in a white reclining chair. He tucks in each end around my body until I'm cocooned inside, and I fight a grin, watching his concentrated effort. "What?" he asks, not looking at me, but still fiddling with his task.

"You're cute."

Blue eyes meet mine, a smirk lifting his stubble-filled cheek. "And I think this stuff is making you high."

"Would that be such a bad thing?" I plop my head against the headrest. "Being the *Dreamer*"—I say the word in sarcastic awe— "needs to have some perks."

He chuckles and sits on a stool, scooting it closer so he can hold my non-IV hand. "I think being able to create anything you can imagine is already a pretty big perk."

I scrunch my mouth to the side. "Yeah, I guess there's that."

"How are you feeling, really?" He runs a worried gaze over me.

I glance to the veins surrounding the stuck needle, watching how the liquid energy lights up their snaking lines like my skin is made of translucent paper. "I was telling the truth before. I do feel better. My headache's gone."

"And your muscles? Are they still sore?"

I gently move around. "Not nearly."

The tenseness in his shoulders eases. "Good."

I lift my hand from his to run it through his raven hair, and he leans into the touch. "This is getting long. I can almost grab it now." I give a testing tug, and his eyes cloud, a wickedness swirling with the twitch of his lips.

"Careful, midnight." He threads his fingers back into mine. "I don't want to be responsible for what would happen if you pulled that again."

I squirm in my seat. "Really, Dev? We're in a hospital, probably the most unsexy place in the world."

He fights a grin. "Well, aren't you in this hospital?"

I frown. "Uh, yeah?"

"Then it's an *incredibly* sexy place."

I snort out a laugh. "Oh *God*. I forgot how cheesy you can be."

He's about to respond, when there's a clearing of a throat. Elena stands in the doorframe with Raymond, not a hair on her blonde head misplaced, while the Vigil engineer looks as if he got stuck in a windstorm. His glasses rest askew on his pert nose, and his lab coat is rumpled along with his hair and untucked shirt. The visual disparity of the two Vigil is almost comical.

"Am I interrupting?"

Dev leans away from me. "If you felt the need to clear your throat, doesn't that give you your answer?"

Elena straightens her already rodlike posture as she walks in. "Yes, well...we wanted to see how our Dreamer was doing." She reaches my side. "From the murmurs around the hospital, I would say you did far and away what I had hoped out there."

"I helped in ending the attack alongside many others, if that's what you mean."

"Modesty is always a good characteristic for Dreamers to have." She glances to Raymond. "Less chance for them to be overtaken by the lure of their powers." He nods in a weirdly clinical way, as if she's spouting a hypothesis about a test subject.

"Elena, was there something else you needed besides checking on me?" I ask, wanting to move on from feeling like a lab rat.

"Yes, there are a few." She folds her hands together in front of her. "First, we wanted to see how the vest held up."

I look down at the thing in question, realizing I never took it off. "Oh, it worked great." I find Raymond's gaze. "Better than great, actually. The recharging capabilities saved my butt a couple times."

"Saved *all* of our butts," Dev adds.

Raymond's chin tips up along with the corner of his lips. "That's splendid. And was it easy to control, the amount of energy coming in and out?"

"Yes, very." I spread my hands along the flexible lightweight material covering my stomach. "I'd like to wear it every time I'm here."

"You will." Elena glances to Raymond. "We think it will be a necessary precaution after tomorrow."

"Tomorrow?"

"That's the other thing I wanted to discuss. Tomorrow you will be introduced to Terra. After hearing the reaction of the guards who fought with you, it's time. Also, I don't think the secret will be much of a secret after tonight—best to get ahead of it."

"What will I need to do? I won't...I won't need to give a speech or anything, will I?" I can feel my face paling at just the thought.

"We'll get into more details in the morning, after you've gotten proper rest." Elena glances to the Navitas bag that slowly drips into my veins. *Great.* Her nonanswer obviously means yes. I swallow. Put me in front of a horde of Metus any day rather than force me to engage in public speaking. I can only hope to convince her what a mistake that will be.

"Do you mind if I take the vest for a while?" Raymond wipes his hands along his pants. "I want to run some diagnostic tests, and we're working on finishing up a few more vests for you so you can switch them out to be recharged."

"Oh, sure." I shift in my chair, and Dev helps me to remove it, careful of my IV tubes. Once out of the snug armor, I feel strangely vulnerable, even with the black protective layer of clothing underneath. I rub at my chest. "You know, I thought about manifesting the vest the other night, but it was too difficult for me to recreate in my mind. The altered Navitas inside feels different from the energy in the usual weapons."

The engineer's brows rise. "Yes, and that's very perceptive of you to pick up. It is different energy, and getting it to activate and be held within the threads takes a precision machine. I wouldn't be doing my job properly if you could merely imagine this and all its capabilities from thin air."

"Well, then two thumbs up for doing a good j—*ow*." I drop my left hand from giving a thumbs-up, forgetting I had the IV for a second.

"Thank you, Raymond." Elena inclines her head to him. "If you have no further questions, I'd like to talk with Molly in private."

"Oh! Yes—no, I mean, no. I have no more questions." He fiddles with my vest. "I'll just bring this back to the lab. Thank you for allowing me to accompany you with today's events." He bows to Elena. "It was truly an honor. And Molly, I look forward to our continued work together."

I smile at the teetering man. "Me too."

He bends at the waist one last time before dipping out of the room.

"Dev, you can close your mouth." Elena waves her hand in his direction, stopping him from saying whatever he was about to say. "You can stay for this. I have no doubt she'd tell you afterward anyway."

He and I share a sheepish glance.

"I have a few other things to attend to before tomorrow, so we can save most of the details of this conversation for our next energy training, but what you did with Tim…" Her blue-jeweled eyes lock with mine. "You succeeded."

I flex and relax my free hand. "Yes. Well, sort of." The image of his angry bubbling skin swims before me.

"You stopped and removed the threat of him becoming a Metus."

I'm unsure if that was a question or not. "Um, yes?"

"Then you succeeded." Walking to the front of the room, she clasps her hands behind her back. "This is quite groundbreaking, your new ability to reverse a usually irreversible process. We will need to explore this further, as well as record your memories soon."

"Record them? Like what you did with the past Dreamers?" I sit up straighter.

"Yes, so we have them on record in case…well, it's better to gather them when they're still fresh in your mind."

I frown. "Elena, you don't need to skirt the issue. You want them in case something should happen to me before my twenty-fifth birthday."

She studies me a moment, a strange respect growing in her gaze. "Yes."

I nod and look away, a familiar tightening twisting in my gut any time I think about the date that looms ever closer and the two choices that are terrifyingly starting to look like one absolute.

Dev touches my shoulder, and I glance to him. His brows are furrowed as he regards me, and I know he wants to ask what I'm thinking, but he holds off because of Elena's presence.

"Well, I'll take my leave." Her perceptiveness for us wanting a moment alone is clear. "But before I go, I want to express how truly proud I am to call you our Dreamer, Molly. You were remarkable tonight, and I believe that what you were able to do with Tim was merely the beginning." She smiles—a rarity. "I will reconnect with you on the announcement plans soon." With a small incline of her head, she's whisked away by her entourage of Vigil guards, who were standing silent outside the door.

I stare at the empty space she once occupied, still lost in thought from her earlier words. *What you were able to do with Tim was merely the beginning.* Phantom pains shoot up my arms with the memories. The agony he was in, *we* were in, the darkness hungry for the easily mutated energy flowing through him. I could feel how pliable we are to become evil when reduced to torment, stripped of our hope. *Hope*—the key to our humanity. What happens when none is left? I frown. Alec. A finger pops my bottom lip away from my teeth, and I blink up to Dev.

"Keep that up and we'll have to sew it back on."

"Sorry, I—there's just a lot on my mind."

"Inevitably so." He inches his way onto my reclined chair. "But let's try to hold off worrying about all of them right now. You've done enough tonight." He brushes back my hair, causing me to close my eyes briefly.

"Have I told you I love you yet today?"

A half smile tugs at his lips. "I was just going to mention how it was about time you did."

I fight a grin. "How courteous of you. At least I don't have to worry about being forgetful when you're around."

"There's a lot you don't have to worry about when I'm around." His gaze suddenly grows serious, resolute.

"Dev—"

"I'm being serious, Molly." He encircles my hands with his. "When you said you had a lot on your mind, I know which one of those things we share. And I meant when I said we'd find a way." His grip tightens. "And we will. I promise you—we will."

I let out a tired breath. "You can't promise that, Dev, and I'm not asking you to."

A crease materializes between his brows, and he momentarily studies our entwined fingers. "You know, there's one thing I've learned from living in Terra—one thing that, no matter what, has always stood the test of time." A fierce sapphire gaze rises to meet mine. "It's that all dreams have ways of coming true."

The determination swirling in his eyes melts me to my core, and I tug him forward, bringing his lips to mine. Our movements are careful at first, a whisper of the heat boiling under the surface. There's a graze, a brush, a tease, and then like a piñata popping, we fall uncontained. He pins me to the back of the chair, his mouth firm and demanding, mine all too eager to please. His hands possess, take, and the moan that escapes me only fuels both our actions. Our surroundings drop away, and just like every time he touches me, looks at me, calls my name, my world briefly becomes perfect, simple. He and I, and in this moment I hold on to it as long as I can. Postponing the responsibilities that will inevitably step into the forefront when we break apart. So for now, I keep us locked, lost, right up until the last drip from the IV pushes into my veins, setting my blood to its final course of rejuvenating heat.

⋗⊨⊙ ⊙⊨⋖

I rub the top of my hand where a slight bruise has blossomed, even though there's no other mark from the freshly removed needle.

"Are you sure you don't want me to come with you?" Dev frowns down at me.

"Yes, go check on Tim. I just need to step outside for second. The brightness of this hospital is making me feel crazy. I need a break from all the"—I glance around to the white on top of white of everything—"lack of color."

"Okay, but I won't be long. I only need to ask when he'll be conscious, for us to come back. I'll meet you out there soon, and then we can go home."

Home. A slight smile tugs at my lips. "That sounds great."

"Good." With a quick kiss, Dev turns toward the section where they are keeping Tim in a sleep-induced coma until he's fully recovered. I head in the opposite direction and make my way back to the front doors.

Stepping outside, I greedily fill my lungs with fresh air. The crowd is long gone, and a quiet after-hours feel has settled over the square. I'm all too pleased to glide into the anonymity of just another Terra civilian strolling the streets. I realize with a frown that this blending ability might all end tomorrow with Elena's announcement. In fact, this might be the last time I'll be able to walk unguarded here too. The thought depresses me. How will the people react? My presence will definitely be questioned. There will be confusion from the Nocturna, and most probably hatred toward their Vigil brethren for keeping such a secret for so long. I only hope the positive reactions will outweigh the negative. I mean, what I was able to do for Tim can't be negated. The skeptics will have to see my presence as a benefit, in that regard. I let out a huff of air. I still can't believe I was able to help him, my gift finally being used for a greater good. Holding out my hands, I take in their normalcy, still baffled that I contain such power.

Flexing and relaxing my fingers by my side, I find a bench close to the hospital's entrance and, on a sigh, collapse onto it. A line of trees behind me casts a shadow across this area, but I'm still able to tip my head up and gaze at the shooting stars above. Millions of sleeping minds zip across the sky, the beauty of them almost overwhelming. A wind dances through the square, and I close my eyes, momentarily taking in the peace. My confusion on which life I'll be forced to choose has slowly been slipping away to reveal only one. One decision, one seemingly obviously way to go. But I push those thoughts away, just as I always do, praying it won't come to that. Even though it feels slightly foolish to have faith in Dev's promise of finding a solution, it's still there—hope, the one gift to mankind that escaped Pandora's box. I have hope that we'll find a way—

The rustling of a nearby bush startles me out of my thoughts. I sit up and narrow my gaze into the area behind me, but it's too dark to make anything out. I listen instead. Silence. Taking another glance around the square, I spot a few Nocturna and Vigil strolling about, and their presence momentarily relaxes me. The surrounding buildings still have the hum of movement, even if it's not as busy as normal. Settling back into the bench, I wonder how much longer Dev will be and if I should go back inside to find him.

In the space between my indecision, a shadow emerges onto the path where I sit, and a chill runs down my spine. Call it intuition, a sixth sense, being a Dreamer—whichever—but instantly I know it's the same shadow that's been lingering out of my sight for weeks. The hovering ghost who's been following my steps in New York, at home. A presence I hoped was merely a paranoid girl's imagining now waits for me to acknowledge it.

With warning goose bumps covering my skin, I slowly turn in its direction. And this time it doesn't retreat into the dark. This time it steps forward, directly into the light. Even with his face newly shaved, I immediately recognize him, and my blood runs cold as my heart putters to a stop. "Dr. Marshall?"

His white teeth flash in the night. "Hello, Molly."

Chapter 45

I ONCE READ somewhere that the dropping sensation you get in your stomach when startled or confronted with a threat is actually all the blood leaving the place where it's not needed and flowing to more necessary body parts and muscles, preparing for fight or flight. So while looking into hazel eyes that I never thought I'd see again, and never in a million years thought I'd see in Terra, I wonder why my brain doesn't presently count as a useful body part. Because it's suddenly drained, empty, zombified. I can do nothing but blink, as if that will dispel his presence, revealing him as merely my hallucination. It doesn't. He stays solid, a reality, and something about the way his smile is set with an unsettling curve gives me a very bad feeling that whatever this is, it isn't a good thing.

With his face cleared of his beard, the youthfulness I saw hidden underneath becomes very apparent. He looks only a few years older than myself, but the fact that he's here allows me to deduce that he could be way beyond me in years. His blond hair is messier than I remember, and his current black Terra garb strikes a more imposing presence than his white lab coat and scrubs.

By some miracle, I find myself able to stand. "What are you...
how is this...I..." My mouth hangs open.

"Yes, a bit of a shock, isn't it?" He slowly glides forward, his
steps alarmingly predatory. "But the feeling was rather mutual when
I first realized who you were, probably greater, in fact."

"You're a...Vigil?" My mind is still set to empty and is having
difficulty putting anything together that's comprehendible.

"I am. And you're the Dreamer." His eyes light up as they take
me in. "It's all rather serendipitous, isn't it? That you should have
gotten hit by lightning while I was in New York. And to think,
I was a day away from leaving to follow another lead in Beijing,
when you were brought in. How lucky I am to have been there and
found you."

Found me? Follow another lead?

"What are you talking about?"

His smile is pitying. "I've been searching a long time for you,
Molly, waiting for you to arrive. I knew by the rising Metus population that someone would be called soon. I just didn't know from
where. We can never predict these things, you see." He inclines his
head, a professor teaching his student. "But luckily, there are only so
many lightning-strike incidents to look into in a year."

"You knew who I was? That I was the Dreamer...when you saw
me in the hospital?"

"Not right away, of course." He waves his hand impatiently.
"There's no test that can be done to reveal that, but then you mentioned your dreams, and well...it was quite obvious from there."
He's right in front of me now, and I tip my head back to meet his
eyes. "But still," he continues. "I didn't exactly know what I was going to do with you once I found you. I had ideas of course—plans,

all involving avenging what was taken from me." I flinch as he reaches out to play with a strand of my ponytail that's draped across my shoulder. Loud internal voices are screaming at me now, telling me to move away and fast, but my legs won't listen. They stay stupid and still, rooted to the spot. "Yes, they would pay. That much was certain. I knew no matter what, they would pay." His face contorts in a deep-seated disdain.

"W…who would pay?"

He blinks to me. "The Metus, of course."

I let out a relieving breath. "Oh."

"And another—*one* other." I swallow away my respite as his gaze clouds over. "But I never thought he'd factor into you, and I didn't think he should. I mean, his kind hadn't even known of your existence here. That is, until recently." There's a conspiratorial tilt to his lips. "Something was forcing us all to collide, it seems. Telling me to watch, to look closely and be patient. And I did, and that's when I saw it. Saw you together, the way he watched you, looked at you. And it became perfectly clear." His eyes flash back to mine, their lucidness a dissolving gleam. "Did you know he used to look at someone else like that? *Exactly* like that. How easy he is to forget his past." He spits the words out like he can't stomach them. "That's when I knew it had to go another way. It made sense then what I needed to do, why you came to me. She was sending me a sign. Telling me what needed to be done to give her peace. I would take care of the Metus after bringing revenge to the man that pushed her into making those choices that day." Warning bells ring loudly in my skull. *He's crazy. Step away. Run.* As his words sink in, with every beat of my barely puttering heart I finally will myself to take a step back, but he merely matches it with his own forward. "So I waited and watched, created distractions to get you alone, but you're never alone, are you, Molly? Someone's always by your side. *He's* always by your side." His lip curls in a sneer. "But he's not now, is he?"

I hold up my hands, warding him off. "Listen, Dr. Marshall, or…whoever you are, I don't know what you want or…what you're trying to achieve here, but I can assure you, there's another way to get it." I chance a look around, hoping someone is close by whom I could call to for help, but the square has suddenly cleared out. It's just him—a man who's quickly revealing all his loose screws—and me. The jovial doctor I thought I knew at the hospital is nowhere to be seen, only a heartbroken, hate-filled shell of a Vigil.

He shakes his head. "There isn't, but I would never expect you to understand. You never knew…" He scowls. "It doesn't matter. You won't remember any of this soon anyway."

A choking breath escapes me as he unsheathes a knife from his side. The foot-long blade's intricate lines glow blue-white in the night, and my power hums in panic, knowing exactly what sort of weapon it is. The memory of rows upon rows of them in the inventions lab fills my vision, and without another thought, I blink back to the present and imagine him throwing the knife away, willing him to collapse to the ground. But nothing happens. He still clutches the blade and walks forward, determination set in his cold, mad eyes. Panicked, I lift my hands, angling a beam of Navitas to shoot straight at him, but it merely hits up against an invisible wall, spraying in every direction but where he stands. *What the f—*

There's a wink of light, and my attention is brought to his bicep. A glowing lightning bolt rests in a band wrapped around his arm. Like being doused with freezing water, I realize my powers are useless against him. *This so isn't good.*

A smile inches across his lips. "Clever invention, isn't it?" He raises his arm, showcasing the band more clearly. "And it couldn't have come at a better time. I'll make sure to tell Dev good-bye for you. And for what it's worth, I truly am sorry you only turned out to be a means to an end, but we all have our roles to play, don't we? This just turned out to be yours." Without another word, he lunges forward, but I spin away before he can grab me, and buy some time by manifesting a large rock. It *thwaks* him in the side of his torso, throwing him off balance. I can't affect his body directly with my powers, but another object will do just fine. He grunts with the impact but rights himself quickly. Readying my stance, I prepare to imagine whatever is needed for that knife to stay very, very far away from me. He takes a step forward again, but just as quickly stills as he glances beyond me.

"Molly? What's going—"

Stupidly, I turn to the sound of Dev's voice, and in that instant lose everything. In my second of averted attention, Dr. Marshall grabs me in his vise grip and swings me in front of his body, my back to his front. With one hand wrapping around my neck, he angles the knife with the other just below my fourth rib—directly at my heart.

With my breath coming out in panicked gasps, I take in the man before us. Dev stands, face leeched of all color, looking as if he's staring at a ghost. "Aaron?"

And there it is, the last puzzle piece I knew would fit but was too terrified of what would be created if I allowed myself to place it.

Dr. Marshall is Aaron, Anebel's Aaron, the supposedly *dead* Aaron. The world tilts, and my body begins to shake with the adrenaline rushing through it. If I weren't connected to the machines back home, I would definitely have woken up by now. The cluster-fuck of this moment mixes rage into my terror.

The surprise in Dev's face quickly evaporates as he takes in the situation. His gaze becomes a storm cloud of fury as it focuses on the threat positioned at my chest. "Let her go." His voice is low, a warning.

"Long time, Devlin." Aaron's grip tightens around my throat, and I hold back a squeak. "It seems I found something of yours that you care about very much. Isn't that rather *amusing*, how quickly you've moved on to the next pretty little thing. And she *is* pretty, isn't she?" His hot breath grates along my cheek. "Do you think she's as pretty as Anebel? Hmm, *do you*?" He shakes me by the neck, and I grow momentarily dizzy. His crazy is beyond anything I've ever experienced, and I'm still in shock that this is the same man I met in the hospital. If I wasn't presently scared out of my mind, I might actually feel sorry for him. But there's no room for sympathy when you're being held by knifepoint, especially by a Conscious knifepoint.

Dev's eyes remain calculating. "If you have an issue with me, then fight *me*. Leave Molly out of this."

"But don't you see? This *is* fighting you, my friend. She's the perfect weapon. A heart for a heart."

Dev frowns. "What are you talking about?"

"Don't play stupid! Anebel should have been mine. She should have been with *me*."

Icy eyes penetrate the man whose nails have begun to cut into my skin. "If I remember correctly, she *was* with you that night."

Aaron gasps, his hold momentarily loosening before— "*It's your fault she's gone*!" A spray of his spittle dashes along my neck, and I squeeze my eyes shut, tears of terror beginning to run down my cheeks, his claws once more digging in. "She always wanted to impress you. I told her we shouldn't go there. Not alone, but she was cocky, like *you* taught her to be. She risked us running into all those Metus because of the stupid way you two competed. She would still be here! Right here!" A sob mixes with his fury.

There's a flash of pain in Dev's features followed by regret, as if he's already drawn this conclusion on his own, has already gone through that stage of blame and grief. "I miss her too," he says softly, "but I'm not the enemy here, and you shouldn't make yourself one either. We're in the middle of a war. We need the Dreamer now more than ever, and if you truly loved Anebel, you would know she'd want you to help put an end to it with us."

"You have no idea what she would have wanted! She told me things only she and I understood, only she and I shared. You never loved her like I did, never!"

The expression of pity in Dev's gaze quickly transfers to rage. "Do *you* think she would have wanted you to grow mad? Look at yourself. What have you been doing all this time? Hiding away and brooding over what could have been? She's gone, Aaron. Gone! You must accept it, like we all have."

"*Dev*." I hiccup in warning as Aaron's grip begins to smother my windpipe. *Reel it in*, I plead with my eyes.

"*Why* must I accept it?" he hisses. "Why are we forced to never mourn our dead? Humans do! The very humans we live to protect and fashion our lives after. Why is this custom then lost on us? No! I *will* not accept her death. She deserves better than that. She deserves to be avenged."

Thump. Thump. Thump. My heart pounds in my ears as I desperately try to affect him with my powers, but it's like trying to mix water and oil—everything slips away from him. And with the knife pinched into my ribs, my mind is too rattled to manifest a third-party object without the threat of harming myself in the process.

"You forget that I loved her too," Dev says, and I glance to him, but he keeps his attention on Aaron. "And felt her loss just as deeply. We both left the city of Terra that day, remember? You can't blame me that I eventually returned."

"But that doesn't mean you deserve a second chance at love. Neither of us does!" With the prick of his knife, I whimper. I actually fucking whimper.

Dev grows panicked. "Aaron." He raises his hands as if trying to appease a rabid dog. "You don't need to do this." He takes a slow step forward. "The Metus are the ones who took her from us." Another step. "She would want us to avenge her with their deaths. *They* are the monsters. *They* are the ones who need to be punished."

The hardness of Aaron's grip eases slightly, and I'm able to take in a large breath of air, but my eyes still stay wide as I watch Dev's careful approach. He glances to me, and we hold each other's gaze, a silent conversation passing. *Please*, I say.

I'll get you out of this, he returns.

"You weren't there." Aaron continues to babble on, his mind seeming to slip further and further away with each word. "You didn't see…her screams…I couldn't do anything to—" His words cut off, finally noticing Dev's gradual advance, and on a hiss, he pulls me tighter against him. I cry out as the blade penetrates through my layers of clothing, its cold titanium precariously stopping on my bare skin. "You don't know what it was like. You didn't see!" An unhinged laugh bubbles out of him. "Oh, but you will! You will! Watch, Devlin, watch as you lose everything just as I did."

Time momentarily stops, my eyes collide with Dev's terror-filled ones, and then it kicks forward on a jab as the knife cuts into my flesh. There's a scream of pain—my scream, as the most agonizing splinters of energy crackle through my body, zooming across every vein. I barely make out the howl of another as Aaron is suddenly knocked away from me, the blade ripping out in the process with a sickening wet pop.

I stand there, oscillating between shock and horror as I glance down to the area where the weapon was momentarily lodged. A dark spot slowly blossoms across my shirt, blood marking a black hole. But I feel nothing now, too locked into watching the cavity of my chest quickly fill with bright blue-white. It moves like a storm cloud, flashing as it expands from the center of my wound. It crackles as it devours, snaps like a whip as it evaporates every one of my cells, the colors churning, pulsing, and swirling. It would almost be beautiful if it weren't representing my death.

"MOLLY!" Dev is in front of me, grabbing my shoulders. He begins to shake me, as if that will dispel what's happening. "Molly! NO, NO!" Wide, desperate, and panicked blue eyes hold on to mine, and I open my mouth to say something, anything, but nothing comes out. "DON'T GO!" he pleads as the light filling me basks his face in white. "Make it stop! *Please*, make it stop!"

But this time I can't. This time I know I truly can do nothing as my body becomes weightless with each section's dissolve, my form fading, bits carried away into the night. My mind grows fuzzy, distant, along with the world around me, and on a last heart-shattered sob, I grasp Dev's hands in mine. "I love you," I say. "I'm so sorry."

And then like ash in the wind, I disappear.

Chapter 46

SIRENS, BLARINGLY LOUD, penetrate the darkness where I float. They yell for me to go, to move, that I no longer belong in this space. I can feel the blackness squeezing me out, forcing me back, and on a kick I'm pushed through.

My eyes open on a tear-filled gasp, and I jolt forward. My skin burns like coals in a fire, my clothes are covered in sweat, and my stomach rolls with vertigo. Quickly, I lean over the side of the bed I find myself in and vomit. Bile grates along my throat as I dispel everything until it's nothing but dry heaves. I rest my forehead on the plush material surrounding me and take in shaky breaths, trying to catch my bearings. Where am I? What happened?

All I know is something isn't right. Something went horribly wrong. Sweeping a frantic gaze around the bright space, I take in the flashing red lights in the corners, their pulse in rhythm to the alarms. My legs are stuck in a cushioned bed, and strange lettering runs like hacked code on screens inlaid into the walls. For a second I think I'm in the Dreamer Containment Center. So much of this looking like so much of that, but then with a crawling chill, I realize I'm awake—back in the Village Portal Bookstore. A stuttering inhale clicks down my diaphragm, and my nails dig into the material around me for purchase, my strength momentarily sucked away. *This can't be right.* But then the images of my last moments in Terra swim before me like a torturing phantom—Dr. Marshall, Aaron, his knife plunging into me, Dev's pleading words, my body disappearing from the center of my wound. *My wound!*

On a cry, I grab for my chest, but it's whole, not filled with light and burning away. I curl my fingers into the work clothes I had on a day ago, wanting to rip them off. They don't belong on me. I should be in black, should be wearing my unifor—

Oh God. I remember! I still remember all of it, all of Terra! The Conscious knife didn't take it away from me. A drop of relief mixes into my panic but is quickly diluted by all my other fears, one in particular that I can feel the validity of deep within my bones. Gripping the plush material surrounding me, I choke on a sob as I climb out, my heart tripping in its racing pace.

Stumbling to one of the screens, I knock into apparatuses and wires that hang around my bed, forcing them out of my path. My joints ache from being torn out of their comatose state too soon, but I ignore the pain. I ignore all of it as I press a sweaty palm against a monitor. It slides down the screen as I try to make sense of the symbols dancing across. It looks like one sentence repeated over and over, but none of it makes sense.

"Why can't I read you?!" I smack the glass. Turning back to the room, I search for anything else that could possibly help, but there's nothing. *Nothing!* Just like the emptiness that's expanding in my veins since the moment I awoke here. It's the one sensation I've been trying to suppress, trying to pretend doesn't exist, for I know what it means. I know *exactly* what it means, but no—*no*, I won't accept that. I *can't*. Digging my fingers into my hair, I squeeze my eyes shut, trying to block out the sirens and continuous flashing lights that are screaming at me to listen to them. *It's gone*! *It's gone*! *It's gone*! They won't stop yelling.

"Shut up! Shut up! Shut uuup!"

A sudden high-pitched whirl invades, and the portal in the corner of the room flashes bright just as Rae bursts through. "*Molly*!?" Frenzied eyes find mine. "Oh thank Terra." He takes three large strides and brings me into his arms.

His hold tightens as I bury my face into his chest, allowing his presence to momentarily silence the surrounding noise, but then I smell the scent of Terra that still clings to his clothes, and I have to push myself away. He frowns, a quick hesitancy in his gaze. "You remember me, don't you? You remember I'm Rae?"

I nod, my lower lip wobbling. "Yes, yes, I remember."

His shoulders slump in relief, but his features remain pained. "I came as quickly as I could. Dev he—we had to deal with Aaron. He's being held in one of our security cells."

I shake my head, not caring about that. There's only one thing that matters right now. My stomach rolls again, and I take in a deep breath, gathering my strength—what little remains. "You have to tell me." I clutch his shirt. "Is it gone? My connection to Terra, did he take it from me?"

His brows pinch in as his gaze sweeps across the monitors in the room. When it lands back on me, the truth is written everywhere. "I'm—I'm so sorry."

And there it is—my destiny cemented in an apology. My breath is leeched from me, my soul being torn away as the world momentarily turns red with my rage, blurring out of focus with disbelief before it quickly desaturates to black and white, to emptiness, to pointlessness, to normal, and on that last thought is when I finally break. With the loss all consuming, I collapse to the ground. Rae is quick to try to help, but I shove him away, my gaze falling to my open palms in my lap, the creases that run through them—my lifeline splitting in two and ending short. Gone.

I'm so sorry.

It's gone.

Curling my hands into fists, I cover what's written, and then I tip my head back, and I scream.

Epilogue

THE PORTAL PULSED in the dark, an angora fish tentacle enticing its prey. So much held on the other side of its light, so much within an arm's reach of an impassable path. The man's eyes began to water from the endless hold it had on him. People rushed past on the street, unaware of the figure in the alley's shadows, oblivious to the suffocating pain wrapping around every one of his cells.

It shouldn't have taken this long.

His body quaked with another bout of barely contained fury, and he'd let it out if he hadn't already a few moments ago. Nothing seemed to give him reprieve. Nothing doused the overwhelming terror from knowing he'd spend another day without seeing her face, without running his hands through her thick midnight hair, or without watching as the edge of her mouth tipped up in amusement when she thought he couldn't see. The city hadn't stopped whispering of the girl who could fly, who held the power of Navitas in her palms—her story quickly becoming myth with each passing day she didn't return. Elena had yet to address her presence, and he was unsure now if she ever would.

This wasn't supposed to happen. They were meant to have more time. They were meant to figure it all out. The ever-present pit in his stomach curled around itself like a snake, the injustice making him sick—the déjà vu. How much was he meant to suffer and why in such the same way?

He growled and pushed off from the wall he was leaning against, beginning to pace. Every bone in his body screamed with revenge, and he licked his lips from the memory of his fist crunching against Aaron's eye socket. Endlessly it connected with a satisfying punch until he was forced to stop. Until crimson blood mixed, neither one nor the other's—just theirs. He still had no idea who pulled him off, and he wasn't one ounce thankful. His next move was meant to be fatal.

They thought Aaron was safe from his wrath by being held in an undisclosed location. Safe until he could undergo a fair trial. *Fair.* The thought almost made him laugh, if it didn't make him sick in the process. No, in Dev's mind, Aaron forfeited being properly treated by the law the night…the night— He let out a forced breath, unable to bring himself to think about it again. This was when he wished he could sleep. Then he could try and convince himself it was all a nightmare, one he could wake up from. But no, he knew in this world that nightmares and bogeymen didn't go away when your eyes opened. Instead they stood right where they were, smiling back. Dev's grip on the strap across his chest tightened. He'd find a way to get to Aaron, and when he did, he was going to take his time.

A silhouette filled the entrance of the alley he hid in, and by the form's curved frame and haloed strawberry hair, he didn't need to see her face to know who it was.

"I heard I could find you here." She stepped into the shadows, Dev's night vision easily picking up the nervousness set in her feline eyes.

"Aurora."

"Waiting for Rae?"

He didn't answer.

She sighed, and now that she was closer, he could see the tired-ness in her features, the heaviness of her lids. Her usual strength and prowess reduced to a barely glowing ember. Her brother's return had not been the celebration it should have been. Dev frowned, forgetting that he was not the only one suffering.

"Have you been to see him?" he asked.

She pressed her lips together as though to keep them from wob-bling. "I can't believe what he's done." She shook her head. "He was never so...this isn't who he is, Dev."

"It isn't who he was."

She swallowed. "He's still my brother."

His eyes met hers. "Are you sure about that?"

An awkward silence followed. They never had awkward silenc-es. Dev glanced beyond her as the portal across the street blazed. His chest lifted, but only a woman popped out to meet an awaiting friend. "Did you need something?" He looked back to Aurora, try-ing to control another bout of frustration he felt coming on. *Why was it taking him so long?*

Her chin tipped up. "I know you. I know you must be planning something for what Aaron..." Her gaze cut away for a moment. "But please, please think before you do anything rash. Remember who he was—who he *is* to me. I just got him—" Her lips pressed together. "Just please, let the law take care of it. That's all I ask."

Dev studied her, allowing her plea to roll through him. "He's been alive for all these years, alive but letting us think he was dead. Letting *you*, his sister, think that. For what? To fulfill a delusional, misplaced avengement to a dead person?" The words stung to say, but he kept going. "Someone he claims to have loved? What about the love he had for you? The one who's followed him through everything. Do you think he even thought about what you wanted when he decided to be a Nocturna guard? That you gave up your own dreams to follow in his footsteps? What leaving you behind, never to be heard from again, would do to you? He's selfish, Aurora. He's always been selfish. And what he did to Molly—" Dev's hands balled into fists. "How can you stand here pleading his case?"

Tears tracked down Aurora's cheeks, her green eyes bright in the dark. "He's my brother," she whispered. "He's still my brother."

Dev shook his head, wishing he could understand, but his current tolerance for anything that was in his way of getting back what he lost was nonexistent.

A bright light shined in the distance again, and this time, thank Terra, Rae exited the portal. He glanced around and stopped on Dev, who brushed past Aurora and stepped out of the alley.

"How is she?"

Rae's shoulders were tense as he walked forward, holding a black box. At the sight of it, Dev's heart pounded. The only form of connection between him and Molly had been through this tiny container that could send small things between their worlds without mutation. "No real change today," he said and looked beyond Dev. "Oh, hi, Aurora." She came to stand near them but not close enough to be a part of their conversation. Rae frowned.

"Has she been eating at least?" Dev wanted to ask a million questions, like if her hair still smelled of honeysuckles, but he thought Rae would probably feel as comfortable answering that as he would to ask.

"Some things. With the help of Becca…" His brows creased together. "It's getting harder to make up excuses for why Molly is the way she is right now. I don't know how much longer I can keep all this a secret from Bec." He gestured to the city. "Molly barely speaks though, so at least I don't have to worry she'll slip up and say something."

Dev's eyes narrowed. "Has she been sleeping? Getting enough rest?"

"That's *all* she wants to do, but it only makes things worse, because when she wakes up, she realizes she didn't come here and collapses into herself again."

Dev glared off into the distance, the ball of rage growing hotter in his gut.

"But we'll find something to fix this." Rae tried to console. "Elena's got the top engineers on it. I promise—we'll find something."

Dev's gaze cut through him. "Don't you know by now? Promises are useless."

Rae shifted, clearly uncomfortable witnessing his friend's slowly dimming faith. "She gave me this to give to you." He handed over the container. "And don't worry. I haven't been sneaking peeks at any of these letters. Terra only knows the type of smut you two must write to one another."

Dev's lips remained still, his ability to smile severed along with his heart. Rae sighed, but Dev ignored him as he removed the lid. A note sat on top, and he picked it up, reading the elegant slanted scrawl of Molly's handwriting.

I expect this back the next time I see you.

Dev's grip tightened around the paper as he moved it aside to peer into the box. His breath caught, and his heart tripped. For there, resting alone in the plush interior, was a tiny swirling seashell.

"What is it?" Aurora asked, walking closer.

With nerves buzzing, Dev gently removed the object as a hesitant feeling of warmth filled his chest. "Hope."

Acknowledgments

Wow, ARE WE really at the end of book two already? How in all of Terra did that happen? Well, probably because of a boatload of some pretty awesome people. The first of which are my family. Ma (Cynthia), Papa (Emil), Alex, Phoenix, and Kelsey, you will always remain my rock, my cozy corner, my warm hug when I need it. Thank you for believing in me to keep chugging forward on this dream of mine. Also, Kelsey, thanks for still wanting to talk to me after all the ignored calls and texts back saying, *Shh, I'm writing.* Your patience is definitely your virtue ;-).

To Dan, I know I've driven you a bit mad at times with my incessant questions dealing with this series. So thank you for your endless, tireless support and for giving me the courage to put my work out there. I'll share my peanut butter with you any day.

To Corinna Barsan and Julia McCarthy, thank you for being my wise wizards and reading the early drafts of *The Divide*. This novel would be half of what it is without your amazing editorial guidance and developmental notes. I bow down in gratitude for having you in my life.

To my dearest editor, Dori Harrell, how can I even begin? Probably first by telling you I love you. You are my angel sent from above, my calming voice among the chaos, and I never ever want to let you go! Thank you for being one of my biggest fans and fielding every crazy question I fling at you, no matter the time of day (or night). Your wit, laser-precision eye, and Einstein-smart notes made this book beautiful.

To my book club gals, Jessica, Lauren, Alicia, Erin, Nicky, Meg, Eman, and Giselle, though most of us are now separated by state lines, you will always remain close. I love you all tremendously.

To Mike, my daytime work husband. Thank you for stepping forward into the unpredictable freelance life with me so I could stretch my wings and really give this writing thing a go. When will then be now? Soon.

To Emma Raveling, you might not know this, but I consider you a great role model in my life. Your writing is forever inspiring, your positivity always infectious and I'm humbled to be a part of your reader family. Thank you for continuing to create worlds we can get lost in.

To all the book bloggers and ARC reviewers who took a chance on this series and have come back for more, I'm able to wake up every day and write because of you. You are the lifeblood of an indie author, and I am humbled to have gotten to know you. Specifically Cassandra (@thebookishcrypt) and Samantha (*The Reading Nook NZ*), you ladies are my version of fairy godmothers. Keep being amazing!

To my self-publishing family, the RWA, and all the amazing authors I've met along the way, you make me feel sane and forever push me forward to be better and keep writing. Specifically Todd Dillard and Shaila Patel. You made me laugh when I needed it most.

To all the family and friends I wasn't able to mention individually but whose endless amount of encouragement and love I feel every day—you are amazing, and I'm truly blessed to be surrounded by so much positivity.

Now, on to more writing!

About the Author

E. J. Mellow is a fantasy writer who resides in Brooklyn, NY. When she's not busy moonlighting in the realm of make-believe, she can be found doodling, buried in a book (usually this one), or playing video games.

The Divide is the second book in her NA contemporary fantasy trilogy, The Dreamland Series.

Made in the USA
Columbia, SC
03 October 2021